IS THIS A DAGGER WHICH I SEE BEFORE ME?

Tirdal dropped forward and flat over a shelf of shale as the round cracked overhead and threw a mist of water up from the stream. Then he was up and moving, and Dagger was there and angry and shooting now. Tirdal dropped sideways in case the human sniper had anticipated the fall. He landed in a pile of sand as a rock erupted chips on the far bank.

That should do it, he thought. Dagger hated to miss more than just about anything else, would be easy to track mentally with that storm of emotion roaring off him, and Tirdal could keep track as he decided how to execute his plan.

Then, only for a moment, he could feel the human as if Dagger were he.

Dagger was pissed. Seriously pissed. The damned Darhel had just dodged the bullets. It was vaguely possible, even with the high speeds of the "dumb" sniper rounds. But the goddamned sensate could feel him take the shot. The only way to stop that was to feel nothing when he killed.

Which took all the fun out of it. What was the point if you couldn't get the rush from the kill? So what was the point of killing the Darhel? Oh, yeah. A billion credits.

So, the next shot, feel nothing. Not until the box was in his hand. And the Darhel was dead.

The link severed as quickly as it had formed, tenuous threads of consciousness snapping away. That was Dagger's mind, then, Tirdal realized. It was crass, paranoid; any emotion, any humanity was weakness to Dagger.

It appeared it was time for a Darhel to enter once again upon the hunt. There was a thrill to that knowledge, with a foreboding cloud hanging over it. This was no game.

The fates of three races and hundreds of planets, perhaps the galaxy, would balance on what Tirdal did next, and how well his mind could fight genetic programming. . . .

BAEN BOOKS by John Ringo

A Hymn Before Battle
Gust Front
When the Devil Dances
Hell's Faire
The Hero (with Michael Z. Williamson)
Cally's War (with Julie Cochrane)
Watch on the Rhine (with Tom Kratman)

There Will Be Dragons
Emerald Sea
Against the Tide

Into the Looking Glass

The Road to Damascus (with Linda Evans)

Ghost

Princess of Wands (forthcoming)

The Prince Roger series
with David Weber:
March Upcountry
March to the Sea
March to the Stars
We Few

BAEN BOOKS by Michael Z. Williamson

Freehold
The Weapon
The Hero (with John Ringo)

THE HERO

JOHN RINGO
AND
MICHAEL Z. WILLIAMSON

THE HERO

Copyright 2004 by John Ringo & Michael Z. Williamson

A Baen Books Original

Baen Publishing Enterprises
P.O. Box 1403
Riverdale, NY 10471
www.baen.com

ISBN-13: 978-1-4165-0914-1
ISBN-10: 1-4165-0914-3

Cover art by Kurt Miller

First paperback printing, November 2005

Library of Congress Cataloging-in-Publication Number
2004004650

Distributed by Simon & Schuster
1230 Avenue of the Americas
New York, NY 10020

Production & book design by Windhaven Press (www.windhaven.com)
Printed in the United States of America

To Robert A. Heinlein,
in hopes that we can pay the debt forward.

Chapter 1

THE ASSEMBLY ROOM of the Deep Reconnaissance Team was as utilitarian and sere as the team itself. The walls, floor and ceiling were a matte-gray unmarked plasteel, blank of lockers, tables or any other appurtenances of human existence. There were two doors on opposite walls, both made of heavy plasteel like a bank vault. The materials were as much a matter of safety as security; power packs and ammunition bins did get damaged, and accidents happen. And when accidents happened with the power packs, catastrophic was the mildest word possible.

Nobody wanted the accidents to happen to the

troops, either. But better to lose a DRT than a base. Or, at least, that was the opinion of the rest of the base.

Ferret was the first one in the room, carrying a snubby punch gun. Four others followed with grav-guns and assorted personal weapons that were officially unauthorized, but few people were inclined to dispute their right to carry them. Pulsers predominated. There was an extra grenade launcher and a couple of large-caliber pistols also. Dagger came in last, easily swinging his sniper-spec gauss rifle.

They were bantering as they entered, Ferret laughing at Thor for taking on Dagger in a shoot-out. "What, you thinking of trying out for the Olympics?" He laughed again as Thor winced.

Thor's account was lighter by five hundred credits. He'd been *sure* that with standard weapons he could outshoot Dagger. After all, the sniper's rifle was a hid-eously expensive and custom piece of equipment that took hours of tuning to set up properly. He would be chagrined at the outcome for days, and could expect to hear it bandied about forever.

Dagger had used a standard grav-rifle, as requested, to put ten rounds in the X ring at five hundred meters as fast as he could pull the trigger, then ten more at a thousand meters nearly as fast. He'd had one flyer at that range, just out of the five and into the four ring. He'd barely taken time to aim, it seemed, and had turned and left the firing line the moment his last round was fired, before any tally showed on the screen. His features hadn't moved until he heard about the flyer, and then had sneered in disgust at himself. The man was inhumanly accurate. It showed in his movements. They were fast but smooth and with never a clumsy bump. Sniping involved stalking as well as shooting, and he was as good at both skills as humans came.

Thor winced again as the rest chuckled. Finally, Gun Doll chimed, "Okay, this is getting boring," and they took the hint and changed subjects.

Dagger still didn't say anything about it as Ferret hit a switch and a set of tables and seats extruded out of the floor. They were sterile gray, just like everything else. Gun Doll eased her lanky frame up against the wall and hit a switch with her elbow—as her hands still cradled a bulky assault cannon—and throbbing music came from all sides. It was one of the abrasive dance tunes she liked, but the volume was quiet enough to prevent complaints. Holograms on the wall flared up, too, displaying unit murals. One of them showed a garish swath of destruction, smashed hovertanks, bent rocket howitzers, crushed combat bots. It started on the left at an insertion pod and terminated on the right at a huge, chiseled NCO wearing the black beret of a DRT commando. His caricature had a heavy grav-gun in his hands, an automatic grenade launcher over one shoulder, a light mortar over the other, knives and hatchets all over his combat harness and a teddy bear sticking out of one pocket. It was captioned, "Excuse me, just passing through." Another showed a drop gone horribly wrong with shattered combat armor scattered all over it, smashed shuttles, artillery still splashing rings of dirt and small killer bots swarming everywhere. At the center was a guy wearing major's tabs, tapping on a long-range communicator. Caption: "I love it when a plan comes together." At that, the artwork was tame compared to pieces that drifted around the nets and were posted on screens here and there, many of them making light of the acronym DRT . . . "Dead Right There." Or sometimes, DRTTT: Dead Right There, There and There. Or the DiRTies. Though few people would say that to one in a bar, unless they were *very* good friends. Masochism was the prime requirement for recon in nasty territory, so DRTs could take a lot of damage. They could also dish out their share and a bit more.

The chat dulled slightly as they started laying out their weapons and stripping them down for cleaning. The team was filthy with mud, sweat, grime and assorted shredded greenery; the weapons were merely dirty from use. Good troops took care of their weapons because their lives depended on them. Between pirates, feral Posleen still romping around from the war that had almost wiped out humanity, and the new Blob menace, these troops expected to see action at any time. The weapons were cared for because they were the difference between life and a cold e-mail to their survivors.

The weapons' receivers were coated with a chameleon surface that assumed the colors and pattern of anything in the vicinity. As they were laid on the table, they shifted to match, becoming all but invisible. Ferret cursed and said, "The surface stays active damned near forever, even when there isn't enough juice left to shoot with." He pressed the surface switch to drop the weapon to neutral gray.

Gorilla, being one of the technical specialists, said, "No, it won't last forever. It will last a while, though.

The surface is small and the environment in here doesn't take much shifting. But I wouldn't try to get that long out of an intruder suit. Otoh, it's easier to detect."

Ferret replied, "Teach your granma to suck Posleen; 'The expert scout uses guile and deception rather than relying on technical devices.'" Shrugging his shoulders he turned back to his weapon.

The troops' sure fingers handled the parts without effort, as they would even in the dark. The dull coated barrels with their internal grav drivers and small bores were shoved to the middle of the table and the receivers to the edge, in a standard layout. In the frame of these, smaller parts, trigger assemblies and sights were set in positions personalized by years of practice. The punch guns were rather simple: an energy unit that slid out and wasn't to be messed with and the frame. Each soldier had his or her own favorite layout, but all were clearly the product of the same basic training. Dagger sat off at a table by himself, his sniper rifle being cared for by hands that almost caressed it. Dagger was like that. Always part of the team, always alone.

Thor pulled the breech of his grav-gun and stared into it while waving his glowing light ball across the table and down to illuminate it from the bore. As he inhaled the astringent tang of burned metal wafting from the tube, he cursed at what he saw. The main problem with the weapons was that the ammunition they had used was substandard. The factory-recommended ammunition was depleted uranium coated with a carbon-based witches' brew and charged with a tiny droplet of antimatter. The antimatter droplet was released by a shot of power and then the charge was scavenged from the AM disintegration. However, the Islendian Republic did not have the facilities to produce such sophisticated ammo, so the grav-guns were driven off external packs and most of the rounds used were simple depleted uranium with a graphite coat.

The problem was that at the incredibly high speeds of the rounds, the carbon and then the uranium sublimed and coated the breech and bore of the rifle with a substance that was damned near uranium-carbon alloy. And nearly as hard to get off . . .

Thor reached into his ruck for a bulb of soda from his "emergency" rations, and paused. "What the hell?" he muttered, finding something hard and not bulb-shaped. He grasped it and pulled it out. It was a rock, about five kilograms' worth. Just a rock.

"You rat bastards," he said disgustedly. It was a running gag. Every time they came back from a mission or a field exercise, some jackass was able to slip a local boulder into his gear. He must have a pile of forty of the damned things in the corner of his barracks room now. No one knew why he kept them. Neither did he, except that they were mementos, sort of. He even had one from Earth.

Everyone laughed aloud, except Dagger, and even he snickered. Gorilla said, "Another rock for your collection, Thor."

"Yeah, yeah. Rocks, concrete core samples from the engineers, always something. Sooner or later someone's going to get me busted for smuggling a Rumakian Sacred Piece of Granite or some shit. And I'll make you guys cough up the duty."

"You'd have to," Ferret said. "Dagger would have all *your* cash." Everyone laughed at that, even Dagger.

The hazing about the shootout picked up again.

"'Hi, my name is Thor, and I can't hit the broad side of a warehouse.'"

"'Dagger, shoot me now before I try to beat you again.'"

"'Duh, me Thor, me think me shoot straight.' 'Dat's okay,' said the young maiden, not wanting to embarrass him, 'I'm thore too!'"

Dagger said nothing. He didn't need to. Thor said nothing, trying to make them pick something else by being boring.

Ferret made a single comment and shut up. "You better be able to shoot better against the Blobs than against Dagger," which let the conversation segue into a discussion of what the next mission might be. There was no question that the next mission would be against the Blobs. There were few other threats currently, and none that required the special skills of DRTs. The question was whether it would be a raid, a recon, another casualty-racking attempt at a snatch or some new vac-brained plan from the whiz kids on the Strategic Staff.

The so-called Blobs, the Tslek, were a recent enemy to the loose federation of planets that made up the Islendian Confederation. They were dark, soft creatures with no fixed form, that extended pseudopods for manipulation. So far, not many humans had seen a Tslek up close. At least not to report back afterwards. Several remote colonies had been lost, their administrative centers smashed into incandescent vapor by what were reported as kinetic weapons but seemed to pack more energy than simple rock falls. As with nukes and antimatter weapons, such devices were forbidden among the civilized races, especially among humans. The shock of the attacks had rippled through space with the first reports. Reconnaissance and special operations craft had been sent out to determine the nature of the threat. Some had come back.

The Tslek occupied an undetermined number of planetary systems near the fringe of human exploration. So far the humans had only found one planet that had a Blob "civilian" presence. Or at least a moderately large presence, because it was difficult to tell the difference between Blobs that were military and civilian. The human task force commander had dropped a series of kinetic strikes in retaliation and retreated. At the moment the situation was something like a "phony war" with both sides probing forward. One could get just as dead in a phony war as a real one, though. The front was insubstantial and shifting, but very real.

So far the Blobs had gotten the best of it; the frontiers in that direction had been hammered with millions of dead colonists as a result. If, or more accurately, when a Blob raiding force got through to the more heavily populated worlds the civilian casualties would be enormous; on the order of billions.

There were indications from scouting ships that the Blobs were planning on attacking towards the Core worlds with a large fleet. The humans were grudgingly willing to accept the casualties that came with this; the normal technique was to let a group attack then slash in behind them with light forces and sever their supply lines. But the line of advance was the question. While Earth and the Core might not care, the Islendian Republic didn't wish to be the route used.

The Blobs apparently had the same needs as humans: hydrogen to refuel their ships, spare parts, oxygen and water and fresh food. They also used the same drive systems as humans, the low energy "valley drive" that would take ships from system to system along "valleys" between stars called transit lanes and the "tunnel drive," originally introduced to the humans and their allies by the enemy Posleen, which at enormous energy cost could "tunnel" at hyperluminal speed through any region of space. This meant that from time to time they had to resupply with hydrogen for their valley drives and antimatter for their tunnel drives, besides taking on other consumables. Some of that could be brought forward by resupply ships. But some of it, fuel especially, was more efficiently gathered along the way. It still made more sense to have ships resupply on food rather than "grow their own"; plants took up space that could be used for ammo and "legs" and weren't as efficient at cleaning the air as recycling systems.

For all these reasons the Blobs were going to need an advanced base on their line of march. It would have certain requirements: it would have to have more than one good transit lane, it would need a Jovian-type planet for fuel and it would probably possess a terrestrial planet with signs of Blob agriculture.

The Blobs didn't strictly need a system with an Earth-like class planet, but that was the way to bet. Not only did it permit areas to grow and process food without the expense of domes and other necessities on moons but it permitted crew rest in decent conditions. The biosphere also was a remarkably good cloaking material for all the normal methods of detection; it meant atmosphere to deflect particles and other life signs to disappear among.

The Blobs did not appear to be stupid and they seemed to use the same general logic system as humans. That meant that they were as aware of the needs as the humans. And they would guess that the humans would know this. So they were probably prepared for a reconnaissance of some sort.

The missions related to this might be very nasty, brutish and short. The team knew this, and tried to avoid admitting it by joking around the subject. Any mission could be their last, and current events were less than promising. A couple of teams had disappeared lately. Nobody knew where they went, or what had happened; they weren't on the need-to-know list about other team missions. They simply received the bald reports that team such-and-so was "missing; presumed lost."

While the team discussed missing comrades, the team commander showed up. He was a familiar enough sight, working with them daily as he did, and standing orders were not to waste time saluting unless a field grade officer was along. They were formal enough for discipline, relaxed enough for camaraderie. What made the team stiffen their postures and grow instantly quiet was the strange creature accompanying the captain. It was a sight almost never seen to human eyes: a Darhel. In uniform.

The group instinctively bristled. Even after almost a millennium of contact the Darhel were not popular.

They had once been virtual slavemasters of the human race. They still had the reputation of being dishonorable, untrustworthy Shylocks. The few humans who dealt with them found them to be as shifty as sand and mean as rattlesnakes; they seemed to take great pleasure not just in making money but in screwing people while they did so. While none of the team had dealt directly with Darhel before, they all knew the stories.

Bringing warnings of the Posleen, voracious interstellar beings who stripped planets as locusts do fields, the Darhel had provided technology and weapons to humanity in exchange for human strategic expertise. That technology had been rationed out in such a fashion that, while the Posleen had been stopped, casualties among the inadequately equipped human forces had been horrific. The Darhel always insisted this had been unavoidable and due to logistical issues, but no one could miss that the end result was a loss of eighty percent of the human race and nearly a century of the remainder being used as mercenaries and pawns, while those "relocated for safety" during the war had wound up as scattered refugees assimilated into alien societies, with a near total loss of their human thought processes. The Darhel, of course, had graciously helped humanity rebuild and resettle Earth, at "reasonable cost," said cost being set by the Darhel. It was not a history to inspire trust. Nor had they actually shared technology—most of what humans had acquired had been reverse engineered from the little that had survived the war.

In the end, of course, it had turned out to be a grievous mistake on the part of the Darhel. They should have either left humanity to its own devices or dealt with it fairly. When it became clear that they had done neither, humanity's response had been . . . human. Some of the Darhel had survived the sporadic programs of extermination practiced by the survivor states. Some.

This Darhel was pale and translucent of skin with cat-pupilled eyes. Most had green or purple irises, this one's were purple with a bare turquoise tinge at the edges. His face was typical of Darhel, narrow and reminiscent of a fox's. His hair resembled that of humans and was the usual silvery black rather than the metallic gold tones seen more rarely. "Gold" and "silver" regarding Darhel hair meant exactly what the words said; the hair was not blond. Darhel had pointed ears that tended to twitch under stress, and sharklike teeth. They didn't smile much. They looked, in fact, like classical fantasy Elves. This one wasn't twitching in stress, and bore a practiced closed-lip smile of greeting. By its eyes, the smile could mean anything . . . or nothing.

To make matters worse, the Darhel wore gunny's stripes. The question was, had he earned them from politicking, as a reward to his Shylock skills, or the hard way, from operating in the field? Almost unnoticed amid the other shocks, he wore the badge of a sensat above his left pocket.

After thousands of years of striving, humans were finally starting to make actual strides in extrasensory perception. The military, especially, had started using them for a variety of purposes. Very few could "read minds" but many of them could sense emotions even at a distance. A few could get a vague sense of the future. There were the expected prejudices against them.

Despite the fact that few could sense, much less decipher, actual thoughts, everyone feared them for that potential ability to delve into the private recesses of the mind. Every sentient being that the humans had met had thoughts that they preferred not see the light of day. Thus, most found sensats uncomfortable companions. Most sensats, in fact, could just barely sense emotions and occasionally very strong and focused thoughts. They might get a vision of the last thing a dying person saw for instance. That didn't make people any happier.

A few were found on the Deep Recon teams. Generally they were empaths who could do things like spot an ambush by the "lying in wait" emotions of the attackers. The Blobs were detectable by the sensats. Indeed, because sensats could detect a Blob kilometers away, the Tslek apparently used extrasensory perception as a normal means of communication.

"Welcome back. I hope it was a good exercise?" the captain greeted them. There was an automatic but halfhearted flurry of mumbles and "sir"s as the team all but ignored him to stare at the Darhel.

The captain had been prepared for that response, and rather than waste time, said, "Let me introduce Tirdal San Rintai." The Darhel nodded at the introduction and waited patiently. "Tirdal is a limited empath, a Class Two, and has completed the qual course for DRT sensat with a secondary skill of medic. He will be accompanying you on the upcoming mission."

There were mutters and barely audible comments, which reached the surface when Dagger said, "No offense, sir, Tirdal"—with a faint nod at the Darhel—"but we've been a team for a long time and operate well together. We don't need unfamiliar personnel in our ranks at the start of a mission, with no prep or training time. It's more likely to screw things up than help."

The captain fixed Dagger with a stare. "You think so, do you? You know what the mission is, then?" Before Dagger could even shake his head, he continued, riding over any other arguments that lurked beneath the surface. "Well, here's the facts: We have a warning order for an insertion on a possible Blob planet, to recover intel and possibly artifacts and prisoners. The only team that ever made it back from one of those had a sensat along. So we are taking a sensat. Period. Tirdal is available, trained and has Level Four sensat scores. He's going with us. Is that all right with you, Sergeant?" His emphasis while staring at Dagger made it clear he was tiring of Dagger's questioning on every mission order. The man could shoot like nobody's business, and outstalk a cheetah, but his regard for authority left much to be desired.

Dagger stared back, firmly though not obviously defiantly, and said firmly, "Understood, sir. Tirdal, welcome to the team."

At that, Tirdal finally betrayed action, stepping forward to shake hands. "I greet you, Dagger. I'm sure we can work together." His voice was sonorous and deep and his grip solid as Dagger took it. Then it was more than solid, a strong, crushing grasp, accompanied by a violet and cyan stare that locked with his eyes and seemed to look through them into the brain behind.

Dagger pressed down on the hand, hard. Besides being a multiplanet-classed shot he was one of the strongest men on a team of very strong men. But he couldn't budge the Darhel's grip. After a moment he felt the Darhel start to press down and it was like having his hand in the grip of a mechanical press. After a moment's struggle his face finally betrayed a flicker of pain and the Darhel, smiling again, faintly, released the pressure.

Dagger didn't betray any surprise outwardly, despite what he felt inside at Tirdal's disturbing presence and strength. "Yeah, no problem," he muttered, trying not to shake his hand in reaction to the pain.

"I look forward to working with you," Tirdal said with a nod, his vertical-pupilled eyes never leaving the face of the sniper.

The others shook hands and introduced themselves. Tirdal nodded to each in turn, saying almost nothing else.

Chapter 2

THE PREMISSION BRIEFING bore no shattering surprises. There was fuzzy vid from a probe flyby, with scientific data on geology and meteorology, botany and zoology. They were fuzzy because the probe was the size of a basketball and had whisked through at meteoric velocities, then done a datadump; anything larger or less covert would have given away the fact that someone was interested in the system.

Mission gear was listed, some as required, some optional. Another list had forbidden items. No shocks there, either: nothing that could give away the location of an inhabited planet, no tech gear that didn't

17

include a self-destruct, nothing personal that was indicative of culture or language, etc. Also tediously routine for the team was the situation. Enemy forces: unknown. Friendly forces: none. Attached assets: none. They were needed at once and had only minimal prep time. There was never time to rehearse it properly, but there was always time to waste a team or two. They would at least get two days to shake down with their new member. The military was generous in its own way. Day One was today, all talk. Day Two would be a field exercise.

"The planet is quite Earth-like," the team commander, nicknamed Bell Toll, said. "Climate is temperate and moderate. I hate to sound too cheerful, but altogether it looks like a walk in the park compared to our usual missions."

"How do we insert?" Gun Doll asked.

One of the intel weenies briefing them replied, "A stealthed survey ship found an open tunnel to the system. It was quite unlikely, but there it was. The system they found contains both multiple Jovians and this high-quality planet. Sensor bots were dropped for their usual sweep, when faint energy emissions and hyper tracks were detected. The bots performed a cursory biosphere sweep and localized the emissions."

"It's our job to do a drop," Bell Toll continued, "move to the area and determine, hopefully without detection, if there is or is not a Blob base in the area. There's something there, but it could be Blobs, free-colonizer humans or pirates. Or even another, unknown, race. It's up to us to determine which. And for that we'll need our sensat.

"Tirdal, attention, please," he asked, and Tirdal

snapped upright. "Tirdal's been in service for quite some time as an intel analyst and interrogator. He's only recently been through the DRT course, but has some experience and time in grade, so, by the chain of command, he will be third in line of command, after me and Shiva. At ease, Tirdal.

"Class Two, for those of you who slept through all the training sessions, means he can detect emotions and thought processes, but not reliably acquire actual thought symbols. Level Four means he can detect out to a variable but undefined range greater than Level Three. He's going to be one of our early warning systems to keep us from walking into a tea party of Blobs. Also, if he can pick up any signs from a distance, we may not have to go in as far. I'm sure you all appreciate the advantage of that." They did. Brave fronts aside, anything that reduced mission risk was a good thing. Everyone took another look at the Darhel, looking as cool as an Oort planet in his brand-new uniform. Most of the stares were curious, but a couple were cold. He didn't seem fazed.

"With all that said, are there any questions not addressed in this briefing or your packets?" There were not. All the questions that the team wanted to ask were on the unofficial forbidden list. "Why are we doing this shit?" "Are we actually expected to survive?" "Is this a good time to ask for a transfer?" Questions that flashed through most of their minds, at least from the second mission onward, but could never be spoken. They were DRT and they hadn't gotten this far by quitting.

"Then you had better get last minute stuff fixed up and check your gear. Zero seven hundred start tomorrow. The initial oporder will be Thursday at zero nine hundred. We'll probably lift sometime around seventeen hundred to nineteen hundred hours. That's all. Tirdal, follow me," he finished with a point of his finger. He knew better than to leave the Darhel alone for now. The team was still unwinding from their last exercise and wouldn't react well to the stress of an incoming alien sensat. He could already hear the grumbles.

Despite shorter legs, the Darhel strode easily down the duraplast hallway alongside the captain, feeling the human's conflicting thoughts. Beneath the turmoil, there was order and confidence. Even more than regular troops, sensats needed to know their commanders were prepared to deal with issues. Tirdal felt the coming question arising before Bell Toll opened his mouth. "So what do you think, Tirdal?"

"Of the situation, Captain? Of the team? Of the preparations?"

"Of the team, for now."

"I don't think they like me much," Tirdal said slowly. He said everything slowly. His voice wasn't taciturn or filtered to be deep and empty, that was just how Darhel spoke. His only expression was a flip of his right ear.

The pictures to either side of them were more formal, line drawings and holos of battles and locales. Bell Toll appeared to study them as he walked, though he'd no doubt seen them thousands of times before.

"They may not like you," the captain said, frowning. "Yet. But small teams require trust and teamwork. Since you're new and haven't been with the team in their exercises, or missions for that matter, you're naturally going to experience a bit of standoffishness. This is just the nature of being new to a team. Don't let it worry you. Do your job and everyone will forget that . . ."

"That I'm a shiftless Darhel freak?" Tirdal supplied with an ear flick.

"If you take that point of view things will be very rough indeed," the captain said, stopping to lock eyes with the Darhel. "And I won't tolerate discrimination."

"Yes, sir," Tirdal agreed, tasting the forceful honesty in the statement. For a wonder, the team commander seemed to accept him at face value: as a "newbie" team member, not a Darhel, not an evil demon Shylock. Still, the captain was keeping him separated from the rest of the team at present. Tirdal partly appreciated that because there was less stress in their thoughts when he wasn't around, but it wasn't a good sign. They'd have to learn to be comfortable to function.

"But you still have to respect their unity and work to earn their trust," Bell Toll said, as if *he* were the sensat. "If you try to mess with the experienced members, they will go hard on you, trust me. You're the new boy, learn to deal."

"Yes, sir. I'm prepared for that."

"Good. They're—we're—going to give you the respect due your rank. But it is up to you to prove that you're worthy to be here, not up to us to prove that we are."

"Yes, sir," Tirdal said as they reached the captain's office.

"I'm sure you've got your own preparations," Bell Toll said as he turned at his door. "Oporder for the exercise is at zero nine hundred. Same briefing room."

Tirdal flicked his ear again, then left as Bell Toll closed the door.

Back in the team's briefing room, the NCO in charge had just returned. He'd arrived late and left early to deal with details, and no one had had a chance to talk to him, yet. Shiva, as he was known, walked in to the middle of the heated discussion about the Darhel. It was rather vehement, and he'd not even sat down before Thor confronted him.

"We gotta goddamned Darhel sensat dumped on us, Sarge," he complained without even a nod of greeting.

"I know, I was here," Shiva said. He was calm. Shiva was always calm. Considering the missions and the troops, it was a good attribute, and he'd made it as long as he had and to his rank because of it.

"Good. What are you going to do about it?" Thor asked.

"Nothing," Shiva replied. "Nothing I can do, and he's the sensat we've got. Sorry, Thor, you'll have to get used to him."

"They probably let the little shrimp ghost Q course," Gorilla put in. "They always go easy on sensats." His voice was deep and gravelly to match his huge size.

"Think so, huh?" Shiva asked, turning toward him.

"Yeah, am I wrong?"

"Well," Shiva drawled, a faint smile of amusement spreading across his face as he spread across the chair in a stretch. "He apparently *maxed* the course. Not 'exceptional,' but 'maxed.' I called Roy over at Course and the instructors were impressed. And most of 'em hated his guts. So there was no favoritism there."

"It's probably just like the way chicks get treated,"

Gun Doll said. "There's so few of us, still, that we stand out. Everyone assumes that women, shrimps, aliens and civvy specialists get special treatment." She looked over at Dagger, who'd hazed her mercilessly upon her arrival, before grudgingly admitting she knew her job. "Right, Dagger?"

Dagger was putting away fine tools from his cleaning and maintenance kit. He was forever tinkering with his rifle, and carried extra tools to that end. It was probably unauthorized for him to do depot level adjustments, but he shot well enough that no one would dare complain. He laid down a probe and shrugged very slightly.

"I put him where I put everyone else. If he does his job, I don't have a problem. If Shiva says he maxed the course, I'll assume he can keep up, keep quiet and back us up." Closing the receiver on his gauss rifle, he cycled the mechanism, pressed the stud, and listened to the snap of the ignition circuit. "If he screws up, it'll make more work for me. Then we have a problem."

Gun Doll, Gorilla and Shiva stared momentarily at each other, not at Dagger. Dagger wasn't paying attention to them. At least not outwardly. It was probably part of his act. He loved to play the cold killer. It was annoying, but it was how Dagger was.

"Dammit, why did it have to be a Darhel? Why not a human sensat?" Thor groused.

"Because we don't have enough," Shiva replied. Human sensats were not only rare, but were needed to produce GalTech materials, because the only way anyone had figured out to produce most of the gear at that level was the way the Indowy did it—by "praying." Actually, it was a complex ritual of meditation and thought, but it was very intensive and those doing it were not generally available nor disposed to lugging huge rucks through dangerous wilderness. The Michia Mentat, the largest school of the sensory arts, kept pretty much to themselves, and had since the Islendian Republic had split from the Solarian Systems Alliance some hundreds of years before. They'd served more in a diplomatic role between the Fringe and the SSA, and part of the treaty had been written to keep them out of military matters. They'd sat out the rebellion, their focus being within, but everyone knew how badly Earth and its allies would have fared had they been involved. "Don't see you going to sensat testing, Thor."

"Could be worse. It could be an Indowy sensat who we'd literally have to carry," Gun Doll said.

"We'll manage," Dagger said and snapped his firing circuit again after his last round of adjustments. It couldn't be coincidence this time. Everyone stared at him.

"Right," Shiva said, breaking the tableau. "If you plan on drinking, getting laid or anything else tonight, get your crap squared away now. If you don't make excuses, I won't have to make explanations, and we'll all be happier. We're departing straight after a two-day run through. So live it up now."

It was well after 1700 hours when the prep work was done. Shiva was still doing administrative stuff, which never ended—the troops had to be certified as to range time, medical appointments and the other minutiae of military life. Bell Toll was scrounging data, trying to wheedle a few facts that could give his people the edge in this op, as well as drafting the orders and acknowledging briefings. This op was going to play hell with their training schedule for the Readiness Standards Evaluation, which since this wasn't, yet, a "declared war," had to be met. That was the military; stick you out on the raw end one day and put you through chickenshit the next.

Thor appointed himself patrol leader of the bar crawl, and proceeded to prod the others. He first cornered Dagger in his room, who replied, "Thanks, but if I'm going to be shooting, I'd like to be as sober as possible." His expression wasn't exactly condescending, but Dagger was very much the psychotic loner. He almost turned into a cloistered monk before a mission, and wasn't much of a partier afterwards. He'd been known to have three beers, once or twice. He'd even had an expensive shot of Earth whisky once. He wasn't cheap, he was just a purist.

Tirdal was next, and looked somewhat confused. Behind him the lights were dim. His desk had been cleared and set with a small candlelike object, a book and some other items Thor couldn't identify from the door. They were some kind of religious or personal gear, and Thor didn't pry. It wasn't politeness; he was embarrassed. To his inquiry about joining the entourage, Tirdal replied, "You wish for us to appear in public as a group, then attempt to find private entertainment, then return to little sleep?"

"That's sort of it," Thor agreed. "It's supposed to be fun and help take the edge off."

Tirdal appeared to consider it for a moment, then replied.

"My presence would create a disturbance among

others that would not be helpful to you, I think. There will be nothing for me to do privately, and if left alone in public, there could be issues. As to 'taking the edge off,' I will meditate most certainly, and review recent events. I also need to study more of both human interaction and technical matters. So I think not. But I do thank you for the invitation. Perhaps when this is over the timing would be more appropriate."

"Well," Thor said, "if you want to observe human interaction, this would be the time."

"I'm aware of that, and the idea is intriguing," Tirdal replied. "But other considerations take priority. I hope, however, that everyone has a good time on your 'bar crawl.'"

"Thanks, then," Thor said a bit awkwardly. "I hope your meditation goes well." It seemed the polite thing to say.

He knocked on Ferret's door and found the specialist leaning back in his bunk with his fingers interlaced behind his head.

"Bar crawl time," Thor said.

"I'm on it," Ferret said, rolling to his feet and slipping his feet into ship-boots.

"Glad to hear it," Thor said, with feeling. There was nothing lonelier than a single-handed bar crawl. "The sarge can't make it, we don't want the captain along, Dagger's being himself and Tirdal doesn't seem to understand the concept."

"Just as well," Ferret had told him. "Either of them would scare chicks away, and we don't need a fight tonight, either."

Thus it was that Gorilla, Ferret, Thor and Gun Doll

went looking for distraction before their appointment to spend two months in space and muck. They met right outside the base gate, where everything a homesick young troop could yearn for was available.

There was the branch of "Feelings, Inc," a company which had staked out space near every base on three planets, to sell cheap trinkets to soldiers as "fine jewelry" for their loved ones back home, wherever home might be. The prices were not cheap.

A vid arcade clattered and dinged, lights flashing through the door. Every machine in the place was cranked to maximum difficulty. Entertainment equipment could be rented at stiff fees, the purveyors sure of their income because troops' ID numbers could be called in to the base if funds were tardy, to be forcibly secured from said troops while their commanders wrote them up for failing to be responsible and for disgracing the service. Only the former mattered to the business in question.

An old electronics storefront had been converted, the sign out front proclaiming "Bambi's Lingerie." It had once added "private showings available" until some wiseass had changed the marquee lettering to read "Ass and head," which had likely been true, Bambi's having been shut down weeks before by the local mayor and police, concerned about the morals of their town. That emphasis on old Solarian "morals" was quaint and hickish on a planet like Islendia.

However, that concern for morals didn't extend to the rest of the strip of small establishments determined to find some way, any way, to liberate all the cash soldiers and spacers might have. Everyone loved the military, as long as the military had cash to burn.

After that, they were free to piss off, or go back on base and quit whining, or spend a complimentary night in the town lockup. The screwing of soldiers wasn't a moral concern, as long as that screwing involved their time and money but not sex. Unless, of course, that sex followed a spending spree in the "Short Time Saloon," the area's only real bar.

Not being homesick young troops, and far more savvy and sophisticated than anyone might think at their ripe ages of twenty or so, they walked right past Soldier Row and paid no attention.

"Dancing," Gun Doll insisted. She was made up in electric blue, including a dye for her bobbed hair. She wore a long overtunic to hide her shoulders and hips. It wasn't that she was unattractive, but her proportions were unusual, with her height and solid skeleton. Men were intimidated, and even more so when they found out she was a DRT. It was exasperating, and she tried to play it down. Instead she played other things up—the garment was slit down to below her navel.

"Drinking," said Gorilla. It was a long-standing argument between them. He wore a jacket and tie over his shorts, trying to look casual from his lofty height. Gorilla never wore makeup, because he felt it looked stupid on his craggy face.

"Drinking and dancing, and lots of chicks," Thor said. Thor had strange styles of fashion, wearing a synthleather jacket at least ten years out of date over striped tights. His bulging thighs and broad shoulders were obvious, he hoped.

Gun Doll said, "Drinking and dancing, hold the chicks."

"Oh, I will," Thor agreed, grinning.

Ferret, wearing jeans and cutaway tunic to show off his pecs, made up lightly and relaxed as always, asked, "Same place as last time, or someplace new?"

"Who got laid last time?" Gorilla asked.

"I did," Gun Doll admitted, "but I had to pimp myself to do it. How about somewhere less snooty?"

"Yeah," Thor agreed, "somewhere where we'll be recognized for the cold, calculating killers and human sex machines we really are."

"So, Thor wants to go to Fantasyland." Ferret grinned, elbowing him.

"Yeah, whatever, there's a bus," Thor said, pointing. "We can get sweaty after we find the chicks."

They boarded the bus just in time to be hanging at the door as it sought cruising altitude of ten meters. The driver gave them a dirty look, because they were violating the law and it would be his ass if anything happened to them. It was obvious from the clash of styles they were military. Their casual attitude about the height said they were some kind of commandos, as did the cropped hair and thick necks and shoulders. Already they were getting looks, and that suited this group fine.

They didn't care about ugly looks or amused glances. All they cared about was attention from other young people, preferably attractive, though "attractive" was a slippery term when alcohol or other intoxicants, their other desire, entered the picture. And all of it would make for great stories later.

As their profession required utter secrecy and low profiles, they made up for the lack of attention when not working. They were loud and brash on the trip, and though they gave no details, that being a prudent standard, there were enough varied commandos stationed there that no one had any doubt they were some of them. That, and the heavier than usual sidearms they carried.

While having guns didn't of itself attract favorable attention, competence combined with them did. When a feral Posleen might trot down any street, suddenly charging to the attack if the urge and voracious appetite tickled its semisentient fancy, the presence of professional killers was a welcome thing. The troops were therefore popular, no matter their young, smartass attitudes. None of the passengers complained about the noise, and a few kept close. Islendia might be urban and modern, but Islendia was also raw and savage. It had been wrested from the Posleen at great cost, and scars across the landscape and crashed Posleen landing craft attested to a generous use of antimatter weapons, when the human settlement had been reinforced.

Being fecund egg layers, the Posleen had been defeated but not wiped out. They came in two classes. "Normals" were semisentient, just bright enough to swing a rock, or, if so equipped, pointshoot a weapon. "God Kings" were larger, sentient and scary. Each God King could control up to fifty or sixty normals, running them around like tabletop gaming counters through a handful of Superior Normals. Posleen were parthenogenetic carnivores that looked like a cross between centaurs, crocodiles and ponies. Their defining attribute was their voracious appetite. Their enemies and prey became sushi and jerky in short order.

When they'd arrived in the sector, armed with star drive and advanced weapons, they'd proceeded to wipe out every planet they came to, like locusts in a field. Then they'd met humanity. Most of the human race had not survived, but, on the other hand, most of the Posleen advance hadn't either. And as the old joke said about "the unstoppable force hitting the immovable object" there had been a lot of side effects. One was "tamed" Darhel. Another was the Tular Posleen.

The Tular Posleen were a settled, trustworthy race who only rarely ate sentient creatures, and even then only other Posleen, and kept to their own planets. The ferals left behind on a hundred planets were simply ravening beasts to be exterminated. And anyone on such a planet who didn't carry a weapon stayed close to those who did.

That had been part of what pushed Islendia, her thirty-odd republic planets and similar number of colonies over the edge to rebellion. Earth had wanted to resume the strict weapon controls and environmental standards it had been working on before the Posleen invasion. At which the blighted and struggling worlds of the Fringe had screamed bloody murder. Not drain a swamp because it might "damage the natural balance," when such balance was already screwed by the presence of Posleen in the bog? Not bloody likely. And suggesting one seek permission for an AI guided autocannon with antimatter shells to deal with said Posleen, just because some Earth bureaucrat thought they were "inappropriate" for civilians wasn't a concept to win the hearts and minds of the Fringers.

Which was why there was now an Islendian Republic. And a rump group of worlds, old, sophisticated and highly developed, seething in the background.

The bus trip wasn't long, only about two hundred

kilometers, through the light of a falling sun and then into the domed warren of the city proper. Islendia was actually an Earth-like moon of a monstrous gas giant, debatably a brown dwarf, that had been christened Juliana. Juliana was coming into full phase as Isel, the system's star, set, the planet a fluffy wash of colors on the horizon, seeming to stretch endlessly. Juliana would rise to show dun and ochre bands punctuated by bright red roils of reacting hydrogen. Its ring formation and myriad satellites made it a rare sight for those tourists who could afford the steep transit fees, and the complex rotation of it and Islendia around Isel led to very strange day cycles.

The troops paid little attention. Not only had they grown up with that tangerine monster hanging over them, they'd seen far more exciting things, from their viewpoint, on other planets. Dagger was from far out on the Fringe, and would likely find it interesting, if he were along and if he were disposed to admitting to a human esthetic weakness. They, who had traveled far, kept their attention focused down at the seething fleshpots below.

The fleshpots were another of Islendia's appeals for the prudish but wealthy residents of the SSA. The lax laws and taxes of Islendia had permitted the relatively poor former colony to build a hefty trade surplus with the more settled inner worlds. Tourists, however, were becoming less common as Earth and its leechlike dependents became more insular.

Something was happening to the inner worlds, something that was rarely spoken of and poorly understood. The visitors, generation by generation, were becoming less and less interested in "Fringer" delights and more and more introspective and studious. On the other hand, that was also easing the political tensions.

The bus kept its altitude all the way in, coasting between ever taller buildings lit in varying colors. The older ones had plain illumination. The newer ones were lit with panels of color and images, turning them into three-dimensional artwork that rose for dozens of meters above the traffic. The advertisements rose higher than the buildings. Despite the domes and a state-of-the-art defense grid, large meteors were a common occurrence on Islendia, because of the nature of the Juliana system, and a twenty-five-megaton blast in the stratosphere instead of on the surface was still bad for structural integrity. None of the buildings rose above thirty stories. It wasn't common for domes to crack, but if they did, the same shockwave would tear the edifices apart. Hence, most activity was indoors and underground, despite the complications of building down instead of up.

The driver landed them atop a platform in front of a complex, still a good ten meters up. The four were already crowding the door before it opened, and erupted as they would from an assault pod under fire, swarming out and toward the broad, anachronistic stairs descending into the Sector A club, its lights dim red to match the décor.

Thor was first, flashing an ID and waving his card at the sensor. He slowed just enough for the dye marker to slap coldly against his hand, and was already reconning the place as he passed inside. It was fortunate they were sober, as the flashing lights and shifting holograms made visibility an iffy proposition, and it was hard to tell substance from image. That was part of Sector A's appeal. He decided on an empty corner booth, and arrived there at a run, beating another man who looked annoyance at him but didn't dispute his claim. The booth was one of many set high on the wall, approachable from below only by a ladder, but low enough for "vertical envelopment" of the floor below. Thor scrambled up the ladder with the rest of the team following.

"Here we go!" Ferret called as he arrived behind Thor, taking the side seat. "A good, clear field of fire."

"For you to puke?" asked Gorilla, whose height gave him an even greater view from the booth's position high on the wall. His back was to that wall, too. The others couldn't see past his imposing bulk.

Thor said, "Ferret, don't get us thrown out by tossing beers, okay? Even if it's a charitable thing to do, it's messy and pisses off the goons."

"Back soon!" Gun Doll yelled cheerfully, as she swung over the railing and dropped. One of the security goons started yelling at her as she bounced across the floor to join a man who was dancing by himself. She made a hand gesture in the goon's direction that was at least as old as starfaring mankind and grabbed the dancing man by the elbow. At first surprised, he smiled shortly and they melted into the growing crowd.

Gorilla said, "Score one, Gun Doll. Are we going to hit on chicks? Or drink first?"

"Drink first," Thor said. "That way when Ferret gets us thrown out it will hurt less."

The place hadn't filled to capacity before they grew bored and left. There was no time to develop an image or a relationship. Their needs were immediate, and constant movement the chosen means of finding company. That it was neither efficient nor cost effective didn't enter into the picture. They'd hit club after club until luck, boredom or morning did them in. Any of them could have explained the folly in their approach, had they stopped to think, but thinking was to be avoided for the moment.

From Sector A they went to Eden, a club lit only by UV lights. Couples and small groups made out in the near-black corners and nooks built in for that purpose. The building was a converted police command post from the early days of Islendian colonization, and had numerous closets, lockers and offices, most now converted into open space, some left as lockable cubbies for trysts.

"Hey, look at the diplopukes!" Ferret said, a bit too loudly. "They're wearing *suits!*"

Gun Doll played off it. "Hush, it's not polite to stare."

The diplomats appeared to be from somewhere in the Solarian Systems Alliance. It was always amusing to see staid, conservative representatives staring in awed embarrassment at painted men and women sweating off their lusts. They arrived expecting yokels. Everyone from their planets knew the Islendian Republic was populated by gun-toting, backwards farmers. Yet those farmers had a deep understanding of sexuality, and a devil-may-care attitude. Tomorrow might bring a meteor too large for the defense net, a feral Posleen to rip one's leg off, or worse, a sport God King leading an oolt of fifty of the damned things to eat a school. So why not eat, drink and screw today, if the work was done and the bills paid?

There was a vivid liveliness to the confederation that was missing in the inner worlds. Although the inner worlds were far more technologically adept, it was the Fringe that produced the poets, artists and actors who created the entertainment the inner worlds craved. The daily drama of survival, the life-and-death nature of life on the Fringe seemed to bring out far more artistry than the placid, safe, lives of the Core.

Whatever the case, the "hicks" were both more alive and more sophisticated than the Core worlders and that life and sophistication was always hard for the Core worlders to fully grasp. Often they saw only a barbaric spectacle, but that spectacle held far more beauty than could be found from Earth to Antares.

Eden led to Mac's Place, to four or five others they wouldn't remember, but would track by the stamps on their arms. On the street somewhere between Sudsy Capone's Laundromat and Bistro, which rated highly for its original theme, and The Orbital Room with its drunken young women and screaming music, Thor was struck by philosophy.

"Isn't it odd," he said, "how we, young, strapping, desirable hunks of flesh, Gorilla excepted, of course, on the prowl and itching to get blown, laid or whatever, have some of the poorest luck?"

"Speak for yourself," Gun Doll snickered. She twirled a man's underwear around her finger. "I had a quickie at Eden while you were busy being hosed by that blonde. And I think that was a guy in trans, anyway—"

Thor interrupted with, "I assure you she was female. *Very* female, and—"

"Yeah? So where's her panties?" Gorilla asked.

"You know the rules. No souvenir, no score for the board."

Sighing, Thor continued, "No, we didn't get that far. My point is, we seem to manage less action than the soft businessmen."

"They've got more money than you ever will," Gun Doll said. "Besides, where's Ferret?" she asked rhetorically.

"Still at Sudsy's," Gorilla chuckled. "Last time I saw him, which is while Thor was taking that tumble in the air dryer, he was sneaking behind the machines with something that was very probably female."

"Yep, saw that," she agreed. "So there goes your profound theory, Thor." Her tongue tripped over the phrase. She'd had a few drinks, too. "The score is one, Ferret and me, half point for you for style because we're being generous, and Gorilla has none yet but the night is young."

Thor pointed out, "It's three ayem and we've got an oh seven hundred formation."

"Yep, young," she agreed. "I think I can score two tonight." She was eyeing a man outside a bar, holding a drink and leaning casually against the wall. "Target acquired, fire for effect," she said. Her voice was sultry and seductive and so out of place with her normal personae and the comment.

Thor and Gorilla chuckled. "Goodnight, Doll. See you in four hours."

She waved her fingers behind her back as she sidled up to the stranger and smiled a smile that promised him a lot of intense, if brief, fun.

Chapter 3

GORILLA HUFFED AS HE rose and ran. Oh seven hundred had come too early. His oh six hundred alarm call even earlier. He wasn't hung over, but he was cranky and fatigued even after a shot of drugs to wake him and stabilize his metabolism. He'd known better than to go drinking before an early call, and he'd done it anyway. He promised himself he'd never do it again, and knew he was lying. It was a character flaw in an otherwise very strong personality. He hadn't found a woman, though he did just often enough that he'd keep abusing himself like that for the unlikely chance of doing so.

39

So here it was, not yet noon and he was sprinting uphill, in assault suit and extra armor, humping a blocky pack full of killer bots and sensor bots, a sharp rock in his boot top stabbing his calf and sweat greasing him.

A warning flashed in his visor, and he dropped, skipping behind a thick bush and dodging whipping thorns. To his left, Gun Doll opened up with her assault cannon as she took a position behind a rock. The noise had three frequencies—the basso roar of the firing, the harmonic note of the rapid rate of fire, and the hypersonic cracks of the projectiles. Under those was the whine of the mechanism, barely audible, and the pitch shifting caused by the recoil mechanism varying slightly. The weapon wasn't as accurate as Dagger's rifle, but then, at twelve thousand rounds per minute at full rate, it didn't need to be. She ducked again to confuse anyone as to her whereabouts.

Gorilla snapped a ball from his kit, tossed it gently out in front into the matted grass on the slope and ignored it. It unrolled into a large insectoid bot and crawled forward. He didn't need to see it; he'd seen thousands of them. It ran a wire behind itself, so he could read its sensors with less chance of detection than via a beam. Meanwhile, he was programming killerbiobots because he knew they'd be needed.

Massive fire sounded right after that flash he'd gotten, ranging from pops and cracks to outright roars, screams and booms. A warning flashed across his visor. "ALARM TRIGGERED. RED TEAM GYSGT TIRDAL. ASSAULT REPULSED, FAILED. POINT BLUE TEAM."

"Oh, blast the little freak," Gorilla muttered under his

breath. He got another message, "CONTINUE WITH EXERCISE FROM FAILURE POINT." He nodded. There was no point in stopping; they were here to learn. They'd pretend nothing had gone wrong, move forward and keep trying. As they'd have to evade the Blue Team defenders, now that they, the Red Team aggressors, were positively located, it would be that much harder. Blue was likely to score several more "wins" as the scenario adapted, before final no-joy was called. And at a case of beer per point, it was going to get expensive.

"That clumsy Darhel can buy the beer," Gorilla muttered.

An incoming message from Shiva said, "Gorilla, can you get us some distractions, please?" Shiva was still calm, even in the face of incoming swarms of dumb and seeking projectiles and "simulated" explosions that still shook the ground and slapped at the air.

"Way ahead of you, Sarge," Gorilla replied. He inhaled a deep breath, smelling scorched earth and metallic explosive residue, got a good map image and pressed a key.

Four of his small killerbiobots charged forward. Each was loaded with a kilo of hyper explosive (simulated). He took in his split screen in a glance, panning across all four "eyeballs" in the drones. They darted and bounced through the brush just like rabbits, which was no surprise; they'd been genetically engineered from that form. As they hit the five hundred meter mark from the defenders, he cut them loose to seek their own martyrdom and launched three flyer forms. Engineered from Islendian peregrinches, they flew out from him in three directions, and at randomly selected moments erupted straight up. They headed over the enemy and stooped into steep dives. Each was rated at .5 kilos and had a four shot canister weapon that fired a swarm of self-seeking flechettes. That done, he glanced again at the sensor bot he had trundling under it all and slugged its eyes' image to the rest of the team. He turned back to his controls and aimed the already orbiting swarm of killerbees in on terminal, across the line that was the best guess for enemy troops.

His screen was twinned in miniature to the captain and the sarge. They could see what was happening if they chose or if their AI decided the info was important, or as, now, when Gorilla pinged them with a red flash. He had two more bots approaching the line and "created a distraction" by the simple expedient of blowing them in place. As the enemy shifted for cover, the sharp sensors on the flyers caught the movement. The swarm was slower, as it had to buzz the information electronically around its collective intellect.

It worked, sort of. Interdiction fire ripped the flyers from the sky. The killerbees took damage, but each "death" only slowed their thoughts, not stopped them. Two of the rabbits disappeared under fire, but the third "exploded" mightily. If all was well, at least two Reds were casualties.

Then an alarm shrieked in Gorilla's ears, a shock tingled his spine, and he said, "Aw, shit," and joined the Darhel, who had already been hit again, in simulated death. He'd been too busy running drones to move. Five seconds was all it took sometimes.

But his distraction had worked; the rest of the team had moved and gotten hid again. Now Gun Doll was hammering away, Thor was providing cross fire with his grav-rifle on full, punctuated with raps from the underslung grenade launcher as fast as he could trigger. His fire stopped as he "died," but Shiva and Ferret were around the other flank. One of Dagger's seeker rounds ripped into a grav-boosted dive over a rock, and the captain tossed some cover fire around it.

The Blue Team fire was much reduced. They were definitely taking casualties. Shiva died, which left Dagger as NCOIC.

Dagger, being Dagger, didn't bother with his remaining team of Gun Doll and Ferret, but just kept shooting. It was good shooting. Still. "Dagger, what do we do?" Doll asked.

"Keep on 'em," was the taciturn reply. It was encouraging, but not very informative.

Gorilla sighed. His last two bios, both rabbits, were bouncing easily as targets. Before he "died" he'd been hoping he could backtrack the shots that would inevitably kill them.

It sort of worked. One was shot, Dagger counterfired, and another Blue died. The other bio was ignored. The AI deemed its blast insufficient for the cover involved. Gun Doll laid down a blanket of fire until she got swatted. An incoming flyer nabbed Dagger, which left the captain with a punch gun and Ferret with a gauss rifle against fortified troops with support weapons and drones.

"I call!" Bell Toll said. "Well, that was succulent."

Dagger was talking at once, which was an indication of just how angry he was. "Tirdal, you ever take a step without tripping something?" It had been the second exercise of three today where the Darhel had blown their cover. The third time he'd been slow to return fire.

Shiva said, "Dagger, did you forget you were Fireteam Leader when I bought it?" His voice was still conversational.

"Enough, everyone," Bell Toll said. "Let's go watch the after action. And don't sweat it. We worked well as a team, at least. Up until close to the end." He didn't mention Dagger, but the thought was clear to even non-sensats. "And even with that, we inflicted one point six to one casualties against a defended position."

A bounce pod arrived to pick them up, dropping down on Shiva's beacon. It descended fast, a dot in the sky becoming an inverted cone that seemed to crash to the ground, its recoil mechanism preventing it from bouncing. They clambered aboard the shelf around the bottom, each backing into a hollow that mostly fit their gear. Gorilla was too tall and had to squat, knees bent. He'd ride it that way the entire trip, swearing colorfully about the machine.

Tirdal was last, attaching the harness across his chest and letting the molecular weave bond with itself. The hardware behind his helmet snaked forward to provide commo and oxygen. There were minor sighs at his tardiness, which ended as the pod abruptly sprung off. Gs rose heavily to more than triple the local level.

The ground shrank below them, the pod reaching a moderate altitude of three thousand meters in about seventeen seconds. It seemed to loiter at the top of its parabolic trajectory, then it began its descent.

The designers of the bounce pod had been clever,

but not very military minded. With very few exceptions, bouncing high over a battlefield was suicidal. With even fewer exceptions, rear-echelon personnel didn't like speed and altitude, especially when strapped to the outside of said conveyance ("vehicle" being too kind a term for the thing). The craft wasn't practical for combat, and terrified the hell out of support troops so they'd refuse to board. Other than a very few specific rescue operations—in deep gorges, for example, and even that was dangerous with protruding shelves of rock—the only use was for getting around a practice range. How the hell the damned thing had made it through selection in the first place, and who the hell had made a buck off it, and which masochistic sons of bitches actually enjoyed pogoing around with their lunches in their throats were long standing topics of bull sessions.

The pod was descending. It was dropping like a rock. Bungee jumpers thought they knew what adrenaline was. If they had any idea . . .

The ground came up fast. Faster. Despite familiarity, everyone except Dagger and Tirdal clenched and gritted their teeth. Dagger was a sociopath about such things, refusing to flinch, and Tirdal didn't have a human perspective on altitude as it became height and then "Oh-shit-we're-going-to-die."

The pod hit the ground, their stomachs dropped into their boots, then they were heading up again, brains rattling in their heads as blood was pulled out of their brains.

Luckily, it was only two bounces in to range control.

Ration packs were the rule for exercises, so the same

for practice. Never mind that they'd be "practicing" with them for the next several weeks. It was SOP.

"Hell, I can't eat after that," Thor said, looking a bit green around the ears.

"Yeah, let's just sit for a bit first," Gun Doll agreed, panting. They both sought seats on the hewn wooden benches available under a shelter roof. Tourists would have found them rustic. To the troops, it was simply an indication of the military's cheap attitude about them. Why spend money for the grunts, when there were conference rooms that needed shamogany tables? They collapsed, still staggering, and dropped their harnesses behind them. Weapons slumped across knees or down to lean against the bench, but still controlled and with muzzles away from each other. An accidental discharge, even with the practice projectiles that evaporated upon hitting armor, would be messily lethal at close range.

Soon, they were all seated, Bell Toll up front with the range instructor, a hologram building between them. "Tirdal," Bell Toll said.

"Sir," the Darhel acknowledged. He and everyone else knew what was coming.

"You've got the dexterity of a herd of goonyaks." The captain's voice wasn't mean, but certainly had a ring of disgust to it.

"Sorry, sir," Tirdal replied. There wasn't much he could say against the charge. It was a human metaphor, and he had been clumsy.

"Dagger," Bell Toll said as he turned.

"Yo," the sniper replied around a mouthful of ration packaging.

"'Yo, *sir*,' if you don't mind." Without waiting for

a response, he said, "'Keep on 'em,' is not a very practical order, would you agree?"

"Ah, hell. I'm sorry, sir. But I was getting good shots and we all knew we were screwed anyway."

"'Screwed anyway.'" There was a moment's pause and the captain said, "If you have that attitude, yes. But look here." He indicated the holo and waited until he had everyone's attention. It only took a moment; they were fundamentally good troops, if high-strung. "Had you paid attention to anything other than *your* shooting, you could have had everyone suppress for Doll, and had her lay fire from here," he waved a pointer into the image, sending minor ripples as he disrupted the transmission, "and then the rest of you could have closed. Think you might have done more damage that way?"

"Yes, sir," Dagger agreed, chastised.

"Good shooting, yes. Keep an eye on other things, too. Gorilla."

"Sir," the hulk replied. He knew it was about not moving enough.

"If you want to sit still and be a target, we can arrange it."

"I know, sir. Overeager on the task."

"Yes, and it cost you. But that was one hell of a job with the critters," was the admission, with a grin. "Can you do that on the run?"

"I can, sir. And will."

"Doll . . ."

They ate, they watched themselves screw up all over again in the holo, and a few snide comments flew at Tirdal, who had made more than his share of mistakes, being the new guy. But he'd also moved fast on the assault, and gotten into good cover. He had some raw edges still, but was no slouch and the rest of them knew it. He said nothing. Neither did they, after the initial cracks.

"Okay, on top of all that," Bell Toll concluded, and everyone focused, "the incidents with feral Posleen are up sixty percent. Three God Kings came trotting into Bergen over the weekend, as you may have heard." There were nods. The three had come in as a coordinated attack, in fact, with almost two hundred normals under their control. They wielded primarily sticks and stones, with a couple of scavenged shotguns and some flammable fluids, but it had taken most of an afternoon for the town militia to round them up and exterminate them. Damage had been described as "moderate," but that included destroyed buildings and forty casualties. At least six casualties had been fatal so far, with others likely to die from their wounds. "Well, Governor General Sunday is not happy, and we're about to start a series of patrols to crop the damned things again. So as soon as we're back from this mission, you can plan on some hunting." To the enthusiastic response he said, "I knew that would make you happy." It didn't make the captain happy. It would play even more hell with the evaluation schedule. But the troops would get to break things and kill Posties, which was the real point of having them.

"So, all in all, we know what we did wrong. And I let it go wrong, to see how things would play out. More practice would be good, but it's what we've got. And we should be avoiding contact on this mission anyway. We'll do one more this afternoon, a sneak instead of a crash. Tirdal, stick close to Ferret and learn how to be quiet. Then we'll dog off and pack for lift."

Tirdal nodded, the others murmured, and lunch was choked down in a hurry at the prospect of wrapping up.

There were still mutters about Tirdal. There would be. But they'd disappear if he worked out to be as quiet as he was determined and stoic.

Chapter 4

THE STEALTH INSERTION SHIP was cramped. No niceties were put in for the psyche of the crew or passengers. It wasn't likely the ship would ever see passengers, except perhaps a courier. Commando teams were regarded more as cargo than passengers in regard to transit.

Pipes ran along bare overheads, lockers lined the bulkheads and passageways, and structural gear poked from every possible bare spot. There was a stink of burned metal from welding during maintenance, a tang of ozone and a musty, sweaty smell of age and dust that hadn't been precipitated by the environmental systems.

Everything was plain white, though slightly faded with age despite regular cleaning and maintenance. The only spot of color was the garishly bright safety-red airlock. Another hatch led to the crew's section of the ship. It was crowded in the compartment, the team crushed close together, with Gorilla hunched nearly double with the barely two meter height of the overhead. "Wish they'd build one sized for normal people," he groused. Really, though, he was used to it. His entire life had been spent in a crouch, he often felt. And the ship was close around everyone, he simply felt it more.

On the deck at their feet was an open hatch through which bright white light streamed from the huge warship they were docked with. The two ships were inverted in relation to each other, G fields in opposite directions and the null-G of the airlocks making transit tricky. The reason for the open hatch was the young navy sublieutenant standing in front of Bell Toll, the stealth ship's copilot and official liaison for the "supercargo."

"Our end is covered," he said. "We've had what looks like either piracy or commerce raiding along the route, especially the approach systems; there's been some ships disappearing in the area. When we're cruising we stand out like a sore thumb and there's not much our popguns could do against a commerce raider or a good pirate ship. Since they're running trade escort, we've simply docked to the *Zivotinovich* for the duration. We'll piggyback with them until we make minimum approach, then continue from there. It'll actually save about six days transit."

"Sounds good, Lieutenant," Bell Toll replied. "The sooner we get there, the better."

"That was what we figured," the navy officer said, nodding. Not that he had any real choice, and not that the Army could do much except bitch through the general staff if they didn't like it. "You want to get comfy aboard *Ziv*?"

"No thanks, son," Bell Toll said with a grimace. "We're trained to peak at the moment; I'd rather hibernate and come out fresh than have us get fat and flabby on a damned cruise ship."

"Sure, I figured," the lieutenant said. Damned Army grunts, he thought. Always looking for rocks to put in their bunks. They weren't happy unless they were wet, sore and eating slop. "But I was told to extend the invitation."

"Oh, it's appreciated, and we probably will on the way back, space permitting. But not now. We're used to mud and cold and need to stay that way," he said, ironically echoing the copilot's thoughts.

"What's *Ziv* doing on this route?" Ferret asked. He'd managed to wedge his way past Gorilla to the scout craft's crew locker. He shrugged out of his pack's straps and started stowing it and his other gear. "I thought they were acting as flagship for Second Fleet."

"They got pulled back for a fusion bottle problem," the lieutenant said from behind him. Ferret hadn't known he was there.

"Great," he said, with a nod, a bit startled. "Let's hope they fixed it properly, or this could be a very enlightening trip."

The lieutenant half-smiled, half-scowled and said, "Well, let's load you below and get moving." The joke wasn't new, and the grunt likely had no idea what could happen. Adjustments to fusion containment fields were fairly common, and there was a broad range of operation that required a yard to adjust and posed no danger, but simply reduced efficiency. And if there was a real breach, it might be a loss of containment, with contamination of the engineering space, which was annoying but not serious. In the exceedingly rare case of a compression in the field and a rupture, it would be over so fast no one would notice.

Bell Toll shook Tirdal's hand as he came aboard from the cutter. It was strictly show, to make sure the scout's crew knew he was officially accepted. See the Darhel with the human commander? Must be some kind of consultant. That was the desired effect, and rumor control should have it through the ship at slightly less than lightspeed. Tirdal secured his gear and watched the others board and load.

Entering was awkward. There was a null-gravity zone filling the hatch. The troops stepped off, spun and drifted down, fast at first, then slowing as they reached the deck, until they touched without impact and walked away. The field was computer controlled and managed everything in it as discrete packets so each person in the field moved at his own rate. Exiting would be done by jumping up lightly and being carried up and out. Turning to account for the opposing field was the only real complication. The interior of the lock was actually low enough that jumping down into it and even crawling out would not be an issue. But the field was there anyway, to help with cargo and inexperienced personnel.

The interior of the bay they'd use for the trip was even more crowded than the compartment "above." One or at most two people could move around in it.

To that end, they loaded one at a time. The interior was merely a corridor with two tiers of bunks bolted in on either side that were currently configured into G couches, legs raised slightly and the backs at a shallow angle. There were four right by the hatch and two each forward and aft. With them installed, the already tight corridor was narrow enough that Gorilla had to turn sideways to fit down it and also bend double. So he took the couch nearest the hatch. His gauss rifle/grenade launcher was secured in a rack on the hull side above his head and he was wearing his combat harness with ammunition, water, holstered pulser, combat knife and other accoutrements. He didn't notice it as a hindrance because he wore it like underwear, taking it off only to shower. He even slept in it most of the time.

Gorilla was not happy in the enclosed space and everybody knew it.

"Nice and snug, Gorilla?" Thor asked. "Need a teddy?" It did look vaguely like a crib, once the safety rail was up.

Padding flowed up from the couches followed by hard memory plastic as reinforcement, fully cocooning the team members and leaving only their heads and necks exposed. Gorilla did not like this procedure either; it was a bit nightmarish for a paranoid claustrophobe. Thor was still kidding him about it as it sealed around his neck. "Maybe the captain can untuck you a bit."

Gorilla said, "On the trip back I'm going to make sure to hide a few bugs and snakes in your couch, Thor."

Thor shut up. He hated snakes.

Masks descended and automatically snuggled for a good fit over the team's noses as the JG and a female corpsman (SBA) from the *Ziv* injected the troopers in their necks. As each was injected, he or she became very still and waxy and pale of skin. It was typical of Hiberzine. The corpsman finished up by touching a control and the memory plastic flowed up and over the exposed part so the team ended up disappearing in their cubicles, so many lumps of dull, gray plastic. Between the Hiberzine and the encasing, the troops were effectively in stasis.

Tirdal was still watching the procedure. The medic turned and asked him, "Are you going to take a bunk now?"

Tirdal flicked his ear and said, "I am not. Hiberzine doesn't work well on Darhel. The side effects are unpleasant."

"That seems strange," the medic said with a frown. "I thought the Darhel invented Hiberzine for yourselves first, then adapted it to humans."

"No," Tirdal said with a dark but bemused look. "It was invented for use on humans, by the Tchpth, at the request of the Darhel, about four thousand of your years ago." He turned and jumped expertly up the hatch and headed for the dreadnought.

As his feet disappeared, the SBA looked at the injector and then at the JG. "I thought we only ran into the Darhel a thousand years ago?"

"So did I." The looks they swapped were confused and faintly disturbed.

Chapter 5

THOR OPENED HIS EYES to see the Darhel as the cocooning material retracted. He sat up and stretched but it was more psychological than because of a real need. To the team no time had passed at all. Hiberzine suppressed all activity at the cellular level. There was no fatigue or strain.

He saw Tirdal waiting, looking pretty much as he had before they went under. The JG and the medic, however, were jumpy. The medic was administering the Hiberzine antidote while the JG made sure everybody was recovering well. It was merely ritual; Hiberzine never had any major side effects. However, its process was still not understood, it not being a human creation, and it was always studied and regarded with a bit of awe.

The others opened their eyes and looked around, taking only a moment to place themselves. As far as they were concerned, nothing had happened. The only real reaction was from Gorilla, who seemed more than glad to be out of the cocoon. He rolled his feet to the deck and sat on the grated floor, just to be out of the bunk.

Bell Toll checked the internal chronometer in the nanocomp in his head and frowned. They'd been "down" for three months and the voyage was supposed to be a month and a half. What had been the delay?

"What the hell happened to the schedule?" he demanded.

"Things with the Blobs have heated up," the pilot said with a worried frown. "There's been another big clash in the sector and high command really wants to know if this is a major staging zone. Because of the fighting we were unable to use the intended system for a jump and had to do a non-tunnel jump, then refuel before doing a second jump. There was a nest of pirates there, which we cleaned out. Busy around the Fringe here," he added with a grimace.

Bell Toll didn't speak; he just grimaced back.

"For local information," the pilot continued, "we'll be checking out an anomaly around the second gas giant while the team is on the planet, and another stealth ship is on the way in support."

Bell Toll nodded but didn't ask questions. The probability was that at least a task force was following the second stealth ship and for all he knew there might be a dozen stealth ships in the system. But he didn't need to know anything else, just who was available for pickup. Nobody was sure if the Blobs interrogated prisoners, or even took them. But operational security was still a standard watchword. What you don't know, you can't tell.

The JG added, "There's a mission update and a standard news update available to you. I flagged it attention to you if you want to plug in and download it. I'm going to check on the insertion."

"Thanks," Bell Toll said to his back as he headed forward. He realized the pilot was another navy type who couldn't or didn't comprehend Army thought processes and didn't want to be around them. Well, the discomfort was mutual.

The team started checking some of the headlines they'd missed over a quarter of a year as Tirdal settled himself in his drop couch. Bell Toll noted the sidelong looks the medic was giving Tirdal and decided that stepping out of the compartment to inquire about that in private was called for. He waved to Shiva to keep everyone else in the small ship, received a nod, and stepped up the bounce field to the deck above.

The sublieutenant was nervous and looked around a lot, as if expecting eavesdroppers.

"What's wrong?" Bell Toll asked him.

"Well," he replied, "it's not going to be on either download, but the Republic lost a lot of ships in the last clash. They held on with fighters but the Blobs really kicked our asses. If the Blobs ever overcome the fighters we are going to be in deep shit."

"That bad, huh?" Bell Toll scowled. Why couldn't he get good news on this trip?

"That bad," the lieutenant agreed. "Also, the Darhel

was acting really weird. Did you train with him before you left?"

Bell Toll shook his head. "Only briefly, why?"

"Just weird," The JG replied. "Kept to himself mostly, worked out in the dreadnought's gym. He didn't even interact with the dreadnought's security team except to show ID, but they definitely were nervous around him, and it got worse as time went on. The first day one of the spacers tried to pick a fight with him."

"How'd that turn out?" Bell Toll asked, his nerves jumping. He didn't like the possible outcomes.

"He avoided it," the pilot said. "Just ignored the insults and the shove and walked past him."

"That was it? No follow-up?" He'd expected the Darhel to fight. A human DRT would. It was disturbing in a way that no retaliation took place.

"Well, not exactly. He walked over to the weights, set up the stack, and bench-pressed nearly five hundred kilos. Like it was nothing. Rep after rep. Everybody got real quiet and just moved away. That was the end of it."

"Goddam," Bell Toll replied softly. He'd had no clue.

"That's not all. After that, he was rarely in the gym at the same time as others but when he was it was always like that. He worked out in two point five gravities, had to turn it down even when heavy grav personnel turned up, and always pushed five or six times what anyone could believe. It just had people spooked. I mean, none of us had any idea how freaking strong the Darhel are."

"Neither did I," Bell Toll replied, surprised himself.

He turned and headed back down to the team. That was definitely something to keep in mind, and to ask about when the time was right. Dammit, no one knew enough about the Darhel. They could teach Intel branch about secrecy.

As he reentered, he asked, "What's new in the news?"

"Besides the military stuff," Shiva said, "which the press got wrong as usual, the Solarian Systems Alliance are going off into philosophical lotusland. It's not that they don't recognize the threat from the Tslek, it's like they just don't care. Their ambassador has been expressing distress, but he's quite adamant that the SSA isn't going to become involved in 'a regional war.' We could just let the next thrust through to teach them a lesson." He was sprawled for comfort, but still stuck in the small berth.

"I often wonder if the SSA are humans or Indowy," Bell Toll replied. The Indowy were a harmless, endearing race of scientists who were inoffensive and had no concept of fighting at all. They'd been being obliterated by the billions when humans were brought into the war. And still they had a noncombative attitude. It was genetic.

"How's that?" Tirdal asked.

It was one of Tirdal's first questions, and with the tension regarding his presence, Bell Toll was grateful for the chance to talk. Not to mention the impending boredom of the metal and plastic walls.

"What do you know about human history since we—" he paused knowing that he couldn't say, "threw you Darhel bastards out"—"secured our place as a galactic race?"

"Very little," Tirdal replied.

"Oh," Bell Toll said. "Well . . . let me synopsize."

"Yes, sir," Tirdal nodded. He appeared ready to hear anything and remember it all. Maybe he was. It was one more creepy measure of him.

"Earth and Barwhon were able to destroy the entire Posleen incursion. They had sufficient population to comb the surface and wipe all the ferals out. And it didn't take them long to get back up to populations in the billions. Most of the Fringe worlds were cut out around the main wave of the Posleen. Remember that we stopped one small advance of them; there were trillions of others going in other directions at the time."

"Yes," Tirdal agreed. "We gave you the technology we couldn't use, to wipe out entire star systems as a means of eradicating them."

"Yes," Bell Toll said. "And the Fringe—specifically the Federation—was secured from those we captured, which are now a buffer zone between the SSA and the Tular Posleen, who were the only ones who came to reason, after we killed enough billions of them.

"Anyway, after Earth recovered, they wanted to resume business as usual."

"Business as usual?" Tirdal asked.

"Yes, stop fighting," Bell Toll said. "It's not natural to us, so they say."

There was a moment's pause, and when Tirdal answered he sounded more distressed and confused than he had since they'd met him.

"Not natural for humans to fight? Your seven million years of evolution has been one long, bloody battle. You had aggressive animals, short supplies, little technology for food and horrible means of communicating. The century before we introduced ourselves alone you exterminated over forty million of your own species. You exterminated over fifteen million of my race in the Dead Years."

"Oh, so you did know something about us when we met," Shiva mused, ignoring the other comment. "We always thought so."

"We've never denied it," Tirdal said.

"No," Shiva said slowly. "But you never admitted it, either."

"Anyway," Bell Toll continued, "Earth and the SSA are trying to, have been trying to, go back to a model a bit like the Indowy. No violence, pretend that technology is just a tool, and concentrate on philosophy. What's our term—?"

"Aristotelian," Shiva supplied.

"Thanks," the captain said with a smile. "And on the Fringe, we face ferals and potential alien threats like the Tslek."

"So you're two distinct cultures in one race?" Tirdal said.

"More than two," Shiva said. "We have dualities about everything."

"Interesting," Tirdal said. They waited for a follow-up comment, but he resumed his reticence.

Bell Toll said, "And that's why we split off, and why the Michia Mentat were busy producing weapons against the Posleen, and didn't get involved in the rebellion. A good thing, too, because that would have scared Earth into drastic action, instead of just deciding we were expensive distractions."

"Which is why we don't have enough sensats of our

own," Shiva said. "The Mentats are still remote, still concerned with personal development and growing technology, not concerned with the mundane world of carnivores and nukes."

"I would like them," Tirdal said.

Everyone else laughed. Tirdal did not.

"So," Shiva said, "I expect this coming war will be us, possibly the Tular, possibly some Darhel, all against the Tslek, while Earth sits fat and happy and tries to undermine our culture from the rear."

Gorilla asked, "You think it's that bad, Captain?"

"I do, Gorilla," he said. "I can tell by the pricking of my thumbs. Unless something comes along to tip the balance in our favor, the Tslek are going to serve us up like Cram on toast. Oh, to hell with that. How are the Greenwood Grendels doing in deathball?"

Shortly, it was time to move from the scoutship's personnel bay to the drop pod. The small, spherical craft would have the team in a circle facing inwards, their G couches contoured against the sides, packs and weapons between and underneath them. They were re-stowing gear, ensuring it was secured very tightly for the pending screaming drop through the atmosphere of the target planet. The commander followed them down, shouldering his gear on the way.

Tirdal was closest to him, following everyone else's lead and fastening his ruck and weapon, a punch gun in his case. Bell Toll glanced at him as he finished and snugged into his drop harness. What else was there about the Darhel that he didn't know but should? He was really starting to wonder about them. All he or anyone else had to go on was Tirdal's performance in the Qual course, which was impressive enough. And could they trust him? "We never denied it." "No, but you never admitted it either." What other secrets were hiding behind those gold-flecked eyes? But without the sensat they were surely in deep shit.

Everybody else was already in position and starting to strap down as Bell Toll locked his own equipment in place. He checked everyone's gear as he strode around the ring, all five paces of it, then did another circuit and checked their straps. Nodding to himself, he slumped into his own padding and started buckling in. When done, he plugged a wire into his helmet. "Pilot, we're secure and ready to drop."

"Acknowledged. All stations secure," was the reply. The hatch dropped, clanged and sealed with a hiss. Whatever happened, they were now committed. It was probably psychosomatic, but Bell Toll always felt as if the atmosphere grew stuffier when that hatch sealed. It certainly had its own plastic and chemical smell that one never got used to.

The stealth ship was on a ballistic track mimicking a comet or other piece of deep-space debris. It had a very effective near black-body exterior and the entire system was made to absorb or deflect detection systems. The target planet had one large rotationally locked satellite, like Earth and the Moon, and the plan was to do a hard break in the shadow of the satellite, relative to the planet, then whip past the planet at a lower speed, catching another slingshot to push it back outsystem. If any of the trajectory was detected it would look like a very low probability meteor pass. Immediately after the braking maneuver all systems would shut down and they would become a hole in space. This would leave them in microgravity but everyone had trained in it before. The microgravity portion would last about a day and then they would be inserting through a low-orbit zone of the planet. The main ship would drop the pod and continue on the way while the pod did a small retro burn, then used atmosphere to brake.

There were some dangers. If there were sensors on the "back" side of the satellite they would detect the braking maneuver. Also, if they had been tracked on the way in, the change in trajectory would be obvious. The only way they would know was if one of the ungodly fast Blob missiles headed their way. At a good fraction of the speed of light it wouldn't take long.

The enemy might shoot the pod down as a precaution. If they weren't worried about getting detected they would shoot down every meteor that had the potential to be an insertion team. But the Blobs had as good an appreciation of tactical silence as humans. So far the technique had worked all the other times it had been used. So far as they knew, anyway. There were always teams and craft that disappeared without anyone knowing why.

The fall into the system was tedious as nothing else can be. Someone once described combat as "Long periods of boredom punctuated by moments of sheer terror." While true, it doesn't relay the underlying tension of that boredom, hoping for action to stop it while hoping not to have any action. The sheer hell it plays with one's nerves is indescribable. Any action at this juncture would mean instant, unfathomable death. The boredom was preferable.

The best thing to do was sleep. However, one can

only sleep so long, especially in microgravity. Each human figured to nap for about four hours of the duration, leaving close to twenty with almost nothing to do but fret.

Gun Doll listened to dance music, her helmet display providing her a light show. That was all she apparently needed to keep her in a half-aware trance. Ferret and Shiva muttered and shook their heads at each other. Strange chick. Ferret would watch news and movies, switching between the two as he got bored with either fantasy or reality. Shiva would tear through documentary shows from a dozen planets, absorbing history, biology, art and culture at an amazing rate. He retained it all, too. His breadth of knowledge was staggering.

Dagger simply stared at nothing. It was another part of his act or his personality. No one was sure which, and no one wanted to or dared ask. Dagger was as strange as Gun Doll, in his own freakish way. Hell, they were all strange. One couldn't be a DRT and be normal. The only thing they all shared was a high tolerance for pain and abuse.

Gorilla kept full surround video and audio going. He wanted nothing to do with reality while cooped up in the ball-shaped coffin. Why anyone with his phobias had ever volunteered, no one would ever know. But he handled it every time. Next to him, Thor read books the really old-fashioned way—text on a screen. Historical fiction, fantasy, travel, romance, adventure, geekpunk futurefic and anything else he could get hold of. Bell Toll often felt Thor would be a much broader troop or even qualify as an officer if he'd read some nonfiction now and then. The man had a voracious appetite for words, but everything he read was escapist. Still, if that helped him cope, the captain wouldn't complain. No matter how removed from reality the man was here, in the field his senses and instincts were good and he could shoot well. He might not fit into a job in the city, but he was just fine in the weeds.

Tirdal was the unknown quantity, and everyone except Dagger took surreptitious glances at him. He seemed absolutely calm, staring dead ahead as Dagger did, right at Dagger, right through Dagger. It was almost as if nothing were in front of him and he was staring into the stars. The faint, enigmatic, almost fox-like smile he bore didn't do much to reassure people. Was the Darhel totally flipped out? Meditating? Dead? No one wanted to ask. Dagger was staring back, staring through Tirdal. It was a creepy tableau.

That just left Bell Toll to keep busy, worrying about his troops, the mission, the upcoming Readiness Standards Evaluation that had to be done, war or no, and little things like his chances for promotion or survival. His mind ran in loops, barely able to concentrate, until he realized he was rehashing the same half-thoughts over and over again, with no conclusions reached. He knew he wouldn't be able to sleep, either. It was a wonderful start to the mission.

After several eternities of sighing, twitching, moaning, frustrated exclamations, stretching and aimless mental drifting, he heard the pilot calling orders through the intercom. "Everyone make final check and confirm gear secure. Stand by for braking maneuvers and microgravity." The cocoons came up, much as they had before, but this time everybody was awake.

Deceleration hit like a hammer as the ship struggled to take off the velocity it had built up dropping in. Actual deceleration was nearly six hundred gravities but apparent decel was only around six. The compensators were being strained even to accomplish that, and all the DRT troops crunched like atmospheric fighter pilots. The G couches helped compensate, fluid pressurizing limbs to keep blood flowing in the core and brain.

Thor made a laconic comment in an attempt to hide his nervousness. "Not so bad. Remember the drop on Haley?" His voice was a bit tight from the pressure.

"Was that the first or second time you tossed your guts?" Ferret asked back. He, too, was trying to sound casual and not succeeding.

Gun Doll said, "Ferret . . . didn't you puke . . . so hard . . . you splashed me . . . on that drop?" The G was harder on her; it often was on women. But she'd never once thrown up on a drop that anyone could recall.

Straining slightly, Bell Toll asked, "Tirdal, how are you managing?"

"Fine," Tirdal replied. "How long is this phase?" There was no strain at all in the Darhel's low, steady voice.

"About another nine minutes," he replied, while pulling up the physiological monitors for the team and glancing at them. Everyone was stressed and elevated. Gorilla was doing his usual confined spaces panic: Pulse 125, respiration 41, all other readings showing clear pain or stress. It wasn't pain. But Gorilla was used to it and knew how to manage it so Bell Toll paid no further attention. The Darhel's readings were also very high but they were in the clearly marked "normal" zone. Heartrate was 186 and that was considered "low normal." His alphas were . . . really strange. But also considered "normal." If those were normal, then Tirdal wasn't the slightest bit bothered. Or maybe Darhel didn't react physiologically. That had to be it. No creature could suffer through such an unnatural state and not react somehow.

Without warning the braking thrust ended and they were in microgravity. The cocoons retracted to the standby position again and everybody except Tirdal moved around within their couches. The couches flattened and conformed to the sitter and Ferret brought up an entertainment package that involved, based on the sound escaping from his helmet, lots of loud shooting and screaming. Gun Doll started nodding her head and making other movements, some of them a tad suggestive, as she twitched to her music. Shiva wondered, not for the first time, if she'd aspired to be a dancer before her body grew too tall and rangy. She wasn't bad looking, but with her height she'd never have the balance to dance—too much hip and shoulder for those long limbs. She obviously found the couch confining.

"Watcha reading, Thor?" Shiva asked, needing a break from the silence.

"Devi Weaver's new one, *Dust of Success*," Thor replied enthusiastically. "Intergalactic space fleet warfare. National politics, unit wrangling, assorted government idiocy and exploding spaceships. Some of it's based on Napoleonic naval warfare and World War II from old Earth."

"You like it?"

"Generally," Thor said. "The politics I can take or leave. But I like exploding spaceships."

"Ever read about the ancient Greek sea battles with rowed ships?" Shiva asked.

"Nah, sounds boring," Thor said.

Shiva sighed and tried to think of another tack. As the only two readers, they should have some common ground.

Even Dagger gave up his blank stare and brought up a shooting game. His was different from Ferret's, the shooting being more deliberate and more widely spaced. The screams were just as ugly, and Dagger had a grin on his face in short order. His wiry body tensed occasionally, unconsciously working the muscles for a crouch or a run, but they were barely perceptible. He moved very little without conscious thought.

There was no set schedule here. The troops needed time to flake off and be ready for whatever followed, so they napped as they wished and sucked paste meals in their couches. Latrine facilities were plumbed into their suits. The routine was practical, covered the essentials and was mentally draining.

"Shiva," Bell Toll said, interrupting his thoughts, "let's run through the scenario again, then the troops can look at the maps as we get them and prepare to unload."

Glad of something to do besides wait, Shiva said, "Yes, sir!" and brought up a tactical screen.

Tirdal simply waited, as he'd done for hours so far.

Some time later, after the troops had reviewed rough maps built from flybys and everyone except Tirdal had complained, the ship came round on its second pass, ready to drop them onto the planet. The pod was in a launcher that was mounted perpendicular to the "line" of the ship's movement. The pilot cut in on everyone's screen and gave them a trajectory chart, with the release point marked with a classic red X. The closure was shown by a blue dot on a curve, while the upper right corner of their visors had a countdown running. The couches enveloped them again, and everyone tensed up. Almost everyone.

As the ship came opposite the insertion point, breaths were held and muscles were taut. There was no real significance to this stage of the insertion, but it was a vector change, and thus of note to the human mentality. And, of course, an error would cause them to crash or whip past into nothing. Recovery in the latter case was iffy. In the former, impossible.

As the timer hit zero and the blue dot hit the X in the display, a WHUMP! sounded through the pod as compressed hydrogen and magnetic flux tossed them from the stealth ship onto a new trajectory toward the planet proper. The felt Gs were extreme but brief, perhaps ten G for two seconds, then microgravity returned.

The pod entered an elliptical orbit that should coincide with a proper entry angle into the atmosphere, at which point flight could begin. Until then, there was nearly an hour of microgravity. Games and music resumed with varying amounts of attention paid to them. No DRT troop would admit to being scared on an insertion, but most were.

The first touches of atmosphere whispered threateningly against the field around the pod, and insertion proper began. The flight through atmosphere was the kind to cause newbies to wet their pants. Even experienced troops found them disorienting. Because of the need for stealth, no powered maneuvers were allowed. The result was a literal tumble through the atmosphere, the forcefields in close to protect the ship and within the atmospheric plasma caused by friction between the craft's "surface" and the rarefied atmosphere. From outside, the craft resembled a meteor. From inside it was a roller coaster crossed with a nape-of-the-earth flight by an insane pilot on drugs. The pod flipped from side to side, barrel-rolled, pitched and cocked in various attitudes and at differing speeds. It tumbled, rolled like a die and occasionally bucked. The internal temperature rose steadily as they dropped deeper, since there was no way to radiate the incoming energy. The occasional dense pocket of atmosphere caused jarring, teeth-clattering jolts. Space inside was at a premium to start with, and the maneuvers made helmets bash into bulkheads and knees into gear. No one spoke, though there were grunts and other utterances at the painful jolts. Occasional curses shot out. The troops mostly kept their eyes closed, not from fear, but to reduce the disorientation. It was the type of ride adrenaline-junkie civilians would pay big money for, and experienced professionals could take or leave, preferably leave.

But it was nothing compared to the finale.

Below the cloud layer, the "wings" melted out and back into brakes to slow the vehicle to a "reasonable" speed. Were it not for the inertial dampers, the crew would have been squashed by the violent deceleration. As it was, only long practice prevented them from heaving their stomachs. It was a harsh change of orientation, the pod being upside down and rolling at better than five thousand meters per second, then suddenly nose down and steady at barely sub-Mach speed for the local environment. The pod was above ocean, and splashed into waves in an angry hiss of steam. It was not a landing per se, but rather a controlled crash and a big splash.

The brakes shifted again in their forcefields and became small fins, and low-power impellers started up. Most of the remainder of the insertion would be under water, and slow. The process was semiautomatic, Bell Toll indicating a route and the craft's AI handling the trip from there. That saved having personnel pilot the craft, to be left stuck during the mission, or having to risk a takeoff and another landing. Besides, most of the procedure was either too complex for a human pilot—like the insertion and braking—or too simple and boring to bother with a pilot.

The pod wasn't streamlined, though it could morph quite a bit. Its forcefields could assume any shape needed. That wasn't an issue. But the speed of sound is much lower in water than in air, and sonic shockwaves under water are rare and almost never a natural phenomenon. Stealth predicated slow, cautious travel. After crossing light-years in days and thousands of kilometers in minutes, the last leg would be hundreds of kilometers in long hours.

Special warfare troops get long, boring training followed by long, boring practice in the art of staying sane while doing nothing. Each has his or her own particular coping mechanism. Good teams are those in which the members have learned not to drive each other to violent rage with annoying quirks, like breathing in an unpleasant fashion or shifting a leg in that manner that makes another want to crack his head after the ten thousandth time. Tirdal was the odd troop in this equation, and the others shifted unconsciously in slight but real bother at the disruption of their familiar relationship.

The pod used propulsion that was as close to silent as was possible for Republic technology. As the ocean grew shallower and the coast approached, the speed would slow even more and even slight noises would become more of a risk. To that end, silence reigned until everyone had triggered isolation circuits in their helmets. At this point all talk was through an intercom circuit, connected by wires, not an RF net, to further reduce stray emissions.

Talk picked up, everyone glad that particular ordeal was over, and wishing to escape from considering the pending risks for at least a few moments.

Almost everyone. Dagger and Tirdal were silent.

"We're down," Gun Doll said.

"Cheated death again," Thor added.

"Yeah," said Gorilla, his pulse dropping below 120. With a screen before him not showing the confines of the pod, and voices in his ears backed up by natural sounds, he could handle it. He could also handle it inside a box if he had to; he had in training. But if the technology was available to be less uncomfortable, he'd use it. "We got a count on how long to shore, Captain?"

"Thirty-seven hours," Bell Toll replied. "Here's the map," he continued as he displayed it for Gorilla and left the link open for anyone else. "We go down around this peninsula, up into this bay and get out near the river delta. Hopefully, it won't be too swampy. We'll move around to here, upriver about twenty klicks, and that's where we start working." The site in question had been known beforehand, but the exact approach hadn't been decided until they were in-system and could get a good view of the terrain.

"Lots of walking," Thor said. It wasn't a complaint, merely an observation. "Gorilla, can you handle that crate of bots for that far?"

"Sure," the hulking troop replied, unconsciously flexing his rock-hard shoulders. The bots weren't light, and were bulky, but his load would decrease as they traveled and the bots were deployed.

"Who's on point?" Gun Doll asked. She always asked for details.

Shiva replied, "I figure to put Ferret up front again, to cover Tirdal in second, you behind him for firepower, Gorilla, the captain, Dagger, me and Thor watching our asses."

There were murmured assents and a "Yes," or two.

"Okay," he continued, "I'll hit you up with individual notes. Feel free to talk amongst yourselves."

Moments later, his voice came through Tirdal's earbuds. "Tirdal, you hear me?"

"I hear you, Shiva," he replied. "What do I need to know?"

"A lot. Keep in mind, you're number three in the chain of command. If I go down, you take my slot. That's not going to be easy with this audience."

"As a specialist, I'm not usually one to take an active leadership role," Tirdal said. His voice was even more inhuman and sonorous through mikes and filters.

"You've got the rank, you've got the training. You'd better be able to take that role," Shiva said urgently. He didn't need the damned Darhel wimping out on them.

"True. I can handle it if they can," Tirdal said. It wasn't exactly an accusation, more of a caution.

"They'll do it," Shiva said, hoping Thor and Dagger wouldn't cause any hassle. He made a note to remind them. "If we lose the captain, too, you have to run the mission." It was clear from his voice he wasn't very happy with an unknown, an alien, a Darhel in that position. But realistically, none of the others would be better. Gun Doll was a social flake, as technically competent as she was. They wouldn't listen to her. Dagger was a nutcase, or at least pretending to be. He'd scare the troops worse than the Blobs. Thor and Ferret lacked the experience and Gorilla had the bots to worry about.

"If I have to, I'll do it," Tirdal reassured him. "I know all the basics. Tactics. Gear. Leaders should be self-secure and give orders, not take votes. I did take the NCO leadership course."

"You maxed that, too, right?" Shiva asked.

"Yes."

"Well, maxing the course doesn't indicate talent or experience. So review anything you need to now in case you're needed."

"Yes, Sergeant," Tirdal agreed.

"One other issue," Shiva said, grimacing to himself. This wasn't an easy one to broach. "Darhel don't think like humans."

"We don't," agreed Tirdal. "What are you referring to?"

"Humans and Darhel have coexisted for a thousand years, and in that time, we've learned almost nothing about you," Shiva said, warming up. "We were damned near your slaves for a hundred years. You're generally much more mercenary and individualistic than humans, correct? And we don't get along well. No insult, just an observation."

"That's generally correct," Tirdal agreed, his voice even flatter.

"What you have to keep in mind is that we're running this on human terms," Shiva said cautiously. "You have to try to operate as we would, not as a Darhel."

"What specifically?" Tirdal asked. It sounded like he was probing.

"Ah, hell, I can't find a diplomatic way to say this . . . our experience says that Darhel are more willing to draw back when things get tough." He didn't use the word "cowardice" but the thought hung in the air. "Darhel don't risk themselves for the group. Darhel aren't willing to go the last yard unless something is in it for them. For humans, when we're in the bad and the scary, we do it for each other. So, I've got to ask: What are you going to cling to when the lives are flushing down the disposal chute?"

"I am here for a mission. I will do what is called for for that mission," Tirdal said. If he was offended, he didn't let it slip into his inflection. "It is hard to explain to a human. For Darhel, to be in a place such as this, doing this, is a philosophical choice. If I was capable of turning against that philosophy, I would not be here in the first place. I am not here for you. Nor for Gun Doll. I am solely here to perform the mission. And I will do that to my utmost."

"Good," Shiva said. "And it's not just you I'll be addressing. Everyone else has to understand that bugging out is a fast way to die. They should all know that, I'll remind them anyway. That leads to the point."

"Yes?" Tirdal asked. His ear flick was invisible inside the helmet.

"Who calls the ball?" Shiva asked. "For the pod to lift, it has to have the command to do so. In reality, there's always a chance of someone wetting pants and running. If they get into the pod, that leaves the rest stranded. I don't know about Darhel, but it is part of human nature, a bad attribute that's too common and hard to suppress. That's why only the commander can call the ball."

"I understand," Tirdal said. "Humans have two sets of attributes; those they use outwardly and display, those inside they fear and can't control. By not discussing those negative attributes, they are subject to a loss of control and reversion to instinct. You really aren't as developed as you'd like to think you are." His voice wasn't accusatory, exactly, but it hit Shiva hard. So much for diplomacy.

"That's good enough for our discussion," Shiva grudgingly admitted. "What that means is, the pod will not respond to anyone who's not ranking. It will make periodic contact with our medical sensors, and will only depart if the senior member orders it. Junior troops will be ignored. And sometimes . . . the fact that a junior troop isn't on board has to be ignored, too. If the mission calls for it. So anyone in charge may have a morale problem squared if things go to hell."

"Is this a warning or an order?" Tirdal asked.

"Both," Shiva said. His expression wasn't visible through the helmet, either.

Tirdal was the first one Shiva spoke to. Dagger was second. Nobody liked Dagger much, either. But he was very good at his job. He was just creepy in demeanor. Nor was he enthusiastic. "The goddamned Elf is number three?"

"Enough of that, Dagger," Shiva warned. "You know this. Deal with it. And it shouldn't come up, anyway."

"No," Dagger said, "Unless things go in the toilet anyway, in which case we can just assume we're dead."

"Dagger, deal with it," Shiva warned again.

"Oh, I'll deal with it," he promised. "Maybe we'll get lucky and the Darhel will die first."

"Dagger!" Shiva's voice was sharp.

"Oh, relax, Sarge. I'm not going to gap him. I'm just pondering possibles."

"He'll do his job. You do yours. Capiche?"

"No problem."

That was a lie, Shiva decided. Dagger was always potentially a problem. But he could do his job, and did, even if he ran command ragged in the process.

Shiva spoke to the rest of the team in turn. Gorilla didn't seem worried. But then, he was a specialist himself, and only along for a job in his own mind. Gun Doll just said, "Well, let's hope it doesn't come to that. And that he's as good as he appears to be."

Thor and Ferret just grunted. They knew they were low men on the pole anyway. Once done, Shiva reported to Bell Toll. "Spoke to everyone, sir."

"Yes, I listened in," was the reply.

"Think it's okay?"

"Yes," Bell Toll said. "Dagger's just nervy and trying to put a face out. The rest aren't a problem. Tirdal sounds as ready as anyone."

"Well, it's the situation we have, sir. It'll just have to do."

"It'll be fine," Bell Toll assured him.

"Yeah. So why am I jittery?"

"You're nervy, too."

"Yeah, that must be it. Think I'll read a bit while we travel, sir," Shiva said. He was never jittery. He'd made his career on being calm and collected.

"Fine, Sarge. We'll review intel again after we sleep, say from oh two hundred to oh seven hundred."

"Yes, sir. I'll tell them."

Even Dagger was playing games now. The trip was too long to keep up his front. Thor and Ferret started a joint shooting game of some kind. That was to be encouraged, as it required coordination between the two. It wasn't as good as a training sim, but it was still interaction. Gorilla kept his screens up, looking at anything rather than the tight quarters. Gun Doll was alternating map games with music.

Tirdal appeared to be meditating. His bio readings were at the very low end of Darhel normal. No programs were running in his helmet. Three hours into it, Gun Doll saw him through her visor while switching from her game back to music. He had a limp look that didn't match the natural body tension of a game. But his eyes looked to be open and alert behind the dim red glow of the pod's lighting reflected off his visor.

"Whatcha doin', Tirdal?" she asked on the common freq, curious.

"Talking to whales," Tirdal said, turning slightly in her direction.

"Very amusing, Tirdal," Shiva muttered. "I didn't know Darhel understood the human sense of humor." He was on the public channel, too.

"Only incompletely," Tirdal replied.

"Well, no matter. But if we're going to work as a team, you need to work hard on fitting in with the rest of us. If it's some private thing you're doing, say so. If not, tell us the truth. We need a handle on you as much as you need one on us.

"So what is it you're doing?"

"Meditating, mostly," Tirdal said without pause. "It helps me focus on the mission. Otherwise, my . . . Sense . . . is alert for Tslek." It was mostly a true statement.

"Hear any?" Shiva grunted.

"Not so much hear, as know. There's no sense yet. When I get one, it will be just a general feeling. Imagine you see city lights on the horizon . . . it's that kind of awareness until I get close enough for details."

"Hell, Tirdal," Gun Doll put in, "we can sense that much." She sounded rather disgusted.

"Of course you can," Tirdal replied, his voice still deep and slow, unstressed. "When we get closer, however, the local life and environment will cloud your senses, whereas mine will get clearer. I'll find individuals, and be able to tell their mental state, as clearly as I can feel your physiological frustration over not getting 'laid' the last night before we left."

There was a moment's pause, then an embarrassed

chuckle all around that shut off quickly as they each realized how open they were to the Darhel's powers.

Thor changed the subject quickly.

"What's the local gravity, Sarge?"

"Er . . . one hundred and twelve percent of Earth normal, Thor," Shiva replied.

"Guess that explains it. It feels about like home."

"You're from Ridloe? Yeah, I guess it would be."

"Reminds me of Talin," Gorilla commented.

"That's where you won that pig screwing contest, right, Gorilla?" Ferret asked.

"Pig wrestling," Gorilla corrected him.

"Sure. I know what I saw." He made a squealing sound. There were more chuckles.

"You can try it next time, Ferret," Gorilla said, easily. It was an old joke. "Those genetically altered razorbacks are vicious."

"Nah," he replied, no witty answer coming to him. It had been a mean pig, and Gorilla hadn't even been drunk. He'd just decided to try the local entertainment and after a few muddy rolls and grapples had tossed the pig against the wall, stunning it and making people leap back, beers sloshing. Even the locals had been impressed.

Talk tapered off again. No one asked Tirdal any more questions. They were afraid of the answers.

Oh one hundred was officially lights out. Gun Doll and Gorilla stayed awake a bit longer, but the others started closing their eyes and trying to sleep right away. The process was made harder by the tight quarters that allowed no movement, the mostly upright position that was not comfortable for natural for humans, and the lack of activity so far. Spasmic twitches betrayed bodies that were not fatigued enough. Still, rest of some kind was necessary. They'd be going for hours, perhaps days once ashore. Fitful sleep was better than no sleep, even if annoying.

There were various drugs, systems and training techniques that had been used over the years to "induce" sleep, not to mention ones that obviated the need for it, removed "boredom" reactions, removed such problems as claustrophobia and otherwise reduced the strain of DRT travel methods.

The problem with most of them, the exception being Hyberzine, was that they had long-term deleterious side effects. By and large the DRTs avoided the pharmacopia available to them and just "toughed it out." And they only took Hyberzine during the extended travel involved in moving from star system to star system.

Maybe some of the pharmacopia would have been appropriate, but there were too many horror stories of drugged troopers losing it on missions to be willing to take the chance.

Chimed tones woke everyone at 0700. Shiva followed them with his own gravelly call.

"Rise and shine, boys and girls. It's another spiffy, action-packed DRT day. A day without pain is a day without sunshine! First, we'll start with a rousing breakfast of eggs Benedict and Celebes Kalosi coffee—"

"Ah, hell, Sarge, give it a break!" Thor snapped. He'd finally gotten to sleep about 0400, tossed and turned in his literal rack and was not feeling rested. He wanted more sleep and wasn't going to get it.

"Everyone acknowledge and I'll stop. Dagger?"

"Yo," was the reply, sounding a bit strained.

"Gun Doll?"

"I'm here," she said, following it with a yawn. It was almost sultry under the rasp.

"Ferret?"

"Yeah, if I have to."

"Gorilla?"

"I hear you."

"Tirdal?"

"I am awake," he replied. He sounded as alert as ever.

"Okay, well, we don't have eggs Benedict, but we do have hot chow, and we won't be using any once on land. So dig in while you can. Only twenty more hours of plastic chow and comfortable racks."

"'Comfortable,' the man says," Ferret griped. "I think there's a conspiracy between the Army and the Navy to make these damned pods as painful as possible, so we'll be glad to get out of them even if it means dying."

"So the secret's out," Shiva replied. "Guess we'll have to kill you on this mission to keep it under wraps."

The usual complaints continued as each pulled a "rat," or ration pack, from his or her ruck. Once opened, the meals were self-heating, a catalyst in the pouch warming the surface. With a little stirring, the contents were piping hot. If a bitching troop is a happy troop, morale was high indeed.

"Anyone want to swap for tuna with noodles? Anything?" Gun Doll asked.

"I got chicken with rice," Gorilla replied. "That work?"

"Please," she said, relieved. Tuna with noodles was appropriate for interrogating prisoners. It wasn't food for people. She could smell Gorilla's revolting chamomile tea, too, but said nothing. If it helped him relax, that was good, and she'd tolerate it. What kind of masochist drank chamomile tea?

Tirdal had Darhel rations. The packaging was obviously different.

"Darhel can't eat human food, Tirdal?" Bell Toll asked. He'd thought they could.

"We can," Tirdal said. "There's a few enzymes we have to avoid, but most of what you eat, I can."

Thor asked, "So why the special rats?"

"It's designed for high energy and is strictly vegetarian," Tirdal replied. "We avoid meat."

"Can't? Or won't eat it?" Dagger asked.

"I can and have, but prefer not to," Tirdal said.

"Afraid to hurt an innocent cow?" Dagger pushed, apparently wanting a reaction.

"Hand me your meat patty," Tirdal said in response. He clearly intended to take up the gauntlet.

"Sure," Dagger agreed, tossing it. Tirdal caught it and, after a brief meditative pause, took a bite. His face as he bit was as expressionless as they had ever seen it but his teeth were obviously designed to cut flesh; they sheared effortlessly through the unrehydrated patty, rather than ripping it like human canines. He chewed slowly, swallowed, and tossed the rest back to Dagger. "Satisfied?"

"No problem," Dagger said. "Just wondering." He hadn't been the only one. One of the training segments for DRTs was a survival course where one ate bugs, snakes and anything else that happened across one's path. If Tirdal couldn't or wouldn't eat meat, he'd skated the course no matter what his records showed.

But Tirdal had clearly been distressed by the act. Or at least it was clear to Dagger. He wasn't sure who else had caught it. Useful to know. It went along with that story that Darhel couldn't kill. That's why they'd blackmailed humans into fighting the Posleen for them. No matter what anyone said, the Darhel was a second-rater.

"Come on, Dagger," Gun Doll put in. "You know I can eat anything you put in front of me. I just don't like the taste of mammals. Icky."

"Just wondering," Dagger said again.

No one commented on the huge volume Tirdal packed away, like a teenager with late-night munchies. Perhaps he ate fewer but larger meals, or smaller daytime meals. Perhaps he was nervous and eating to compensate. It might be that he had a higher metabolism; he had mentioned that the food was "higher energy." Or maybe he was just a pig. It wasn't anything important, and no one felt friendly enough to inquire, especially after Dagger's hazing made everyone feel awkward.

The team spent the morning reviewing their data and doing isometric exercises in place. The pod was too small to allow more than two troops to move around at a time, and even then, there was too little room to do anything other than walk circles. The cramped confines were one of the things they'd trained for. That didn't make it pleasant. They were only too glad to walk those circles, around and around in front of teammates who either ignored them or stared through with dopey eyes, seeing but not noticing. After lunch, most of them brought up displays of open space to fight the growing claustrophobia one couldn't avoid after hours in a closet. Gorilla had even kept his screens up while eating and sleeping.

Bell Toll said, "We're heading north on our last leg, if anyone's interested." Everyone clicked over to the map to see. "The bay is a glacial formation, which is interesting as we're at the thirty-seventh latitude. There's some odd climatology here. It's deep and narrow, and the river delta is fairly solid and not marshy once we get inland. It shouldn't be hard to walk. I can't get a good image on the shore, yet, so we'll assume heavy growth. If it's not, we're lucky."

"So with that in mind, everyone get some sleep," Shiva said. "We'll wake, eat and run ashore. Local dark is when, sir?"

"Actually," Bell Toll said, "that will put us ashore right about local dark, if we get six hours rest and allow two hours for eating and prep."

"You heard the man," Shiva said. "Nighty-night."

Chapter 6

THE WAKE-UP CHIMES were drowned out by Shiva's strong voice singing, "OH! What a beautiful morning!" followed by even louder bitching from Dagger, Thor and Ferret.

"It's time," Shiva reminded them. "Grab your last, hot, home-cooked meal, kiss your screen of your mama goodbye and get ready to suck mud."

The meal was abbreviated and interrupted by the sorting of gear. Rucks, harnesses, helmet displays and clothes were all checked, with Shiva and Bell Toll scanning a troubleshooting program to see if the troops missed any problems. Gorilla had calmed down and seemed almost cheerful. He most of all would be glad to get out of the ball and on land, even if it was hostile land. Conversely, Gun Doll and Ferret were tensing up a bit more than the others, but no more than they had on previous operations. Tirdal was still physiologically normal. His alpha history didn't seem to match up with him getting any sleep, but the Darhel were so thoroughly nonhuman in character that it was impossible to say.

"Feet Dry," Bell Toll announced as they reached a depth that would allow no further submerged progress. "Vent and unplug." Everyone took one last opportunity to relieve themselves, then disconnected the equipment that made that possible. The Darhel's anatomy was strange, but it was the type of event that no one wanted to discuss, so no questions were asked. Wiped off with towels in lieu of showers and fastened into assault suits, everyone took a last bite or two and squatted with their gear. That made the center of the ball a packed, elbow-to-elbow mess.

"Tirdal, do you sense anything?" Bell Toll asked. He felt stupid saying the words, they sounded overly melodramatic, but there wasn't any other way to put it.

"Animals of some kind," Tirdal replied, not bothering to comment on the captain's evident discomfiture with the request. "Primitive thoughts regarding hunger and pain. Nothing else. Nothing sentient nearby with the exception of the team."

"Thanks. Gorilla, go."

At a signal from Gorilla, the first robot was released from a side hatch. It floated clear of the pod and swam quietly across the choppy surface trailing a hair-fine control wire, its progress slowed by the shore currents.

Its paddlelike legs propelled it, and after an impatient time it reached the pebbly beach.

This bot had been chosen for its unobtrusiveness. It looked like a giant pill bug. While it was convenient that it was low to the ground and matched many fauna, it was also a compact and efficient design. Once it touched land, its "antennae" made a sniff for chemicals, sounds and motion. Sensing nothing, it shifted its legs from paddles to tractioned feet and trundled up the rocky terrain into the nearby weeds.

The camera feed came on at once, visible on everyone's visor in any part of the spectrum they chose to look at. Gorilla said, "Infrared Three appears to have the best image," and there were grunts of acknowledgment as people sought that view.

"Temperate forest?" Gun Doll asked, examining the dark patches of growth.

"Sort of," Bell Toll said. "I'm not sure if those trees are actually deciduous. Cycad or palmlike. The undergrowth is heavy." It was. The screens showed a thick, tangled variety of bushes. Over the bushes loomed broad, spreading trees reminiscent of palmettos and rubber trees. Above them were tall, spindly forest giants, with leaves spiny like cacti. The vegetation was packed in at the shoreline where access to sunlight was the greatest. The ground was thick loam with much rotten vegetation, riddled with holes made by animals. A molten sun was dropping behind the trees, in a pink and blue mural of sky.

"There's an animal," Dagger said, his eyes always sharp for movement.

"I see it," Gorilla said, and adjusted one of the cameras for a closer view. The controller on the front of his harness was set up for fingers or voice, though voice control was rarely used. If he was too busy shooting to have a free hand, then he'd shout orders, but that was to be avoided. "That is the biggest freaking cockroach I have ever seen," he said, bringing it into sharp focus for everyone.

"More like a trilobite or silverfish," Bell Toll said.

"Whatever. It's an insect," Gorilla said. "If you're afraid of bugs, you're in trouble."

"Aren't you afraid of bugs, Gorilla?" Thor asked, pushing awfully closely to Gorilla's real phobias.

"Only from the inside," Gorilla said, eliciting chuckles. "Which might be possible here. There's another one, different species. It appears insectoids are the dominant animal form around here."

"Likely, but let's not assume too much," Bell Toll put in. "There could be monstrous birds who eat those things."

"Good point, Captain."

"Holy crap, look at the jaws on that bastard!" Ferret said. He lit the creature in question with a cursor.

"Those are some serious mandibles," Shiva agreed. The bug in question was shearing through plant stalks about ten centimeters thick. The stalks didn't look like spongy weed, but appeared to be rather woody, like bamboo. As the plants fell, the bug handled them with lobsterlike pincers, feeding them into its mouth as a kid would French fries. They disappeared about as fast.

"Question is, does anything prey on that?" Ferret asked.

"Will it reassure you if I say that the bot found fecal matter and determined it to contain meat residue?" Gorilla said.

"No," Ferret admitted with a shiver.

"I sense no carnivores at present," Tirdal said. "If there are any nearby, they are not conscious or self-aware."

"Mammaloid!" Bell Toll said. "There!" A circle glowed around that part of the image, and Gorilla zoomed in.

"Looks a bit like a capybara," he said.

"Capybara?" Tirdal asked.

"A large rodent creature from Earth."

"Thank you."

"There's a small flyer," Shiva said, spotting flitting movement.

"Whoa, too fast! Hold on," Gorilla protested, sequencing the images and numbering them for review. He brought a close-up image of the flyer up for everyone.

The flyer was also mammalian, a bit like a bat but with a longer snout. It and the capybara analog were both shaded from yellow to brown. Their claws were long but curved.

"Herd," Gorilla said, shifting the image in a blur to the south. The browsers were bugs, and huge, at least a meter tall at the "shoulder." Their carapaces were striped for camouflage, and they flickered through the darkening shadows, seeming to phase in and out.

"No signs of Blobs or other intelligent life? No technology visible?" Bell Toll asked.

"Nothing, sir. Rats, bats and bugs," was the reply.

"Go ahead, then," Bell Toll said, ordering the next step.

"Yes, sir," Gorilla replied, thumbing another control. The wire to the first bot was severed, giving it easier range of movement. Four more bots kicked loose, swam ashore and trundled into the weeds. Behind them, the pod extended two tubes just below the choppy waves, their mouths sealed by forcefields.

As the bots moved ashore and spread their electronic senses for threats, the team shifted and prepared to debark.

Ferret was the first up, shoving his gear into one tube before sliding himself into the other. He often wondered if this was what a baby felt like at birth. The passage was long, dark, confined and made it hard to breathe. The traction field grabbed him and drew him up until his hands reached the lip. Drawing a deep breath, he slipped up into the chill water. Reaching into the other hatch, he grabbed his punch gun first, then his ruck, which was surrounded by a flotation jacket. The near one hundred kilograms was too much to swim with. Gingerly, he let his helmet break the surface with a soft ripple, then rose with gentle frog kicks until his nostrils just cleared the troughs of the choppy waves.

What the sensors had filtered out and not bothered to mention was that it was raining. Rain interfered with vid image, and it wasn't heavy enough to be considered a terrain threat. It would give cover to both them and any threats. It was one of those cold, constant rains that fit the term "a great day for DRTs and ducks."

"Pouring cold rain, but no immediate threats," he reported back in a whisper, the sensors of his helmet deducing the voice as a transmission.

"Understood, break," Shiva said from below. "Tirdal, you're up. Stand to and stand by."

"Yes, sir," he agreed, repeating Ferret's procedure with the tubes.

"Go," Shiva said a few moments later. Tirdal felt the field grab him, and he was drawn up the tube. He took a breath as he passed through the forcefield, then he was in water. He grabbed his punch gun and ruck and surfaced near Ferret.

Ferret wondered how Tirdal was doing. Tirdal's breath sounded strained and he was paddling hard to stay afloat. Moments later, he seemed fine, and his motion slowed to near nothing. Some mod of his suit was handling flotation. Was swimming that tough for Darhel? Ferret wondered. Perhaps he was denser than humans. Or maybe he lacked the proper angle to his limbs. No matter. He seemed fine now. But damn, did he glow on infrared. Either he was strained, or that was some metabolism he had.

With a nod, Ferret swam forward, low in the water, towing his ruck. He couldn't fault Tirdal for being strained. This was one bitch of a swim, through chop, loaded with gear and, he found out as he neared shore, through muck and weed. Regardless of the local weather, that water was cold, too. He made adequate time: five minutes for a hundred meters, riding up and down in the waves, dunking occasionally. Months of training had taught him to throttle his breathing at the first splash of water in his nose. It itched and dripped horribly, but he'd take care of that upon landing.

As he neared the breaker line, he began crawling through the shallows. The suit was tough enough to be a ballistic shield, but it was thin and the pressure of sand and gravel through it chewed his knees to raw meat that stung in the salt water now draining out. In theory the suit could be sealed as an impermeable membrane. For cold climate that was fine; in this weather they wanted ventilation and drainage. As the waves dropped below his torso, he drew his ruck up next to him. He deflated the cushion, which had four more gas cylinders to inflate it, should they need to cross more water. A few seconds of wriggling got the ruck onto his shoulders, with him sitting. Rolling to his side, then to his abused knees, he rose to a low crouch and shimmied up into the shore weeds, cleared his boot soles of gunk, then edged into the taller grass for cover. A quick glance in his rear view showed Tirdal halfway to shore, Gun Doll afloat and almost invisible behind him. That confirmed, he kept his eyes open in front for any possible threats. The hissing waves of rain damped sound, especially on the water.

And Tirdal was good, much better than he had appeared in training. Were it not for the rear image, he wouldn't have known the Darhel was there. Tirdal slipped to his left about five meters and hunkered down, his punch gun trained outward but his expression seeming to be turning inward. Ferret took that chance to blow his nose, a finger over one nostril to concentrate airflow. Snot, salt water and sand spewed from one side, then the other. He kept it quiet and low to the ground, wiped off on his sleeve and rose back to a low crawl below the grasstops.

Gun Doll was ashore on his right momentarily. While large for a woman, indeed larger than Ferret or Dagger, she was much smaller than Gorilla, and her load was almost as huge. Besides her tribarreled support cannon, she had power packs, ammunition and some of the commo gear. The sheer energy put out by her more massive weapon meant high-capacity heat sinks that added to the mass she carried. She moved slowly, sinking into the muddy sand as she humped up the beach.

The three moved cautiously forward into the drooping forest edge, nerves reaching out for any threat, as Gorilla came in behind. He had an oversized ruck stuffed with technical gear. Added to his huge bulk, it forced him to lie down to minimize his profile. The captain was next, then Dagger. Again they shifted forward, then Shiva and Thor brought up the rear.

Gorilla sent a signal that ordered his bots ahead. Slowly, they clambered through the growth. Their brains were sufficient for most terrain problems. Occasionally, one would pause when it could find no clear or quiet path, and await a nudge from Gorilla, who was watching miniature windows in his HUD. The team slithered along behind the rolling perimeter, alert for anything the broad senses and limited mentation of the bots might miss.

A hundred meters in, one of the bots was attacked by an insect form as it extended the perimeter. The segmented, clawed carnivore grasped the bot in an embrace similar to that of a praying mantis and tried to bite through its carapace just behind the head, mandibles skidding off the tough molecular surface of the bot. The bot reacted as programmed, extending monomolecular spikes that shredded the abdomen of the predator. Everyone paused as the attacking insect twitched and wriggled in death. The bot then dragged the dead body off under a broad, feathery bush to conceal it before resuming its position for the march.

"I'd hate to see an aquatic version of that," Ferret commented in a whisper. "The Loch Ness Lobster." There were snickers from Shiva and Bell Toll in response. The rest hadn't been to Earth and likely didn't get the reference. Tirdal almost certainly didn't, and who knew what he would laugh at? Dagger may have gotten it, but loved his icy façade. Still, two chuckles on an obscure reference wasn't bad.

Behind them and forgotten for now, the ship slowly sank beneath the waves and retreated to the depths for camouflage. Later, it would move to a ready point near the extraction zone and await their return. If no message reached it after two weeks there, it would move to a different extraction point farther south for ninety-six hours. There was a tertiary position to the north for emergencies that would be available for ninety-six more hours; everyone hoped to avoid that, since it would mean mission failure and hiding near what would probably be a Blob military installation with their presence known. If none of those plans worked, the pod would assume the team dead and follow the planned escape route to try to get the information back to the Republic.

Bell Toll referred to the maps on the helmet systems. They'd be traveling for about ten days, over a small range of hills or low mountains, then to an overlook point. From there, whatever they found, they would take a different route back to the new pickup point.

"Anything?" he asked Tirdal. Their helmets used a comm system, originally developed by the semimythical Aldenata, that was understood to be impenetrably secure. Still, it was dangerous to encourage excess talk and a habit one should not develop, as it would carry over to those times when one wasn't using commo. And since no one knew how the damned thing actually worked at the scientific level, most troops didn't really trust it.

"I don't believe I sense any Tslek, but the background from the whole . . . lifeweb . . . makes it awkward to tell," the sensat admitted. "I can only sense for a certain distance."

"How far?"

"Not very. Several kilometers at most. The emanation is not 'attenuated' by distance but nearer thoughts, feelings, are clearer, more in focus. Depending upon the amount of life, beyond a certain point everything is a sort of gray background hum, like light on a snowy day. I do not explain it well, but this forest is teeming with animal life. There are no Tslek near. Beyond that I cannot say."

"Good enough," he said. Transmitting to everyone, he ordered, "Forward. Nav points are highlighted on your maps."

Ten days of infiltration is not like ten days of camping. All night, they moved through the drenching rain as it ran in rivulets down their necks and into their suits, dragging slivers of plant and muck with it. It stung at the scrapes from the initial crawl and irritated every bruise and scratch taken en route. The bots moved ahead, the troops followed, those in front cautiously, those behind alert for any threat from the rear. Roots reached out to trip, rocks to mash, rough grass and leaves to saw and cut bare flesh. The gravity was slightly higher than Earth normal, but they were strong. What was more tiring than the additional weight was the change in inertia and balance the unfamiliar field caused. Quite often, their route would force them to a crawl under choking vines or over boulders and it was then that the gravity pulled at them. The air was strange and humid, redolent with rot and growth, with a faint bite of salt from the ocean.

Rations were cold, chewed as they marched, the trash carefully stuffed into gear to take along. Litter in camp attracts pests. Litter in the field attracts enemy stalkers. Here, it could do both. They paused every two hours and rested, shaking mud and sharp sticks from boots, thorns from clothing and wiping grime from necks and faces. A quick check all around and a few swallows of water, then the pace would resume. They urinated in a jug brought for the purpose, so as to reduce the chance of a chemical trace. It would be emptied when they camped and the contents properly buried. The only advantage Ferret had on point was that he didn't have to lug the jug. A disadvantage was that while crawling, he was likely to, and occasionally did, slide a hand forward into a cold, greasy pile of animal droppings. The insectoids left feces that resembled a cross between worm casts and lizard goo, in piles as large as that from cows.

Bell Toll was impressed by Tirdal. He'd understood Darhel were very urban, their planets mostly citified and commercial. If so, Tirdal had learned well, as he moved quietly and with economy. He certainly seemed as strong as was rumored, and traveled easily whether at an erect stride or bent low for concealment. It was obvious that he was following Ferret's lead, though, and he didn't seem to be paying attention to what was going on around them. Was that due to his urban background? Or his reliance on his Sense? Or a combination of the two? Either way, he made a note not to put Tirdal on point.

Every planet, every biome had its own unique traits. The least obvious but most important here was the lack of animal noises. The insectoids apparently communicated by chemical or other signals, and the mammaloids didn't use sounds lest they be detected by predators. This quietness served a positive function, in that there were no sudden silences of wildlife to give away the team's presence. It also was a hindrance in that there was less background noise to mask their movement.

It was also eerie as hell. The bushes swished and rattled; the fernlike leaves rustled softly. Light breezes swirled and phased the sound of the continuous rain into something from a relaxation soundtrack. Mud splattered and squelched. As they passed, the team heard a scuttling of bugs, wrestling for mates, running away from predators, capturing prey, fighting, mating. Occasionally, branches would thump. And over that . . . nothing.

Then, as the team splashed through a shallow stream, there was something.

Out of nowhere it came, buzzing and flapping past Ferret's face, then Gun Doll's.

"Shit!" he muttered. Gun Doll limited her response to a gasp.

Weapons swung around and eyes sought targets, until Ferret said, "No threat. Just those damned bats."

"All clear here," Gun Doll reported. "Though I swear one plastered itself across the visor and flashed me."

"Was it good for you?" Thor muttered with mirth.

"Best hung thing I've seen on this trip," she replied.

"Quiet down!" Shiva ordered. Everyone was tense and needed the release, but that was enough and it was now time to go back to work. In his visor, everyone had warmed up slightly, Ferret and Gun Doll by several degrees. They faded back to "normal" as the adrenaline wore off. "Normal" out here was high, metabolisms working furiously. This was the kind of infiltration they could market for weight loss. If civilians thought that new fad of pseudo-boot camps for "health" was exciting, they should try this.

"Dawn soon, Shiva," Bell Toll said, shortly after the bat assault. "Set us up for camp, please."

"Yes, sir," he acknowledged, and spoke to them all. "Camping time, people. Any ideas?"

Thor replied, "There's a small clearing to our left. Slight elevation, thick growth."

"That might work. Let me take a peek. Hold, troops." Shiva eased back behind Thor, took a glance at the site suggested, and decided it would serve.

Normally, a depression would be preferable, being better concealed. In wet conditions, though, one wanted to avoid drowning. The risk of discovery being minimal at present, higher ground was preferred. Concealment was still wanted, though. This was a spongy hummock of ground surrounded by low areas, ringed by a thick tangle of reaching limbs entwined with vines and twigs. The entrance Thor had found was low to the ground, covered above.

"Bivouac site, fall back by numbers," Shiva ordered, taking a position near the weedy passage and motioning

Thor within. Bell Toll followed, then the others in order, Shiva and Ferret backing in last.

Camp didn't take long to pitch. They each had a thin membrane to cover their suits, thickened on the underside to provide enough padding to provide insulation and cushion the skin against sores. Trained troops made their own beds by scooping out a couple of handfuls of dirt to make depressions for hips and shoulders. Overhead, they drew freshly plucked—not cut—weeds and stems. That growth would stay fresher longer, and there'd be no bare white, or here, bright green, cut wood to illuminate their presence to an enemy. Gorilla's bots stalked out to form a perimeter, their sensors, microphones and a laser web providing reasonable assurance that an approaching threat would not be a surprise. Dagger dug a shallow latrine slit to one side and poured in the enzymes that would quickly reduce the contents to raw molecules. He followed that with the contents of the jug.

While they'd eaten on the march, dinner was a tradition that helped maintain the body's circadian rhythms. They each quietly munched, slurped and sucked a rat pack. The best that could be said was that the packs were nourishing, and each one lowered the mass one had to hump by half a kilogram. Shiva's voice came through the web again, "Watch in reverse rotation. Sorry, Thor."

"No offense," Thor replied. "Next time I'll camp us in a bog." His tone made it obvious he wasn't very bothered. He took a crouch near the middle, rifle cradled in his arms, and prepared to sit patiently. The rest rolled over to face outward, weapons inside their bags with them, and blanked their helmet visors against impending light. There was no way to make the wet go away.

Thor sat still in the rain, hunkered under his poncho. Periodically he'd turn to take in the perimeter, after which he'd take a slightly different position facing a different direction at random. He kept the images from the bots in his view, with his sensors set to alert him if anything large moved. He had one tense moment as a pair of fat beetles waddled by, but was undisturbed otherwise.

Two hours later, Bell Toll awoke and crawled out to relieve him.

"How was sunrise?" he asked in a whisper.

"Couldn't see much, sir," Thor replied. "Gray, then misty, then this," he said with a gesture that was almost a wave but only about a handsbreadth wide. "Rain stopped about an hour ago."

"Good. I hope," Bell Toll said. "It's going to be hot and muggy." He looked around at the soft textures of lingering mist, trailing into wisps that split and wove wraithlike through the trees. "But we should dry as we get inland from these coastal swamps a bit. G'night, Thor. I relieve you."

"G'night, sir." Thor crawled over to the vacant spot he'd prepared earlier and rolled out to sleep.

The day passed fitfully, sleep aided by training and exhaustion, hindered by the itching damp, the bugs, the still, humid air, the bright light softened only slightly by foliage and atmosphere, and gravity different from those the bodies had grown used to. Still, it was rest, and if today was unsatisfying, perhaps the next would be better, with acclimatization and more arduous labor to drain them. Or perhaps they'd be dead. The philosophy of the soldier is one based on adaptation to the unpleasant.

Tirdal's shift was as boring as the others, but Dagger watched him surreptitiously. Dagger still didn't trust the Elf, even if the others had accepted him. He held still and Tirdal gave no sign of knowing he was awake, though if he could sense as they said, he probably did.

They all woke at dusk, Ferret on the last watch already up and ready.

"You know the drill, folks," Shiva said. "Strike camp. Hygiene and prepare to march." Everyone used the slit, filling it in as they went, and Thor, last, tossed the saved sod back atop it, flattening it out with his heel. Bathing being out of the question, a quick wipe with spongy pads laden with activated nanos served to wipe grit from eyes and kill bacteria. Tirdal scurried around, scuffing and brushing at grass and bushes, until the very people who'd slept on an area couldn't see a worn spot. He also found three tiny slivers of plastic left from rat packs. There was grudging admiration for his work. "How'd you do that?" Thor asked.

"It's a Sense," Tirdal replied. "The plants don't have emotion, but they have a . . . 'normalness.' I move them around until they seem most normal. That's the best I can describe it in English. It only works when very close."

"However it's described, it works," Shiva commented. Even Dagger nodded appreciatively. The clearing looked untouched.

The trash stowed and a final check made they moved out, Gorilla's bots leading the way. Their power packs would be good for at least a couple of weeks, and they could recharge somewhat in daylight, using nano-sized thermocouples under their outer shells.

This night was much like the last, except that it was not raining and gradually dried out. The suits stuck to bodies, causing itching until the moisture capillaried out and evaporated. The permeability could be adjusted, but it still took time for moisture to vent. Heads itched under the web harnesses of helmets. The ground was drying as they rose from the coastal wetlands. The squelching goo had become sticky mud, now hard-packed earth.

They'd only been hiking about an hour when Tirdal spoke urgently through his microphone, "Ferret, drop now!"

Ferret's reflexes were good. He threw himself flat among stalky weeds as a large animal leapt through the space he'd occupied. He rolled and fired, missing, the weeds crackling and breaking as he tumbled. The creature dug in as it landed, spun and charged. Tirdal's shot was wide, the hollow *poounk!* of the punch gun resonating as the beam shattered plant stems. Then Gun Doll's autocannon spoke with a *BRAAAPPP!* that shook the ears even with its muffling. The heavy, hypervelocity needles tore at the insect, then their antimatter cores, just a spare few micrograms, blew it to slimy chunks.

The troops were professionals. The rest were already in a perimeter, covering each other and prepared to fire.

"Report!" Bell Toll snapped.

"I sensed a sole predator form," Tirdal said. "I warned Ferret, who evaded it and appears unhurt. Gun Doll's fire killed it. No other senses, no immediate threats that I can tell."

"Understood. Stand to until we make sure we're still secure," the commander ordered. The weapons weren't as loud as chemically driven weapons or explosives, but were loud and alien enough in this environment. Hopefully, either nothing had been around to hear, or the growth had muffled it down to distant thunder or other natural noises.

For long minutes they were all but motionless, eyes and sensors alert for any hint of a threat.

"I call secure," Bell Toll finally said. "Bring in the perimeter. The shot appeared strange, let's review the video."

He scrolled through frames of the fight as seen on Tirdal's and Gun Doll's helmets until he found those he sought.

"There," he said. "The darts didn't penetrate the carapace. The antimatter did all the damage." The frames showed gouges left by the projectiles, their velocity too high for them to be captured on this equipment. It wasn't until one of the explosive rounds caught the shell that the creature had really been damaged.

"That's impossible," Dagger said. "I want a shot at a piece of that."

"Actually, Dagger," Shiva put in, "that's a good idea. We better see how the weapons handle it. Keep a perimeter, folks."

A plate-sized section of the carapace, still dripping with yellow insect goo, was placed against the base of a tree.

"Punch gun first," Shiva decided. "Tirdal, give it a try."

Tirdal nodded, aimed and fired. The *poounk!* of his weapon was followed by a clatter, and the section of exoskeleton jumped. It spun, landed flat and kicked up earth. Gun Doll walked over, held it up.

"Nothing," she said. She replaced it against the roots. That was impressive. The energy toroid from a punch gun would drive a hole through most material, to a depth of several meters. It was a great area-effect and antipersonnel weapon. Apparently, its blast was too diffuse for this.

Thor's rifle round, a standard one with no antimatter, ricocheted. So did Dagger's more potent round. His antiarmor round punched through. Gun Doll fired another short burst of just AP. Then another. After twenty rounds, she succeeded in smashing through. Shiva fired an antimatter round set to zero penetration, and the explosion tore the piece to shreds as it if were cooked crab shell.

"Interesting," he mused, examining a scorched, steaming fragment. "It looks like we need to set for surface detonation."

"What about the punch guns?" Bell Toll asked. "Any ideas?"

"I guess we hope for a trauma effect or a stun," Ferret said.

"Just keep in mind that a surface shot on a larger animal might not damage any vital organs," Shiva said. "Hell, we don't even know where their organs are, assuming they have any in the first place. So be very cautious."

There were nods and grunts as weapons were adjusted, then the slogging continued.

Another couple of hours passed uninterrupted before Gorilla said, "Hold."

Ferret stopped, halfway forward in a crawl. It was a

trained reflex, and he didn't flatten from that position until Gorilla said, "Secure," indicating they could get comfortable but not move from their positions.

He fed a video to them, which he was getting from two of the bots.

"Captain, check this out," he said on the open channel, so everyone could follow it.

The scene was something from a horror show. A pack of small predators were attacking a larger herbivore, like carnivorous roaches atop a giant ladybug. The roan-colored domed plant eater was big enough to fill a small bedroom. The gray roachlike predators swarming it with angry, twitching antennae were the size of German Shepherds. Whatever their mandibles were made of was tough enough to shear chunks from the bulletproof shell of their victim.

The team watched, still as dormant reptiles with fingers ready on triggers in case they were attacked next. The large creature galloped in a circle, knocking down saplings up to fifteen centimeters thick, and shaking the ground. One of the attackers tumbled underneath and was stepped on, convulsing into a ball around its middle. Fronds were torn loose from the trees, and the weeds and ground cover were plowed into confused furrows by kicking feet. The animal had insectoid legs that ended in what were effectively hooves of the same insane super-chitin, sharp as boar's tusks and with a sheen under the mud coating them.

Even from more than a hundred meters away, the trees could be seen to whip back and forth from the melee, as the now wounded megabeetle bucked and kicked. Those hooves were vicious, but not really placed to help much.

It was hobbling now, as one of the attackers had sheared off a leg. Then another leg on the same side was crippled and started to give. As its motions slowed, the slender killers concentrated on that side, snipping off an antenna, then another leg, a protruding piece of flank and the last leg on that side.

"Gorilla, let's see that," Bell Toll ordered. The attackers were on the far side from them.

"On it," Gorilla agreed, and the view shifted as the ambulating intel bots crept in a circle, scanners focused on the grisly scene.

As the view shifted past the still alive and twitching bulk, Ferret said, "Oh, yuk."

"Yeah," agreed Gun Doll. The rest were silent but agreed with the sentiment.

The six surviving carnivores had sliced holes between the top and bottom shells, and were rapidly eating their way inside. As the team watched, one of them disappeared with a kick of legs, like a rat down a burrow. Only this burrow was into the tender flesh of the dappled, pretty and still squirming body of the beetle. The others followed suit.

"I take back what I said about not being scared of bugs," Gorilla said. "If one of those gets me, shoot me decently."

"Or just frag me quick," Dagger said. Even Dagger.

"Right," Bell Toll said. "Gorilla, Ferret, let's detour way around there. And if those . . . things . . . come close, shoot first and tell me afterwards. Don't wait to ask permission."

"Yes, sir," echoed gladly through the earpieces.

Chapter 7

THEY BIVOUACKED AGAIN before dawn, and rose at sunset to keep moving. The local day was a little over nineteen hours, and at this latitude and season they moved for thirteen of it. That odd schedule also had a tiring effect. They went to sleep more easily, but it was neither comfortable nor resting sleep, merely a change of routine for the body.

"Man, this sucks," Thor bitched softly as he leaned against a tree and tore at a rat pack. "Bites, stings, aches, scratches. You'd think they'd give us armored combat suits for something this long."

"Good luck, Thor," Doll replied, also quietly. "We're

lucky we've got chameleons. You know how rare the good stuff is."

"Yeah," Thor said, darkly. "Too cheap to spend the money."

"That's not it at all. Didn't you know?" Shiva said.

"Know what?"

"Ah," Shiva replied, settling into a squat over a stump of tree, after he'd poked it with a stick to ensure it didn't contain any squirming biters. "Listen, young student, to the history of our kind."

There were snickers, but Thor and Doll paid attention. Gorilla finished messing with his controller and took two long, low steps over. From his outward perch behind a boulder, Dagger cocked an ear in, too. Bell Toll nodded assent to Shiva, and Tirdal sat carefully near Ferret.

"First of all, all this technology is GalTech," Shiva began. "Some of it is Indowy, some Tchpth, some Darhel . . . and a hell of a lot of it Aldenata, acquired from caches and not understood. We can build this commo gear, but we still have no idea how it works, a thousand odd years after we first ran into it. Some we reverse engineered from what the Darhel sold us, because they won't tell us how it works. No offense, Tirdal."

"None taken," he replied with a nod practiced to look human. "That's not my field, and they don't tell me about such things either. Our people are . . . castes? Sects? Regarding specialties. We do not do the communications gear that you speak of anyway. Darhel technology relates almost entirely to what you would call 'information technology.'"

"I guess I knew that but had never put it in words," Bell Toll said. "Go on, Shiva."

"So it's limited to start with," Shiva continued. "Then, things like the suits especially have to be grown in a tank with psi control. It takes a lot of mind power, which is where the Michia Mentat got their position." He paused for a moment, then said, "I suppose we're developing castes, too." He looked faintly disturbed.

"Anyway, at the time of the Rebellion, we, meaning the Islendian Federation, before we became a republic, had settled a bunch of planets, mostly Posleen blight worlds, and were between the SSA and the Tular. Not an enviable position. Earth started this long-term disarmament, expecting us to follow suit. We didn't, because we still have Posleen to worry about. And now the Blobs, too.

"So we had most of the military installations, a share of the GalTech weapons, and almost all of the weapons humans built. We were the perimeter, still are. Earth has the money and the politicians. And it's a good thing it worked out that way, or we wouldn't be here."

"I could handle not being here," Thor joked, though he knew what Shiva meant.

Ferret said, "Shut up, Thor, I want to hear this."

"We had skirmishes for almost a hundred years, with the SSA on one side, the terrorists all over and the feral Posleen and some last holdout oolts along the border," Shiva continued. It was obvious that history was his specialty and passion.

"The terrorist groups were mostly Fringer Freedom groups, people who wanted to separate off from the Core worlds with a smattering of local ethnic separatists. They didn't have a lot of general support, either group, but they scared a lot of people and made a lot of noise. And they forced more and more military to be diverted into the Fringe.

"Finally, Earth began to realize it couldn't dictate terms to us; that was the time they were trying to impose martial law. Most of their ground combat forces were from Fringe planets. Virtually all of their officers were from Fringe worlds. A good bit of their heavy industry was in Fringe worlds. Damned near every single base was in the Fringe. We had the training, but they had the stranglehold on GalTech. The Michia kept neutral, of course, which is likely good, or we'd have human blight worlds, too. They would have been a powerful enough ally that Earth would have had to waste systems to stop them. And they would have scorched their own share.

"Anyway, the Fleet commander in the Islendia sector was Patrick Sunday."

"Him I've heard of," Thor said.

"Who hasn't," Shiva smiled. "He was from the Core worlds and his family had been military for as long as the SSA had been around. But, despite that, he could see the way the wind was blowing. He made a deal with the SSA. The Fringe was in virtual separation from the Core. Taxes weren't getting paid, orders among the military were being ignored and planets were starting to figure they were 'on their own' and developing local militias. And in the midst of this were probes from the Tular, rising piracy and, of course, the odd terrorist.

"The SSA finally gave up. Sunday convinced the majority of bomb throwers and their 'unaffiliated' supporters to come in 'hands up.' They were amnestied but prevented from taking office. The ones that didn't go for it were ruthlessly hunted down, by their former 'colleagues' among others. And Earth permitted the Republic to split off."

"It couldn't have been as easy as that," Dagger said. "Where's the money?"

"It wasn't easy by any stretch of the imagination," Shiva admitted. "But, on the other hand, no planets were turned into slag and no suns were detonated. Easy is a relative term.

"And, really, Earth only relented because we had most of the regular hardware, but did not have GalTech in large quantities. We would have been a threat they couldn't ignore, and not been believable as allies. It was lucky, because we basically outgrew each other. Had we been weaker, or stronger, it would have been a fight."

"So that's why ACS are rare in the Fringe," he said, looking at Thor, "and reserved for very special occasions, and be glad you don't have one, because usually when we toss them into the meat grinder, it means things are royally succulent and people die. Be glad you have that chameleon at least. And we're DRT because we're masochists. Not because we get to kill a lot of things. We're trip wires."

"I guess that explains it," Thor said. He believed it, but he didn't like it. "But I got to wear ACS once, on Tenarif. It was wonderful."

"Oh?" Bell Toll said. "I didn't see that in your file."

"It wasn't official," he said. "And it was while I was still infantry. Remember, I qual'd DRT last year."

"Yeah, so what about it?" Dagger asked.

"Oh, damn," Thor said, a glazed look in his eyes. "The suit supports you. You want to sleep, you lie down. It can wake you or put you under. It gives artificial neural feedback like bare skin would. It does nanosurgery to fix small wounds." He held up his welted hands, scored with saw-edged grass and bites. It was easier to sense one's surroundings with bare hands than with gloved, but there was a price to pay. "It uses stasis for major wounds. The AID talks to you, feeds you info, cuts out the crap you don't need and prioritizes the critical stuff. It'll stop damned near anything incoming, and you have real antimatter beads for weapons, no powerpack needed. Hell, it massages tired muscles. It'll sing you a lullaby if you really want. I got to wear one for a week during an exercise, as a backfill."

"I'd heard that about them," Gorilla said, scratching the grimy stubble under his chin thoughtfully. The suits kept hair groomed, too. "Be nice for sleeping." His length meant that he often woke with cricks in his neck on deployments, after squeezing into awkward little nooks to hide and rest.

"Yeah, well speaking of sleeping," Shiva said, "it's time to do that very thing. And I won't sing you a lullaby, Thor."

"No problem," Thor said with a grin. "Maybe Doll will massage my shoulders."

"Sure," she said. "With a rock."

Thor was on watch again. The rest lay back to sleep. Tirdal sat up, awake, through Thor's watch before he retired.

"Meditating, Tirdal? Or just can't sleep?"

There was no reply. Tirdal sat motionless in an

almost lotus with his eyes focused on eternity, and it creeped Thor to hell. Eventually, he turned away from the Darhel, not wanting to see those staring eyes. He could still feel them.

The next night took them into foothills. The peninsula they'd come from rose steadily to a ridge that joined a mountain range, and they'd be following the higher ground until they reached a plain.

It was near midnight when Gorilla ordered, "Down!" in a harsh whisper. Everyone dropped silently into the weeds. Ahead, distantly, there was a crashing, rustling sound, muffled by the thickness of the woods. Breaths were restrained, motion frozen, hands gripping weapons and waiting for a threat, a release, anything to break the crisp, dry tension.

"Stand by," Gorilla said. He ran a diagnostic, then said, "There's a cliff ahead. One of the bots fell and is out of commission."

"Destroyed?" Bell Toll asked. "Aren't those things hard to damage?"

"Not when they dislodge rocks on the way down and get crushed under a two hundred kilogram boulder."

Shiva said, "So watch where you put your feet."

The cliff appeared in their night vision as they approached, a dark line angling from the right. They were forced to take a narrow path along the edge of the ridge, the cliff gradually turning to tumbled, rocky bluff then to sharp slope before merging with the line of the hills. They walked with one leg bent against the incline, gripping vines and branches for stability as strained muscles trembled on the rocky ledge. The previous day's rain had mostly run off and dried, but enough dampness remained beneath fallen spiky leaves to create a slipping hazard, exacerbated by the surreal contrast created by night vision. As the bluff became a steep slope, Bell Toll stopped.

"Angle us down, Ferret. There should be a leveling at the two-hundred-meter contour."

"Got it, sir," he replied.

They'd gone only a few meters before Ferret could be heard to mutter, "Ouch!" over the net. In moments, everyone was twitching and cursing as small creatures chewed at their exposed skin, their bites and acidic saliva causing sharp stinging pains. A nest of something had been disturbed, and the occupants were protesting this incursion.

Shiva suddenly clutched at his helmet, fought with the straps and yanked it off. He didn't cry out, but the expression on his face was mean. They'd been at his ears and neck.

"Retreat one hundred meters, leapfrog by numbers, now!" Bell Toll ordered and the troops scrambled to obey. Noise discipline suffered somewhat; the minor but painful injuries were very distracting.

"Keep the perimeter. Shiva, Tirdal, get people treated. Thor, Gun Doll, let us know if anything moves closer. And somebody give me a report!" Bell Toll said.

"Antlike form," Ferret said, "but looks more like a roach. And the little fuckers bite like angry rats. Think they can fly or jump. I was sliding up on a downed log and out they came."

"Got it. So watch for downed logs. Shiva, are you okay?"

"Yes, sir," Shiva replied. "Going to have huge welts

on my cheeks, ears and neck, but I'll manage." As he spoke, Tirdal was spraying an anesthetic/antiseptic salve onto the bites.

"I think I see a fragment of mandible," Tirdal said. "I'll need to pull it out. Permission to use light, sir?" Darhel had better night vision than humans, but it was a minuscule piece of sting he was trying for.

"Yes, toss up a cover and keep it dim."

Tirdal pulled his bedroll from the bottom of his ruck, spread it and drew it over their heads. Thus shielded, he could illuminate the wound. There was indeed a small, barbed piece of shell there, and he worried it gently out with a needle and tweezers as Shiva muttered, "Son . . . of . . . a . . . bitch!"

"Done," Tirdal said. "It is oozing blood and should be allowed to drain. I see no need to lance it further."

"Thanks, Tirdal," Shiva acknowledged. "Your turn."

Tirdal held up his hands, which had a dozen small welts on them, though Shiva didn't recall him making any noise or fuss. He took the Darhel targeted nanos and sprayed Tirdal's hands down. There were a couple of stings buried in the skin, but they came out easily. Drops of violet Darhel blood flowed briefly.

That done, the two of them worked the others over. Ferret was worst, with bites to his neck and almost up to his elbows where some of the fire ants, for want of a better name, had crawled under his cuffs. Dagger was almost as stoic as Tirdal. Gun Doll demonstrated a rich skill of invective, the backs of her hands being badly swollen. Thor, who'd been last, had one single bite.

"Lucky bastard," Gorilla commented. He'd taken more than a few himself.

Everyone treated, trash and gear recovered, they resumed, Ferret leading them around the nest and avoiding other rotten trunks. There was no hurry and no need to repeat the experience.

That day they slept among old, weathered boulders, hunched against their bases or sprawled over their curves, the local sun pattering across them through long leaves. They woke stiff and sore, stretching and flexing to work out kinks.

"Well, shit," Gorilla muttered.

"What?" Bell Toll and Shiva asked together.

"Lost another bot," he groused. "Checking . . ." he muttered and fussed with his controller.

"I need cover while I go get it," he said after a moment.

"On it," Dagger agreed, leaning over a boulder and ready to shoot. Thor went with Gorilla as close support, and the two hiked out fifty meters to get the device. The rest policed the area, then took cover amongst the formation, awaiting the prognosis.

"Servos shot on one side," he announced. "Looks like cumulative wear and tear, grit inside and all those kilometers of walking. I can't fix it here. This is the oldest one I have, anyway. Want me to lug it along, Sarge? The sensors still work; it can sit watch."

"We should be fine," Shiva said after thinking. "It won't help in a battle, it is mass we don't need to carry, and there's little enough to sense between here and there. We have more bots and the sentries will just have to be alert."

"Gotcha. Let me set the destruct."

Thirty minutes later, the team well down the slope and the sun still just up, an enzymic reaction followed by a small, hot fire took place in a hollow under a massive boulder. As well as the bot, all their accumulated trash was disposed of in the convenient inferno. It left a congealed puddle of metals and plastic residue. The latter would crack and dust with "age" in a few hours, leaving little evidence of their passage.

Down the hill they moved. Downhill is not fun in the dark, loaded with gear, footing unsure, mud, debris and leaves that can slip or trip or entangle. They were cautious, following single file along Ferret's chosen route. Gun Doll's load caused her to slip here and there, once even puckering the tough fabric of her suit as she passed a broken limb while tobogganing down the slope on her hip. She limped slightly after that, especially when forced to put her entire weight on her right foot. Her only external reaction was to swallow a couple of pain pills and reach inside her suit to slap a nanite patch to her skin when they rested.

"I'll be fine. Can't dance here, anyway."

They were all taking damage. That was part of the job. Aches, pains, bruises and nicks, exhaustion and fatigue, blisters on the feet, and collarbones grinding under the mass of rucks that strained the limits of the human body were familiar, if despised. Then they were ignored as mere background. No one took this job without understanding its risks, and while griping was a pastime, whining was not acceptable.

Shortly, the ground started to flatten out to hummocky woods. Here and there the depressions contained puddles or mud, often with some local algae and slime analogs afloat. Ferret moved them between such obstacles when possible, both for comfort and because splashing mud and water were hindrances and noise hazards. Above them, saplings and limbs of heavier trees had been sheared off by some recent severe wind or tornado. The spearlike bases stabbed at the sky while the broken sections bowed low.

Those and other occasional breaks in the canopy showed the stars wheeling overhead, bright and clear through a sky unbothered by industrial effluent or the lights of civilization. The local moon was ruddy rather than bluish, and showed a small crescent.

"Pretty," Thor remarked at break time, tilting his faceplate for a quick glance up.

"I've never seen stars so bright," Tirdal said. "Our planets have little wilderness."

"We only get to see them out past the Fringe," Ferret said.

"It almost—" Tirdal said, then twisted. He'd Sensed something. It was a large insectoid akin to the one that had jumped Ferret, mandibles wide and skipping forward. He dodged as it came, raising his punch gun and firing a shot that went wide. The bug landed beyond him, twisted in an odd eight-legged bounce and came back. It was in midleap, ready to shear off chunks with those appalling jaws, when it fractured and tumbled with a sharp crack. It landed on him, but in a fall rather than a leap. Gun Doll and Shiva bounded over and rolled the wriggling corpse off him. The head was sitting by itself about two meters away, antennae and mandibles still twitching in a grotesque imitation of life.

Dagger was alongside shortly, asking, "Are you all right?"

"I am," Tirdal replied, sounding breathless. It might have been from the exertion of a fifty plus kilogram bug landing on him and the resulting wrestling match, or perhaps he was distressed at last. "Did you shoot it, Dagger?"

"Yup. Through the neck, contact fused. I don't know where the brain is, but I figured if the head was separated, it was less of a threat."

"Good shot!" Gun Doll said, impressed.

"Thanks," Dagger acknowledged.

"I owe you one, Dagger," Tirdal said. "Let me know. I'll take a shot for you."

"Really?" Dagger asked. It didn't sound very Darhel.

"Surely. But only in the leg."

After a moment's pause, there were repressed laughs and snorks.

"Are you otherwise okay, Tirdal?" Shiva asked.

"Fine, and ready to move," he said.

"Everyone else?" Shiva asked around. Getting nods, he said, "Then let's hump."

They'd made good time so far. The next couple of days slowed progress immensely. They came to a narrow chunk of grassland that led into the savanna proper to the north. The grass forms and bushes were tall enough for cover, but hindered visibility.

Gorilla switched the bots to manual and had them crawl out slowly under the grass. He guided them with an inertial joystick attached by a wire to his helmet, which was attached in turn to a small module, to which the wires on the bots were connected. The hair-thin threads that the bots unspooled as they went were fairly tough, but were considered one-use items. Rewinding them would take additional mechanisms aboard the bots and the wires would be covered in crud anyway, even if they didn't break. He had a package of spares in his ruck, but they were a finite resource. With less cover for the troops and clear ground for the bots, it made sense to use them for a time.

"What do you want to do, Captain?" he asked, slaving his image to the captain's channel.

"I want to see more," Bell Toll said after a moment's pondering. "Can you send up some flyers?"

"Right away," he agreed. Clear ground was the bane of infiltrating troops, and they were understandably cautious. Still, if it were safe, cutting across would save much time over detouring to the south.

Gorilla reached back into yet another compartment of his seemingly bottomless ruck and pulled out a handful of feathery stuff. He lofted it gently into the air and the bundle of small drones untangled and flapped free to fly above the ort's likely route, buzzing and circling like dragonflies while feeding imagery back to him. They spread out and fluttered "randomly," each one a dumb eye sending back a single view that switched between infrared and enhanced low light, the twelve such views sorted by an AI and displayed for Dagger and the captain. They could operate as a collective, like a swarm of bees, but were less detectable singly.

The flock detoured wide around a family herd of something rhinoceros sized, arching shellbacks visible above grass while the snouts stayed near ground.

"Herd beasts," Gorilla said. "Likely not very intelligent. But dangerous if they have hooves like that beetle thing did."

While this was going on, Bell Toll decided that scientists would have a field day here. The local life was insectoid on a scale never seen anywhere else, and they grew those armored carapaces that could stop small arms fire. What else was new and arcane?

"Well, that answers that question," Gorilla said with a tinge of disgust.

"What?" Bell Toll asked.

"The local flyers will attack my drones. I've lost two of the dozen," he explained.

"Might make sense to limit the number you have airborne, then, if you've done a scan of the area," Bell Toll advised.

"Will do." He brought eight of the remaining ones back, letting them alight on his shoulders like so many pets, though one wouldn't normally wad pets into a ball, albeit carefully, and stuff them into airtight pouches on one's harness.

"Okay," Bell Toll said, "we may as well get going. It's likely going to take two nights to do this. We'll need to stop in plenty of time to pitch a camp. And no one trip anything. Ferret, lead on, then Doll. Tirdal, you'll follow Gorilla. Let me know if you sense anything."

"Understood, and will do," Tirdal acknowledged. A human might have felt slighted, being bumped in position as a threat to stealth. No one knew how a Darhel took it, nor did they care. No mistakes that could spook a herd would be allowed.

They made a good three kilometers in a low, slow crawl through and under the grass, getting dusty and sweaty and occasionally smeared by the mountain-ous piles of bug droppings that smaller scarab-forms were chewing into little piles to rot or wash into the ground. The stuff didn't smell like anything on a human world, nor likely a Darhel one, but it stank just the same, a rotting odor of fermented plant life and anaerobic bacteria.

About an hour before local dawn, just as Bell Toll and Shiva were getting antsy, Ferret reported, "Got a depression here. Dry. Good spot to dig in."

"Outstanding. Everyone stay put," Shiva said. He shimmied through the formation until he could see what Ferret saw. "Yes, that'll do fine. Let's get in quick, dawn's coming."

That day found them skulking in the hollow for cover, wrapped well in blonde grass, with half-cylindrical camouflage screens overhead. They were close together, and kept two on watch at a time, dug into shallow fighting positions to the north and south. Nothing happened until after noon, and the sleeping went fitfully.

Just after the primary peaked in the blue sky that was brightly decorated with towering, puffy cumulus, local life intruded when a herd of smaller grazers browsed through on Gorilla and Bell Toll's watch. They approached slowly and started to wander by. Then, as if drawn to the smells from the camp, they turned towards it.

"What do we do, sir?" Gorilla asked.

"We don't spook them, first of all," Bell Toll said. "Let's just hope they drift past. We won't bother them if they won't bother us."

"Yes, sir," Gorilla agreed, but kept a tight grip on his weapon. He held that pose while a family group of six crawled right over him, feet carefully avoiding the unsteady surface of his back after one step, mandibles clipping grass near him, then brushing against him, nuzzling his right cheek and ear. He was freaked but unhurt, and clamped down on his sphincters and nerves as the pony-sized creatures decided he wasn't food and moved on. "Glad that's over," he muttered.

"It might get worse," the captain reminded him.

"Thanks, sir. You're all heart."

True to form, it did get worse. The local pseudo-mammalian bat analogs ranged in size up to something like a pterosaur, and five of those rode thermals lazily around the grassland. Then, apparently sharp-eyed, they came over to investigate. Shortly, they were orbiting the bivouac like horrific vultures gone awry. The shadows were big enough to have provided shade for the team, if one were to perch spread-winged.

"What the hell do we do now, sir?" Gorilla asked.

"Well, don't shoot. That'll be obvious and might stir them up."

"Yes, sir. But I would like to do something to get rid of them," he insisted. "It's like having a floating billboard announcing our presence. And I think they're getting lower. I'd rather not be lunch either, seeing as those things can likely carry off one of these grass chewers."

"Right. Got one of your bots out there?" Bell Toll asked, an idea forming. Heck, it might work.

"About fifty meters in front of me, sir," Gorilla agreed. "I think I see where you're going. We have it stagger about and see if one will attack it."

"Yes," Bell Toll confirmed. "But be ready to scoot if they freak. We don't know how similar they are to Earth vultures or Garambi rocs."

"No problem, sir. Want me to shoot if they freak?"

"Only if you're being attacked directly. Do it now, they're definitely lower."

"Yes, sir." He called up the bot as he clutched his gauss rifle closely, and sent the lumbering creature out at a trot, circling as if injured on its right side.

One of the long-snouted flyers peeled off, looking amazingly like a fighter aircraft in an historical vid. It dove, wings spread rather than in a stoop, and opened its mouth. The teeth within were obviously meant for cracking shells and rending flesh. And it was huge. It might measure eight meters across the wings.

Then it was on the drone, wings flared to airbrake, neck cracking down like a whip and jaws snapping shut. The mock beetle reacted exactly as programmed, and the molecularly thin spikes drove out, taking it through the jaw and face. It squawked, rather quieter than an earth creature, dropped to the ground and thrashed about, its clawed and fingered wingtips beating at the inedible, hurtful little morsel stuck in its mouth. Confused and wounded, it alternated between trying to flap away and flopping around in agony. The defensive needles withdrew back into the drone, but the damage was done. Staggering and disoriented, the creature fell over and twitched.

Sensing something beyond their ken but clearly uncouth, the other four flapped for altitude and soared away to seek more familiar prey.

"That is done," Gorilla said, with a sigh of relief. "I think I'm going to crawl back and drain before I wet my pants. That okay, sir?"

"Nerve wracking, yeah," Bell Toll said. "It's shift time, so says me. Wake Dagger and do what you gotta do. And don't waste time. I'm next."

When they prepped to move out at nightfall, Gorilla discovered the drone had been damaged worse than he'd thought. Reluctantly, he dropped it into the latrine slit, where its enzymes and destruct device would be unnoticed beneath the ground.

Across the mini-veldt, the woods began again. This ridge was the one from which they would hopefully see their target. They slept at the base, dug in well under weeds, and posted sentries in pairs with Gorilla's small flying bots perched on trees, sensors wide open for any hints. He stayed up most of the day, popping chemicals to keep himself awake. That night would begin the infiltration proper.

Chapter 8

THE CLIMB UP the ridge was steep, with footing made treacherous by a scree slope of shattered flat shards of ancient lava under the tangled skein of weeds. Pieces slipped and skipped downhill, tore lose under boots and gloved fingers and threw dust even through the plants. That combined with alien pollen to create swollen, oozing sinuses and itching eyes. Even through the gloves, chips and nicks from the impact trauma of the rocks caused niggling discomfort. Then the splinters worked their way in, along with thorns and burrs. Balance was precarious, and Gun Doll and Gorilla skidded several meters down the abrasive surface because of their awkward loads. Swearing and griping, they forced their way back up. Tirdal was clearly exerting himself, to the secret delight of some of the others, but his denser build kept him slipping and sliding as he dug fingers and toes into what solid surface he could find.

After several hundred meters of angled frustration, they found plants solid enough to grip. That made the climb easier, though it added sore shoulders to the tally of aches and pains. The coarse, fibrous stalks with leaves like nettles gave way to low, flexible bushes, then to trees. The terrain was thoroughly un-Earthly; Earth hills would have had loam followed by broken rock with solid basalt higher up. This was flaky followed by loam-covered solid surface with more slate-like shingles above the treeline. What odd eruption and surface effects had caused this? A shallow lake, perhaps, that cracked the lava, boiled away, only to ooze out again from the ground and shatter the bottom? Or had it all slid down from above? Exposed by weather or animals and then eroded?

The ridge was long and twisty, which was why Bell Toll had decided to go over rather than around. A small part of him wondered if that had been the right choice, even though intellectually he knew it was.

A few moments later, another colony of antlike insects attacked. These were larger, almost five centimeters long, and they chewed at the tough fabric of the suits as if it were some other form's carapace. "Hold still!" Gorilla spoke up. "They're big enough to bite. I'm sending out bots."

The little flyers Gorilla had rose into the breeze and alighted on each of the troops, skittering along limbs and gear and flicking the little pests off.

"Captain, Thor, hold still. There's more on you and they killed all the flyers. We'll have to take them off by hand."

"Hurry, Gorilla," Bell Toll suggested. "I can feel the damned things getting through the fabric."

"Right there."

Shortly, all the gnawing annoyances had been accounted for. Bell Toll hadn't been exaggerating. There were two holes through the fabric of his suit and one halfway through his right shoulder strap. It was a molecularly grown fabric, knitted and then woven into something tough enough to stop knives, most pistol ammo and even slow kinetic rifle rounds. The mandibles from those creatures had shredded it. But there was no injury and nothing to be done about the damage, so the advance resumed.

They rested briefly and silently once among the bushes, and again in the lower trees. It was as swelteringly hot tonight as the day had been. Sweat was pouring from all of them, and even Tirdal had a sheen to his waxy features. His breath was ragged but controlled.

"Nice night for a walk, eh?" Shiva teased. There were faint mutters or snickers in response. "You okay, Tirdal?" he asked, looking over.

"I'm fine," was the response. "I'm concentrating on Sensing, and meditating to calm my body."

"Too much exercise even for you to ignore, Tirdal?" Dagger asked.

"Dagger, I have never pretended to be more than I am. If anyone here carries a false face, it is not I."

"Right, if you can jaw, you can climb," Shiva said, cutting off more talk. "Back to it." There were groans and muttered comments from Thor and Gun Doll.

But they were softly voiced, pro forma protests, and the ordeal resumed.

"I do think I'm beginning to sense Tslek," Tirdal said as they resumed the climb. "There's a pattern of thought there."

"Details?" Bell Toll asked.

"None yet, sir. Just indications of presence."

"Right, we'll take it as a warning. Concealment and discipline, folks. I don't have to tell you."

"You don't, but will anyway," Shiva said. "And I'll echo that. No dumbassing."

The ascent through the trees was fairly rapid, the roots being as useful for traction as they were for tripping. All it took was caution to navigate them. Some of the trees resembled pines with knotty roots, straight and tall with tapering branches. They oozed their own sticky, syrupy sap, too, as Ferret and Tirdal found when they slipped by too closely to one. After that, they tried to avoid the trunks.

By the time they reached the ridge, the growth was back to scrub forms and sparse trees, with stark shadows cast by the moon, leaving lit areas the color of dried blood. They took to cautious crawling and occasional darts across barren ground. Their coveralls adapted to the local colors and shifted their IR emissions, but that latter came at a cost: heat retained inside. Powered armor had a substantial heat sink capability. The Intruder Chameleon Suits the team wore could handle it only for a short time. They were glad to shelter behind an outcropping below the military crest of the hill and let the heat disperse to the breeze. Even if it was a muggy night, it was cooler out there than in the suits.

"Okay," Bell Toll said, a hint of satisfaction in his voice, "we're ready to rock. Gorilla, Dagger, sneak us a peek."

This was the way of DRTs. Days of slogging and pain had brought them here, all of it merely the commute to work. Now the mission proper began. Rucks were left under a shelf of rock to enable faster and easier movement. They'd recover them when done. If they were forced to abandon them, it was likely to be a situation so hot that they wouldn't live long enough for the extra supplies to be missed.

Dagger slithered forward and higher, suit sealed and scanners in hand. As Gorilla unfolded a bot from his ruck, the captain looked at Tirdal again. His expressions were readable to the others now, and he was clearly concentrating.

"Got something?" Bell Toll asked.

"Perhaps," Tirdal said with a flick of his ears. "I'm sure there's a Tslek there. I can feel it. That's the problem."

"Why's that a problem?"

"Captain . . . I only sense one," he explained.

"One." Bell Toll bristled alert, hair on his neck standing up and goosebumps running down his arms despite the heat.

"Yes."

"That is very not good, Tirdal. Are you sure?"

"I'm sure I sense one. There could be others hidden behind unknown shields, or blocking me, or sensing me and affecting my mind, though I don't think that's the case. But I only feel one of them."

"Are they underground maybe?"

"No, I'd still sense them," he assured the captain. "And this one is . . . not worried. Not military. It feels like a caretaker going through a routine."

"I'm not showing any Blob genetic material on my sensors," Dagger interjected. "No nonnative molecular activity except us. Though we are making a lot of 'noise' that might hide things. And I don't see anything down there—" he indicated the far side of the ridge "—that indicates much travel by anything bigger than a rat. All clean. Spooky," he admitted.

"That doesn't make sense," Shiva said. "Any kind of base, even inactive, even if it's just a supply drop not yet built into a base, should have patrols and sentries. Technicians. Enough shifts to work around the clock. Thirty, forty at least. More likely a couple of hundred. Minimum."

"I know," Tirdal agreed. "But I sense one. Only one."

"Well, I admit to being freaked," Thor said. "What do we do?"

"We wait for Gorilla's bots to tell us what they see," Shiva replied. "We check around here. Then we decide from there."

"Right," Bell Toll said. "Gorilla, ready?"

"Ready, sir," he agreed. He set a small "animal" down and let it scamper off.

"If this was a big base, you'd expect patrols," Dagger muttered. "I'm not even getting particulates or aromatics from metal or plastic, which you always get with bots. If they've been running patrols they are really stealthy. And there's no reason for that kind of stealth. They didn't know we were coming."

"Did they?" Thor asked. "Could they?"

"No way," Ferret assured him with a choppy shake of his head. "And if they could, we'd be dead already. Why wait? But why no patrols, even if only bots? It doesn't make sense." He was trying to reassure himself, too.

"Tirdal," Thor asked, "are you sure you've got the right feel? How can you know what a Blob feels like if you've never felt one before?"

"I can't explain color to the blind. I know. Believe me or not, but I'm telling you what I have." Tirdal gave him a look that was almost a glare.

"Relax, Thor," Bell Toll ordered. "Gorilla, how's the bot?"

"Running, sir. Or walking, more accurately. Got it on molecular wire. Halfway down the slope and nothing so far."

"Describe, please."

"It's a glacial valley, very heavily forested once past the lava. On the far side there are some dark spots that are probably caves. It is just possible to see under the canopy . . . wait, I have movement. Here's the image," he said as he plugged them all in to his view. "Bringing up mag now."

There was definitely movement. "Are those bots?" Gun Doll asked. She lit a cursor and waved it over the area in question.

"Might be," Gorilla agreed. "We'll get a better view shortly. Stand by."

The view faded as the bot scurried ahead, shutting down most of its sensors as it entered the thicker growth. It ran with only its navigation and warning circuits live, as Gorilla coaxed it through the brush.

The team sat still, patiently, as he moved it in closer. This was something they trained for almost beyond all else. The stars shifted overhead, occasional small forms scurried past, including one as big as a fox. It was a half hour and more before Gorilla said, "Got it. Here." The images came back on screen.

There was a cleared area, and within and around it was activity. Vertical maintenance bots moved around vehicles and performed functions. Sensor globes flew slow orbits around the area, weaving around trees and other obstacles like so many intelligent tennis balls. Armored combat bots, unlike Alliance or Republic gear but obvious as to design, rolled around the perimeter.

There was a pause as Gorilla's bot detected and moved around a mine. At Gorilla's prompt, the screen lit with locations of sensors, mines and self-guided weapons, the drone detecting their faint idle signals and extrapolating. It wasn't yet as accurate as it would get after prolonged exposure, but it was good enough.

As the bot's view panned across the edge of the encampment it revealed a group of Blobs moving in a wedge formation. The patrol ambled and flopped across the clearing and into another part of the woods in a gait that seemed impossible.

Everyone had seen the patrol. Bell Toll looked over at Tirdal, who deliberately shrugged, that not being a Darhel gesture.

"I'm not sure what those are. But I don't sense them. Nor any distortion from the machines. I sense one Tslek only. Still."

"Something else is bothering me," Dagger said. "That clearing is too small. It's as if it's supposed to look like a base, but isn't one."

"How do you mean?" Thor asked.

"I see it too," Gun Doll said. "A proper facility would have a second perimeter, the trees would be downed and either removed or placed as revetments. They have no safe zone, and any attacker on foot or skimmer can come right up to the edge."

"This doesn't make sense," Thor said. "They understand security and threat discipline as well as we do. Why are they being so stupid?"

"Maybe they aren't," Dagger said. He had everyone's attention. No matter his façade, the man could stalk anything and find any hole in a perimeter. Under the sweaty grime and ragged, unshaven whiskers, his eyes had a sharp, squinty cynicism. He wasn't assuming the Tslek didn't know exactly what they were doing.

"What do you mean, Dagger?" Shiva asked into the pause.

"Tirdal says he senses one only. Let's assume that's true. We have one Blob. We have a lot of gizmos. We have a crappy perimeter a troop of Space Scouts could crack. We have a formation of what look like Blobs stomping around like a dictator's guard. Sensors get no good reading of any minor effects like waste. I say it's a decoy."

Shiva and Bell Toll frowned. Shiva spoke first.

"This is a big camp. If this is a decoy, those are holograms . . . so an insertion team would come someplace like right here," he said, jabbing his finger at the ground, "see all this and boogie in a hurry, without doing a detailed check. They'd see what the Blobs wanted them to see and not start a fight with a force that size. But why?"

"Because they want us to call in a report of a major facility building up and request space support," Bell Toll extrapolated. "The Navy sends a major force in, and somewhere they're waiting to cream it."

"Tirdal, you say they might be able to block you?" Gun Doll asked.

"It's possible, of course," he admitted. "It's never

happened, but I can't rule it out. They'd be just as likely, more so, to note your signatures. I can . . . suppress mine. Do as a matter of course. Humans, nonsensat humans, do not."

"What are you thinking, Doll?" Shiva asked.

"If they tracked us coming in and want us to leave with that intel, we're fine. If they haven't pinged on us yet, we don't want them to. We can't assume those are holograms."

"One way to find out," Gorilla put in. "The biotic mole."

"We didn't bring it this far to not use it," Bell Toll said reasonably. "Do it. But be careful."

"Believe me, sir, seeing that dance down there makes me very careful," Gorilla replied.

The item in question was a hamsterlike bio-animate. Grown from Earth rodents, it was a "dumb" biorobotic brain with tiny sensors encased in a real and retarded animal that had just enough brainpower to eat, excrete and move where told. It wasn't good for any detailed scans, but it excelled at missions like this. Even if detected, it would look like one of the local minor mammals.

"Send it scurrying in, however it's supposed to move, and have it contact something, preferably a dumb bot," Bell Toll ordered. "We'll go from there. Gun Doll."

"Sir?"

"Get the transmitter ready. If we get doinked, the report has to go out before we die. But don't push it without my orders."

"Yes, sir," she agreed. And if it came to that they were well and truly fucked, because the emergency transmitter would burn a signal through subspace that would be easily readable at the Navy's station thirty-five light-years away. They might as well set off fireworks and wave their arms.

"Primary plan is to walk out with the data, no matter what it is," Bell Toll reiterated. "I'd rather fly out than fight. So don't get horny. This is a walk, not a dance."

Gorilla was done digging in his ruck, and had the tiny creature in his hand. It sat there, dumb and still, its only sign of life being the little turd it chose to drop right then. Ignoring the minor distraction, Gorilla traced instructions on the touchpad in front of him, then set the creature atop the larger standard "pill bug" that would carry it to the perimeter. He gathered up the pair and shimmied higher toward the crest. There was no real reason, just the psychology of being a bit closer. Tirdal followed behind. The few meters would help him sense better. This was not a good situation. Behind him, Dagger came up with his sensors, and squirmed between two rocks like a lizard.

Gorilla put the bigger bot down and sent it on its way. He'd programmed it to pick a course and meander down as if feeding. He could adjust its path if need indicated, through the wire it was laying behind itself as it scurried under ledges and behind rocks, making good use of the terrain. At every pause it sent another image back.

"I hate to rush you, Gorilla," Bell Toll said, "but it's about three hours until dawn and we'll need to be making trail soon."

"Gotcha, sir. Let me get it into the trees and I can speed things up."

And he did. Once the rock started giving way, he

dialed the creature up to a fast trot, using what image there was to "drive" the bot through the woods. Its own circuits gave it a certain amount of decision making, and with his interpretation of the terrain ahead, it traveled quickly.

"Less than three thousand meters to go," he reported. "Slowing back down."

The device stopped a safe (they hoped) two hundred meters from the outer perimeter. The viewster biobot dropped off its back and darted for cover under thick grass. It too was programmed to move "naturally." In this case, it snuffled forward until it found a small game trail and trotted along it toward the site. To any sort of sensor it would look like what it was, a furry little animal. There were no electronic systems on it, no evidence that it was a construct. It would be invisible unless the sensors were designed to search for nonautochthonous life forms.

In a spot of good news, it appeared they were not, because the little creature was able to penetrate without any of the sensors going off. Further in there would probably be "clean" zones into which even a mouse couldn't penetrate. But the outer sections were relatively easy, with only local terrain, predators and the biobot's diminutive size as obstacles.

It took another solid hour for the creature to do its penetration, just one of many small mammaloids running around in the area. Once it did, it found a rock under which were several of the local roach lookalikes. They were edible to earth creatures and the viewster hunted them avidly until another party of Blobs, or perhaps the same one, came back through. When it saw the low, gray creatures it quickly scuttled across their path where the swift moving creatures would run over it and continue on their way.

"Here we go," Gorilla said, and everyone watched the repeated image from his controller. The "Tslek" flopped and rolled right over the sensor-creature, leaving it, and the nearby grass and twigs, unharmed. They were excellent holograms, but nothing more.

And the base was a trap.

The encounter had been in clear view of the sensors Dagger and Gorilla had deployed and that was that. Gorilla looked at Tirdal, who stared back but didn't even change expression, then down at the team. Whatever was there was apparently a fake.

"I can send the viewster into a few emplacements and possibly get more information, sir, but the likelihood of detection increases with each exposure. And I think the answer we have is short and sweet."

Bell Toll shook his head for a negative, then used hisses and hand signals to get the attention of the rest and order them back. The Aldenata tech-based communicators they had were absolutely secure, but he wasn't going to trust them this close to an enemy base that was obviously set to trip them up. It might, in fact, be best to go back to old-fashioned laser signals, even if it limited them to a line-of-sight formation. After this, they had to exfiltrate by a different route to avoid possible detection, then get the acquired intel back to the sector command. The slim facts they had would nevertheless rule out many wrong avenues in this game of deception. Negatives could sometimes, in fact, prove more valuable than concrete answers.

But that was for the analysts to decide. Their job was to hump back out and stay alive.

Following Gorilla's preprogrammed orders, the viewster headed back up the game trail as the two recon troops and Tirdal slid down the reverse slope of the ridge. The larger bot had already headed back over so Gorilla told it and its companion to head out on point. The reverse trip would actually be shorter than the insertion and they should be able to make it in a week. It would be a tense week of careful movement and thorough concealment. Whether or not the Tslek had planned for them to find the site, they had to assume that the Tslek knew they'd found the deception. So being found now would mean death. A pawn stays alive only so long as its purpose is served, and from a Tslek viewpoint they were now a liability even had they been valuable before.

The team bivouacked again within the trees, the nearness to the Blobs being a slightly better risk than trying to slog out fast, risking noise and discovery as they traversed terrain in daylight. They'd save the forced march for tomorrow night.

Later that day, the viewster came darting back over the shards of the ridge and found the place where it had been told to report. It sat patiently under a ledge and waited an hour for signals or orders, but there was nothing there. Having lost contact with its control it snuffled around until it found a hole in the ground, crawled in and died. Specially bred internal bacteria would dissolve it in under three hours, leaving nothing but a smell and some bones. At some level, everything is expendable.

Chapter 9

THEIR RETURN ROUTE cut through the low hills that had intervened before. For a while they followed some game trails that paralleled the hills. The hills probably were ancient remnants of mountains, worn down from staggering ranges, most likely foothills of the taller mountains that rose to east and west of the glacial valley and river plain in between. There were other signs of old vulcanism, indicating that this area had had a violent youth.

Once away from the Tslek "installation," they moved quickly and surely, and off the game trails. Predators loved game trails for obvious reasons, and no one wanted a fight. There was no other reason to be more than normally cautious, and every reason to get off-planet as soon as possible, so they slogged fast. Ferret made good time and showed considerable skill at finding routes with fair footing and clear space to hike, while still keeping tall growth around them for concealment. He rarely caused them to backtrack around obstacles, though he did have them detour around another log that might contain a nest of the biting ant things. Tirdal watched and tried to deduce how Ferret did this. It was a skill he had no experience in.

The second night out, they came to a fairly deep and strong stream that had cut a chasm through the rocks ahead.

"We'll have to detour downstream until we find a place to ford," Ferret said. "Unless we're going to build a moly-rope bridge?"

"No," Shiva said. "Safer and likely faster to go around. Five minutes to rest and on we go."

The path downstream was a rubble and boulder-strewn igneous mass with trees growing at chaotic angles near the edge, straight and tall further back. The soil was rich and fragrant, made dark and fertile by minerals from the broken rocks and well-rotted foliage. It wasn't a hard route for trained troops, as it was downhill with lots of handholds. They swiftly covered three kilometers of steep, rocky bank as the bots led the way.

"Flat ground ahead," Gorilla advised.

Ten minutes later, the ground began to level. They were back out onto glacial plain. No sooner had they reached a stretch that looked promising for a crossing,

Gorilla called, "Whoa! Anomaly!" His voice was soft but urgent.

"What type?" Bell Toll asked as Shiva waved the troops into a perimeter.

"Not here," Gorilla answered with a shake of his head. "Forward and west. Energy reading of some kind. It's small and not moving."

"Isn't that just great?" Bell Toll asked facetiously. "Okay, keep the bots safely back but find out what you can. Everyone sit tight here. Tirdal, what've you got for me? Can you sense it?"

"Yes, I can now," he nodded. "It's very faint. It's not Tslek. There's something there, but it doesn't even seem alive. Just . . . there, present. And it has a psychic component. More than that I cannot say. But definitely not alive."

"Okay, Ferret will lead, you move up closer to him and keep alert. Remember that he has more experience at sneaking. Gorilla, get your bots out wide and move slowly; we don't want to spook whatever it is, but we've got to take a look ourselves. Shiva, plot us two escape routes—one slow and cautious, one go-to-hell. Everyone ping me acknowledgment . . . okay, let's do it."

Tirdal and Ferret dropped their rucks and crept forward. The relayed image from Gorilla's bots helped them keep to low ground and clear of the knotted webs of roots. The ground was soft and mushy again, and it soaked through their suits, the wetness permeating the air with the smell of damp and rotting life. The only animals they saw were the smallest scavengers and stem-eating types. While crawling, they were below the umbrellalike canopies of bushes. Their route through the looping roots of the trees took them past a local anthill analog, busily trafficked by beetle-creatures less than a centimeter long. Ferret shook off a few that tried to bite and sting, taking him for some dead source of protein.

"Ouch," he muttered. "Gonna have welts from that. They aren't as bad as those other little bastards, but watch them, Tirdal."

"I see them," Tirdal said. "Stand by." He pulled a scrap of uneaten ration from his smaller ruck and waved it past the nest, then dropped it a meter away. It was a sugary cookie and the eager little monsters swarmed it and ignored him.

"Let's see the bot's-eye view," Ferret asked. Gorilla obliged and relayed a near-ground-level image in the visible spectrum. There was an almost-clearing ahead; one of those spots where the trees thinned enough for a dropship insertion or a small camp. The bots had stopped there. They'd been programmed to pause if they encountered anything with a pattern not on file as "natural," and what was here certainly wasn't.

"Is that what we're looking at?" Ferret asked.

"At and for," Gorilla replied. "I dunno what it is."

All that could be seen was a thin spot in the trees. Within were some lumps and mounds. They resembled burial cairns from some lost civilization, weathered and beaten for ages. There was a wrongness to the area that even the humans could feel.

"The source is in there somewhere," Gorilla said. "No threats show. I've got both bots watching it and the flyers perched on trees on the far side. Nothing except local life."

"Gorilla," Bell Toll said, "send a bot in slowly.

One step at a time. Ferret and Tirdal can pull up to the edge. We'll stay back for support. Thor and Shiva, keep an eye on our asses." There were pings of acknowledgment and the team moved.

They'd shifted perhaps five meters when Gorilla said, "Stop." Everyone froze, fingers on triggers, until he said, "No threat, but I've IDed the source. Central mound, right there. Power emanations, but very low."

"Okay," Bell Toll acknowledged. "Let's move in. Ferret and Tirdal wait where you are. Gun Doll and I will take a supporting position on the left. Dagger and Shiva on the right. Gorilla will pull up and relieve Ferret, then Ferret advances."

Upon closer inspection, the area wasn't a clearing at all. It was tree covered, like the surrounding terrain, but in a radius around the central mound the trees were slightly stunted and there were stones poking up through the loam. It was the lack of animals and the stunted trees that gave it an odd feel.

"Radiation?" asked Bell Toll.

"Not much above background levels," Gorilla said after studying his sensors.

"There's a minor pulse to the emitted frequency," Dagger added. "It's steady. Nothing dangerous to us, but I suppose after enough years it builds up. There also might be chemicals in the soil, depending on what this device is. The surface here reads differently. And those stones are odd."

They were among the mounds, now. Ferret and Thor had their backs in, as did Gun Doll, her automatic cannon moving in slow sweeps as she studied the trees.

Tirdal brushed at one of the stones and examined the striations revealed beneath the clinging dirt. It was an extruded block, not carved native stone.

"Plascrete," he said softly.

The others shifted carefully over to him.

"What did you say?" Bell Toll asked.

"Plascrete," he repeated. "Look at the extrusion marks and the texture. It was produced on site with no concern for prettiness."

Gun Doll ran her fingers over the chipped corners of the revealed mass.

"How old does plascrete have to be to crack and crumble like that?"

"Very old, I would guess . . . and Sense," Tirdal said.

Spreading out and examining other revealed rocks determined that the place was a ruin. It was some sort of very old building or fortification, hundreds, possibly thousands of years old. All that was left were a few mounds of tumbled plascrete overgrown with misshapen, gene-damaged trees and tangled vines. In the cold drizzle and half-light, it was an eerie, disturbing scene.

Gorilla had the bot dig into the lump, carefully. It made quiet incursions by drill, split cracks between the holes with a pneumatic ram and gingerly pulled out sections. It then made another cut, slightly deeper. Ferret, Dagger and Shiva stayed in an outer perimeter, nerves naked wires, alert for any threatening movement, or any movement at all. The other half of the troop formed to contain anything that might erupt from within the dig.

"Energy source," Tirdal said.

"Yes?" prompted Bell Toll.

"I'm not sure. Just some source of energy. They all feel somewhat alike . . . heat, radio, UV . . . just a sense of intruding rays, not enough to be harmful."

"Got that, Gorilla?" Bell Toll asked.

"Got it," he nodded softly, adjusting the bot to dig wider before going deeper. "We're going to have to either hide these blocks the bot is cutting, or stick them back when done. A pile will be a giveaway."

"Yes," Bell Toll agreed. "But it can't be much deeper now, can it?"

In answer, Tirdal said, "There."

"Yeah, the bot sees it now," Gorilla agreed, looking at his screen. "I'm clearing around it. It's a root power source of some kind, encased in plasteel."

Bell Toll dialed up enhancement and resolution on his helmet and tried to get a glimpse into the hole, past the ludicrously hulking limbs of the small bot.

"Oh, shit," he said softly.

"What?" asked Gun Doll, being closest. She pulled up her own screen and said, "'Oh, shit' is right."

Enough of the case was revealed for its architecture to become apparent. That combined with the energy readings made it familiar to anyone who studied history or matters military.

It was an Aldenata artifact. Apparently a functional one.

The Aldenata were extinct. It had been they who had bred the Posleen for war, and screwed it up so as to leave the Posleen a marauding threat. They'd created the Darhel, who could administrate but not fight to defend themselves. The Indowy, Tchpth and possibly the humans had been tampered with by them, also. Besides the damaged races of this part of the galaxy, they'd left a few installations and a very few artifacts. Whatever had done them in had been thorough. No one knew. Or at least, no humans. The other races didn't discuss it much.

The box wasn't that large, about a half meter on a side and vaguely oblong. There were two queerly formed handles on it that the bots used to drag it to the surface. A careful cleaning by Gorilla and Gun Doll revealed that it had controls on the surface and some inscribed characters.

"It could be anything or nothing," Gun Doll said, as she wiped away dirt to reveal the text and pulled out a ruled scale and camera. They couldn't decipher it here, but they could get images for file.

"Yes, but any industrial corporation would pay a cool billion credits for it," Bell Toll said. Even if it wasn't sold, the soldiers could expect enough of a bonus for it that they'd be able to live comfortably for the rest of their lives.

"So, ten percent of a billion, split eight ways . . ." muttered Dagger, sliding up alongside to peer into the hole. He was figuring the likely salvage percentage they'd get if the government did sell it.

"Dagger, get back out where you belong," Bell Toll snapped quietly. The sniper's eyes were needed where they could track incoming Blobs, not calculating profits.

"Yeah, sure," he agreed and slithered away again.

"Captain, should I get some images for our researchers?" Tirdal asked. "We do have more experience with Aldenata equipment than you."

"That's partly because you won't share the info you

do have, but go ahead," Bell Toll said, some prejudice slipping past at last. Tirdal ignored it and took several views of the device.

They turned over a few more rocks and had the bots drill around the area, test bores to see if anything else registered. There was nothing else that stood out.

"I'm getting nothing else," concurred Tirdal. "All I feel is the power from this," he indicated the device, "and it feels as if it's idling, waiting."

There was nothing left but for a full archaeological expedition, which could be expected if the humans ever took the world.

"Well, let's clean up the area and move out," Bell Toll ordered. "We'll take the box with us and let the experts fiddle with it."

Gorilla got the bots to work replacing the chunks of plascrete, while the soldiers took turns scraping and digging at the bot tracks and drag marks of the rocks as only trained Special Operations troops can.

"I can easily determine the damage at this close range," Tirdal said when they were finished, "but it's likely not obvious to a routine observer at any distance."

"I can see it," Dagger challenged. "If I can, others can if they look hard enough. But there shouldn't be any real searches before we bug out."

"Nevertheless, let's try to cover our tracks in and out," Shiva suggested.

"I concur," Bell Toll said. The work resumed amid sighs.

The trick to a good concealment is not to do too much, or a site becomes a "garden," neat and obvious rather than rough and nondescript. In true Zen fashion, doing little is harder than doing much. But by dusk, rain starting, there was little evidence that anything untoward had happened. An organized search might show something, but no casual examination. If they'd done their jobs properly, rain would wash away any remaining signs in short order. Of course, any major flaws in the dig would show more clearly as rain eroded soft earth. It was best they move quickly, just in case.

Bell Toll took the bulky artifact and strapped it onto his pack under a chameleon cover. He grunted with the effort of lifting it—while not outrageously massive, it wasn't light by any means.

Slogging through mud is a military tradition from as far back as humans have been fighting, which is always. It's something every military organization has to get used to, but, despite jokes, no one ever gets used to. Mud slows the steps, sticks to the boots then oozes inside, cold, wet, gooey, gritty and sharp in spots. It splashes as high as one's head, no matter how high that might be, and is generally unpleasant. Every generation, the designers insist they've developed a "mud proof" boot, and every generation the troops laugh hysterically as mud squishes past seals, flush surfaces or joints.

The team was squelching along the nearby river, mud alternating with trickles and puddles of water, the dark, dank bank on one side with the tendrils of tree branches arching in ghostlike fingers over them to the water's edge. They should be well shielded from most sensors. Even thermal imaging wasn't likely to detect their chilled, clammy hides through the scattering foliage.

Ahead, they were seeking a ford. Some further distance from the Tslek facility was desired, and crossing the watercourse should decrease the likelihood of anything coming for them. While they could swim, even burdened as they were, there was no need to exert unnecessary energy.

The first ford they found wasn't as hospitable as Bell Toll had hoped. Certainly it was shallower than upstream, but it was on a moderate slope that gave the shallow water good velocity over rocks. It wasn't going to be that much easier to cross here.

"Keep low," Bell Toll advised in a whisper. Everyone nodded. Besides keeping their silhouettes concealed, it would keep them stable in the current. They were as wet as they could get already, anyway. "Ferret, out you go."

"Ferrets don't like swimming," the little point troop replied, but he said it as he moved out on the rocky shallows they'd been using, toward deeper water.

Ferret stepped down off the shelf, one hand on a protruding root near the bank, and began wading. The bubbling, ankle-deep stream near the edge turned to rippling and waving knee-deep currents within a couple of steps, then to a pounding torrent that ripped at him, seen as dark and light infrared and enhanced visible traces across his visor. He leaned forward and grabbed a rock that rose from the water, and worked his way around into the calm downstream of it. Kneeling and reaching, he caught another handhold and crossed the channel between the two, water shoving at his chest and splashing into his face. He worked his way across by keeping solid hold of the rocks as his feet slid on smooth, moss-slickened pebbles underneath and water raged past him. He was two thirds of the way over when he reached a deep, rushing current about two meters wide. It didn't take much observation to conclude that he wasn't going to cross it alone. And it would likely look worse in daylight.

Ferret studied the voracious swirl for long seconds. Then he began crawling backwards. Once he reached the previous slab of weathered limestone he called back on his transmitter, it being too loud to shout even if noise discipline allowed it. "It's too swift. Gorilla can likely get over; he's taller and heavier. We're going to need to belay," he said.

"Goddammit. Understood," Bell Toll replied.

Shortly, Gorilla began splashing and crawling from the bank. His larger mass was of benefit, and he made steady progress through the tugging current and was alongside in moments.

"Hold my ruck and tell me what you need," he said as he swung his albatross-long limbs free from the harness.

"Deep and swift," Ferret said, pointing. "If you can shove across we'll run the rope. Otherwise, that bastard is going to take someone for a ride."

"Got it," he nodded.

Gorilla had a tough time of it himself, and Ferret was glad he'd asked for aid. The two-meter tall troop splashed into the water and only kept his head above by maintaining a firm grip on Ferret's proffered hand. He reached across, angled by the strong current, scrabbling for purchase. The flow underneath was unbelievable, stretching him out starfishlike. After several minutes of clutching, he retreated. Sitting under the rock, he shouted up to Ferret, "I think it would be easier to move further downstream. But let me try something."

He sought a chunk of rock about as wide and flat as his hand. He plunged his hand in and wrenched free one that seemed appropriate.

"Tie the rope around that," he demanded. "Toss it and I'll pull myself across."

It sounded reasonable, and Ferret gave the rock two loops and two half hitches. At a nod and a point from Gorilla, he tossed it over the depths and between the large boulder and a projecting knob just upstream. He pulled and it caught. Gorilla seized the cord and was across in seconds.

Then came the task of tying his ruck near the far end of the line, tossing the free length and drawing it across. Everyone and all their gear was going to get soaked from this. They'd only thought themselves wet so far.

Ferret was ignominiously hauled over, then made it the rest of the way in a combination hop, skip and plunge. There was no real cover on the far bank, so he settled back into the water downstream of another bit of rock.

"Secure," he reported. "Give me some company."

At a nod from Shiva, Tirdal trudged down and over. His dense form was of some help here, and he kept his position despite the flow. At the rope where Gorilla still waited, he planted his ruck and let Gorilla tow it across. That accomplished, he grasped the rope and slid over. He disappeared beneath the shifting surface, leaving only his hand as an indicator. That hand was joined by his other, and he made his way in fitful, sliding jerks across. As he bumped the far boulder, he extended a hand and clenched it twice, until Gorilla reached down and heaved him up, or tried to. It took both of them, Tirdal shoving with his feet, Gorilla heaving on the rope and straining back with his feet, before the Darhel's head surfaced. He could be audibly heard to gasp in a breath as his massive form rose up onto the rock.

"Holy shit . . . Tirdal," Gorilla asked between gasps. "What do . . . you weigh?"

"I'm considerably denser in bone and muscle mass than a human," Tirdal said without answering him. He continued doggedly over and took Ferret's position, as the short human squirmed onto the bank proper.

The procedure repeated. Only Ferret had been light enough to swim with his gear. Gun Doll slung her cannon over, then her gear and then herself. She massed less than her rangy size indicated and swung in the current like a flag in a stiff breeze until Gorilla caught her hand. Once across, she leaned against the mud, covering the rest of the squad while Tirdal guarded her and Ferret acted as a sensor wire against anything from the front. Ferret had adapted to his social calling of mine-tripper, and had become philosophical about it. He did hope for promotion within a few missions, though.

Dagger went through contortions to pass his sniper rifle across to Gorilla without getting it into the water. It wasn't the wetness that worried him, but the risk of banging it out of alignment between the rocks. Truthfully, it was built much sturdier than that, and he was just obsessive, but Gorilla humored him and took it by the muzzle, even though the long extension of mass from his hand pulled muscles in his forearm. Dagger would spend a goodly time fussing over it and drying it later, he was sure.

Shiva, Bell Toll with the artifact and Thor followed, and they were all across. Soaked, slimed with mud and moss, bedecked with bits of weed, they blended in even better than they had before. It was bone-chillingly cold even with the warm air. The best way to slow the conduction of heat through the water was to dial down the permeability of the suits. That left them wrinkling like prunes inside squelching, water-tight shells. Once warmed, they'd turn the permeability up until they steamed dry.

"Gorilla, give us a good scan," Bell Toll ordered.

"Will do, but only one bot made it across. The other one took a soaking—must have a hole in the shell somewhere—and won't work until dry," he replied. "Want me to send flyers, too?"

Bell Toll thought for a few moments. It was likely they'd lose some more to predators, but the team was exfiltrating and the drones were intended for use. The risk of discovery was negligible, and the data they'd provide could be considerable.

"Please," he said. "As soon as they're out, we'll move. At least we've had our bath."

"Yeah, and it's only April," Ferret joked. He felt free to comment now. After all, he'd blazed the path across this giant roach hotel, its marshes, cliffs, plains, to the Tslek, the Aldenata box and that godawful river. There'd been two other planets before that, too.

"We're looking for somewhere to hole up for the day," Shiva said. "We want hard cover and conceal-ment, just in case. Be sharp."

Once more they moved out, following Gorilla's technobugs.

No matter their training and experience, this was

an arduous mission. All of them were dinged and nicked from the trip so far, all fatigued and near exhaustion from the odd day cycle, higher gravity, strange air and odd environment. All were strained mentally from the risks and possible threats, as well as the incredible aloneness of being the only humans on the planet, the only ones within thirty-five light-years, for all intents the only ones in the universe, for nothing anyone else could do would help them in an emergency. Mundane annoyances like the boring rations and blisters were just teasing flirts to remind them of the rest.

Then there was Tirdal. The Darhel slogged along steadily, quietly, doing his part and doing it adequately well with no complaints at all. That just made empathizing with him that much harder. That, and he might peer into one's soul. Tirdal was still very much the outcast. No one could get a handle on him, but they weren't much trying, either. If he wound up staying with the team beyond this mission, perhaps that would change. It remained to be seen.

The introspective and tactical silence was broken by Ferret saying, "I think that might work . . . over there." He lit the area referenced and everyone looked over. It was a large outcropping, still within the trees, with a series of smaller projections lower down the slope.

"Stay cool," Shiva ordered. "What do you think, sir?"

Bell Toll waved Ferret forward and moved up to see for himself. "Ought to do fine, Sarge. Bed 'em down."

"Got it. Ferret and Gorilla, do a perimeter sweep.

Gun Doll, cover them from right there," he indicated an outcropping. "Everyone else, dig in."

Gun Doll sighed in relief as she set her cannon down on its spiky monopod. The gyroscopic stabilizers would keep it steady and level, ready to swing at a touch. That done, she ripped off her helmet and gave her matted hair and the scalp underneath it a good scratch. "Going numb under here," she muttered, barely audibly, to no one. Days of the helmet's mass across the webbing, even with the foam padding she'd added, was a growing distraction. The dandruff didn't bother her, it was just part of the job, and would clean up once home. Besides, there was no one here but the guys.

Shortly, Gorilla had his sensors out, doubled to act as mines at his order. They were far more expendable now than they had been early on and the potential threats were greater. Equipment was expendable, people were not.

Shortly, they were in place, the flyer bot sensors atop the rocks, three small killer bots lurking downhill, and the sole surviving pill bug uphill and watching. Shiva directed the troops to individual spots where they'd be hidden but able to provide interlocking fire, and had them roll out their bags. The latrine was dead center for convenience and security. "Not going to be deep, Sarge," Dagger said. "Rocks less than a half meter down, of course."

"It'll do," he said by way of acknowledgment and dismissal.

While Shiva handled the housekeeping, Bell Toll examined the artifact. He ran his fingertips over the surface, seeking controls or seams. There were none apparent in this light. Shrugging inwardly, he reached into his gear and pulled out a tracer-transponder. It wasn't really necessary, and he was probably over-reacting, but they'd all hate to lose such a prize. It couldn't hurt to mark it, so he did. He slapped it onto a corner and the molecularly thin film of it fused with the artifact's surface and became effectively part of it and invisible.

Dagger had slipped alongside him, undetected until the last moment. Bell Toll started slightly, but kept it from showing. Dammit, he hated when the sniper did that. He did it just because he could, and it only encouraged him if he thought he'd got one over on you.

"Yes, Dagger? Are you here to take advantage of the commander's open-door policy?" he asked.

"Nah, just wanted another gander at the box, sir. I didn't get a good look earlier," he said, moving in close. He was shoulder to shoulder now, and it made Bell Toll uncomfortable. Frankly, he'd rather have Tirdal that close than Dagger. One was unknown, the other a pain.

"Well, this is the artifact, Dagger. Artifact, meet Dagger," he said, trying to inject some levity into the situation.

"Charmed," Dagger joked. Hell, he wasn't that bad, Bell Toll thought. Just another kid with something to prove. Give him five years and he'd mellow. When he'd first arrived he'd been all attitude, now it was partly an act. He'd get over it, and if there were opportunities to let him act like a mature person, they should be encouraged.

Dagger was poring over the device in the growing

light. His fingers traced the raised symbols that might be long dead controls, followed the contours and hefting it. "What is it and why is it here?" he asked, mostly to himself.

"We might never know," Bell Toll said. "Some can be opened inside a stasis field, though some are equipped to self-destruct. Others are unresponsive. The fact that this one still has latent power is a good sign."

"Any guess what it might be, sir?" Dagger asked, his sharp, perfect eyes still focused on the box, examining every line, every dirt-filled pit.

"No clue. A ship's control box, unlikely. A base computer, possible, though I'd think they'd have extracted it when the base was abandoned, or an enemy would have seized it. Anything else I couldn't say. I've had briefings, but I'm no expert." He shrugged.

Dagger shrugged also. "I see what are obviously seams, but I don't see a way to make them budge. We going to take turns humping this?"

"No, Dagger," Bell Toll replied, smiling. "In this case, the commander will assume the horrible burden of carting the cargo, thus to spare his troops a strain that wasn't in the original plan. Besides, it's my ass if we lose it."

"Yeah, I could just see that one. 'We found this Aldenata artifact and dropped it in a lake. So sorry, but it really was cool at the time.' I can't see them buying that."

"Right," Bell Toll chuckled. "Well, I'm going to wrap it back up, so show and tell is over."

"Right, sir. I'll keep an eye out tonight. And I can set some of my sensors to act as additional alarms if you'd like."

"Please," he agreed as Dagger walked in a crouch back across to his gear. He reflected that Dagger wasn't so bad when his interests were challenged. It was boredom that made him awkward.

It was dinnertime again. Hopefully, there'd be few more of those on this patrol. As shifting, flashing sparks of false dawn warned of the coming light, they plowed into their food. Hunger helped and so did long practice, as well as awareness that they'd be out of here in very few sleeps.

"Tuna again," Gun Doll bitched. "Who eats this crap?"

"Sorry, Doll," Thor said. "But I'm not swapping my pork fritter."

"Doesn't matter," she said, resignation and a sigh in her voice. "I'll eat it."

Dagger said, "Be right back. Gotta drain the vein," as he rose and walked toward the large rock.

"Why didn't you go in the stream like the rest of us?" Thor joked. Then he wondered why the sniper was walking out past the rocks, and with his rifle. "Hey, Dagger, the slit is over th—"

As he passed the rock, Dagger grabbed a neural grenade from the pouch on his harness and tossed it back into the middle of the team.

Chapter 10

TIRDAL FELT DAGGER'S aggression smack him. It was palpable, vicious, and thoroughly emotionless under the surface. The incoming feeling was so strong, it was one of the few visual senses he'd ever had. The feeling hit him and rolled over him, creating a link for a bare fraction of a second. He could feel the callous smirk on his/Dagger's face, see the grenade arc from his/Dagger's hand. The sudden image of a fangar, a predator on Shartan, came through clearly. Dagger was not only committing mass murder, he was enjoying it. It was an intense moment, the sensat equivalent of orgasm, personal and powerful. They were Tirdal's specialty. He couldn't always "feel" people in his area. But he always knew when they were participating in a kill.

He also knew that there wasn't time to stop it. His punch gun would go right through the boulder the sniper was using as a shield against the neural lash but the grenade was already in the air as the Darhel surged to his feet. Stopping to kill the sniper would just leave the entire team dead on the ground. Their vital information, and the possibly more vital artifact, would never make it back.

This thought process occurred in an instant and Tirdal knew what he had to do. Saving the team was out of the question; he couldn't reach the grenade and throw it out of range in time. All he could do was avoid the death himself. And keep the box, which had to be Dagger's target, out of the hands of the sniper turned traitor.

But to do everything that he had to do, it would be necessary to use tal hormones. Which was another problem.

Tirdal summoned the tal, letting the natural anger at the sniper's betrayal slither a tiny tendril past hard-held defenses. The mere touch of anger triggered the tal gland, dumping a modicum of hormone into the Darhel's system and slowing his subjective time and the world around him as he reached for the box.

The captain was slowly looking at him in consternation but Tirdal didn't pay any attention; the captain, who was a decent person, really, was dead and didn't know it. Tirdal's knife-blade hand struck the officer's wrist, breaking it and releasing the hold on the box. As soon as he had the box secured Tirdal turned and dove over the boulder behind him. The whole world seemed to slow as he could see both Shiva's and Gun Doll's looks of horror at the sight of the grenade out of the corners of his eyes. His vision split, one eye tracking on potential threats to the right as the other looked to the left where the grenade was coming in. Humans couldn't do that, he remembered. It might be useful knowledge later.

He had the box, his punch gun and his combat harness with its small patrol pack. What he didn't have was his rucksack. But as soon as he had the bulk of the granite between him and the grenade he intended to teach the sniper a few things about Darhel.

One of which was that they really hated traitors. At least Bane Sidhe Darhel did.

He leapt up and back, and one hand struck the top of the boulder to correct his course with a twist. Fingers tougher than granite left small scars as they drove him forward and down into the tangled undergrowth. The landing would receive no praise from his master, and he felt one shoulder give. But then he was flat on the ground, if somewhat battered, when the neural grenade gave its snarl.

Breathing slowly and deeply to prevent lintatai, Tirdal spun around on his belly and, carefully controlling his tal reaction, fired back along the line towards the spot the sniper had thrown from. Carefully. He was just shooting boulders and dirt. Not a person. If the person happened to be in the way that would be a pure accident. But not a kill. Never a kill.

Ferret was turning his head as Thor spoke, and realized something was wrong. He didn't know what that thing flying in from behind the boulder was at first, but he knew it was bad.

Luckily, he had been setting up his position behind a low finger of rock, to at least have the illusion of privacy. He ducked flat and hoped he'd be covered from whatever stupid stunt Dagger was pulling. He didn't care if he got laughed at for putting his face in the dirt. If this was a joke, it was a bad one.

He felt the angry lash of the grenade, and knew he was wounded. At first, that's all it was, an agonizing rip through his body, bright flashes in his eyes. But he was alive. He concentrated on that. His awareness returned, with his feet kicking convulsively. The pain resolved as a searing, cramping burn from his mid-calves down. He'd been mostly covered from the rays of the blast, but his feet had protruded beyond the rock and been exposed, and it hurt, oh shit it hurt.

Now he had to move. That couldn't have been by accident, and Dagger would be coming back to kill him. He also noticed as he scanned the area that the bodies in front of him didn't include Tirdal. Was that damned Darhel in on this? Not good. Whatever was happening was not good. He scrabbled for a gap between the rocks and tried to squirm through, but got stuck. It would be easy to push himself through with his feet, except his feet were not working, except that the nerves were working and they fucking hurt. There was firing behind him and that was a bad sign.

By sheer force that strained a tricep into a sting that paled compared to his feet, he wiggled out. He held still as he saw Tirdal go jogging past below, headed downstream with the artifact.

Oh, son of a bitch, he thought. Had it all been a

setup to get that artifact? Or had Tirdal and Dagger cut a deal this evening? "Captain?" he whispered into his commo, craving a reassuring voice. There was no reply. He knew they were dead, but he had to check. Scrolling through channels, he tried, "Sarge? Doll? Thor? Gorilla?" with no responses. Panic set in as he realized he was in command now, with two traitors, and it didn't matter a damn, because he was going to be killed. And even if he wasn't killed, the neural damage to his ankles and feet meant he might get gangrene and die shortly anyway. He couldn't very well amputate, and he had no way of repairing nerves in the field. Was gangrene possible? He didn't know. Not that it mattered; he was lame.

He scrabbled higher up the slope, keeping low, keeping hidden. This part he could do on hands and knees for now, though he'd have to watch where his dangling feet went or he'd leave a clear sign of his passing. He didn't just need to worry about Blobs now, this was Dagger who would be stalking him. And Tirdal could probe his mind. He wasn't sure there was anywhere safe at this point, but he couldn't just lie there and wait for a shot.

Ferret was scared. He wasn't afraid to admit it. He was just old enough to grasp mortality, and it was staring hard at him. He couldn't see any way of coming out of this alive, but the few hours or days he might have were precious beyond anything else.

Carefully, he made his way uphill under waving fronds and tangled stems. Height would give him a better chance at a shot, as long as he could stay hidden, because Dagger's sensors and eyes would be looking for him, and the way he'd shot against Thor was just terrifying. And Tirdal had been following Ferret the entire trip, with that Sense of his, staring into his soul.

Ferret took a deep, slow breath and tried to calm down. He knew he was panicking, he knew he was in shock, and he knew his pulse was beating way too fast for health.

There was a dimple in the earth, thickly overgrown with greenery, and slightly damp. It would shield him for now. His heat would balance out the evaporative cooling of the earth, and he should be able to blend into the background. He elbowed and kneed his way around to the far side and slithered in.

Dagger was happy. That was a rare thing. But a billion credits could buy a lot of happiness. With a billion credits he could move himself to Kali and spend the rest of his life abusing worshippers. He could have himself rejuvenated as many times as he wished and when even rejuv failed could have his brain transferred to a new body and go on having fun. Maybe a woman's body. Maybe he'd do that anyway, just for the kicks. A billion credits were going to buy a lot of pleasure.

He stood up as soon as the grenade settled down, stepped down and glanced around the clearing at the spasming and very dead bodies. Good. They were all assholes anyway. Where the hell was the . . .

Tirdal couldn't localize the satisfied emotion but he heard a movement that wasn't thrashing and fired along the vector. But as he did he sensed the surprise and flight emotions as well. He ripped out a series of shots to either side of where he thought the sniper had been but realized that he'd missed. It wasn't really surprising. It was all he could do at this moment, though. Dagger might dodge into a beam. What was the motive here? Was simple greed enough to cause a trained professional to kill his teammates? Or did Dagger harbor some deeper issue? The human mind was a difficult thing to understand. For now, the motives weren't important. Tirdal kept shooting as he skittered down the hill with the artifact, leaving obvious drag marks but needing distance and time.

Dagger dove and rolled, knowing what was going to happen. He also noted that the damned box was gone. The heat detector on his rifle had the Darhel more or less pinpointed so he let loose a hornet round and got the hell out of Dodge, keeping those rocks between them as a punch gun poounked behind him. Then there was more firing. It wasn't very accurate yet but that could change. What the hell had happened? He'd seen that damned Darhel in the clearing. He'd made sure of it, because killing the damned smart-ass Elf was the frosting on the cake. Certainly it had sensed him, but how in the fuck had that little bastard got the box and lit out over the rocks into a shadow zone before the grenade had fuzed?

Tirdal's shoulder was hurting but he ignored it as he stood up and started to the side. It was that moment that the hornet round came flying around the boulder.

The hornet round could track on several items but the chameleon suit was giving off enough heat that that was the easiest. It lofted at a relatively low velocity until it decided it had a good track then went into high-speed acquisition.

The shot had been just a hope and a prayer for Dagger. The defensive sensors on Tirdal's harness spotted the energy release on launch and as the device came around the rock a beam of high-intensity protons met it. The protons caused the body of the device to emit its own personal EMP field, tearing apart most of the electronics that controlled it. The weapon had lined up for its attack run but the EMP shut down its systems and although it continued towards the Darhel it was at far below killing velocity.

The projectile still slammed into Tirdal at over a thousand meters per second. Bullets, or even hypervelocity beads, don't knock people down, but the impact cracked his lower chest plate and knocked the air out of his lungs. He managed to roll away from the rocks to a new cover position, wincing in pain and controlling his breathing to maintain consciousness. He hunched deeply under an alcove in the slope and kept his punch gun pointed up and out, in case Dagger should appear in front of him. Then he got his brain working again, through a miasma of sparks in his vision and a roaring in his ears.

He could Sense the silence from the camp. He was not good at picking up humans with his normal senses, but the background hum of life, human life, was gone from the small camp. And he could Sense the sniper out there, somewhere. The empathic sense that had been honed by the Bane Sidhe disciplines was not precise. It could tell him if something was very near or very distant. Everything in between was gray. The sniper was leaving "near" though. Which meant he was probably finding a good place to take a shot, which meant it was time to move out.

There were things up there in the rocks that Tirdal needed. His gear. His food, which was designed for his enzymic limitations as well as to provide the high calorie content he needed. Clean water. Some of the killer bots that Gorilla had carried would help with the sniper. On the other hand, wandering into the camp was out of the question. Before long Dagger would find a good hide and the next sensation Tirdal would pick up was the feeling as he squeezed the delicate neural trigger of his rifle.

He glanced at the box that was the center of the difficulty then looked around. The area was rolling and lightly wooded, the bones of the earth sticking up through the loam. If he kept to low ground and the trees, the chances were the sniper would not be able to get a shot at him. Of course, that would really add to the travel time.

If he could break contact with Dagger, he might be able to take to the ridges and outrun him. Darhel were descended from heavy-grav predators; this world was to him as Mars was to a human and humans moved like so many cattle. He could easily outdistance Dagger.

On the other hand, there was no question that Dagger had the advantage on him. The sniper had much more experience in the field than Tirdal, whose training was mostly mental and personal. And Dagger's rifle had about ten times the range that his weapon did. That meant that Tirdal had to either leave him far behind, or get in tight and kill him, assuming he could do so without going into tal overload and suffering the consequences. That also would be a failure of the mission. He grimaced. It was one of the few expressions that was the same for both races.

Ideally, since he couldn't get the artifact out past the human fleet anyway, he should just destroy it here. But it would take more energy than a punch gun to pierce that molecularly bound shell with its forcefield reinforcement. He'd just have to carry it until he could arrange disposition. Neither Dagger, nor any other human for that matter, could be allowed to access the damnable device.

Dagger would expect him to go for the camp. Then he would expect him to run for it. And, frankly, Tirdal couldn't figure out any other options. But, since he already knew he wasn't going to go for the material in the camp, it was time to run, before Dagger came to the same conclusion.

He trotted downslope towards the watercourse, then began paralleling it towards the west. Somewhere to the south, presumably, Dagger would be holing up, waiting for him to head for the camp. That should give him the time to break contact.

Dagger slid slowly into place under another shelf up the hill and extended his rifle. That damned punch gun made the Darhel too much of a danger at short range and that damned harness eliminated most of his smart rounds. But the free-flight projectiles would work well enough. That was so like a Darhel. There was always something they had to stick their manipulative fingers into. If he'd had the good grace to die with the rest, Dagger would be nearly home by now.

He panned the holographic sight from side to side

and swore. In the hollow below the team members had twisted into the characteristic spasming posture from the neural grenade but he didn't pay them any attention. He didn't need any of the commo gear. He hesitated over Gorilla's load of bots but this fight was going to be mano a mano; screw the electronic pieces of shit. He thought again about the local detector off Ferret's harness and the tracker control off the captain. Better take those. The only heat emanations were from the cooling bodies; the devious little son of a bitch Darhel was gone.

Or was he just well hidden? The sight would pick up the slightest trace of heat but it was possible to spoof it. Just closing the uniforms like they were space suits would do it for a bit. Of course, you risked dying of heat prostration on a warm morning like this. With the remaining moisture in the suits from earlier, Tirdal should be stewing like a chicken. But he could be doing that, buttoned up and staying really still until Dagger moved.

That was unlikely, though. He should have gotten at least a trace by now and the computer was saying the area was deserted. The fucking Elf had run. With the goddamned artifact.

And it wasn't likely he could outrun, outwit and outthink Dagger. First of all, the captain had put a tracer on the box. He hadn't made a big deal of it, had actually been sort of cagey, like he knew it might come up missing. Did the Darhel know? Probably not, or he wouldn't have wasted time grabbing it. In fact, why had he? The box's mass was a hindrance to him that Dagger could exploit. His own greed had burdened him instead of Dagger with the bulky artifact, and it could be used to track him. Dumb. Second of all, there wasn't another tracker in the Galaxy like Dagger. He could track a Himmit on rock. Tracking a city-bred Darhel wasn't going to be too hard.

He thought about the stuff he wanted. Ferret had a lifesigns tracker that could pick up complex nervous systems out to a hundred meters or so. It also picked up genetic traces like blood or hair. It was designed to pick up humans but it probably worked for Darhel as well. It didn't pick up Blobs, but between it and the tracer on the box he should be able to find the Elf bastard and put him down. The captain's tracer had a corresponding box to follow it. With those, even a blind man could find the Darhel. Then it was payday. But if Tirdal was there waiting, Dagger would be blown to bloody bits by the slap of a punch gun. Best not to risk it. Besides, he didn't need gadgets. This was a battle of wits.

Dammit, yes he did need them. Fear wasn't going to dissuade him from doing this properly. Taking another scan across the area, he decided it was safe and darted down in long, low strides, hunched over. He kept the rifle slung, using its harness sling to hold it straight along his back over his ruck. It was a bit awkward, but left both hands free for his rail pistol and his knife. Reaching the depression, he looked for Ferret's body. It had been over there and now it was . . . not. Shit. Ferret was also alive. That was a stick in the ass he didn't need.

There were faint but clear marks. Ferret had wriggled away through the rocks. That meant he was probably injured. His survival was still another complication though, dammit. The trail grew faint, and a quick scan didn't show any heat trace, so he was either gone or hiding. Still, Dagger knew he'd have to be fast, in case one or the other showed back up.

Anyway, on to that asshole captain. He snickered again. The thought came to him, "That'll teach you to have me dig the shitter."

The captain was facing away. So, the coward had tried to run rather than fight. Typical. you could always expect the commissioned orifices to fight from the rear. And what the hell had happened to his wrist? It was not just broken, it was shattered. The fingers and forearm were swollen, the bones crunched so hard the limb would have flopped like a sausage if the muscles weren't cranked down tight from the neural effect. He must have landed on it very oddly. No matter, it wasn't important. What was important was finding where the bastard had stuffed the tracker, and quickly.

Oh, wasn't that just fucking lovely. The asshole had it in his thigh pocket, and his suit was permeable to vent moisture, which also meant that the oozing shit and piss from his clenched then relaxed sphincters had drained down and into it. As he rolled the body over, he took one look at that face, which was more confused than anything. Stupid bastard probably hadn't had any idea what was happening, even when it came down to it. Typical. Dagger hawked quietly and spat across his nose and mouth. "Next time, die neatly you piece of shit," he whispered. Then he was up and running, kicking Gun Doll's sprawled and twisted form in the crotch as he ran, just because. Flaky bitch.

He moved out and back to the east, fast but cautiously. Fortunately there was that range of hills between them and the Blob base; with any luck there wouldn't be any Blob presence over here. He angled carefully upslope, keeping low and keeping trees between him and the open grave of his former buddies. It would be interesting, he thought, to see how the local life disposed of the corpses. Would they do as Earth carrion and eat the eyes first? Strip the bodies, even inside their suits, to bare bones? Or would something jackallike chew the bones at once? What of the gear? Buried, dragged away as trophies or curiosities as rats would do, or left to form new "artifacts" for some other race to find a thousand years hence?

It wasn't an interesting enough question to risk a billion dollar box over, though. But it could amuse his idle moments in the coming years. Maybe he'd commission a picture. Or hell, on Kali he could pay to have it reenacted with prisoners and watch how they decayed. Import a truck full of bugs and mix up some drinks.

He reached a slight knob about two hundred meters away that offered good visibility. The sun was just rising past it, burning off the haze that had coalesced only a few minutes before, and adding another element of excitement to this contest. The Elf would have an easier time detecting movement in daylight. So would Ferret, though he wasn't much of a threat. So would Dagger. But it negated some of his instruments, like the heat sensors. That pumpkin-orange ball would soon be a sun near as bright as Earth's, and was, by the time he'd shimmied around the clearing to the high point. It rose quickly with this short day.

He settled under a mass of leaves, his chameleon

gear blending in nicely. Using his scope, he scanned the area again but there wasn't any sign of the Elf. Good. Well, bad, but he'd deal with that at once. There wasn't any sign of Ferret. The little twerp really was a good sneak. Not good either. Though he might be dead in the weeds. It wasn't important, but it would be nice to know.

Obviously Tirdal had gone the other way. So, it was time to head back down, and look for the signs of his passing. That would be like tracking a rhino through a ceramics exhibition. The Elf really had no clue in the woods. He was certainly quiet, but without Ferret to follow, he would leave plenty of sign.

As to Ferret, if he hadn't popped up yet, either he was injured, or he'd decently crawled off to die. No worries.

Tirdal should have been able to break contact easily. What he had not anticipated was the amount of damage to his chest plate. His suit was broached, and blood leaked from the small hole.

The Darhel chest plate was not just ersatz ribs. It had evolved as both a protection for the heart, lungs and a nerve node that the Darhel had in the same general area as humans, and as a functional diaphragm. Tirdal started off at a good pace, but after a couple of kilometers the tingling pain in his chest exploded into searing agony. He did a quick medical scan and it confirmed his worst fears. What he had hoped was just a hairline fracture in fact was a crack almost across the plate. Using it to suck in and out, especially at high rates of speed, was impossible. He'd be lucky if he could move as fast as the sniper, much less outrun him. Holding the box awkwardly across his shoulder pulled the plate up and sideways, making it hurt worse with every step. He swapped sides, shifting the punch gun to his left and the artifact to the right. That was a bit better. He vaguely recalled that humans were typically oriented to use one side only, usually the right. He'd keep that in mind.

It was then that Tirdal realized that the sniper must kill him. Even if Dagger decided to cut his losses—though the only one so far had been Tirdal's acquisition of the box—and leave, the pod wouldn't take off without Tirdal. Unless Tirdal was dead. Nor could Tirdal approach the extraction point until Dagger was dead, because that was the point of failure—they both had to go there, and neither could leave the other alive.

That was for later, though. For the present, he had broken contact, he had defined the parameters of the immediate mission, and now he had to secure the tactical advantage and locate his target. All the text from training came back to him, and he realized how thoroughly humans avoided discussing actualities while burying them in platitudes. He knew exactly what he had to do. He had no idea how he was to proceed. It was probably one of those "you'll be taught this at your destination unit" bits, like so many others. How odd that humans required all this ritual and what they considered privation to look within and determine if one had the mettle for the job. A Darhel simply meditated, considered the question, and decided if it was something he could grasp. Then the training would begin. The human "training," however, was nothing but that focusing of thought, that grounding of self, with the essential details left out. Tirdal felt horribly cheated.

Lacking the proper training, the problems then must be resolved through reason. Dagger would seek high ground, attempt to determine where Tirdal was, then pursue to a range that would allow him a shot and no closer. The obvious signs of cowardice Tirdal had seen precluded him from engaging at close range. Therefore, Tirdal needed to find a new area. It should be one not conducive to long-range shooting.

He looked at the river through the trees and debated. Darhel were dense; they had more bone ratio than humans and their muscles were significantly denser than those of most humans. They had very little fat ratio. So they tended to sink like stones. He had learned to use underwater breathing gear and could construct an adequate float. Water was familiar to him. But floating down the river, while it might permit him to throw the sniper off the trail, would be a good form of suicide. If Dagger did follow the river, he'd have the high ground for a shot and the best cover. If he didn't follow, it was a draw. Draw meant death, because the pod would leave them there.

The only answer, no matter how poor, was to stay in the woods. How long would Dagger wait? Would he wait most of the day to determine if the Darhel would come back? Or had he already raided the camp and started on the trail?

Tirdal thought about the mind that had been revealed in that one moment of assault. It was . . . slimy. Conceited and emotionless, unless the hint of cruel pleasure in the taking of life was an emotion. It was not like the Blobs, who were very clearly vicious in thought process. Not like most humans, who were quite happy to avoid confrontation most of the time. Similar, really, to some of the baser Darhel he had been exposed to. He understood them, even if it was only intellectually. Dagger's motives and cause were clearly different, but the results were similar.

Such a mind as Dagger's would accept the normal belief of Darhel as cowardly traitors. When the Darhel did not immediately appear he would follow. In fact, he was probably trailing Tirdal at this moment.

He started walking as he thought. There was every reason to put some distance between himself and the sniper. He focused his thoughts on the pain, letting insira training grapple the pain until it existed only at a second level below consciousness. With his submind keeping track of the injury, he was able to devote all his concentration to the matter at hand. He moved at a safe walk, twisting and slipping through the branches and over the roots. After a few trudging steps, he adjusted his posture to deal with the pain signals from his submind and slowed slightly. That position reduced the agony to a sharp bite, but it would exacerbate things when the soft tissue tightened up. The box atop his shoulders didn't help.

The other consideration was that a personality like Dagger's would not take chances. Dagger would find a good spot on the projected path and try to ambush him. That was all the more reason to stay ahead. And he'd have to stay ahead for an Earth week, nine local days, because that was the timeframe on the first pickup. Dagger had at least a week to track down Tirdal and the box and kill him. Then there were the eight days after that . . .

Meeting the first pickup was not a requirement. The pod would change positions twice before leaving the planet for all time. The question was whether he thought he could live in competition with the sniper.

Darhel can manage without rest for a considerable time. Their muscles can build up fatigue toxins the way some Earth animals can develop an oxygen debt. So Tirdal could easily go up to three days without sleep, even injured. He could push to a week without extreme side effects. Beyond that it got tricky. It would be best to end this quickly. And if he could figure out Dagger's rest periods, he could use those to advantage.

On the negative side, Tirdal had a number of handicaps. He was not competent in the woods. He was injured. But the injury would heal, quickly. Quicker than Dagger could imagine. The woods skills though . . . those were a problem. Then there was the minor matter of tal, lintatai and having to kill. Dagger had already shown how easily humans could kill. It was a considerably tougher task for a Darhel. Then there was the metabolic issue. Already he was hungry and he only had a protocarb converter to depend on. He could convert just about anything to food but foraging would still take some time. And it would leave marks, because it took a lot of random plant life to yield enough fat and protein, especially when one didn't recognize the plant forms or take the time to dig for roots. Besides the signs left by foraging, it gave the sniper more time to find him. He'd need more food to stay awake, which meant more signs.

It was as likely as not that the contest would be

decided in a day or two. But that was planning on the basis of losing. Plan to win with fallbacks.

So, if he did the expected, ran for the pickup point where the pod was waiting, he could assume he would be intercepted. Although he might survive a couple of ambushes, he would probably succumb eventually.

If he ran for unknown territory he might be able to turn the tables. Dagger would be at a disadvantage, never knowing where Tirdal would show up.

Decision made, Tirdal turned to the north. He'd have to cross this river at once and move away from the extraction point, drawing Dagger with him, to end the scenario before the pod defaulted to the north.

He wouldn't bother with the chameleon effect of his suit for now, he decided. It used power that he should save for sensors and the proton discharge in case of more hornet rounds. That power use was detectable and he was leaving a trail Dagger could follow anyway. The local distortion would not be much help without good concealment first.

He waded out into the stream, which was a hundred meters wide at this point. The current was slow but insistent, pulling at him and urging him downstream. He adjusted his pace and angle, careful of the mass above his shoulders which affected his balance, and pushed on. The depth rose to his waist, slowing his rate to near nothing. Then it was at his chest, the current relentless in its urge. His neck. Taking a deep breath, he strode forward and under.

The water was reasonably clear, sediment from upstream having settled just beyond the rapids, sediment stirred by his feet disappearing quickly. Occasional shells, eellike local fish and bits of debris swept by. He plodded along, feeling the surface lap at his hands. The temperature was cold by human standards, refreshing by his; Darhel was a cool world. The water was only a couple of meters deep, but the pressure and current squeezed his injured chest. That was going to be an ongoing problem on this stalk.

Soon, his hands were under, which was good for concealment, bad for his growing need for oxygen. He could last a bit further, though, and the bed started rising, rocks giving way to a smooth, sandy bank. He rose nearly to the top of his head, hopped up and exchanged lungfuls of air, his chestplate not liking that, either. He was swept several meters downstream before his feet regained purchase. Once they did, he resumed walking. The bed rose once again, then suddenly dropped away, leaving him tumbling. Deep channel. But was it near the center or offset to one side?

He caught solid surface again, twisted twice in the current and stood upon it. He felt with his Sense and his senses for bearing, and got them. The ground rose rapidly in one direction, and that would be the bank. It was a good thing; he needed air again and had too much mass to get above the surface by swimming. In fact, he needed air so badly the pressure in his lungs hurt more than the spreading bruise and strain of his chest. He forced his feet forward, shoving them into the mucky clay here and drawing them back out, desperate to reach the surface soon.

Then he was above it, the water swirling around his neck as he panted for breath. His muscles ached from the aftereffects of tal, the exertion and the oxygen starvation, but he was up and out, sprawled among weeds and able to rest.

Except he couldn't rest. Dagger wouldn't be far behind, and might see this clumsy crushing of greenery for what it was. He got his knees and elbows under him, pushed up while taking deep draughts of air to heal himself, and grabbed the artifact he didn't recall dropping. It was time to put distance between himself and his enemy. He disappeared into the forests, pondering ways to create confusion and interfere with Dagger's plans.

Ferret sipped water from the tube at his chin, forced himself to chew a slimy, rubbery bit of rat pack chicken, and waited for the painkiller to take effect. He'd swallowed a wound nano, too, though they were meant for healing small cuts and blisters, lest they get infected. What it could do for massive neural trauma, he didn't know. But it might at least prolong the inevitable.

At that, he was getting some pins and needles feeling back into his right ankle. It was excruciating to bend it, but he could do so. The left still hung limply. He wasn't sure how nerves so thoroughly dead as to make a limb useless could still send screaming jolts of pain through him. He was on fire up to his hips and balls.

There'd been scuffling noises from within the camp earlier. Part of him had wanted to crawl over and help, but it might be Dagger or Tirdal back for loot. Anyway, the medical gear was with Shiva, who was there. It was best that he stay hidden, though it gnawed at him. It smacked of cowardice, even though that was his duty right now. He had to stop that box from leaving with the Darhel.

Nothing had happened for an hour, and he'd been able to recover from some of the shock with the help of some meds. That, however, was about the extent of his pharmacopeia and the range of his medical skills. The only human medic on the planet was that goddamned Darhel, who was making off with the artifact.

He decided it had to be a spur of the moment decision between Tirdal and Dagger. To think the whole mission was a setup was paranoid. Besides, if the Darhel had wanted it, they had ships of their own, or Tirdal would have steered them clear of the site after having the humans clear the Blobs, or he would have grenaded them there. That was the type of cowardly attack he expected from them. But it had been Dagger. Dagger, who had shown so much interest in the box. The two of them must have had a quick debate over splitting the money, then gone to work.

But he couldn't just lie here and wait to die, or be found by those two scum and killed. He had to get moving. As they'd be heading for the extraction point, he'd have to do so, too. The only hope was to get there first and hold them off, force them to deal with him. That would likely kill him anyway, but he couldn't let them take that artifact. Those things were dangerous, and especially when up for bid to any lunatic or group of extremists out there.

The bitch of it was, he could save himself, possibly. Gun Doll's transmitter would burn a signal out, and he knew enough about it to be able to make it do so. That would bring in a force. With only one Tslek there, the odds were excellent that he could stay hidden. Even if the Tslek got a force there first, he could be well away from them. But that would start a huge battle, cost hundreds or thousands of casualties, and the box would already be gone. If he did that for just his life, he'd be saved, yes. Then he'd be put away forever. That was just not the type of fame he wanted, and that life wasn't preferable to death, really. He couldn't do that to people.

Could a force get here fast enough to matter, if he could protect the pod for a few days? Was he likely to live that long? The artifact was important enough to make that call, even if he wasn't.

It might bear thinking about.

First, he should try to figure out where they were. Dammit, Tirdal could read minds, and Dagger had gear at least as good as his. He didn't dare pursue them, yet he had to. The artifact had to be recovered, and he'd likely have to kill both of them to do it. And he wasn't sure he could.

Taking a slow, deep breath, Ferret got himself calm enough to consider everything. The important fact was that he was already effectively dead. He was in excruciating pain. Nothing could get worse, from a personal point of view. Every moment was a gift of borrowed time, and he intended to use each one of them. All that was left was professional accomplishment and duty. Though it might be that no one would ever know what he did.

He rolled slowly over, feet full of phantom pain that couldn't exist with the damaged nerves, but did. Every shift of his boots over the rough surface of the ground was static up into his thighs. He clamped down on the pain and managed to reach into his ruck for the lifesigns tracker. He opened its case, brought it up at minimum and began searching for residual DNA, pheromones or heat. He canceled everything that indicated himself and let it search and ponder.

There was something down by the stream that wasn't local. The readings didn't match Dagger's profile. Tirdal had gone that way. So it was Tirdal.

Ferret considered for only a moment. Tirdal would be easier to track than Dagger, easier to approach. The man—alien—wasn't the best in the woods, in fact was downright clumsy in a few ways. Also, he had a punch gun, which was a much shorter range weapon than the rifle Dagger had. Tirdal was injured, and wasn't going to be very stealthy, assuming Ferret could stalk him. So Tirdal was the logical one to pursue first. That and he had the artifact. Get that and he had a hell of a bargaining chip to use with Dagger.

That decided him. He drew his feet under him, rose carefully through the waving leaves, alert for threats, and explored the range of motion of his shrieking, cramping legs. Nausea and pain washed over him, and he tried not to strangle on saliva or bite his cheeks as he grimaced tightly. Swaying from poor feedback, he steadied himself.

He could walk. Not well, but it was possible. His right ankle bent as he wanted, the left was insensate but did move mechanically if he thought about it. He would need support though, as he couldn't tell what was under his foot, or how it was moving unless he looked at it.

There were straight, sturdy saplings within stumbling distance, and his knife cut through one easily enough with three light chops. He trimmed it to a good length, with a side branch to use as support. It would work as a crutch. Now he'd have to lose some of the mass he carried, however.

He'd keep two grenades, one power pack for the punch gun and his knife as weapons. The rest could be buried. The tracker he'd keep, of course. Two rat packs would supplement the marginal crap he'd be able to get out of the food converter. He wouldn't need rope, gloves or most of what was in his larger ruck. He could just use the patrol pack, if he detached it.

Thus unburdened, he could limp more steadily. And his nerves were hurting less. Either the painkillers and nanos were having some effect, or the nerves were dying. For now, either was acceptable.

Learning to use his feet as mere appendages rather than as limbs, he headed downhill, very slowly and cautiously, probing ahead with the crutch and hopping down to meet it, every jolt another brand into his legs. He wasn't going to try for anything in the camp. It was an easy threat zone, and likely booby trapped. He'd just have to rely on his wits and his gun.

Dagger settled down in his next hide and checked his bearings. The point was a slight rise overlooking a clearing along the river. His hide was a circle of trees, open above but thickly interlaced from about forty centimeters off the ground to a couple of meters up. It was peaceful in a way, like the practice range. And as with the range, there would be a target. He had a good view from underneath out across the river valley.

The Darhel would have to go well out of his way to not cross the clearing and the last time Dagger checked the Elf had been moving slowly. There had also been traces of violet blood; the hornet must have scored even if it didn't kill the little creep.

He idly glanced at the tracker on the box and frowned. It was well to the north, nowhere near a line to the pod. What in the hell did the damned Elf think it was doing? Then it hit him. The Elf wanted to play games. Okay. No problem. The only game in town was "Dagger wins." But he'd have to pay more attention to the tracker. Eventually he'd get the Elf to rights.

Later, though. He was faster than the Elf and could easily catch up. Time for some lunch. He pulled some leaves off the nearest tree and root stems from the ground and put them in his converter. Maybe the processor could imitate something unusual. He scrolled through the list of delicacies on the menu. Ah, calf brains. That sounded interesting.

Chapter 11

TIRDAL CROUCHED DOWN and took a drink of water. The trickling stream here probably meandered down to reach the large river to the south, but in this area it ran between clay banks. There were plenty of hiding places and it would have been a fair place to rest for a bit, if he had any idea how far he was from the sniper. The problem was that he was the hunted. Dagger could hit him at any time so he had no time to slow down and rest.

Turning that around would be tough. Unlike the sniper he couldn't track people, didn't have the slightest idea how. He had vague memories of stories about broken twigs, footprints in weeds and similar signs, but he had no realistic hope of doing anything. He'd observed Ferret enough to know that it was part training, part talent and part philosophy. Even if he had talent and developed the thinking, he had no way to get the training, and a mistake while learning would be lethal. His Sense would spot such unusual signs . . . from less than a meter away. Only if he stumbled across Dagger's trail would it help. And he was trying to stay away from Dagger. Until the sniper fired he only had a vague sense that he was near or far.

When Dagger fired he would have to use the tal hormones. But using them had a high degree of danger. He was still bemused at his luck back at the camp; that use far exceeded anything he had tried in the past. He looked at the box and flicked an ear. Damn the Aldenata, as humans would say. It was similar to an ancient Darhel curse. For now, it was needful to seek higher ground, and that took him back the way they had come. He could move all day, must move all night, and try to lure Dagger close.

That had been interesting, Dagger thought. He should definitely try some of the more esoteric foods when he had the money. And when he bagged the Elf, he'd see what Darhel tasted like. Chicken, most likely, but who could say? There was so little known about the damned things. In fact, if he got a handy kill, he should drag the corpse with him. An in-depth analysis of a Darhel corpse would be useful to humans, and likely some lab would pay a few credits for the body. It couldn't match the billion or more he'd negotiate for the box, but it could account for the pain in the ass factor the goddammed thing was causing him. Also, it was evidence to support his position.

Anyway, he had an Elf to stalk. He looped the tracker around his neck to keep it readily accessible, raised his rifle into low port and felt its comforting heft, then checked the surroundings and moved out.

How the hell had the little bastard crossed the river? Dagger wondered, amazed. Well, shit, he needed to get moving. He'd underestimated the Darhel, and that was not good. He took a route directly toward the stream, pushing his way through the brush and not worrying about a trail. Ferret might follow, but Dagger was sure he'd have the upper hand. Sneaking was Ferret's thing. Shooting was not. Not that he couldn't shoot, but he needed a reason. All Dagger needed was a target.

Once he reached the stream, he realized that crossing it would be a bitch. He looped his rifle into a diagonal position, waded out and angled against the current. He'd have to swim, and that was going to be harder than hell. As the depth reached his chest, which put him further out than Tirdal had been, being taller, he pushed off and began stroking.

It wasn't that the water was cold, though it was. It wasn't that drag of all his gear and the suit slowed his strokes and caused muscle strain, though it did. It wasn't even the intermittent cracking of his helmeted head against the rifle barrel and the neck strain caused by tense muscles and all that mass on his head. The combination, however, sucked. He was being dragged downstream, and was soon tired. Yes, he was making progress, but it was slow. Then he inhaled in between strokes and caught a lungful of water that made his lungs spasm. He coughed and cringed, choking and gagging. How had that little freak made it across? And he hadn't even drifted far downstream. No matter. He was nearly across now, and was able to snag an overhanging branch. It kept him from losing more distance—he'd lost at least five hundred meters so far—as he recovered his breathing. Panting, wincing, he got it under control and swam in, dragging the branch with him until it became more liability against his lateral progress than anchor against being swept downstream. A few hard, urgent kicks and he reached shallow water.

He angled at once upstream, intending to cut Tirdal's path and follow it, simply to avoid blazing a new trail. It would be easier to follow the Darhel, avoid the areas where he got snagged, and overtake him from directly behind. He kept his eyes open to the sides for signs of passage . . . like those branches there, the fronds broken and inverted. Something had passed them recently. Looking down and along a line from the river, he saw bent stems and then a bootprint. There. The incompetent little troll was his. He turned to follow and smiled to himself.

Ferret found the stream a relief. He was burning with metabolic heat, from exertion and stress and pain, even with his suit as permeable as it could get. Also, the water took weight and pressure off his feet. He wasn't heavily burdened, and while he was swept a considerable distance downstream, he had no major problems, though his shoulders ached fiercely and his strained tricep burned before he reached the midpoint, as he swam using hands alone. That drifting in the current also brought him past a section of bank that looked very much as if someone had clambered from the water. He'd have to come back to that. His attention came back to his progress, his punch gun on its harness cracking his right elbow and chest as he swam, his improvised crutch catching on his left arm and leg. It might not have been the best idea to shove it through his harness like that. But if he dragged it out now, he might be able to use it to reach bottom.

He tried it and it worked. He reached, stuck it into the mud and was pulled downstream of it by the current. Then he could twist and plant it again and repeat the procedure. It wasn't efficient, but it saved a lot of wear on his arms and stopped him from being swept too far. He could also tell depth, though sometimes it was by shoving the stick down and getting nothing.

Farther downstream, his knees reached bottom and he crawled out on hands and knees, rather than get his feet stuck in mud or risk tripping over rocks. As a result, he was smeared and greased with dank, wet loam before he reached high ground. Then he had to cross a boggy area, the bank here being higher than nearby ground in this rolling terrain. At least he could move relatively fast on hands and knees, even if it was awkward to keep his feet raised behind him. He should be safe here; neither Tirdal nor Dagger should be this far downstream.

It was painful to rise upright, even with his crutch. Damned excruciating. The words didn't do it justice until he whispered under his breath, "This hurts like a motherfucker," while leaking tears from squinted eyes. That felt right. Sometimes, profanity was necessary, rather than just punctuation. This was one of those times.

He was getting the hang of walking, as much as it hurt. He could now move in a step-limp, step-limp that made for okay progress. His left foot was at an angle so he could shove off with it, assisted with the stick. His right was working just fine, except that every step felt as if he were walking on hot coals, and hurt worse as he staggered to throw his left foot out in front. When all his weight hit a foot, he winced and stiffened.

It didn't take long to get to the area where whoever or whatever had scrabbled out of the water. He crept again, easing in under the feathery undergrowth like a lizard or snake. His punch gun was cradled over his arms, and he favored the left elbow to drag himself forward, so his right hand was slightly rearward in case he needed to shoot in a hurry. His crutch kept bumping his helmet from where it was lashed across his pack, and his head itched outrageously as it dried under the helmet, all slimy with sweat again.

The bank had been rather chewed. That set of prints was clearly Dagger's, so that other set with the odd cant were Tirdal's. They were already teamed up, then. Damn. That was no good.

Then, a fleck of mud slipped from the tread pattern of Dagger's track into the muddy water. Ferret took a closer, more scientific look. It wouldn't do to make assumptions.

Tirdal's tracks were older and softer. Perhaps thirty minutes old, though it would depend on the mud here. Dagger's were perhaps five or ten minutes old. So they were aiming for a meeting point.

Ferret couldn't pass them, but he could certainly find them at that meeting point. Dagger was now the primary target, then, because of his greater ranged weapon and readiness to kill. He had a momentary flashback to that shootout between Dagger and Thor, and shivered. Yes, Dagger had to go first and quickly. Tirdal was an unknown, except that Ferret could hide and track better than he.

They clearly didn't expect to be followed, though, so it was time to stop dallying. He shoved back up to his feet with the aid of his crutch, and kept going.

The foothills were well forested, and Tirdal trudged on. The trees were good cover. They were also a hindrance, with undergrowth and roots. These were not like the cultivated copses or semiwild prairie on Darhel. These were thick, tangled forests out of some early epoch of planetary development. Also, he knew he was leaving a trail Dagger could follow. That wasn't much help for his intended ambush; it was better to be invisible so as not to be outmaneuvered. Another problem, after all night splashing in water and half a day of running with an artifact on his back was his innate lack of body fat. The strength and endurance of a Darhel did not come without a cost. Although the chemical analog they used instead of ATP was more efficient, the lack of long-term energy storage meant that after a day or two of high-energy activity the Darhel was drawing entirely upon muscle mass. He needed that mass. Also, the lack of fat and blood sugar slowed his reactions.

Most of the food coming out of his converter had been from plant matter. Although it was high in complex sugars there was minimal useable protein or fat. Some plants existed somewhere in this biome to provide both, but he didn't have the time to seek them out. The unpleasant fact was that he needed to eat some meat. He'd trained for it, even if he didn't like it. Even if every fiber of his mind screamed at the idea.

There was another small brook ahead, green and thick along its banks and the mossy rocks it trickled over. That was a good bet for easy-to-corner food. Leaning over slowly to avoid spooking them, he was rewarded by the sight of potential meals crawling and swimming in a group among trailing tendrils of weeds. He gratefully dropped his burdens and settled down.

He reached an arm in to snag one. Then he had to try again. By the third try he had its reactions figured out and at least snagged a tail as it slithered free. The sixth attempt found him with a handful of wriggling creature.

It was slimy and had external gills even though it had legs like a reptile. Possibly it and its ilk were a third animal family that the explorer bots had missed. Perhaps it was a larval version of the "mammalian" types. Whichever, the creatures would be a good protein source and they even scanned as edible to his simple sensor kit.

Now if he could only eat one.

The problem was not disgust; the squirming, wriggling thing in his hand had triggered atavistic cravings he hadn't even realized existed. But they were also triggering other reactions and Tirdal wrestled with his autonomic processes. The tal gland, sensing the coming moment of kill, had gone into preorgasmic spasm. If the gland overcame the Darhel's hard-held control it would dump its contents into his system, permitting him to bolt the food at lightning speed and vanish at a run.

And, not coincidentally, trigger the genetic "zombie" switch installed by the long-gone Aldenata.

If the molecular detectors scattered throughout the Darhel's brain reached a certain level of tal hormone they would activate, triggering the condition called "lintatai." If that happened the Darhel would sit there quite happily until Dagger came along and took the box. Or until he keeled over from dehydration, for he would neither eat nor drink nor perform any other fully voluntary function without orders.

So in wrestling with his tal gland he wrestled for his very life.

Using ever scrap of the Jem disciplines he had trained in for so many, many years he got the incredibly seductive urge under control. Tal release was truly orgasmic and his body shuddered in pleasure from even the mere inkling of it. There were many among the Darhel who were tal addicts, playing chicken with their own bodies by watching violent shows or simulating violent behavior. But only the Bane Sidhe had learned, through the opposite approach of rigid control, how to suppress the gland and control it. Use it when needed and otherwise shut those feelings and emotions away. It was only the Bane Sidhe Darhel and their Michon cousins, in fifty thousand years, who had learned to kill and live to tell about it.

But even the Bane Sidhe had never killed and eaten quivering prey, the ultimate reason for the tal gland. The ultimate goal of the predators called Darhel. The flawed, frustrated predators called Darhel.

Tirdal the Darhel took the newt analog in shaking hands and drew a deep breath. The mind is a mirror of the soul. The soul is a mirror of the mind. The mirror of the pond reflects the stillness of the sky. With his mind a blank he twisted the creature's neck.

The damned Elf was making better time than he could have believed. The blood had dried up and the Darhel kept moving. For the last few hours it had been in a straight line and the tracker on the box showed Dagger to be gaining. Apparently the Elf had stopped by a stream, and since he was only a couple of kilometers away, Dagger figured he could catch up quickly. But the hell if he was going to get close to that punch gun. So where to set up?

The country was moderately hilly and forested, not good sniping country. But the trees were starting to open up and the country was rising, a good sign. Somewhere ahead was that plateau they'd crossed, or one like it. If the stupid Elf kept straight he'd come right into sniping country and then he'd be dead meat.

On the other hand if he stayed in the lowlands or the foothill forests he might occasionally be visible anyway. So it might make sense to just head for the hills and try to intercept. If that didn't work and the Elf stayed in the lowlands he could always backtrack.

On the other hand, maybe there was a better way to spook him.

The commo system that the teams used was beyond state of the art; it was derived from one of the Aldenata systems and was completely untraceable. It was also voice only and missed some of the register so the voices came out sounding funny. But it permitted communication without any fear the Blobs would detect it.

Dagger used that now. He opened up the frequency and contacted the Darhel.

❖   ❖   ❖

Tirdal calmly picked a bit of pseudonewt out of his teeth and sucked on it. Not bad. It did, in fact, taste like the human chicken he'd been forced to try in training. He had been using the Jem disciplines all through the day, controlling his fear, his tal release during the escape, while eating, while trying not to breathe water; now he was constantly in a state of what humans would call "Zen." Or perhaps it was like the endorphin high they got from stress or pain. He flicked an ear in humor. The bit of food removed, he shifted his slung punch gun back to the ready position. Then his communicator clicked.

"You realize you're one dead Darhel."

For a moment only, he jolted. Then discipline took over and he brought his awareness back where it belonged. For Dagger to break the silence meant he was afraid. He didn't think his skills alone were up to the task of defeating Tirdal, so he was going for the psychological edge. Tirdal had planned on doing the same thing. He'd just intended to wait a day or two and let Dagger grow worried. This, however, was an opening, and a useful one.

"We are all dead, Dagger," he replied. "From the moment of birth our end begins. Some come sooner than others, some later, but all inevitable."

"Yeah, very philosophical. And your end comes soon, Elf." Dagger's voice was strained already. The anger was palpable right through a low-grade comm channel. That was step one. But how to exploit it?

"Really, Hubert, insults are not necessary." Tirdal knew Dagger's real name was uncommon. It might be a sore spot for him.

Apparently it was. Dagger's voice was tight when he replied. "Call me that again, Elf, and I'll shoot you joint by joint. Ankles first, then knees. Arms. Then I'll kiss you with the muzzle of this baby and blow your fucking spine out."

"I won't call you 'Hubert' if you don't call me 'Elf.' Truly, Dagger, you seem distraught. What would you like to talk about?" Tirdal asked, keeping his low voice conversational.

There was no reply.

Dagger was annoyed. He'd wanted more of a reaction. The Darhel was a cocky little freak, but that would change. Still, he needed a reaction from something. Ferret was likely a better bet to screw with. He switched frequencies.

"So, Ferret, still hiding in the weeds?" he asked.

There was a slight gasp of surprise. Dagger chuckled to himself. There was the score he wanted.

Ferret replied, "No, Dagger, I'm hunting you two bastards. Want to bet I can't nail you?"

Dagger pondered that for a moment. It was several seconds before it sank in. Ferret thought he and Tirdal were allies! Oh, that was rich. He had to shut off his mike for a few moments and laugh deeply, muffling it in his suit just in case. Oh, man.

He could see how it happened, too. The box was gone, Dagger and Tirdal were gone, what else would he assume? But hey, no reason not to play that for all it was worth. This would be fun.

"Think you can nail Tirdal?" he said. "I wouldn't be too sure. He's better than that act of his makes him out to be. And you know I'm beyond you."

"We'll see, you murderous fucks," Ferret said. There was pain in his voice, and it wasn't emotional. Injured? Likely.

"Why, Ferret, did you catch some of the neural effect? Wow, that has to suck."

Ferret's reply was clearly angry but restrained. "I'm fine, asshole. You worry about yourself."

"Right. See you at two thousand meters. Unless you'd prefer closer? Click!" Dagger replied, the last sound uncannily like the faint snap of his firing circuit.

Hey . . . he could tease the freaking Darhel with this, too. That he and Ferret were allies. Anything to keep them on edge. He'd play them off each other. Maybe Ferret would even do the Darhel for him. That could be amusing once he nailed the kid.

Dagger smirked, barely avoided laughing again, and continued after Tirdal. Ferret wasn't an issue anymore.

Ferret shook. He'd given away too much info in that conversation. Communications security. How often had that been drilled into them? Anything you say, or what you don't say, can be hints. And Dagger wasn't stupid, far from it, no matter how nuts he was. So the best thing to do was keep quiet and not respond to provocation.

Besides, he had the lifesigns tracker. If they didn't know if he was alive or dead, he had a much better strategic position. And he did know they were alive at present, Tirdal injured.

For the first time that day, Ferret smiled. It wasn't pretty through his dirty and strained face, but it was genuine.

He didn't smile for long. Biology had caught up with him, and he had to take a dump badly. What he couldn't figure out was a way to do it while keeping a low profile, an eye out for predators or enemies, and while not putting weight on his legs. Last resort would just be to do it in the suit, but if it was possible to avoid that, he'd prefer to. No one liked sitting or walking in shit.

After a few frantic seconds of searching, he found a downed, rotten log with slimy fungus on it. Still, it was a seat of sorts, and with one hand to balance against his crutch and one to hold the punch gun, he managed to take care of business, then slip agonizingly back to the ground. When done, he couldn't kick dirt over the evidence, so he settled for using the butt of his weapon as a shovel.

That done, he rose painfully to his knees and resumed his stalk, slow and steady. The prey has to avoid leaving a trace and watch for obstacles. The tracker has to avoid running up on his prey, or being attacked from the rear. Hopefully, those two wouldn't be moving too fast with that artifact, though they could certainly move fast with one to lead and one to cover. But he recalled that Tirdal had been somewhat slower due to his shorter legs. And there was nothing else to do but follow, at this point. He'd have to think of a way to change that. Meanwhile, that twisted leaf and those bent stalks told him which way to go.

Tirdal kept moving. Patience was the key. Remain calm, remain awake and alert. Anger, hunger, pain and fatigue would lead to Dagger making mistakes, and those mistakes could be turned to Tirdal's advantage.

As to the present, more food was indicated; he needed strength. He wondered if it would be easier or more of a strain to kill again. He pondered the relative risks for a few minutes while eating reconstituted "bean curd" produced by his food converter. That decided him. He'd risk it. Human military rations were barely edible.

So, this could be used as a training exercise. He needed to learn more stealth and how to hunt, and there was food on the paw or leg in this forest. Beetles, he recalled from lectures in DRT school, were eighty-five percent useable protein. It was likely these analogs would be similar, allowing for greater mass of exoskeleton and organ. Still, there should be lots of protein there. The problem was catching a beetle and opening it up afterwards.

Dropping into a crouch, he squatted silently and used his senses and Sense to seek local life . . . and there was one of the browsing beetle creatures, about ten meters ahead. He could just see its sensory stalks examining leaves, with far more grace and flexibility than an equivalent insect form would have on Earth or Darhel.

He eased forward, alert for movement of the plants that disturbed his Sense, watching for anything he might brush against, feeling for anything underneath that might shift. It was arduous and took a lot of concentration, but he believed that he could get the hang of it with enough weeks' practice. Of course, this would be over in days or hours, but he filed the knowledge and the need for study in this field. Nor was this insect as bright as Dagger. It was genetically programmed for the noises made by the local predators, and Tirdal was soon within five meters. He examined the terrain, which was firmly packed humus with leafy undergrowth and trees, clear enough for a charge.

Dagger, or any other human would have been amazed at what happened next. Tirdal leaned forward and shoved off with his feet like a sprinter or tackle. The box followed a higher trajectory so it would stay near him and not be left behind, his punch gun was tucked in tight under his left arm. The beetle's antennae twitched straight up, and it followed them as its legs flexed. But before it could move, Tirdal had snatched the rim of its shell on the fly and rolled out. His chest plate caused him to cringe in pain, but he forced the sensations back. Pain was a warning, nothing more, and he knew he was injured. Further pain was of no use.

The insect was awkard to kill, though not hard. It wiggled in his grasp and tried to find purchase, its legs brushing his arm periodically. After a few probes, he was able to insert his knife blade between the edges at the rim of its shell and, with a mighty, convulsive kick with ten legs, it died. He pried it open to find clean, white meat, and focused his Jem discipline to keep the tal to a trickle. That was not an easy task, for his pulse was thundering in his ears. It was not exertion; he'd barely put forth any. It was, instead, the clawing rage of the beast within demanding release. But he beat it down and proceeded to eat.

Above that, his overmind considered the event. The stalk had been adequate, the attack good. That rollout, however, would have alerted everything within a kilometer. There were still dead leaves and spiky needles hanging from his hair, and one, stuck between suit and skin, was poking him sharply. That part of the attack needed work. His punch gun was still in place, and the box was a bare meter away. Well done.

After slicing the meat up with his teeth and swallowing it in the slivery pieces his dentition demanded, he made an attempt at sucking tissue from the legs, since he couldn't seem to crack them with his hands, or even with his knife hilt against a tree.

That delicate meat refused to yield. He bit, sucked and probed with his tongue, but it wouldn't separate. It was right then that it happened.

While he was conscious for attacks, considering strategy and concentrating on food, that inner beast came howling up toward the surface. It craved that meat more than he did, and it needed release.

Tirdal dropped the husks and shook as his self-control and Jem discipline fought a quick, painful battle. Tal could not be allowed to win. Lintatai, no matter how blissfully pleasing, was death. He was sweating profusely now, struggling even more. When the opponent advances, the warrior retreats, the warrior evades. The warrior seeks battle on his own terms only. The opponent's force must be bent as a tree in the storm . . . but this opponent was himself, and retreat was not possible. It was a frontal clash, and his consciousness was fading into dusky haze.

Then he was back. How close had he come, he wondered. But he had not succumbed. Lesson learned: eat fast, dispose of corpse, keep moving. Complacency and contempt were not to be allowed. Every time he courted tal, it would be like this he realized, and he felt a cloud descend. Centuries of philosophy, training and triage had not yet defeated the genetic tampering of the Aldenata. How many other races had been left damaged and incomplete by their deific meddling? The Posleen, the humans, Indowy, Tchpth, Himmit, Ruorgla . . . and those were the ones known to the Darhel. Were even the Tslek bastard offspring of the Aldenata?

Still, he had much to report to his Masters, should he survive this. They would be grateful of the knowledge, and it would further the Art.

"Hello, Tirdal." His musing was interrupted by another transmission.

"What can I do for you, Dagger?" he replied, glad of the distraction.

"You can die, you little freak," Dagger snarled. What was taking so long? Even given greater strength, the Darhel lacked the legs and hips to move quickly. Dagger should be catching up to him, should have caught him by now.

"What a coincidence, Dagger, I was about to ask the same of you." The Elf's voice was almost conversational, as if he wasn't under any stress at all, just taking a walk in the park.

"Yes, you'd need that, wouldn't you?" Dagger taunted. "After all, you can't do the deed yourself."

"It is very difficult for Darhel to kill," Tirdal admitted. "But it can be done. And in your case, it will be a pleasure."

"Good luck on that, then," Dagger said, smiling. "I mean, you leaving a trail like a lovesick blunderbeast is bound to make my task easier and yours harder."

"I thought you could use the advantage, Dagger," Tirdal replied. "You humans are so weak it is laughable." He still didn't sound worried. Screw the little bastard.

Dagger needed something to prod with, and saw just the thing. "Hey, look what I just found! It's a rock! Not only a rock, Tirdal, but a turned rock, damp underneath. And this crushed leaf here seems to have your boot's tread pattern on it. Unless there's another Darhel here with number forty-three boots, right boot with a V-shaped cut in the third tread, it's yours. How about that?" The trail really wasn't that easy, but he'd seen the bootprint earlier and did have a goodly number of blazes to follow. That and the tracker. But the little fuck was moving at a hell of a clip.

Tirdal replied at once, "Good for you, Dagger. If you can maintain that pace nineteen hours a day here for the next ten local days, you can meet me at the pod and we can fight this out. The gravity is high for you, low for me, and woods skill aside, we both know which of us is the more intelligent." He didn't sound worried. Dammit, Dagger had him pegged, knew his every step, and the goddamned Elf acted as if it were no big deal.

"If you were really smart, Tirdal, you would have died at once when it would have been painless," he said. As soon as he did, he knew it sounded weak. He tried another tack. "Of course, you're a coward, like all Darhel. Can't fight. Won't fight. You not only used humans to fight your wars, you felt the need to bully and screw us into it by keeping back the weapons tech we needed. Live humans are a threat to you, and you know it."

"Dagger," came the reply, "I've been very patient so far. Now, if you don't want to see me angry, at least come up with an intelligent argument or a real threat. And your simplistic, childlike knowledge of politico-historical events is amusing.

"Remember, also, that killing is a mental discipline, not concerned with the physicalities of rocks and leaves. I've been letting you live because my philosophy calls for it. You mistake that for cowardice. That's not my issue. But if we continue this, you will find out what a Bane Sidhe is. Do you recall that term, Dagger?"

"Never heard of it," he snapped. "Some Darhel boogeyman?"

"No, Dagger," Tirdal replied. It had to be a deliberate condescending tone in his voice as he said, "Perhaps you've heard it as 'banshee.' A Bane Sidhe is a demon who calls men to their deaths. Though I won't be calling, I'll be visiting personally. And I intend to make it very personal." That sonorous voice was suddenly a vicious slap with a gravelly undertone. "I'm going to kill you, Dagger. I intend to rip your heart out through your ribs while it's still beating, and, because it's such an issue for you, I intend to eat it, raw, while your dying corpse watches."

"My, my, aren't we bent out of shape about that pack of assholes getting nerved," Dagger said, trying to chuckle. His opponent didn't sound like a shivering, neurotic sensat without combat experience. He sounded like a killer, almost like Dagger himself. He knew it was all act, but he trembled despite himself. That low, deep voice that sounded so cold and calm had been mean. Could the little bastard actually mean it?

"They don't even enter into this, Dagger," he heard. "That's an issue for your chain of command. I'm going to kill you for trying to, in your terms, 'fuck me over.'"

"Fuck you over?" Dagger asked, outraged, fear forgotten. "Who's got the goddamned box here? And what do you expect to do with it if I let you live?"

Tirdal said, "The box is none of your concern, since it's only money to you. But since you ask, I intend to take it to the proper authorities."

"Proper authorities?" Dagger yelled, incredulous. "Proper authorities? It's worth a billion credits. A billion. Even after taxes, as if we couldn't figure out some way to avoid them, it's a goddamned fortune. 'Fortune' isn't even enough of a word. It's like winning the lottery, except it's been earned the hard way. That money is mine, ours if you weren't being a fool about it. You want to take it to the authorities? Hell, if you weren't such an asshole, I could cut you in. I even know who to fence it through."

Tirdal replied, "For some reason that last fact doesn't surprise me. So that's your motive here? You killed your whole team for money?"

"Yes, Tirdal," Dagger laughed. He'd outflanked this Elf who thought himself some kind of genius. "That's pretty much it. Call it a weakness, but a billion credits is worth more to me than those whining little wussies. And I get to use you as an alibi. 'The Darhel freaked out under stress, couldn't handle facing the enemy.' You're perfect. You tossed the grenade in panic, I hunted you down and took care of it. I'm a hero. Then I take leave to console myself over the loss of my friends and disappear. Next thing no one hears, I've got women lined up to blow me four times a day and a mansion full of slaves." He was babbling, he realized. Dammit, keep control.

"Fascinating," Tirdal replied. "I'm sure a psychiatrist—

is that what you call them?—would have a fine time analyzing your neuroses. Or are they psychoses? I'm not up on human mental ailments. There are just too many of them to keep track of. You may even harbor some as-yet unknown ones. But your cupidity tells me you'd make a rather good Darhel, or at least what you think of as a Darhel."

Dagger was panting now, and not from exertion. Dammit, why was he having a panic attack over this? He had those when confronting things. That was the point of being a sniper, the point of keeping people terrified. It avoided confrontation. And the Darhel was in the next county, he told himself. He shouldn't be twitching like this. "W-what," he said, then got control, "you're just going to turn it in for a reward? Not even a finder's fee? What kind of Darhel does that make you?"

Again, no hesitation before the reply. "The kind with pride in himself, his clan and his race. Not to mention the survival of his race. And your race, Dagger. There are Fringe planets with contacts to species we don't have proper relations with. Do you really want them having access to whatever is in there?"

"How altruistic," Dagger replied. "All thought for others. Selflessness and charity. You'd make a wonderful human wuss."

"And with that insult, Dagger, we are done for now. Goodbye."

"Tirdal? Tirdal? Come back you cowardly little Elf, we aren't done talking!" he shouted.

It appeared, however, that they were, for now.

Chapter 12

FERRET'S LEGS WEREN'T hurting as much. He figured that was good, tactically. He was almost back to a reasonable pace, and had tossed the crutch. He was still limping as he moved, but he was moving by himself. Medically, he figured the lessening pain presaged massive tissue damage from gangrene or something similar. He actually might survive if he could get these two beaten and call the pod. There were good AI medical facilities aboard. He still considered that tantalizing chance, now far behind him, of using Doll's transmitter for backup. He really, personally, didn't care if a war started, instead of all this back and forth. But command would not be happy with his sorry ass, even if he survived. Anyway, it was only a chance, and he'd abandoned that for this track. Fretting wasn't going to help.

The voice in his earphones surprised him. "So, Ferret, how are you doing?"

He clamped his mouth tightly shut, lips thin. The longer he could wait before speaking to Dagger, the more of a threat he'd appear. Let Dagger get scared. That was a weapon all by itself.

"Ferret? I know you're there, you half-assed moron."

Nothing. And Dagger was sounding a bit distressed.

"Okay, Ferret, I'll play your game. Just wait until I see a glimpse of you again. It'll be the last. Goodbye."

Dagger had definitely been disturbed. Good.

The signs on his tracker were not making sense. They still showed Tirdal to be several minutes, almost half an hour, ahead of Dagger. Dagger was about a half hour ahead of Ferret. So why hadn't Tirdal stopped to let Dagger catch up? They'd still have plenty of lead.

Of course, they didn't know how far ahead of Ferret they were. Dagger was likely playing for time, hoping Ferret's wounds would do him in.

Unless they planned to spread out and make Ferret choose, so they could envelope him. If so, it was even more important that he keep silent. He was the best tracker of the three.

He wished he knew what they were planning though. And that he had someone to talk to. And that it would stop hurting.

✧   ✧   ✧

Tirdal left Dagger to fret. What was the human expression? "Stew in his own juices." That was it. And it was doubly appropriate. This level of exertion caused tremendous metabolic stress and perspiration. From what he knew of human physiology and medical treatment, it had to be about as unpleasant for Dagger. Which was good. Dagger might handle the heat better, but Tirdal had greater stamina and resistance, he was sure. The worse things got here, the more advantageous it would be.

There was danger, he admitted. Dagger could track better, and had a weapon with much greater range. He also sounded completely insane at this point. Had he been already, and it was simply surfacing now? Had it been hidden by a social façade? Or was it something latent, triggered by his impulsive actions? Did being alone emphasize human emotions? That was always true to some extent, but was it worse in this instance?

No time for that now, he thought. It was time to put kilometers between them, and stay in the woods while doing so. He rose carefully back to his feet and secured the artifact, then resumed his march. Behind him was the shell of his lunch, its legs still occasionally twitching even though there was no body or mind attached to it. Insects were so barely sentient they were very hard to kill properly. Whereas sentient animals were easy to kill, in theory, except for that mental activity involved.

The local sun was well on its way down. That would change things immensely. He could see innately better than Dagger, but Dagger was very skilled with night vision. Also, Tirdal's hotter metabolism would shine in that night vision. However, Dagger had now been awake for nineteen hours. Certainly he could go longer, but aside from thirst and hunger, Tirdal wasn't particularly stressed. And Dagger was. The situation should change in Tirdal's favor shortly. All that was needed was calm and patience. The waves turn rock to sand. Sand smoothes all signs. Be as the waves; persistent, calm, undeterred . . .

Dagger was furious at being cut off and ignored. It was a pity those assholes hadn't bought it with the rest, because they were really sticking him in the ass. Some alien freak and the FNG were causing him, him! to change plans and waste time. The jumped up twerps seemed to think that they not only were relevant, but were some kind of martyrs.

The anger helped a little with other things, too. His heart was thumping as he strode along. One of his secret phobias when young was the dark. He'd thought he was over it. He'd been through nighttime training, done the survival school gig, been on hundreds of exercises and a dozen real world missions. He started as a branch reached out and stroked his cheek, then he thrust it away roughly. He wasn't afraid, dammit. He kept the anger fresh in his mind, but it was fading, albeit slowly.

But human settlements always had some light and bustle at night. The populous planets had enough light pollution so that one could always see the warm glow of a city on the horizon. Military encampments had generators and activity. Here, there was absolutely nothing. Nothing except that Blob site, all holograms.

Nothing except local creatures that would eat him. No one but the Darhel, fleeing him, though he had made his threats sound real. No one but Ferret, who was out there but not talking. No one but the ghosts of his former teammates. His mind was playing tricks on him. There was the trancelike beat of Gun Doll's music. Gorilla's snores came to him, and the captain's cynical presence and Shiva's calm. He turned to look behind him, as he had every couple of minutes. There was nothing behind him, and he knew it, but it was spooky as hell out here. And there might be something behind him, with those local creepie-crawlies.

In truth, anyone would have been afraid. It hit every evolutionary button humans have. It was dark, too quiet, full of threats and lonely. But Dagger's ego had never seen it in those terms. He'd been suppressing his weaknesses behind a mask for so long that their appearance terrified him. One must face fears to overcome them, and Dagger had spent his life avoiding them.

But he had to keep moving. The frigging Darhel was still humping away, damn him. When would the little rat tire? A hazy part of his mind recalled that the Darhel was alleged to have maxed the course, and he started to wonder if that was true. Then he realized that maxing it didn't indicate an upper limit on the bastard's abilities, but a lower one. That was frightening.

Nah, he couldn't be that good. Dagger had seen some real shit. He was letting himself get scared over nothing. Nothing. What kind of wuss was afraid of the dark? He could shoot the bugs as fast as they could attack, and Tirdal was a long way away.

He yelped as something stabbed him in the ribs, then recovered. He swallowed and hit the limb aside furiously.

Then he went berserk.

There was no obvious outer change, though he did increase his pace to a rough, rapid stride, moving in a low lope. He slapped branches aside and didn't realize he was sacrificing stealth for speed. All he knew was that he was catching that damned Darhel, and he was not afraid of the dark. He tripped over a stray root, and it only served to elevate his rage to a higher plane. He was panting, hyperventilating, heedless of his own safety, but all that mattered was catching that damned Darhel.

Ferret kept pushing his pace faster as his legs went blissfully numb. The pins and needles feeling went the entire length now, and he barely felt the brush he rubbed against. It was a good thing that he was stalking, and he'd have to keep it that way, because he was certainly leaving a trail. But at least the pain was gone. It was odd to not feel his feet, but they were working, even if the left one was a puppet's wooden foot rather than a real one.

The coming dark would be of help to him. Unless those two, Dagger specifically, as Tirdal wasn't very good, were keeping a good watch behind, he shouldn't run up on them. But once he did see an IR readout, he should easily be able to follow at distance. Too, it was harder to move stealthily in the dark. Dagger might not leave much, but Tirdal would, and the two together should be easy.

A wave of dizziness hit him, and he squatted down

to catch his breath, or tried to. He sprawled flat in the weeds, feeling them scrape past him and smelling the released sap of several types. The ground smelled slightly slimy, and he'd probably slipped on the surface as stems rolled well-greased between that and his boots. Balance shot because of my feet, he thought to himself. He reminded himself to be cautious. He had no tactile feedback from down there.

He wondered if the nausea was due to his damaged feet, but that couldn't be it this fast. He realized it was a combination of shock, pain, drugs and lack of food and sleep. He'd been awake almost twenty-eight hours, after days of little sleep, and was in rough shape. And he couldn't stop now. The best thing for him was to bull through and hope they had to rest at some point, soon. In fact, they were sure to, unless he presented an immediate threat. Another reason to keep quiet.

Still, they had the advantage. If they rested, they could take turns on watch. Ferret had only himself. But, by resting, they weren't moving.

He checked his tracker again. Tirdal's lead was less. But they had both widened the gap from them to him. So he'd have to do what he could to increase his pace. Sighing, he reached into his kit for more painkillers and a stronger stimulant. He hated to use them; the painkiller reduced his awareness somewhat, and the stim nauseated him. If he were to have a chance of catching up, however, they were necessary.

That done, he opened the last rat to chew on while he marched, tucked it into his belt, and started moving. Step forward with the right foot until weight hit the knee, then shove the left foot forward. As soon as weight was on it, step forward with the right and push with the left. He resumed his rolling, limping gait, and decided the speed was adequate. The pain was less than it had been, and as the fresh analgesic kicked in, he'd move it up faster.

The tracks weren't hard to follow, even in the dark. Ferret had grown up on a Fringe world, and had hunted since he was five. To him, the terrain was a book to be read. More bent leaves and abused stems told him someone had passed this way. That scratch on a tree and that bare sweep through brush indicated a long weapon: Dagger's. Those flat areas were due to feet with a different geometry than a human's: Tirdal's.

Then there was the mark left through the stems by a larger local form. He studied that at a near-jog as he crossed it. Yes, something had trotted through there quickly, in pursuit of something smaller. That meant a predator. A predator was even worse in his limping condition, and in that he'd prefer not to fire and give away his location. He wasn't sure he could handle one with a knife, but that appeared to be his best option for secrecy. As to shooting, it was likely a better option for survival. Of course, both depended on a weapon being able to get through those appalling exoskeletons the local life wore.

It was right then that the predator in question trotted past again. It was about rabbit sized, and it was followed by three more just like it. It was probably his limping gait sending rhythmic but uneven vibrations through the ground that attracted them. Whatever it was, Ferret saw the ground cover twitch and sway, saw the wave of motion turn suddenly towards him and charge. He yanked his field knife clear of its sheath and tried to intercept them.

The first one was easy. He had the blade down in time and the stupid creature tried to bite it. The blade of the knife was a high-density polymer, with a ceramic edge molecularly bonded to it. The bug sheared its own jaw off on the almost molecule-fine edge. For just a moment, it was clearly visible in Ferret's goggles, a wriggling, Japanese beetle shape as long as his foot. Then it fell under a seedling.

The other three tried to attack at once. The first leapt, and Ferret dodged by falling. He hadn't intended to do that, and it sent fresh spikes of pain through his legs, but he avoided a bite. A whack at the temporarily confused bug didn't cleave its chitin, but did crush its legs under itself, as it had no time to retract them. It wriggled and twitched in place in the weeds, but wasn't going to be a problem.

The other two, however, were on him. One was chewing at his right boot. At least, he hoped it was just his right boot. While his foot was insensate, he still needed it to function for this hike. Then the second one started attacking his rucksack, chittering in his ear and scaring him badly.

First, the one on the foot. It was the easier one to reach. Methodically and calmly, he inserted the blade, unsharpened edge down, between his foot and the bug, and hoped to hell it didn't try to crawl up the blade and munch his arm. It clung to his boot for a moment, then came loose. The tip pinned it against the bark of a tree, resisted for a moment, then skewered it. It thrashed angrily.

Quickly, he pulled the releases on his ruck's strap,

let it drop, and turned to impale the other pest. With soft ground underneath, he wasn't able to pierce it, but it did stumble off quickly.

Ferret panted for breath, suddenly wider awake than even the drugs had made him, a warm flush of adrenaline coursing through him. He whipped his head around to see if there were any others nearby.

It was clear. He carefully resheathed his knife, took a quick glance at his boot and was reassured that integrity was good, even if the tough surface was badly scored and peeled. Then he reattached the clips on his pack, shouldered it, shrugged it and adjusted it. Of course, just for a minor annoyance, he couldn't get the straps back to the original position. It rode differently on his shoulders and would take some time to get used to. But he was alive, mostly unhurt save for a skinned knuckle on his already bug-bit hand and a sore hip, and was up and moving again at once.

It was fear that drove Dagger to call Ferret, though he would never have admitted it. Just the sound of a human voice, or, even if Ferret refused to answer, the knowledge that he was there, reduced his fear of this black hell he was moving through. This black hell that turned bright and grainy under enhancement, fronds and branches reaching out like wings or arms to grasp at him, brush at his legs, or worse, his head. His teeth were clattering and his knees shaking, but he pressed on. Damn that Darhel, he had to catch that little freak, or this was all a bad screwup to try to explain. He'd catch a firing squad if they convicted him, and without the box for assets, he had no way to get out of the Republic.

"Ready to give up yet, Ferret?" he asked. Just the act of talking made the fear retreat slightly, as it emphasized his humanity.

There was no reply, so he continued, "You know we're going to flank you and kill you, you crippled little loser."

Still nothing.

"But I want to be fair, Ferret. Tell me who to send regards to, and I'll tell them you died bravely."

At that, there was a response. "Bravely how, Dagger?" Ferret's voice was angry. Good. Dagger could almost hear the teeth grinding. "Bravely against you? Or are you going to blame this on the Darhel and kill him, too? Because you sure as hell can't blame this on the Blobs and be believed."

Dagger had no immediate reply, and hesitated just long enough. Ferret continued, "That's it, isn't it? He's not really your ally, he's a convenience."

Dagger snarled. This wasn't the way he'd planned it.

But Ferret was still talking. "I wonder if I can convince him of that? Hey, Dagger? Be awfully bad for you if we started hunting you instead, wouldn't it?"

That he could respond to. "Not at all, Ferret. I don't mind superimposing a target on your face and watching the splatter. Be good for a laugh. And you don't think a fucking Darhel is going to give me any trouble, do you? Do you imagine he's going to believe you? 'Oh, I haven't spoken to you yet, but I'm really on your side.' That will fly."

"Him? Trouble? No," Ferret replied. "But I can stalk you better than you can stalk me. And you have to sleep sometime. I don't really need to talk to Tirdal, anyway. I know where you both are. Later, asshole. The next sound you hear will be your chest exploding."

Dagger growled again and decided he'd better talk to Tirdal quickly. If he could keep these two afraid of each other, he could play them off.

"Hey, Tirdal," he called.

"Yes, Dagger? Are we done with insults?"

"For now, Tirdal, for now," Dagger said, grinning even though no one could see him. "I have a surprise for you."

"Oh? A gift of some kind? What's the occasion?" Tirdal was doing his best to sound light and cheerful, almost human. With that deep, slow voice it didn't work well. Instead, it was ghastly.

"Sort of, Tirdal," Dagger said, nodding to himself. "Ferret is still alive and is right with me. You recall how well he can track?"

"Interesting, Dagger. You realize, of course, I find that very hard to believe. If you really had an ally, I would have been flanked in short order, or one of you would have secured the box before you 'fragged' your entire team." Tirdal did not sound distressed. That reasonable, logical tone of his was one more reason Dagger was going to see him dead.

Tirdal obviously hadn't Sensed Ferret, he realized! He thought this was a bluff, but he should know. If he didn't, then that defined a limit on his Sense. Excellent to know.

"Well, it was a lucky fluke," Dagger said, grasping for control. He really needed to rehearse his comments before talking to the damned Elf. "But once we realized how much we both hate Darhel, and the value of the box, it became easy. We both get you dead, we each get money. It's a good deal all around. Except, of course, for you, because you'll be dead. The fact that you can't Sense him gives us even more of an advantage, not that we need it. You're dead."

"Very well, Dagger," Tirdal replied. "You have an ally. It's amazing how much of an advantage you feel you need over a lowly Darhel. It makes me think that you aren't as formidable as you'd like everyone to believe you think you are."

That stung a little, once he sorted it out. Tirdal knew how to use the language better than Dagger did. He must have spent years studying to be that sarcastic. But there were a billion credits at stake, and words weren't going to change things.

"Tirdal, I don't mind being generous with a billion. That's why I was offering to cut you in. But you won't take it, so it just leaves more for me and Ferret. As to being fair, why should I bother? We all know that Ferret's the best tracker, I'm the best shooter, and you're nothing. We're not trying to prove some macho point, we're simply going to kill you."

"So you say, Dagger. To borrow a cliché, 'First, you have to catch me.' Goodbye again."

Dagger knew better than to waste time replying. Tirdal wasn't going to listen. Still, those seeds of doubt had been planted in him. If he kept playing them off each other, they would both be allies to him, while they imagined they were against him. It was even possible Ferret would do in the Darhel for him, if Dagger could get close enough to flank and let Ferret take him from behind. And Dagger could backtrack the discharge from a weapon easily.

Yes, this should turn out okay, after all.

The sooner dawn came or they cleared the woods, the happier Dagger would be. This was not pleasant. He grimaced. "I'm not a fucking coward. It's just dark." It didn't reassure him. Dammit, there was nothing here except a few bugs he could outshoot.

And Ferret. Why was Ferret still alive? He stopped again, back to a tree, then turned in a circle, back still to it, searching through his scope for any activity in infrared. Little bugs, but no predator forms yet. And no sign of Ferret.

Ferret decided he needed to hear from Tirdal. He'd have to be doubly cautious what he said and felt, with that little freak probing at his mind, but he also needed intelligence. Whatever he could get from the Darhel would help. It likely wouldn't be much; there wasn't much inflection in that rich, deep voice, and as an alien, Tirdal had to deliberately emphasize his voice. If he chose not to, it was simply a monotone. Ferret would have to discern intent from very few clues. It was a whole new type of tracking.

Taking an extra breath for steadiness, he chose the channel and said, "Tirdal."

"Ferret," came the reply. "So you are alive." Ferret lowered the volume. He had wanted it loud for best hearing of minute details, or any background noise that wasn't filtered, but the level was interfering with his ability to hear his own environment. In the dark closeness of the trees, his hearing was a prime sense.

"Surprised, Tirdal?" he asked. "You know Dagger's not really an ally to you. He's just using you as a convenience to grab all the money for himself."

Tirdal replied, "As a Darhel, allegedly what you'd call a 'capitalist,' I'm amazed at the avarice of humans. Money is a tool one uses to accomplish work. Yet you very often seem to think of it as a status symbol. Just what will you do with half a billion credits, Ferret? Wasn't potentially thirteen million as a share enough? Especially as it was a fortuitous find rather than an earned development?"

What game was this? "I'm not here for the money, Tirdal. I'm here to see you two assholes dead, and the box in the hands of the Republic's science bureau." There was another scuffled weed. He was still on the trail.

"Now, Ferret, that's just amusing and insulting to my intelligence."

"How do you figure?" Ferret asked. The alien twerp was disturbing. He exuded a . . . confidence.

"Ferret, if you'd meant to ally with me, you'd have called while Dagger and I were swapping fire, and offered to help."

"Waaah?" Ferret replied. "I heard you assholes shooting the wounded. I heard you. Then you came running past with the artifact, while Dagger looted the bodies. How stupid do you think I am?" He couldn't believe Tirdal was even trying that line. Had Dagger sold him that thoroughly on the idea? Did he have that low an opinion of Ferret? The insult made him furious. Ferret was no political genius, nor very urbane, but he was intelligent and very good at his chosen specialty. He was reassured himself that moment by another scuff in the dirt. Dagger had passed this way.

What the hell was Tirdal playing? Did he think

Ferret could be dismissed? If he really thought the two humans were a team, why wasn't he more scared? Or did he have an ace for dealing with the sniper? That was likely why he was disturbed at Ferret's existence. Ferret was another threat he hadn't planned on. Except he knew already from Dagger.

Had Dagger not told him? Was it possible they were both playing their own games with that box? That was an idea. Dagger had fragged the team, Tirdal had taken the moment to swipe the box. Now they were both fighting each other. So Ferret would only have to fight one at a time, because neither was going to lend a hand. That was a good theory, and would explain why they weren't traveling together. His thoughts were interrupted by Tirdal speaking.

"I don't think you're stupid, Ferret. Which is why I'm not going to listen to you try to ally with me at this point. I've seen the technique on human vid shows. Dagger plays malicious and evil, you play honorable. I won't be swayed. Now, do you have anything valid to input? Or shall we resume the hunt?"

That taunting question threw Ferret back into a rage. He couldn't believe Tirdal, holding the billion credit box, was going to play innocent victim. "Oh, it's a hunt all right," Ferret replied. "And you can just fucking die, Darhel."

"That's been the plan all along, Ferret. It is unfortunate that it takes two humans to equal one Darhel. Goodbye."

"You asshole!" Ferret near-shouted into his microphone, barely remembering his noise discipline.

There was no reply.

❖   ❖   ❖

Tirdal let his Sense and senses reach out into the darkness. Without the undisciplined thoughts of humans shouting at him from mere meters away, he could feel the environment. It was raw and primal, but not unfriendly. Few of the insectoids noticed his presence, save as the passage of a creature. He was too large for most to be concerned with, and did not display the chemical signs of threat. To others, he did not appear as prey, and was thus ignored. Some felt his movement and became alert, seeking a meal, but in all cases it was simple hunger, no hatred or anger. There was only one glowing flame of anger out there, and it was far away. Distant it was, though white-hot in its intensity. Ferret wasn't discernible yet. Tirdal focused his Sense and sought.

There. Behind Dagger, and very faint. So Ferret was playing catch-up. Nor was he as obsessed as Dagger. He would be hard to track, but was farther away, so less of a threat. It was likely the two of them would meet up shortly. That would increase the threat. What Tirdal would have to watch for would be the two of them spreading out to channel him.

It was possible they weren't really allies, but from Tirdal's viewpoint, they were both threats. He'd have to be certain he didn't get into terrain that would help pin him for one or the other. Both wanted him dead.

There weren't any other humans. He made sure. It was disturbing that Ferret had snuck past his awareness, as close as he'd been for much of it. It might be that the pain of the neural effect had stunned him, though a mind in pain should have registered. Possibly the collective shriek from four other human minds had drowned him out. Still, it wouldn't do to rely on his Sense alone. It clearly had limits.

There were no other humans, but there was hunger. He was being followed, flanked, stalked by several larger predators and at least one mammalian flyer. He could feel the approaches, most of which veered off as he left a particularly defined territory or simply moved beyond the range to be interesting. There were some, though, that were steadily closing. Occasionally, one would drop out of the pursuit, only to be replaced by another.

Then there was that one. It was moving closer and the hunger it felt was strong, driving. It was going to attack, he felt sure. That was a crisis, but one he could deal with. Summoning the Jem discipline, he forced the tal to a lower level, anticipating its surge when he killed. He hefted his punch gun and prepared to respond. It would be soon, he felt. The creature was to his left and running, now was agitated and there was an animal eagerness.

Now. The charge came as he passed a thick tree bole. The animal was in mid leap, chittering very softly, and in a trajectory to seize Tirdal by the head. That was also a trajectory that put it in perfect position for a punch gun shot, though there was no way such a primitive form could anticipate what was about to happen.

Tirdal turned to meet the rush, raised his weapon and shot. The shot would have been instructive to a human observer. It was smooth, effortless, and caught the animal right in the underside of its head as Tirdal dropped underneath its path. It was not the shot of a clumsy creature unable to kill.

Then Tirdal got slapped by his Sense.

The insect in question was the local evolutionary equivalent of a leopard. It was a large, competent solo hunter with good instincts and high intelligence. It had consciousness and self-awareness, and it reacted to the shot. As Tirdal's shot had been perfectly placed, its mind screamed in agony at having most of its face burned off. Then it landed on that face and tumbled so as to break its neck.

DEATH! Tirdal felt it, staggered, dropped. Feedback through his Sense let him feel the creature's swift but painful end. Stabbing electric icicles drove into his brain from the violent, emotional outburst, and tal squirted into his bloodstream. It met the pain, washed it aside as a flood does debris, and roared toward his brain and self. He didn't even feel the damaged edges of his chest plate grind against nerves.

He was on all fours, shaking, quivering, moaning as delicious tremors rolled over him and heat flushed out from the base of his skull. He'd left himself exposed to the creature's emotions, and now was receiving the rewards. It was sweet, and no longer cloying but thick and syrupy. But it moved with such speed, he was overwhelmed and couldn't respond.

Lintatai. He could feel it. He'd thought he'd felt it while sucking meat from crablike claws, but that was a shadow of this. It suffused his entire being, rippling down his spine and out to his toes and fingertips. It rolled in waves through his brain until he could see and hear it, as powerful as a tropical storm over the ocean.

Then it stopped. It didn't retreat, but it grew no more powerful, as some hidden part of his determination slammed down doors on his Sense and halted the influx. His iron discipline and training yanked him to an eddy in the wash, where he could maintain his Self just long enough to think. He rode the crest, slipped behind it and floundered for only a moment. Then he was in control. He was still awash in a sea of powerful sensations, but he was alert and aware.

He'd thought he was gritting his teeth, but had sliced into his lower lip when he bit down. Wet earth was abrading his cheek and in his nostrils. Tendrils of weeds curled over him, twitching in the breeze of his tortured breathing. All these were real, present and he clutched at them for strength. The cool air. The darkness. He'd voided himself as he lost control, but even as unpleasant as that was, it was a real sensation. He thought to reach out, but his self-control took over. No Sense. None at all. The risk of attack was less dangerous than that of any more tal.

It took long minutes of slow, measured breathing to reach an acceptable level. He opened the front of his suit to let heat vent to the atmosphere. The coolness of evaporating sweat helped, as it was something else real and external. His strength and balance returned, but he remained prone, head on one outstretched arm that was cramping from its circulation-killing grip on the punch gun. He'd wait a while longer before rising.

The lesson here was that he had to rein in his Sense when fighting. It could be an intelligence asset until hostilities began, but then it must be locked away. Some things should not be felt, and battle was one of them. Battle must be a cerebral matter, lest it subvert the mind. So he'd fight as a human did. That was how it was done.

A smile, all teeth, spread across his face. Another valuable lesson had been learned. And it was one he could use at once. Dagger thought he enjoyed killing? Thought he was dangerous?

Dagger had no idea.

Chapter 13

DARK TURNED SLOWLY to formless grayness, then to twilight. Inside, Dagger calmed and returned gradually to what passed as normal for him. His breathing slowed from ragged heaves to pants and finally to just exerted breathing. He would not admit it even to himself, but he was glad of the light.

He sought refuge in bullying, as he had always done. "Good morning, Tirdal. Have you had breakfast yet?"

"Why, yes, Dagger, thank you. I had one of the smaller flyer forms. They taste somewhat like duck, or at least that's as close as human animals come. I would compare it more to the bligrol of Darhel. But of course, you've never tasted such."

"Tirdal, we both know you're lying about the meat," he retorted, angered. The little asshole was so unflappable. Well, he'd flap shortly, when Dagger blew his fucking head off his shoulders.

"You seem sure of your statements, Dagger. So why talk to me? Does it make you feel less lonely? Does contradiction please you? Does denying reality and being contrary fill your psyche? If you drown, should I look upstream for you?"

Dagger ignored the incoming attack and kept taunting, probing as he slogged forward in pursuit. Dammit, there had to be a handle somewhere. "Tell me, Tirdal, will you still take that round in the leg for me?"

"Certainly, Dagger. Where do you want me to meet you?" was Tirdal's reply as he crunched through the brush. The ground here was covered with something akin to dried pine needles from the variety of trees on this slope. They were slightly slippery, tending to slide and roll over each other, and he bent down to lower his center of gravity with the box over his shoulder. It hurt his chest less, too, though it made for greater exertion at the unnatural angle.

"Why don't I meet you, Tirdal?"

"Name the place, Dagger. Unless you're afraid?" Tirdal sparred. "And will you bring Ferret with you? Or will he be stalking you? Or just keeping you company in the dark?"

"Sounds to me like you're hiding your own cowardice, Darhel boy."

"Why is that, Dagger? I've said I will meet you. If you really wish, you know how to track me; that advantage is yours. You profess patience, yet are eager for me to reduce your task. Who here is more afraid? And afraid not only of dying, but of failing in one's alleged area of expertise. And against an urbanite Darhel. Perhaps you are not the tracker you would have others believe you are. Certainly you are not the brave killer."

There was a shift in Dagger's attitude. It was swift, sudden. "Well, even if we concede the point, Tirdal, the fact is that I'm a killer and you aren't." Just like that. Conciliatory, even if only slightly. Less argumentative. What was going on there?

"If it suits you to believe so, Dagger, I'll concede the point," he returned.

"Hey, screw you, Darhel," Dagger shouted. "I'm trying to . . . oh, to hell with it."

That was the end of that conversation, Tirdal thought. But what had Dagger so riled?

He thought as he traveled, trusting that the problem would resolve itself in time. Shortly, his self-awareness prodded him. What was it?

His Sense. That was it. As this had gone on, it had gradually increased in sensitivity. He could feel a direction on Dagger, as he could with things that were very close. Yet Dagger was still quite some distance away, he knew. It had to be related to the continuous flow and recent push of tal. Historical details were hazy, but the Darhel had at one time tracked their prey, scarce as it was, across vicious terrain, following the thought images. That had to be what was happening here. It was probably a good thing he didn't have the full Sense of his ancestors, on a world as populous with life as this. The combined input would likely have driven him insane at once.

The odd thing was that Dagger was not directly behind him, but was following obliquely, as if shadowing. That was interesting. "Dagger," he said, intending to harass him with that bit of knowledge.

But that might not be a good idea. Upon consideration, the less he admitted, the better. Especially since he didn't know how Dagger was doing that.

"What is it, Darhel?" Dagger replied, sounding highly agitated.

"How are you doing for rations, Dagger?" he asked instead. "Besides the flyer, I've had two local lizards and a large insectoid to eat. They do taste somewhat like chicken. I think I understand that human joke now."

"We both know you can't kill, Darhel," Dagger replied, repeating his previous comments, "So don't bullshit me." It was clear, both from his voice and from a niggle to Tirdal's Sense that Dagger had not eaten anything not from his processor. Interesting. Either he couldn't hunt, or was squeamish about raw meat, and Tirdal's blithe comments about it were more spikes in him. Best not to exploit that, yet, either. All these things could be used in their time.

That time might be soon, too, Tirdal realized. The forest was thinning, leaving a large oblate circular area that was likely due to some old burn. It was several kilometers across. Unless he turned to cut across Dagger's course, he had to enter flat ground, which was a very unappealing option. He could go around, but that would slow him, and Ferret might fan out to flank him. Dagger could cut across, safe with his greater ranged weapon, but Tirdal could not. But he knew now what Dagger's problem was. It was fatigue and fear of failure. And it had all come overnight. Was Dagger afraid of the dark, too? Was that why he was probing, pushing, trying to provoke a quick end? If so, even more patience was called for.

He paused to examine the terrain. There was always something not seen at first glance that would help. There was what he sought; a stream coming down from the north had cut a gully through the loose soil of this rich field. That's what he needed. Through there he could move at a decent pace, and even if Dagger found him, he'd get few shots, and those would be obstructed. Girding himself mentally, he trotted toward the shallow creek.

Ferret was tired. This was as bad as Hell Week in DRT school, and he was amused after a fashion. He'd never thought he'd have to push himself that hard again. Yet here he was, injured, partially maimed, hungry, exhausted and strung out, his mind hazed with drugs despite his best efforts to keep the doses minimal. The initial pain had eased considerably; he now had numb feet and a dull ache that manifested itself as he walked. But a new irritation was about. His knees and good ankle were aching from the exertion of carrying unresponsive feet. His hips were starting to feel it, too. And he was still stumbling and inefficient, causing overall muscle cramps and strain.

He'd been stuffing leaves into his converter as he walked, and eating the patties it put out. Sure, you could adjust them for flavor, but they lacked real texture and weren't the highest protein food. In fact, the leaves hereabout were almost worthless. Vitamins typically were unique to a planet, he didn't really need minerals except potassium for this short a time frame, and fat and protein came from roots and seeds. What he was eating was going to come out about the same way it went in, which would hurt like hell. Still, it kept the edge off the hunger, even if he was craving rat pack tuna with noodles.

Something came to him and he paused in thought. Something about the signs he followed was bugging him. Just to double check, he raised the tracker.

Oh, shit. He was still following Tirdal. Dagger, however, was not leaving any sign. Not ahead, anyway. So assume he'd peeled off to outflank one or the other. Icy adrenaline rippled through him yet again, though it didn't jolt his tired body, simply made him flush.

He thought back for a few moments. He'd seen sign of Dagger recently. Say, five minutes ago. The sign had been about fifteen to twenty-five minutes old, as he'd been gaining during the dark, which was more evidence of his greater competence over them. Still, no Dagger at present. Dagger several minutes away.

That was potentially very good if Dagger was after Tirdal, and potentially deadly if Ferret was the target. Suddenly, he felt very exposed, and his neck and head tickled in fear. His scalp had gone itchy-numb from the helmet's harness, and he'd been planning to take it off for a bit, but thought now he would wait. Not that the helmet would do a damned bit of good against a gauss bead, but it might slow down fragments or a very long-range shot. Or deflect a bead enough to keep him alive. Anyway, it made him feel less naked.

He decided it would be good to make contact again. He might as well let those two know he was still here. And there were a few answers he wanted. Or at least questions he would ask. The answers might not be forthcoming, but that would be useful, too. And he might find out why Dagger had pulled off.

"Tirdal," he called.

It was only a moment before Tirdal replied, "Yes, Ferret?"

"I'm still following you, Tirdal," he said.

"Of course you are," was the response. "There's not much else to do until we reach the pod's extraction points, is there?"

"True enough," he agreed. "Tirdal, you asked why I didn't contact you when Dagger fragged everybody. I could ask you that same question, couldn't I? Your silence then says a lot."

"It says either I thought everyone was dead, or that I wanted to be alone and unbothered. You have to decide, of course, though it's rather moot. None of us can trust the others."

"And why should I, Tirdal?" he asked. "You took the box. Why do you have it?"

"I took it to keep it from Dagger," Tirdal replied.

"Fair enough," Ferret said. "But why do you still have it? You could hide it, and ambush Dagger if he came for it."

"That would be silly," Tirdal replied. "We all know I'm not skilled at tracking."

"True," Ferret said. "But Dagger seems to be following you just fine. So why not try the ambush? Or, since he can't get off the planet without you, just leave him the damned box. He'd have to carry it as well, and you could just stalk him as he neared the ship."

"I can't take that risk, Ferret," Tirdal replied. "I have to keep the artifact."

"Why?"

"I have told you."

"Those are pretty thin reasons. You're inconveniencing yourself, and helping Dagger." Ferret was arguing. Something was wrong here, and he didn't know what it was. But the situation didn't make sense.

"There are reasons I think are valid for this," Tirdal said.

"Like what?" Ferret asked too quickly. He really wanted to know.

There was silence. "Yeah, I thought so," Ferret continued. "You want that artifact as much as Dagger does. You're both scum."

"Ferret," Tirdal replied, "I can't convince you what I'm doing is for your own good."

"'For my own good.' Sure. Humans are happiest as slaves, right?" he retorted.

Tirdal said, "I really am sorry, Ferret." Then there was silence.

Well, if he wouldn't talk, perhaps Dagger would. Ferret also knew something Dagger wanted kept secret.

"So, Dagger, was that dark night scary and creepy?"

"Ferret, you're still alive. I told Tirdal he should circle back and bag you, but he's too nice."

"Oh, stuff it, Dagger. We all know you two are just avoiding each other. That's why you're attempting a flank." That was a dangerous comment, though he didn't specify who Dagger might be flanking. But if he was forced to reconsider it, he'd likely wait on Ferret and bag Tirdal first. At least Ferret hoped that was how it would play out.

Continuing, he said, "He wants that billion as bad as you do. In fact, I'm planning to help him kill you first, because he's the easier one."

Dagger replied, "So, you recognize me as a threat. That's good, Ferret. I'll make sure you get a nice, clean shot through the head. Will that make you feel any better?"

Ferret ignored the implication. "I'm coming for you, Dagger. You're between me and Tirdal, so it's tactically smart. And it'll be fun, too. I never realized killing could be fun. Thanks for that."

"Of course it's fun, Ferret. That's the point of it. Usually, they have no idea they're about to die. You stare through the scope and watch them go straight to hell. It's kicky. But sometimes, they know it's coming, and they know when they've made a critical mistake. That's going to be you. And I'm going to enjoy the expression on your face as I blow it to jelly."

"You really need help, you know that, Dagger?" Ferret replied. Still, the threat had bothered him. He felt vulnerable again. Was Dagger watching him? No, not from that range in the trees. Still. He'd have to watch for Dagger to circle back and stalk him. The rules were changing in this new war.

Dagger laughed. "They picked the right man for each job. You're the skulker and sneaker. I'm the killer. And the Darhel is just a number."

"You haven't managed to catch that number yet, pal. Looks like he's making good time. Of course, he might just make it to the pod before we do, and leave us here. Hmm?"

There was a moment's pause. Dagger apparently was reconsidering his position. "I don't think so, Ferret. I know something you two don't. He's not leaving with the box."

That had worked, Ferret realized. Dagger was more thoughtful and less reactive. Could he push him more? Perhaps. "You do realize I've been talking to him, Dagger?" he prodded. "And we both know what your intent is. We can sit down and talk, but first we have to kill you. Luckily, with you at an oblique, that won't be hard when we reach the right spot. We'll both have clear fields of fire, and good approaches."

"Why wait, Ferret?" Dagger asked. "I'll kill you as soon as I get a shot. So will Tirdal. Then we'll settle things mano a Elf. But you won't be around to see it."

"Nice theory, Dagger. You could tell that to a shrink, if you were going to be alive to go home." He closed the circuit. Dagger was a bit distressed, but so was he. He didn't need to rile himself up in front of a soulless sociopath, even by audio.

Instead, he threw himself forward, forcing his feet to carry him. After so many hours of limping, he had it down. His ambling gait was at least as fast as a brisk stride. First he'd kill Dagger, then he'd kill that Darhel. If he couldn't get out of this alive, he could certainly keep them from doing so.

Dagger, like Tirdal, saw that the terrain was changing, and smiled mirthlessly. That put the ball back in his court. Tirdal could either head out onto the grass and get shot, or turn back toward him and get shot, or head around and let Dagger flank him and get shot. If the former, it was easy—he'd be in plain view, his death clear in the scope so it could be replayed again and again. If one of the latter two, he could build a hasty blind and get the little twerp up close. Then he could see his face as he died, helpless. There was a frisson of delight in those thoughts. If the little asshole went around, like the coward he was, Dagger could get ahead of him. And that's exactly what the tracer showed him to be doing.

Ferret was the problem. That little son of a bitch was like a rash that wouldn't go away. Dagger wasn't sure precisely where he was, either. Likely tracking Tirdal now, but he couldn't be sure. He had been vague enough that he might be behind Dagger. Cursing again, Dagger wished Ferret had had the manners to die when the grenade went off.

If Ferret were physically capable and had his faculties, he might already have teamed up with the Darhel. That he hadn't was a good indicator for Dagger. Not that it mattered. Dagger knew it was them against him. Whether they teamed up or not was a minor issue. Neither of them could trust the other, though, when it came down to it. He'd have to ensure it stayed that way.

Still, Ferret couldn't be too close. He was talking. People who were talking weren't shooting. What Dagger needed was to pin Tirdal down in a hurry. After that, he could simply lie in wait for Ferret; he had the longer-ranged weapon. Also, Dagger outranked him, so he could call the ball and just wait. There were lots of options. So Tirdal first.

He jogged forward in a crouch to where the trees

subsided to scrub, then eased to his knees and into a crawl, the rifle dragging behind his shoulder. This was where it all paid off. He ignored the flitting flies and scurrying beetles. The day was warm and dry, the pioneer weeds ahead resilient and tough, and Dagger was slim, vicious and expert at infiltration. Pleasure rose in him, displacing the last vestiges of his former worries.

Twenty minutes later he growled in frustration. There were too many life-forms moving about this blaze, creating motion that distracted him. The tracer showed the box to be running across from southeast to northwest, and he could see nothing in that direction. There was no way to take a shot from here. The damned sensor in his helmet was crude and not much use to him, as it showed most of the higher life-forms. If he had Ferret's tracker, there was a setting for a finer definition to resolve only humans or possibly Darhel. Terrain and position were his thing. The enemy's thoughts were for the psych boys and point. He just took the shots.

Of course, Ferret did have that tracker, and might have him pinned down to a few meters. Granted, a punch gun didn't have the range of a gauss rifle, but that little jackass was becoming a major pain and a real threat. He also wasn't talking. Dagger assumed he was tracking Tirdal, that they both were, as he had the artifact and would be easier to kill.

After that it would get interesting. Neither he nor Ferret would want to be burdened with the box, but neither would want to be too far away. Dagger had the better weapon, so he'd just have to keep Ferret at bay until he could kill him, or until they came to a deal, so Dagger could kill him more easily. But Ferret wasn't going to be easy to fool, and could track.

But first was to bag that Darhel. It didn't really matter who did it, but Dagger preferred to have the kill for score, and to be sure the bastard was dead this time.

Should he climb a tree? There were a few, scraggly and flimsy looking, but there should be one that would give him a meter or two of elevation. That should be enough. The Darhel wasn't within range with his punch gun, so why not? Ferret should be out of range also, so if he did this quickly he could be back on the ground for cover.

This was definitely a task for chameleon camouflage, though. He brushed on the effect and watched as his surface texture rippled and became all but invisible. The field would be detectable, but it was low enough power not to be easy to localize. So all Ferret would know without a stalk would be that Dagger was nearby, which he already knew.

Dagger rose to a crouch and stalked through the grass toward his chosen perch, which was a pseudofern that nevertheless had branches. The skin was green and soft rather than barklike, but the limbs were low enough for him to easily reach them. He clambered aloft and scanned along the streambed. There was movement, but it appeared to be just herbivores watering along it, and they were far downstream of where the tracer last placed Tirdal. He switched from scope to tracer, back to scope, and finally saw movement behind a tuft of crabby grass. There the little bastard was! He was using the overgrown banks for cover.

Dagger pondered, considering the shot first. Dagger

never rushed, at least not in his own mind. A hornet round would flip over the bank and make a kill, but the Darhel's harness would likely destroy it in final trajectory. No good. However, if he could get a good shot with a basic projectile, hypersonic and dumb, that would do it. It took more skill to make such a shot, but this was Dagger. Everyone knew he was the best, and the little weasel was about to, too. Or rather, he wasn't. He loaded the round while smiling thin-lipped, and targeted the next break in cover.

There. A flicker of movement at the edge of the opening and then the Darhel was just there. It was trotting, slowly, favoring its right side. The box was in its left hand and its punch gun was in its right. There wasn't much time to adjust for the shot, but there was enough.

The Darhel was moving at maybe eight klicks per hour. Time of flight was half a second. Say a one-meter lead. Breeeeeathe.

As always, it was better than sex. The Republic military tried to weed out the "over the edge" special operations types. But no system was perfect. And Dagger was, and always had been, the perfect psychopath. For him, being the team sniper was all about power. You were the hunter. You watched your target and waited for the perfect time and took it out. It was the ultimate power over another sentient and it was better than anything else. It was a heady drug that paid for itself over and over again when you were gapping the enemy.

The shot was perfect. Dagger watched the round by observing through his scope fluctuations in the heat waves in the air and it tracked in directly to where the Darhel . . . no longer was.

❖   ❖   ❖

Tirdal's Sense tingled, and he felt Dagger's grin. He knew he'd been sighted, but the only thing to do was keep moving doggedly forward. He felt compelled to increase his pace, but the fractured chest plate was still hurting severely, and he didn't want to risk damaging any organs. He kept steadily at it, sloshing through the shallow stream and trying to keep his head down while still making time. He hunched as he rose over rocks, stood painfully upright where it was low and smooth, and kept his Sense aware.

Dagger was exuding cruelty, frustration, egotism and hate. Then, suddenly, they faded to nothing. How odd. Nothing material had been known to affect the Sense, only distance. Yet Dagger was easily within range.

Tirdal realized what was happening just in time. Dagger was in a trance state, preparing to shoot. His emotions were down as he focused on the task and entered alpha state. That was it.

Then an overwhelming wave of cruel pleasure rushed by. Dagger had fired and the round was on the way.

Tirdal felt the rush of emotions from the shot and sprang backwards, causing another tearing sensation in his chest, made worse by the mass of the artifact yanking at his arms. Then, ignoring the pain, he leapt across the open area as the first shot flew by, and rolled down flat. His helmet systems were buzzing like mad, careting the location of the sniper, but Dagger was well out of range of his punch gun. He could feel the hate and frustration of the sniper drop to nothing again and realized that it would be this cat and mouse all the way across the meadow. It was time to push Dagger again.

Calming his breathing so Dagger wouldn't hear the exertion and pain, he said, "I can keep this up all the way, Dagger. You transmit your emotions so easily. Even the beetles are more reticent. At this range, I have literally seconds to know you're planning a shot . . . from that tree, and to evade it. So why don't you give up now and I'll promise you a safe flight home and a fair trial for mutiny, theft and the murder of your team?"

The only answer was an intense wall of rage blowing over him. That, and a volley of five hornet rounds that came whizzing overhead and dove for him. His harness cracked out its defensive signals, and the two that were close thudded harmlessly into dirt, showering it in small fountains. One careened off a rock with a sharp sound, while the last two, far ahead, hit two of the herbivores in the small herd. The rounds didn't penetrate their armor but they must have stung. The beasts stirred and began to move at a trot.

Quickly, Tirdal splashed along and caught up with them, using their agitated movement for cover.

"Really, Dagger, emotional outbursts will not solve the problem," he said, taunting. Jem discipline had to be different from human martial arts, but there was obviously some similarity. He would give Dagger the simplest, most childish instructions to insult him further.

By now he was among the animals, moving slowly and deliberately to keep them between him and Dagger. "First, let's consider our center. Look within while breathing slowly, and find the 'hradir,' what you would call a pool, except it is a sphere. It is round so as to be even, calm and unruffled by waves. Our emotions cause waves upon it, but like any volume of water, it absorbs the energy and holds it within. If that is too complicated, think of a soap bubble. That often works best for those with chaotic minds, or children."

The only reply was two more shots. The first was near enough for Tirdal to throw himself prone as one of the creatures shook and reared back. The other was quite some meters away and indicated that Dagger really didn't know where he was at this point.

Ferret heard the shot far ahead and dropped down for cover. While it was only a joke that he could hide behind a leaf, he was good, and was invisible in an instant. Then he analyzed the threat. He had his sensors maxed and they confirmed that faint cracking sound to be a gauss rifle, sniper type. The gear quickly assessed sound pressure, atmosphere, general terrain, and flashed an estimated distance up. There were seven more shots in two volleys. So Dagger hadn't hit with his first round. That was interesting. Was he in fact shooting at Tirdal and missing? Or at other threats? Ferret decided he'd keep alert for any more local forms. He recalled vividly that they were armored against most rounds. Was Dagger dealing with several small ones or one tough one? Or was Tirdal attacking him and drawing his fire?

No way to tell. And the information he'd acquired really didn't tell him anything he didn't already know from his own senses and the lifesigns gear. It was confirmation, though, and that was a help. Slowly, he rose and moved forward. Now would be the time to make headway on them.

The trees were thinning, so the best guess was that they were shooting it out on flat ground. Dagger likely had sought a tree or other high point. If he used his chameleon, he'd be hard enough to see, and Darhel couldn't kill, which was why Tirdal was running.

Correction: Darhel had never been known to kill. But Tirdal certainly seemed different. So assume he'd find it awkward but not impossible. Hesitation would likely be his undoing, and he was smart enough to know it, so he'd be hiding.

Time to talk to Tirdal again.

"Tirdal, Dagger is between us, approximately. Should we attempt to flank him?"

Tirdal came on in only a moment. "That would be a good idea, Ferret, if I could be sure of where you were, and if we could trust each other. As it is, I expect you to shoot as soon as you locate me. So I'm afraid I can't agree."

"Dammit, Tirdal, Dagger's the greater threat here." The alien was so . . . alien. Precise, logical. Any human would be at least disturbed if not worried. Tirdal was not. It was infuriating.

"I agree. But it's also likely you consider me to be the easier kill. Therefore, to expose myself would be to invite the two of you to try for me first. That's the rough part of a three-way war, Ferret. Whoever moves first, dies."

Sighing, Ferret acceded to the inevitable. He wasn't going to persuade Tirdal yet. He'd have to bide his time. For now, threats would make things worse. So he said, "Okay, Tirdal, I guess we can't work a deal now. But keep it in mind. Dagger's the threat we have to eliminate, then we can try to come to a deal." Though if he got a lucky shot at Tirdal, he'd damned well take it.

"Fair enough, Ferret. Good hunting."

"Yeah, you too," he grudgingly admitted. "As long as it's Dagger you're hunting."

"Of course I can't be convincing in that regard. Now if you don't mind, Ferret, I think we're done for now."

Tired, aggravated, head itching and now going numb, Ferret limped on, and decided to harass Dagger some more. If he could push Dagger into exposing himself or making any mistake at all, they might get rid of him. It would also be a bargaining chip with Tirdal.

He smiled for a moment. Every part of him was either numb or screaming in agony. He'd always thought he didn't want to die in bed, but he was beginning to think it had advantages.

"So, Dagger, it's not going too well, is it?"

"Sooo, you think you can see. Tell me, Ferret, where are you?" Dagger asked back, voice light.

"Dammit, Dagger, you coward," Ferret exploded. "I'm tempted to tell you so I can blow you away."

"You're going to stop me?" Dagger replied with a snicker. "Are you trying to suck up to Tirdal the same way? You know he's with me, don't you? That's why he's not helping you." The last part was reasonable, but bullshit. Dagger wasn't as tough as he tried to be, and Ferret had always known that. And in the last . . . had it only been two days? It seemed like months . . . every moral weakness the man had had come out to play.

"He's not helping me because he's a gutless freak," Ferret said. "We both know that. I'm not afraid of him, but you should be afraid of me."

"But, Ferret, my friend, aren't you suffering neural

effects? Are you going to limp up and bag me?" Dammit, Dagger knew how to twist things. That insult was worse because it was true. Ferret choked back tears and forced his quavering voice under control. Every step sent metal spikes through his legs. Every stumble from a foot that couldn't find its own footing was another jarring jolt through the heel and up. Muscles were cramping up in his legs, in his hips, even in his neck and shoulders from wincing and reacting. His much-lightened ruck wasn't helping either, in that regard. The cumulative effect was causing a severe headache under his helmet-numbed scalp. That was causing sporadic nausea, which made it hard for him to even swallow water.

"Oh, the neural effects were minor. I'm still walking, still talking, and still have a few weapons. I wouldn't count on having range on me. You may be a better shot, but I have tactical position, and Gun Doll's cannon," he lied.

That seemed to make Dagger pay attention. "You're lying," he said. "Or you would have mentioned it earlier."

"Sure I'm lying, Dagger. Come here and find out. Want to meet at two thousand meters and we'll each give it our best?"

There was no reply for a moment, and Ferret pressed home his advantage. "How about something more manly? Let's say a hundred meters. Or fifty. Something a real man can call a challenge? I've seen what Doll could do to a target at fifty meters with this monster. Be kinda fitting to have her hardware splash you across half the continent. Ready, old pal?"

"Ferret," Dagger replied, and it sounded for a

moment as if he had caught something in his throat, "I don't play macho, you know that. I see you, I kill you. So if you really have that cannon, you better use it."

"Oh, I will, Dagger," Ferret promised, feeling a rush that revitalized him yet again. He hated running on drugs and nerves, though. "I will."

Chapter 14

DAGGER WAS REALLY getting pissed, and really getting tired. These two cockroaches hadn't died, weren't falling back, and weren't nearly as afraid as they should be. They should both be dead. They should both be rotting bug chow. And he wasn't going to get a long range shot, and wasn't going to get close. Except he needed to.

The bitch of it was, there was no way to bow out if he wanted to. He'd be tried for treason, mutiny, desertion, murder and anything else they could find to tack on, then either shot in the neck or tossed in a vacuum chamber. He'd committed so many capital crimes, there was no way to turn back. He'd known what he was doing when he tossed that grenade, had been prepared to risk the bugs and the possibility of Blob ships as he left, because that risk existed anyway, and the payoff was huge. But this was just a nightmare.

Thinking back to his shooting, the goddamned Elf was right, Dagger decided. He normally moved right up until the shot was taken, then shifted. To make this kill would require getting closer, or much calmer, or both. At close range, the time of flight would be impossible for the Darhel to avoid. So first he'd try the calm. It would be fitting to use the Darhel's own smartass comments against him. He knew when a shot was good, so the trick was to restrain the satisfaction until after he hit. Then he could laugh his ass off.

The scope picked up a heat ripple that wasn't like the herbivores, behind them and a rill of dirt. Back to work. He slowly squeezed the stud and watched, still in trance like at a match, as the parabolic cone of the bullet's path arced toward the ripple.

As if reading his mind, because he was, the annoying little creep dropped before the bullet hit. Dust rose on the bank beyond him. Sighing, growling, holding back his anger, Dagger tried again. Good shot, and this time he closed his eyes. He'd give the round time to do its magic to avoid anticipation. But he'd known it was a good shot, and that was all it took, apparently, for the asshole to pick up a reading. He wasn't there when the round went past. It ripped through more grass, sending stems flying, but didn't touch the Darhel. Son of a bitch.

The little bastard was rapidly getting out of range, too. While the weapon was rated for fifteen thousand meters, one rarely saw an opponent over three kilometers. The Darhel had been within a klick of him there for a few moments, and he'd been so tied up in trying to get the shot that he hadn't pursued. Blast it. The little rat had got him so wound up he hadn't been thinking.

Dropping down from the tree, he headed off in pursuit, crouched low. He wasn't afraid to admit to himself that Ferret was a threat. He was still at an adequate range for bagging Tirdal, outside that of the punch gun, close enough to see by eye and maneuver. That might not be close enough, though. The shadows were getting long, and night fell quickly here. He'd have to stick closer.

He'd also, he realized, have to take a stim. He'd been running for nearly thirty-six hours now, and hadn't slept, had barely eaten, and hadn't even had that much to drink. Hopefully, that injured little troll wasn't any better off and would lag back soon. He wondered what supplies Ferret had? He knew he was last, and could rest in theory. He could stop for food certainly.

What game was Ferret playing anyway? Was he trying to score points by stopping Dagger? Or stopping Tirdal? He'd thought for a while the two were allies, which was laughable. He must have seen Tirdal with the artifact and made a logical but wrong conclusion. If he could steer him toward Tirdal first, that would take a lot of stress off Dagger. Smiling, he opened up the circuit. "Hey, Ferret," he called.

"There you are, Dagger. So, you missed Tirdal with seven shots. Too bad." Ferret was gleeful underneath. Time to put a stop to that.

Lying, and hating himself for it, Dagger said, "I hit seven times, Ferret. You know I always do. That's not why I'm calling."

"Right, so what's your point?" Ferret asked.

Smiling broadly, Dagger said, "You recall that Tirdal is a gunnery sergeant, and ranking being here. He gets to call the pod. It might be best if you were to concentrate your efforts on him first, then worry about me."

"So, he did screw you over, huh?"

"Of course he did, Ferret," Dagger said. The best way to deal with a story change was to make the lie big, and condescending. "Did you actually believe I'd ally with that Darhel freak? I'm insulted." As soon as he said, it, he realized he was insulted. Did Ferret actually think he'd ally with the dirty little Elf? Dammit, every time he had to deal with them, these assholes were a pain.

"Dagger, you'd pimp your mother for a buck. Everyone saw the hard-on you had for that box. Hell, we half expected you to fuck it right there."

"Didn't see that grenade coming, though, did you?" Dagger said, and laughed.

"No deal, Dagger," was Ferret's cold reply. "You die first. And thanks for letting me know you really are afraid, as well as a lousy shot in a crunch."

Silence.

Dagger squeezed his rifle in white-knuckled frustration. That was not how he'd wanted it to go. These two scumsuckers were tying him in knots. Remember, he thought, people who are talking are not shooting. So it was time for Dagger to stop talking.

He checked the tracer again. The Darhel was about two kilometers away. No risk from the punch gun. He dropped into the river's channel to get more water. It would have to be processed by his suit before he could drink it, but it made sense to fill up while he could. He swallowed the stim, washed it down with the warm, flat dregs from his suit's integral canteen, then stuck down a siphon tube to suck water into it for later. That done, he strode out, intending to close with the Darhel.

It was amazing how fast dusk fell with this planet's rotation. The shadows were long before he reached the woodline on the far side of the clearing. Tirdal was still ahead, a good two kilometers, and still moving at a swift pace.

Had he been in the Darhel's position, he would have stopped to set up an ambush. That the little crud didn't, but just kept running, was proof of his cowardice. If they kept heading north they'd hit that savanna, and then he'd either have to get in the open or head back toward Dagger, and Dagger would gap the little freak. He smiled again at that cheerful thought. It wouldn't be long now.

Once inside the woods, everything changed. It was dark. The sun behind him flickered like flames through the shifting growth, throwing thick shadows that grew thicker and more substantial as the light faded, until he was once again in pitch blackness. He kept the IR and enhanced screens up on his visor so he wouldn't have to see the stark nothingness. He now knew how Gorilla felt. He'd made fun of Gorilla's phobia for months before he'd given up. Now it struck home. His own fear was something he accepted and denied simultaneously, and that made it something he'd never actually dealt with.

A tree stepped in front of him, or seemed to. Another reached out its limbs and clutched at him. Hands of roots caught his feet, and he moved at a light run, once again turning every dozen steps to scan around. The trees were cavorting and laughing at him, snagging on his rifle barrel and leaning in toward him.

It had to be a side effect of fatigue and stims, he thought. He couldn't be afraid. There was nothing here to worry about.

As he thought that, batlike wings fluttered past his face.

He screamed.

Tirdal didn't hear the scream, but the sensors on his suit did and reported the anomaly as a possibly wounded "teammate." He grinned at the confirmation of his deduction. So Dagger was afraid at night. It was unfortunate he couldn't take the opportunity to just kill him, but the recent kill of the predator made him realize that killing a sentient would toss him into the abyss of lintatai. It was still necessary to be patient and seek the right circumstances for an encounter.

In the meantime, however, there was no reason not to stick a few pins in his opponent. "Oh, Dagger," he said into the communicator, "how are you doing?"

"F-fine, you little freak," was the reply.

"Interesting, Dagger, you sound relieved to hear my voice," he said, goading.

"Well, I'd rather hear your screams, of course," Dagger said, sounding as if he were trying to be brave. "And as long as you're on air, there's a chance of that."

"I see," Tirdal said. "It couldn't be that you're afraid of the dark?"

Dagger laughed and it sounded forced. "What would make you think that?"

Tirdal scanned back on his sensor log and played the amplified sound in question, with the bellowing noises of nearer animals cacophonous over it. "That's not your scream of panic, Dagger? Or was it a stubbed toe?"

"You filthy little motherf—" Dagger spewed a stream of profanity for over a minute.

When he slowed for breath, Tirdal said, "Dagger, that was neither creative nor clever, though I'm sure it was heartfelt. Also, most of those suggestions are impossible for humans, much less Darhel. They do tell me much about your personal tastes though. But since you have nothing to say that's productive, we should end this conversation. Unless you'd like my company in the dark?"

The profanity resumed, louder and even more hysterical. It appeared that Dagger very much wanted company in the dark, but would never say so.

"Very well, Dagger," Tirdal said after he wound down once again. "I'm closing this channel. And perhaps I should come and put you out of your misery now. Look for me in the shadows," he added in a lugubrious voice picked from a human "vampire" movie. He wouldn't attack, of course. But if Dagger thought so, it would be . . . amusing.

Tirdal brought his attention back to putting distance between them. Perhaps Dagger would curl up in a faint until daylight. Though despite his phobias and moral cowardice, the man was, in fact, brave in many ways, "bravery" being defined as continuing despite one's fears. If only he'd understood that, he would have turned out a much better human being. Instead, he had apparently spent his life trying to compensate. Such a waste of potential.

There was movement ahead, and he froze. He eased down into a squat and slipped over behind a tangle of bush. He hefted the punch gun, hoping he wouldn't have to use it. He summoned Jem, ready to lock the tal down if a kill were necessary. Cautiously, he let his Sense feel ahead.

His vision had a slightly greater frequency range than that of humans, so he didn't really need his night vision gear most of the time. He brought it up now, because whatever was there was just beyond the range of acuity. A glance let him relax. Browsers. The disturbance ahead was large herbivores in a clearing chittering faintly as they snipped off the local woody grass that was not unlike bamboo or felda. Still, he should avoid them.

Or should he? The herd was large and a detour might bring him to predators stalking them. They hadn't shown any real interest in the team as they'd crossed the veldt, he remembered from the insertion four days ago. Was it only four days? So he might as well go through, cautiously, and trust their noise and form to give Dagger even more fits.

Drawing his Sense in to only a few tens of meters, he stood and walked slowly, weapon raised so as to create a distraction if need be, and approached the creatures.

The crashing, crunching sounds of stalks being pruned and chewed were rather impressive, he thought. These creatures were easily the size of large horses or even buffalo on Earth. No animal from growth-poor Darhel could compare. They towered over him, noting his passage with brief waves and twitches of antennae, but took no further notice. He was not food, nor predator, and so didn't enter into their world. He kept his distance just the same, lest he spook them. They actually had improved his progress by shearing the ground smooth in this area, and he was through rather quickly.

He reentered the woods proper and it became thick, dark and oppressive once again. Humidity was greater, condensing into a fog in the dropping temperatures, and seemed to close in around him. His pace slowed and he had to meander and detour often. The terrain had changed, and this appeared to be what he'd heard called "second growth." It was tangled and dense, with quick-growing soft trees, weeds and vines knotted through them and wrapping around the taller trees dispersed through the mess. He thought about hacking his way, discarded the idea because of the obvious signs it would leave, and settled for crawling under and through, pacing around and occasionally scrambling over. There were thorny plants here, too, and some took vengeance for his intrusion in the form of cuts and scratches. He sighed. Those would be beacons to Ferret's sensors, but the alternative was to take a long detour. Ferret needn't worry about leaving traces, Dagger and Tirdal must. It was still a stalemate that had to be broken.

Taking a device from his gear, he planted it at the base of a fern analog. It might not be needed, but he wasn't going to use it anywhere else, and if all else failed it was a little mass removed from his gear. He'd been lucky to have it, but now it was time to get rid of it. He programmed the mechanism, hoisted the box back to his shoulder and kept walking.

He was only about a kilometer past the herd, he estimated, when Dagger screamed again. This time, he could hear it over the background white noise of the forest.

"Ah, Dagger, I see you've found the herd," he said.

Ferret heard the screams, too. At first, he'd thought perhaps Tirdal had scored. There had been no weapons fire, though. So, yes, Dagger was a city boy who couldn't handle the deep dark. And he was following Tirdal again. Excellent. He wouldn't say anything yet, but he'd save it for the right moment. He'd also have to keep a good eye out for whatever critter had scared Dagger.

That also told him that Dagger was using a tracer. He'd gone off the track, and been able to spot Tirdal well enough to shoot at him, assuming that had been what he did in the meadow. He'd climbed a tree to shoot, so assume Tirdal had been the target. Had he climbed a tree? Ferret hadn't seen it, but deduced it. He could be wrong. Fatigue was screwing with his mind. But hell, he had to have some basis for his conclusions, so yes, Dagger had climbed a tree to shoot and missed. Hornet rounds at a target out of direct sight?

But he had peeled off and then come back to resume the stalk. So there was a tracer and it had to be on the box. Likely Shiva or Bell Toll had put it on there as a paranoid measure. More likely Bell Toll. So if Ferret bagged Tirdal, he could use the box as bait. If he nailed Dagger, he could track the Darhel, and use a weapon with greater range to get Tirdal. All useful.

The bad news was that he was lagging behind. Pain and drugs, hunger and fatigue were taking a terrible toll on him. He'd have to hope for something to break the stalemate, or for one of the others to buy it and make it a simple fight. That might be too much to hope for.

Under the other distractions, Ferret kept wondering if gangrene or other rot was setting in. The nausea was getting worse. True, he'd experienced that before, sometimes to the point of gagging on his tongue as sleep and awake fought for control, but this felt different. He hoped it was environmental, with the odd gravity and light. He feared it was his own fate catching up.

Still, if the worst he could do was be a distraction until one or the other of those bloodsuckers killed the other, that would be a start. After that, he'd just have to see. Maybe he could get close enough for a crippling shot. If they all starved to death here, or got chewed by cockroaches, it would be hard on Ferret, but good for the human race.

He realized he wasn't bothered by that outcome, and that realization scared him. It was ironic. He was more disturbed by his mindset change than by his impending death.

Taking another deep breath to relieve some of the pain in his chest, he pushed forward. The dark was his friend. Dagger was meat if he had anything to say about it.

❖   ❖   ❖

"I suppose you think that was funny, Darhel?" Dagger rasped. His voice had a bite to it that indicated he was on the ragged edge of self control. He didn't notice that himself. What he did notice was the indicators of something entering that thicket over there, and Darhel bloodstains. The cocky little bastard had now screwed up, and Dagger would kill him. Slowly, too.

"Funny, Dagger?" came the reply. "No, I thought the bare ground would make you feel more comfortable than all those spooky trees, so I led you to it. Why, did the herd of harmless grazers scare you?"

Dagger shut off his transmitter, checked it to be sure, then growled quietly, teeth clenched until his jaw turned white. He had to kill something, and he had to kill something right now. There! It was a foot-sized beetle, climbing up a tree a couple of meters away. He strode over, raised his rifle, and smashed the fucking thing flat with the butt. Goo squirted out the edges, and he smashed it again. The legs thrashed and wiggled as he smashed and smashed.

He was panting for breath, sheened with sweat and could feel his heart hammering in his chest and his pulse in his ears. But he was calm enough now to pay attention again. He looked around, partly in fear, though he denied it, and partly for intel, which he focused on.

There was a faint heat trail left here. The little fuck couldn't be more than a klick ahead, maybe less. Forgetting his fear, forgetting stalking discipline, Dagger rushed forward. His phobia was still there, however, and it was causing him to be overeager. Closeness to the Darhel was companionship to the unconscious part of his mind. It meant he'd be safe.

He followed the blood and genetic trail, and could easily see the signs of passage. The Darhel not only had no idea how to sneak through the woods, he'd often picked some of the thickest crud to crawl through.

It should have made Dagger happy, but it didn't. This incompetent little Elf was traipsing along like a child, and had been able to avoid Dagger for two days. It was pure luck, and it was insulting. He wasn't going to allow the bastard to think he was better than Dagger. He was going to catch him and hurt him.

In fact, he was going to leave him here, crippled, to starve to death or be eaten by bugs. To hell with killing him. He'd do the Darhel the favor. Since it couldn't kill him, he wouldn't kill it. And he'd do the same for Ferret, too. One human to another. A smile crossed his face as he emerged from a tangle of vines and found clear forest floor.

He'd taken only three steps when his suit's systems shrieked a warning in his ears.

He reacted from training and fear, and dropped flat. He just made it, but as he dove, he felt a vicious sting in his right calf. What the hell? He scrabbled for his pistol, never releasing his grip on his rifle, while spinning around on his back, his good leg propelling him. Wide-eyed in hysteria, pulse and respiration hammering at him, he sought the Darhel.

Nothing. Nothing here. But there was a smell of steaming wood and a report scrolling across his screen in symbols. It had been a directional projectile mine, and it had to have been set by the Darhel. It was low on the base of that tree, and its flechette actually might have hit hard enough to cripple him if he hadn't been so fast.

Goddamn that Darhel! The little bastard should be dead! Dragging himself to a sitting position, he slapped a nano-bandage on the wound. It was only superficial, and if he'd got the patch on quickly enough, he should avoid most of the tautness that went with it.

But it did prove that he was close, and that the Darhel, coward that he was, couldn't kill him directly. He got his hyperventilation under control. He had enough oxygen; he didn't need to breathe for a few seconds. Only when he felt the breathing reflex resume its normal demands did he speak. "Hey, Darhel," he said. "You missed."

"How unfortunate, Dagger," came the response. "I shall endeavor to learn from my mistakes."

"You aren't going to live to make any more, pal," Dagger assured him. He felt confident again, and it had nothing to do with the rising gray of dawn.

"Well, thank you, Dagger, but with as long a life as Darhel can expect, some errors are inevitable. While superior beings, we are not perfect."

It was obviously a deliberate misunderstanding and a goad. He didn't want to listen to any more of that, so he shut off the communicator.

Ferret heard the crack of the flechette mine, and smiled. It was a distinctive sound, and it meant Dagger and Tirdal were mixing it up. Delightful. His nerves reached out for anything dangerous as he closed on the area. His infrared and Dagger's would see each other at about the same range, but he was following. He also sealed his suit for the time being, no matter if he cooked like a pot of bubbling spaghetti sauce. He needed every advantage he could get for right now, no matter the cost. If he could get close enough for just a glimpse of Dagger, he'd try to stir him into a firefight in predawn dark.

It wasn't long, though in the sweltering thickness of his closed suit it seemed like hours, before he came across the area where the mine had been emplaced. There was molecular residue and there were pheromones, and his tracker updated its records. Both Dagger and Tirdal had passed this way, and not too long ago. Dagger had thrashed around, but didn't appear seriously injured, but there was residue that might indicate a surface wound. Tirdal, however, definitely was wounded. Blood was sufficiently present to register.

Now might be time to talk to both of them. Ferret opened a broadcast channel and said, "So, guys, what now? Dagger's scared beyond reason, and Tirdal is bleeding. It looks like I've got all the advantages here." He kept his voice cheerful, under tight control, so as not to betray the pain he was feeling. He hoped he wasn't letting out any hints that the sensat could pick up. So far, though, he seemed to have been safe. Tirdal really did need to be close to resolve details.

Tirdal replied first, "Well, Dagger, it appears you are fighting this alone. In fact, we all are. Two against whichever one makes the first critical mistake."

Dagger replied, and quickly, "That will be you, Darhel. You're the one bleeding."

"You pin all your hopes on a minor wound," Tirdal said, "and ignore the psychological issues. No, I think Ferret and I are in much better shape in the ways that matter."

Ferret cut in, not wanting to be left out of this. He was not the plucky comic relief. "I may be the only one uninjured," he put in. "Dagger appears to have taken some damage himself. I think your mine nailed him."

"Scratched myself on a stick," Dagger insisted at once. "Not that it matters. I can kill both of you with one hand taped."

Ferret said, "I'll take that bet, Dagger. Will you do it now?"

For the moment, Dagger was silent.

Tirdal said, "Dagger, the fact that you've had to lie about allies who appear not to support you indicates your position is precarious in your own mind. That weakness of spirit will be your undoing, regardless of any physical threats."

"Tell me, Tirdal," Dagger replied now, "what is the sound of one Darhel dying? Why are we having this stupid chat? Everyone comfy now? Can we stop talking and start killing? I know I can, you two seem to be reluctant." There was a ragged edge to his voice.

"Trying to find a way to shut down the communications, Dagger?" Tirdal asked with a lilt in his voice. "You must remember that only the senior troop can do that. I think this exchange is useful, and would like it to continue."

"I'm dropping out again," Ferret said. "I've got work to do. But if you kill him, Tirdal, and bury the artifact where I can find it, I promise I won't kill you."

"I'm sorry, Ferret, but I can't make a deal like that."

"That's because you're too cowardly to kill," Dagger snarled.

"I figured that, Tirdal. Pity I can't let you live to enjoy that billion. Later, assholes."

He closed his channel for now. That had been instructive. He and Dagger were both argumentative and childish, likely due to fatigue, and the damned Darhel sounded fresh as a daisy. But Tirdal knew Dagger didn't have Ferret as an ally. Dagger knew Ferret was in the loop. And Ferret knew they were both sellouts he'd have to kill.

Sighing, he checked his rate of movement and stumped along faster, feeling a new pounding in his calves.

Chapter 15

THE COMING DAYLIGHT was a necessary salve to Dagger's sanity, but it wasn't enough. Between fatigue and poor rations, he was lagging badly. Now he was wounded, too. He knew he had to catch Tirdal today, end this today, or he wasn't going to be in shape to do it ever. Then there was Ferret. The little twerp was one hell of a tracker, and tough as nails to still be following. He wasn't even in it for the money. The asshole was doing this from duty, and seemed to think it would matter.

He reached for his canteen straw and sucked at it, but got nothing. He'd been sweating all night and had sucked it dry. He was going to have to take a break and get some real food, as well as more water. The weather wasn't excessively warm at the moment, but he was exerting himself a lot. Hell, he had to be exhaling a quart of water a day, never mind what he was pissing away. If he'd had any idea there'd be a real fight after the grenade, he would have made sure he had some rations with him. He'd dropped his ruck because he hadn't figured to need anything for those few seconds. He was lucky to have the rifle; he hadn't needed it, but just never put it down if he could help it. The wisdom of that habit was obvious now. He could kick himself for not thinking of food when he grabbed supplies. But who would have thought it? He vaguely remembered a week in training regarding logistics and support tail. He'd slept through most of it, eager only for the afternoon's shooting and running.

It was ironic, he thought, the position he was in. The reason he always harassed people about their food choices was because he really wasn't as hardcore as he pretended. He hated raw meat, and he hated bugs, worms and larvae. Now, he was in a position where he had to either eat them or die. He'd trained for it, hated every minute of it, took vengeance upon the world by harassing all others about it, and now had to do it himself. It served to wake him slightly, the rage did. The universe seemed to take delight in fucking him over his discovery of the box. But he'd get out of this, and it would just make the memory that much sweeter.

Somewhere here there had to be some of those flyers or small mammals. He needed food, but would have to be a hell of a lot hungrier to eat raw bug. So mammal it was. Something with its bones on the inside. He kept an eye on the terrain for any area that might contain them, and tried not to think of all the bugs he saw. He was connecting them with food, and that brought back bad memories of that week of training.

Shortly thereafter, he found a depression with scattered puddles. There were lizards there, and he decided that lizard was close enough, being at least a chordate. All he had to do now was get one.

He could have snuck in and snagged one, but that took time. Consciously, he was confident of his ability to stalk, and repressed any thoughts that he might not be. Intellectually, the faster he ate the better. Somewhere below that, he desired to shoot something. That would make him feel better, get out some aggression, and was less involved than trying to grapple a reptile. Shooting was natural for him, and the rail pistol was near silent. If he adjusted the velocity down below sonic speed, there wouldn't even be a crack from the round. Ten seconds with the controls, five seconds to aim, breathe and pop! he had a lizard. Two more pops gave him two more, as they looked small. The rest scattered, but he'd gotten three in less than three seconds.

He moved up and grabbed the corpses, headless or nearly so from the hydrostatic shock of small beads. He whipped out his knife as he did so. He chopped off the remains of the heads and the feet and laid them on a log. With quick strokes he slit and gutted them, sectioned them into legs and torsos, and grabbed the first hind leg.

He hesitated just long enough to get his brain in control and shut off his senses. Then he bit into the warm, rubbery flesh and tore it loose from the bone. It was slimy and stringy in his mouth, and he choked it down, coughing and trying not to vomit. Perhaps if he'd shot them yesterday, he could have had them dried and chewy by now, instead of as something resembling raw squid. He bit again, almost regurgitated the first bite along with it, and chewed, avoiding touching it with his tongue until enough saliva built up and allowed him to force it back and down.

Grimacing, he stuffed the rest into a pocket, wiped his hands free of sticky lizard blood on his suit, and stood up. He'd need water so he could wash this stuff down in small bites like medicine. He just couldn't make himself actually chew the stuff. And the taste would linger until he got to some water.

Tirdal had lied, if he'd actually eaten the damned things at all. They tasted nothing like chicken.

Tirdal, for his part, had his own demons to wrestle with. The cat and mouse game, just as it would cause multiple adrenaline reactions with humans, was causing his system to flood with tal hormone. This was dangerous, but to get the absolute most out of his system he had to use it. He had to release the demon and risk the overload, risk the zombie state of lintatai, if he was going to win against the sniper. He'd stretched out his Sense yesterday and been able to see what Dagger was doing. Only by maintaining that state could he gain enough intelligence to outthink and outmaneuver Dagger.

Then there was his need for more food. While Dagger could last quite some time on converted weeds, and likely could shoot an animal and eat it with little worry, he thought, Tirdal had to struggle with each creature in his psyche, but had to, had to, eat several each day. Worse, he was approaching his own fatigue limit, this being forty-seven hours into the chase. Food would keep him going, though he could already feel the stress and damage to his muscles caused by the drain his metabolism placed on his body mass. He was alert for more food now, seeking creatures with the least intellect. If they were self-aware, he could find himself over the canyon of lintatai again.

He found two large roach type creatures and was able to pry them apart and feast on the succulent white meat without extreme discomfort while walking. The terrain was becoming easier, which was good in that he would leave fewer signs for Dagger and could move faster, but bad in that he deduced the savanna was ahead again. He would be forced to enter the broad plain, and Dagger's shooting range and visibility would both improve dramatically. Still, Dagger had to be feeling severe fatigue. Another day would likely destroy his effectiveness, and Tirdal had been trained in patience.

He found it ironic that he was trying to outwait a human professional in the art. Still, the end result would be instructive, assuming, of course, that he survived to report back. It would be instructive only to him if he failed.

The terrain was very open now, the trees sparsely spread and the undergrowth thickening into scrub again, here where the sunlight was greater. It changed to thick grass on the continental plain ahead. Tirdal dropped to a crawl and slipped under what growth he could, seeking some kind of cover to use ahead. It was very awkward to crawl on the points of his elbows while clutching the box behind his head.

There was a wash from a stream, perhaps the same one he used as before. It was narrower and shallower than the one in the woods south of here, which would make sense, the terrain here being a broad plateau above the rich forest beneath it and the ancient hills. No matter. The cut would provide cover, possible food, water, cooling to refresh him, help mask his IR signature and other lifeforms to create confusion. It would safely take him some distance.

Ferret decided to have another whack at Tirdal. If he could get him to team up, they might outflank Dagger, the real threat; then they could discuss the box. It might be they'd have to kill each other over it, but they could try, dammit.

"Tirdal," he said, "we need to deal with Dagger."

"Of course we do, Ferret," Tirdal replied. Ferret was sighing in relief as he continued, "And Dagger and I need to deal with you, and the two of you with me." Ferret gritted his teeth in frustration, but Tirdal was still talking. "An ironic situation, to say the least. Dagger's motives are obvious: money. Yours appear to be driven by loyalty, but of course we can't believe that. Mine are driven by a similar loyalty, complicated by other issues. You know you can't trust Dagger and believe you can't trust me. I know I can't trust Dagger and know I can't trust you under the circumstances, though if I could explain things, you would agree, I hope. Dagger knows we'll both kill him, given the chance. Darhel don't really have irony, but I begin to understand it. A perverse concept."

"So we agree on Dagger," Ferret said. "We take care of him, then we can talk. You followed me the entire mission; you must know what I'm like."

"It would be a tempting offer, Ferret," Tirdal replied, "except that I have no way of knowing whether or not you're offering the same deal to Dagger. The artifact is the catalyst for all this trouble."

"Hide the damned box, Tirdal!" Ferret snapped, almost pleading. He really didn't want to fight both of them. He really didn't want to kill Tirdal. Tirdal had seemed like a decent enough guy. Alien. Whatever. He really didn't want either of them to kill him, or for fate to catch up with his wounds. "I don't need it! I just need to know that you don't have it, and certainly that Dagger doesn't. If you can't get it off the planet first, we're safe to hunt Dagger. Then we can go together—you tell me where the box is, I take it, you control the pod. Balance of power."

"It would be a reasonable suggestion under most circumstances, Ferret, but at present I can't do that. I have to maintain control of this artifact. I realize that creates distrust on your part. I can't help that."

Ferret, frustrated by talk, said, "Tirdal, I'm on your side, dammit."

"That's probably true, Ferret," Tirdal said, "but we both know I can't afford to believe that."

"Dammit!" Ferret said, frustration in his voice. "Can't you read my mind?"

"I can't answer that question, Ferret, though the answer should be obvious." Ferret likely was telling the truth. The whole scenario wasn't organized enough to be a conspiracy. Ferret did seem to have pure motives. Of course, those were human motives, not Darhel. And as harsh as it was, there was no reason for Tirdal to team up with a crippled human, and every reason to split Dagger's attention. It was doubtful that humans appreciated that logic.

"Okay, Tirdal, can you tell me where Dagger is? And I'll go take a few shots at him."

"I suppose there's no harm in telling you that, Ferret. Though shooting at him wouldn't be sufficient proof. If you are able to wound him or kill him, it will show you have a greater interest in either the artifact or your own life than in Dagger's existence. You see the problem we face." If he could get Ferret to do that, it would improve Tirdal's odds. If he could get Ferret to panic, he might be able to confirm his mindset, as he had with Dagger. But it would take a strong emotion.

"However, Dagger is behind me in terrain that is opening up. I can't be more specific than that. As to his grid coordinates, stand by." He considered carefully how to not give his position away. He really didn't have Dagger localized that well, but if Ferret headed that way, it was less trouble for him. Ferret might also try the same stunt with Dagger. Either way, it made sense to share intelligence about the common enemy. Irony was truly a fascinating concept. "Based on the pod's position as we deployed as zero meridian, here's Dagger's grid," he said, and read off the numbers. "That should place him within five hundred meters. I'd bet on it being less than half that, but I can't guarantee it."

"Got it, Tirdal," Ferret said. Wow. That was only about a kilometer ahead. They were moving as slowly as he was. Of course, three days of fatigue, wounds and the device were burdening them all. "I'll try to bag him. Then you'll join me after that?" he asked. His voice was rising.

"I can't do that, sorry," Tirdal replied, voice still even, very even.

"Dammit, Tirdal, I'm on your side! Please!" Ferret said, growing panicky.

"I don't know human voices well enough to ascertain their qualities. You're distressed, that's all. It's an honest emotion, but not specific enough. You could be being threatened by Dagger, or you could just be in pain."

Ferret sounded sad, hurt, when he replied, "Then fuck you, you alien turd."

Tirdal was still having trouble with the concept of human stress. They could almost appear to change sides on a whim, especially when angry. Yet usually, there was one side they stuck to. Though they did act on the cusp of the moment sometimes, often unpredictably and illogically. They might go outside the available choices and do something utterly irrelevant.

What would Ferret and Dagger reasonably do? What might they do that wasn't reasonable? Speculation was necessary, even if likely to be wrong.

Dagger saw the trees tapering to scrub and knew the grassland was ahead. Now would be a good time to detour off to the east and seek high ground. If he could get up on the bluffs he saw, he would be in a good position to parallel Tirdal and get off good shots. He was aching, wiped out and suffering from thirst and hunger, but this would be over soon and he could rest and even cook some meat. He had to admit the little twerp had put up one hell of a struggle. Not bad for a soft, urban wimp.

Drawing a ragged breath through his parched throat, he shrugged deeper into the straps of his ruck and resumed walking. His step was lighter, though. The end was in sight.

The slope up toward the bluff was steeper than it looked, which, come to think of it, was a good sign. More height meant a better field of view, meant easier shooting. He leaned far into the pace, and rested by putting his gloved hands down and pulling himself along by tufts of grass and rocks. The stems came up to his head when he did that, and mothlike insectoids fluttered up in his face. He caught one as he inhaled, which got crushed between his lips. He spat dry fluff and insect wings, grimacing in distaste. Dammit. He needed water.

Well, there wasn't any water, and wouldn't be until he headed down. So it would be best to stop bitching and get the job done. He could and did drag out a freeze-dried package of fruit he'd hoarded from the rat packs. It was fibrous and tough, but melted slowly in his mouth with what little saliva he had, providing some refreshment and much needed sugar. The physical and psychological boost helped him increase his pace slightly.

The terrain was leveling out and he was on a long fingerlike rill that headed into the forested foothills. Really, this was the long way around back to the Blob site, and he was amazed that the Darhel was doing that.

Was it possible the Darhel were in league with the Blobs? Dagger considered that, brain working furiously. It just might be. Tirdal didn't seem worried about the Blobs; he did seem afraid of Dagger, despite his banter. It would explain much. When he got back, he'd have to report that.

Report what, Dagger? We're not going back. Oh, long enough to write a report, so I suppose we can mention it, but really, who gives a damn? Kali was waiting, and Earth, the Alliance and the Republic could go die.

But as to right now, if Tirdal San Whatever was working with the Blobs and could reach them with his mind, Dagger was screwed. But there was nothing he could do about it, so he would just keep going. And really, Tirdal had had two days to do something and hadn't. It was worth reporting as additional cover to confuse the trail—it might even create conspiracy theories as to Dagger's "disappearance" if he said it in a few bars. Good idea. But there was no threat here.

Correction: there was one threat. He was the threat to Tirdal. Ferret was a non-starter. It was a shame he couldn't cut the little guy in on a deal, at least to start with.

Just then, Ferret called.

Ferret was now in a quandary. He was close to Dagger. He didn't want to get too close. Enough into punch gun range to line up a good shot and nail the asshole was all it would take. And a wound would be as good as a kill. As long as the man was incapacitated, he could be dealt with. It would be easier to close at dark, apart from IR signature. It would be easier to close in daylight with good visibility, apart from the equal visibility he'd show. It would be best to do it soon, before pain and fatigue knocked him over. He'd staggered several times recently, and thought he'd had a momentary blackout as he walked. It might have been just the hypnotic effect of pain, but either way, it was time to end this. He didn't have the strength to go another day, he was sure.

Perhaps he should use that pain for effect now? Appear helpless to Dagger so as to be underestimated, or to present himself as bait. Yeah, what the hell. Enough running through the woods, it was time to bring it to a head. Part of him didn't care anymore.

"Look, Dagger," he said, "I don't care if you keep the bloody artifact. I don't care if the little alien turd dies. I just want off this rock. Can't we work out a deal?" It was a sellout, maybe. Worst case, he'd try to talk Dagger into giving him a ride somewhere before he took off. Best case, Dagger might make a mistake and Ferret would kill him. The problem in that was that if he were sole survivor, he'd have to have a very good story to back up his case.

But Ferret didn't want to die. He realized that of a sudden. He had to clamp down tight to avoid getting a stutter, because he felt, knew at that moment that he was going to die before he could get to the pod. Part of him might not care, but another part did. Death from stranding, or gangrene, or by Dagger was scarier, more absolutely gut-puckering than death from the Blobs or feral Posties.

"That might be possible, Ferret, but you'd have to prove your bona fides. So, you kill Tirdal and you have a deal." Dagger replied.

Ferret didn't need to be a sensat to know that Dagger had no intention of following through on that bargain, but was just fishing for help. The man was transparent scum. Worse, he didn't seem to care.

"Then you help me find him. I don't have most of my gear," Ferret lied.

"Oh, Tirdal won't be hard to find." Dagger could almost be seen to smirk through the voice-only transmission. "He's just out on the savanna, west of the ridge I'm standing on."

Ferret paused a moment before he replied. Had Dagger known he'd let out that bit of information? He just placed himself relative to Tirdal and the landscape. Ferret couldn't think of a deliberate reason he'd do that. He must have just let it slip out. The next question was, had he realized his possibly lethal error? Or was it a gaffe he was still unaware of? Either way, Ferret had a momentary advantage and was going to push it.

In his mind, however, he was triumphantly shouting, So that's where you are, you fucking scumbag. Between the grid and that admission, Ferret had him pinned. He was on that rise ahead and to the east. It was a block perhaps two hundred meters square and longer north-south than east-west.

Controlling his voice, Ferret said, "Okay, Dagger, I'll track the freak down and nail him if I can. Worst case, I'll spot him for you. I'll get the box, and you come and talk things over. Deal?"

"Sure, Ferret," Dagger replied. He had an easy, smug tone that didn't betray failure. Was he really unaware that he'd given his location away? "We can always talk things over."

"So let's do it," Ferret said. "I'll head west and pin

him and call you back when I'm ready. Whichever way he runs, we'll have cross fire."

"Looking forward to it, Ferret," Dagger agreed.

Ferret called Tirdal at once. "Tirdal, Dagger is on that ridge. He's trying to line up for a shot on you."

"Of course he is, Ferret. This is hardly news," Tirdal replied. He didn't sound surprised.

Well, no, he wouldn't be. It was, after all, entirely reasonable.

"Yes, Tirdal," Ferret said, "but he's waiting for me to bag you. He thinks I'll do it."

"I also think you might, given the circumstances. Even if you were not disposed to previously, you have nothing to lose by killing me and blaming me, and the two of you sharing any income. Or just bargaining with him for your life. Though I think you would be foolish to trust anything he says."

"I don't trust the murdering scum, Tirdal. I do trust you," Ferret said.

"That would be a useful turn of events," Tirdal agreed, not really sounding enthusiastic even by the standards of a Darhel. "However, there's no effective way to prove it."

"So let me tell you this, Tirdal," Ferret said. It was part treaty offer, part desperation, and part professional need. "I'm wounded. I need medical attention."

"You really have my sympathies, Ferret, but I can't possibly get that close to you."

"Tirdal," Ferret replied, "you tell me what I should do. You're the medic."

"That's fair enough, Ferret," Tirdal agreed. At last. Something. "Describe the nature of your wounds."

Ferret said, "I took some of the neural grenade. Both

feet and lower part of the left leg. I've got partial feeling in my right ankle, and the rest is a combination of numb and fucking painful. I can walk with difficulty. I took painkillers, a stabilizer, and a minor wound med."

"If that's true, Ferret," Tirdal replied, "I'm surprised you can walk at all."

"Much better than Dagger thinks I can, though it hurts like hell. Not as well as I need to."

"Describe the pain, in detail," Tirdal asked.

Taking a breath before thinking about the agony, Ferret said, "It was a massive jolt through my body, like an electric shock. Then it was just excruciating in my legs. After some rest and the painkillers, it's just my feet and ankles, and the right one has partial feeling. The feet have no sensation, but when I move them, stabbing pains shoot up to my knees. A bunch of secondary effects like nausea I'm not worried about. But I expect gangrene after a while."

"Gangrene is unlikely, as long as you maintain circulation," Tirdal said. His voice was the same, but he sounded a tiny bit friendlier, or at least not actively hostile. Amazing what being a cripple did for people's mindset. "To that end, walking is helping you. As no central nervous tissue has been damaged, you should, eventually, make a full recovery. It will take months without therapy, hours or days with proper meds."

"Really, Tirdal? It's not permanent?" Ferret was elated. He might actually live through this? He forced calm and caution back upon himself. He still had a battle to fight. And he was coming out of the woods, so he'd have to crawl.

"It shouldn't be," Tirdal said. "Humans have recovered from neural lash before."

"All right, Tirdal, then I need to get medication. Do you have that?" Crawling was easier than walking, if slower. But he had both of the others located within a few hundred meters. As long as he was alert, he should be fine. And if meds were available . . .

Tirdal's response was slow. "Ferret, it's an external effect for nerve inductance and is often described as 'excruciating.' My general module can mimic the effect well enough, though it's both extremely painful and easy to find with good scanners. Dagger would likely locate me. Also, you need a nanite to rebuild the tissue. I have that, too. But, Ferret, we can't get that close."

Panicking for real, now, Ferret replied, "Dammit, Tirdal, I've got to have help! Can't you leave the equipment somewhere and let me find it?" He'd been whipsawed by pending doom and survival for three days now. He was about at his limit.

Again, a pause. "That might be possible. They are not of use to me, as they are human specific. Your best bet would have been to acquire Shiva's gear before you left the bivouac."

Tirdal felt the pain under Ferret's last reply. And at that moment, human anguish matched with human pain through Ferret just to that edge where Tirdal could feel him, Sense him.

Ferret was telling the truth.

Of course, Ferret was still crippled. "Ferret," he said, "I am forced by circumstances to believe you are what you say. I can Sense you. I will meet you. I would, however, prefer that you disarm. I will also need to ask other things of you."

"Disarm?" came the panicked reply. "I can't do that!"

"You need not dispose of your weapons," Tirdal said. "You must simply not have them at hand when I meet you. In sight, nearby will suffice. Once you are treated, we can discuss strategy."

"And what about you? Do you disarm?"

Tirdal had known he would ask that, and replied, "I have the medical care you need, and the billion credit artifact. My bargaining position is much stronger. You understand that I am risking much, we both are, by doing this."

"Right," Ferret replied. "I guess I knew that."

"So tell me where you are, Ferret. I may have to have you move some distance to a safer location."

"Yes, I know, Tirdal," Ferret replied. And again, Tirdal could feel his honesty. Revealing his location was a very personal, frightening act under the circumstances. It was intimate, in its own way, and Ferret's psyche couldn't cover that. The flash came to Tirdal for a second only, but it was enough. Ferret was what he said. "I'm at the edge of the forest, likely south of you about fourteen hundred meters."

Tirdal considered. He really couldn't go back, or he'd be exposing himself to Dagger over very flat ground. He had marginal terrain here for cover, but it was better than nothing. If he was able to treat Ferret, who had made it this far with a crippling wound, they'd have the tactical advantage. However, Ferret would ask questions, and Tirdal would have to have answers. He couldn't come up with a convincing lie, and didn't dare tell the truth.

Also, treating Ferret would take time, and there

was no way Dagger was going to leave them alone to do that. Really, the philosophy of life was the true path. The wounded and weak must be allowed to die that the breed could improve. There was certainly no time here to change it.

Of course, humans didn't think that way for themselves, and didn't even grasp it as an alien concept. Nor was it something he wanted to broach with Ferret at this point. It might serve later, if he needed a panic as a distraction.

"That's really not a good place at the moment, Ferret," he said. "Exposure is high. Can you travel more?"

"I can move," Ferret replied, sounding unsure. "But I can't go forever."

"You shouldn't need to," Tirdal said. "If you can last until dark, we can meet and get you treated. All three of us need rest, and Dagger is less likely to try approaching both of us at night. Also, we can take things in shifts, provided we can come to an agreement." Tirdal didn't need rest that badly; he was just now reaching the level of fatigue that created disorientation. How the two humans were managing was a mystery. They were truly amazing creatures, to be studied further. He realized, however, that making them think he needed rest was good disinformation. Ferret was likely to let some minor amount slip to Dagger, which would keep Dagger off guard. Also, he could use Ferret as bait that way, and perhaps get the sniper between them. This endless draw had to be ended.

Ferret's reply was full of regret and resignation. "Yes, Tirdal. I can last until dark."

"Then let us keep each other informed and meet then," Tirdal said.

"Right."

Dagger was glad to have heard from Ferret. It meant he was failing and couldn't go much longer. In truth, Dagger was amazed he'd done as well as he had. But now it was time for the real expert to end this. He'd casually let slip his own location, hoping Ferret would try to approach him in an eager bid to get a shot. There was no chance of that; he had theoretically a fifteen thousand meter effective range. Ferret's was line of sight, but the beam of a punch gun decayed rapidly from internal effects of the photons and atmosphere. Besides, he could see the tree line from here, clearly through his scope. If Ferret moved, he'd nail him.

And speaking of which, he was reaching a good place to start spotting and shooting from. He moved to a kneeling position, automatically mindful of concealment. He'd been doing it so long it was instinct. Even from that height, though, he could see the panoramic spread of the plains with late afternoon sun to light everything. The grasses were waving in ripples of yellow and pale green, occasional blues and tans of other vegetation visible in patches. There were dots of herds shuffling across in various directions. The wind was generally toward him from the southwest, which likely didn't matter here but was never a bad thing.

Now to find his target. That was how he always thought of his enemies: targets. He recalled once giving a lecture to a class who were on a field trip to the base. The teacher had been a cute little thing, but wouldn't give him the time of day. Since he couldn't get in her pants, he'd decided to freak her out. One of the students had asked the age-old question, "How can you shoot someone?"

He'd given half his gaze to the student, half to the teacher, and replied, "You just superimpose a target over their forehead and shoot the target." Her expression had been precious.

And Tirdal was about to get a target superimposed on him. As soon as Dagger relocated the little freak.

Dagger raised his scope and its panoply of sensors and got to work, sitting cross-legged in the grass. He kept an eye out for intrusions or threats, because there were a couple of superbeetles wandering around in the middle distance. It wouldn't do to have one of them attack or even just spook him. Ferret would recognize a spook if he saw one, and close in on him. Tirdal might not, but even so, it didn't fit Dagger's image of his own competence.

The box was over there. He squinted down to take a cursory look, then raised the rifle slowly until the scope covered that same area. It was a sandy riverbank, and apparently Tirdal was keeping below the crest of it. There was movement, lots of movement of animals burrowing through the tall grass. No particular one stood out. Tirdal was there somewhere, but Dagger wasn't able to tell for sure. Still, sooner or later he'd show himself. Dagger lowered the scope, and grabbed cords from a front pocket of his harness. The first plugged the tracer into his helmet display. That would make it easier to follow. The second plugged into the scope, so he could snag a quick look at magnification or in various spectra to zero in. He'd raise the rifle to proper position to shoot, of course, but in the meantime the scope would serve extra duty.

Now it was time to wait. It was warm though not hot, but between exercise and sunlight, Dagger was sweating. At least he was still sweating. If the sweats stopped, it meant heat exhaustion, followed shortly by death. There was no one here to treat him.

Ferret noticed movement out of the corner of his eye and turned his head. "Shit, Tirdal, you've got a flock of giant bats moving in."

There was a moments' pause before Tirdal replied, "I see them. They are not overhead yet, though."

"I think they will be soon. What happened on the way in? Do you remember what the captain said about them?" There were six of the things, circling in the sun and moving across the savanna. They obviously saw something they liked. Ferret realized he was actually afraid it might be Tirdal. Of course, the same things might come after him shortly.

"I missed that discussion also, Ferret. I think it was between the captain and Gorilla," Tirdal said. "But there's nothing I can do about them at this point."

"Tirdal!" he said urgently. "They're not only carnivorous, but if Dagger figures out they've spotted you, you're toast."

"I realize that," was the calm reply. "However, there is nothing I can do at this point," he repeated. "I am open to suggestions."

Ferret thought it was rather obvious. "Shoot them some bait," he said. "If they have fresh meat they don't have to worry about, they'll ignore you."

"Of course," Tirdal said. "If I could find game within range that I could kill with a punch gun, that would be an excellent suggestion." There was a moment's hesitation before he said, "And if I could withstand another psychic blow from killing something that has a consciousness."

It hit Ferret at once. Of course. There were a lot of sensat Darhel. It seemed as if they were all that way. Everyone had assumed that it was mostly their sensats volunteered, but there didn't seem to be any that weren't. If the emotions of those around them were present like that, no wonder they avoided crowds. And no wonder it was hard to kill, or be around killing. "Ah, hell, Tirdal," he said, "I'm sorry. I didn't know."

"Nor were you supposed to, Ferret. Nor any humans. But it's somewhat obvious now and still leaves me in a quandary. If you can get close enough to perhaps hit one, I will trust you to do so. Especially as I don't have much choice."

Ferret thought about that for just a moment. "Tirdal, as soon as one of us fires, Dagger will track the shot. So we want to shoot at him only. If he isn't ducking bolts, he's going to be shooting back." Meanwhile, the pterosaur flyers were steady. They seemed to have acquired a target.

"Patching through," Tirdal said and at once, Ferret could hear Dagger say, "So, Tirdal, the flappies tell me you smell like chicken yourself."

"What are you referring to, Dagger?" Tirdal asked, pushing just a hint of curiosity into his voice.

Either it wasn't good enough, or Dagger was too shrewd to be misled. "They're circling over you, my friend."

"Oh, those," Tirdal said. "I see them, Dagger. Some distance away. Ferret might be there, as he seemed nearly dead last time I spoke to him. Why don't you go investigate?" Ferret snickered under his breath. Yes, Dagger, go investigate and I'll shoot your sorry ass in the back.

"I really don't think so, Tirdal," Dagger said.

"No? Why don't you call him, then? Ferret seems to have stopped responding, and I can't Sense him anymore. In fact, he was rather weak the entire way through this."

"Right. I'm not as dumb as you look, Elf. But I will see you soon."

"As you keep saying, Dagger. It's been over three days now. You make promises like a human politician."

"Bye, Elf," Dagger said. The channel closed.

Tirdal said, "Well, Ferret, that's where we stand."

"Yeah," Ferret said. Just then, Dagger called him. He patched it back to Tirdal as a courtesy.

"Oh, Ferret, are you there?"

Ferret kept totally still as Dagger continued, "I'm about to take a shot at the Darhel. You know I'll get him. And then, buddy, pal, I'm not going to kill you. I'm just going to leave you here. I don't reckon you can last six weeks of transit time back, plus six more weeks of transit time here, assuming anyone decides to corroborate our findings. You might want to just do yourself now, or snuggle up to the Blob base and hope for a nice clean nuke."

He absolutely burned to call the man a psychopath, a freak, a piece of shit, anything. But he had to say absolutely nothing. He gritted his teeth and took it.

"Very well, Ferret. If you're dead, you won't notice. Rest in peace."

The channel closed, and at once Ferret said, "Tirdal, I think we all know where we stand now."

"Yes, Ferret. Very much," was the reply.

"Fine. But when we bag this son of a whore, you are going to tell me why you have the box."

"Ferret, unlike Dagger, I won't lie to you. That information is not going to be available. There are things I cannot discuss, just as you have things in the Republican Army you can't tell Darhels. But we do know where we stand regarding Dagger."

Sighing in frustration and pain, Ferret said, "Okay, Tirdal. I'll trust you for now. But I have no ideas about those flyers."

"Nor I," Tirdal said.

Dagger sat patiently, waiting. It was what he was best at. He often got frustrated on long crawls or chases, but not while waiting. There was always a payoff in a good shot. The sun was bright, his gear chafing and his helmet was heavy. He'd take that off, not being worried about incoming fire, except that he needed the imaging screen. The discomfort was minor enough. His cottony mouth and cracked lips were far more annoying, as was the rumble in his belly and the fatigue dragging at his eyelids. He kept twitching from tiredness, almost asleep and then back awake.

He didn't believe Ferret was dead yet. Soon, certainly, and Dagger would be glad to help with the process. But he was alive now. The tracer showed the box to be down there, about under those gliding reptiles, so that's where Tirdal was. Ferret was playing silent. That was a pity. It was also a bit of a pain in the ass. But he'd nail Tirdal shortly, then get back to Ferret.

Ah, there was the trace. It was moving steadily, enabling him to compare it to terrain features, and there was low bank ahead where he might get a shot. Nodding slightly to himself, Dagger rolled forward into a crawl and eased up to the edge of the bluff. He stopped about a meter back from where the edge rolled down to meet a cliff face of earth and tumbled growth. The grass curled over him and he was nearly invisible. Once he triggered the chameleon circuit, he effectively was invisible.

His visor still showed him the tactical display, and he waited, ready to kill that image and go to the scope proper, which was nestled against the matching window on the visor built into the sniper's visor. He had the rifle in a good position, and squeezed the control that extruded the bipod legs. They sought the surface, spread out their paddlelike feet, and the rifle was as steady as it was going to get. All he had to do now was wait.

The dot moved north, closer to that shallow area, where he could see the narrow waters widen and ripple around the rocks, glinting in the light. Dammit, that water looked cool and tasty. Soon, he told himself. Don't get distracted.

There! Bare hints of Tirdal's chameleon helmet showed above the edge, just ripples, but Dagger knew what they were. The rifle's rounds could punch right through that soft sand. If the first shot was only a wound, it wouldn't matter. Once Tirdal slowed, Dagger would get into position and take him out joint by joint. Or try to get Ferret to do it for him, which could mean he'd need even less effort. He focused through the scope, through the target, inhaled and relaxed, letting part of the breath escape, then held firm and watched the image. Tirdal intersected the third line of the reticle, which should be enough lead. The oscillations caused by Dagger's tremors were as slight as they could get, almost nonexistent, even considering his condition, and he squeezed the stud. The rifle recoiled in the slight fashion gauss weapons did, twitched slightly and steadied. There was the crack of the projectile's hypersonic passage, the wounded air trying forlornly to keep pace with a thoroughly unnatural event, and in his scope he could see the flat, barely arced passage it left, heat-damaged air molecules showing on the screen. Dirt flew from the bank . . .

And the little bastard fell!

Chapter 16

FERRET HEARD THE SHOT. It was close enough to be a good crack. A quick scan with his sensors narrowed the source to a grid about one hundred meters on a side. And Dagger was within that box. Sure enough, it was up on the ridgeline. But without a scope, there was no way to get a good shot. He couldn't start picking away at random, because Dagger would backtrack the energy discharge. It was frustrating.

What he could do was slug the intel to Tirdal, assuming, hoping, Tirdal was still alive. That would show where he stood on things, and with two of them tracking Dagger, just maybe they could get him on the run. It would have to get dark again, too. That, added to the rest, might give them the edge they needed.

But assuming they succeeded, Tirdal was going to have to have some very believable answers to some tough questions.

He attached the grid to a transmission and sent it to Tirdal. Then he sent it to Dagger, just to let him know he was being watched. Ferret grinned a rictus that would have scared even him, if he'd had a mirror. Pain, fear, fatigue and grime gave him a visage to scare a gargoyle.

Tirdal felt the shot and launched himself into the wash, artifact flying clear. The bead cracked past, showering him with loose sand and bits of grass. That had been close enough for him to not only hear, but feel the slap of the shockwave. Then he realized it had hit him, slicing through his ruck and his shoulder. It was a minor wound, but would be extremely painful, as the mass of the ruck would rest on it. Still, he couldn't have Dagger thinking he'd succeeded.

"That was a good shot, Dagger," Tirdal taunted, keeping tight rein on his voice and the growing agony underneath. "Not good enough for an intelligent target, of course, but good enough for a rock or a dummy on the pop-up range." He rolled down deeper to secure the artifact again.

"My shooting is plenty good enough, Elf," Dagger snarled back in rage. "You're just a filthy little cheat." He definitely sounded upset over Tirdal's evasion. He seemed to feel that Tirdal not dying was an insult. Well, there were more insults where that came from.

"Cheating, Dagger? Is not the unofficial motto of

the DRTs 'If you ain't cheating, you ain't trying'? By that argument, your control and coordination is also cheating, because not everyone can do it. No, if this game is to be played properly, each player must use his resources. Surely as great a shooter as yourself can predict my evasions . . . given time. In fact, if you're as smart as you believe you are, you should have seen a pattern already." That was a dangerous statement. Tirdal wasn't aware of falling into a pattern yet, but he just might have. But he had to goad Dagger into thinking even less, to level the field between them.

At that moment, the signal from Ferret came in. He cleared the screen and allowed it to appear, and studied the map revealed. His Darhel gear could come up with much of the same data for him, but of course Ferret didn't know that. And this did prove Ferret was an ally, at least until Dagger was taken out of the equation. After that, they'd have to see.

"As for cheating," he said with a deliberately human tone of malicious amusement, "it wasn't I who tossed a grenade into a resting party while hiding behind a rock."

That seemed to have done the trick, Tirdal thought, as four shots ripped overhead of his cover, blasting dirt into the water. And his Sense showed him Dagger's surroundings, the link between them suddenly solid. He saw the scope image, saw himself as a tiny form that had moved just in time and sunk out of sight. The sun was over there, so Dagger was on that bluff to the east, as Ferret had said. Tirdal brought the image of that back from his memory and confirmed with an image from the suit sensors' cameras. Dagger was . . . right about there, and that might just be in range of the punch gun, if he took the shot now. The punch gun, he reminded himself, was a speed of light weapon. All he had to do was account for the .7416 seconds of recharge time and dodge for cover in between shots. He set the artifact down and got to work.

The suit's computer set up the map for him, and he shifted to a slightly less steep section of the parched dun gully. Then he was up and *poounk!* firing, dropping, shoving to the right off a protruding rock, up and *poounk!* then down and left to the flat piece of shale and up and *poounk!* and left again to a hardened chunk of clay and fire and right and fire and left and again from the same location, as random as an ordered mind could manage.

A Sense came to him, but it was not of Dagger firing, it was of Dagger panicking. Tirdal grinned his toothy grin. Securing the artifact, he moved out.

Ferret just lay still and rested as the firefight ensued. Dagger was clearly not shooting well. Interesting. He was terrifying on the range, great in exercises, had done well enough against the bugs that had jumped them. As to real battles, Ferret knew of his record, but wasn't aware of any specific commendations for his shooting. Things did tend to go to hell in an engagement, true. But Dagger's cold, calculating façade was just that. He clearly wasn't that impressive a shot when it came down to it. That was good to know.

For now, Ferret inhaled the fetid odors, the grass and strange pollens, the dirt and casts left by things like worms. The local sun was to the west and into Dagger's eyes. After the four shots, he had the sniper located pretty much within a ten meter square, allowing for sonic distortion from the grass. He was sure that if he could get a look up that way, he could pin Dagger down exactly. He might even get a good shot off, as extreme as the range was.

Then Tirdal was shooting back. So Darhel could shoot and mean it. Whatever philosophy kept them from engaging in war was a guideline only. Tirdal and likely others had obviously gotten over it. It was about time, he thought, that they took some of the load. It was also, he realized as an afterthought, about time that humans kept an eye on them. Militant Darhels would be bad, with the greater access to GalTech they had.

For a moment, Ferret just lay there and grinned. Then his fatigue-sodden brain realized this was the time to move. He pulled his knees in at once and started crawling under the waving stalks, hoping to close a few meters with Dagger. If this could be repeated a few times, he'd be close enough for a good shot from cover, well inside his practical range.

Of course, it would have to be a good shot. He'd get the one only, then Dagger would shoot back. He might hit, too, even if he wasn't showing the greatest aptitude at present. Obviously, Tirdal was dodging. Ferret had less agility at the moment.

Dagger's view was disrupted by the incoming map from Ferret. He scanned it at once, wondering what it was, as he hadn't triggered anything he was aware of. It took a moment for him to realize it was a map of his location. The little bastard was alive and had teamed up with the Darhel. Well, that was fine, because Dagger had planned on killing him anyway, and this would just make it that much nicer. He growled anyway. Asshole.

Then he flinched as the first shot snapped into the cliff. Tirdal was shooting back! He actually could do it. That wasn't a pleasant thought, if it was going to be a real fight.

Still, it was extreme range for the punch gun, and the Elf had little skill at aimed fire. He hunched to take a shot in case the little bastard showed up again, and he did, but over there. Dirt showered down from the first explosive hit, and the second bolt hit off to Dagger's left, then another hit beneath him some meters, then another. His flinch had turned to a wince but he was now coming out of it. The pathetic little bastard couldn't shoot for shit. Even with a punch gun, Dagger could have done better. He cursed himself, angry inside for letting the little twerp make him afraid.

Then the world shifted under him and the bluff started to slide forward toward the trees.

He rose to his knees and tried to scrabble backwards, but it was too late. The landslide was in full motion. He did manage to get far enough back to be against the fresh new bluff face as everything else collapsed under him, and the fall was not far, only about eight meters. The crumbling dirt gave him a soft surface to land on, and then through. It blew up around him and began to compact again.

Holding his breath and trying not to panic, he threw his arms around until he felt air. He half dug, half swam his way up and snorted in a dusty lungful of air. Clouds of the red clay still lingered in the air, and he could smell the earthy aroma of the newly dug dirt, as well as the silicate tang caused by the punch gun's beam burning dirt to vapor. He spit dirt and wished again for water.

He whipped his head around, terrified that Tirdal or Ferret would be right there. He clutched for his rifle, but it was still buried in the soil. His right knee struck it as he thrashed, and he reached in as far as his shoulder to get hold of it.

Dragging it out was a struggle itself, and the weapon was packed with dirt. He'd have to find cover soon and field strip it. For now, he banged the muzzle as clean as he could get it and fired a round point blank into the dirt. The projectile didn't make much noise, barely having time to create a shockwave. It did shower dirt and clean the muzzle the rest of the way. Likely, some had plated inside the barrel, but it would have to do for now. He tried to stand and fell instead, feeling dizziness, nausea and pain. What now?

"What now" was obvious. He'd twisted an ankle in the fall, was suffering the beginnings of heat exhaustion, and was burned out with fatigue. He needed rest, water, real food and medical care. What shape was that little turd in? Apparently he had water and didn't need food . . . no, wait, he needed a lot of food . . . maybe he had eaten animals. All right, then what was with his aversion to killing? Maybe it was killing sentients? Some kind of feedback into his brain? Hell, it might just take a few shots of large beasts near him to stun him. Why hadn't he thought of that earlier? And what of rest? What about Ferret? How was that little punk handling? True, he could stop for water, being last, but the injuries and fatigue couldn't be helping him.

Dagger realized he'd have to rest. Had to. He simply couldn't go on at this pace, and dammit, it was getting dark again. He let gravity pull him down into the soft earth to catch a few breaths.

Then another blast of a punch gun threw dirt in his face.

He dropped down lower, and rolled off to one side, away from the shot. His brain, experienced at this even if disoriented at the moment, realized the shot had come from the south. That had to be Ferret, then. If the two of them were linking up, Dagger was in a bad place, caught in crossfire. He whipped up his rifle, let the scope follow the rapidly dissipating plasma sheath back the way the shot had come, and marked the location.

Then he slithered down the slope, trading range and position for safety and concealment. So the little asshole was back there, and trying to be clever. He would see about that. It took him only a moment to light the spot on his reticle and squeeze off a round. Ferret might have moved from that spot, but if not, he was dead. If he had, he was about to learn that Dagger could track him back just as well.

Ferret had moved, and fired again right after Dagger did. Dagger rolled, squirmed back, and shot again. His remaining fear flushed from him. This was what he lived for: a challenge to the wits and reflexes. "Bring it on, Ferret," he said into the communicator. "I've got your name on a bead."

Ferret heard that and realized he'd made a mistake. He should have tried to get closer with Dagger distracted. He'd figured a shot then, with Dagger busy, had a good chance and was relatively safe. He hadn't thought the man could discern direction and threat so fast, then respond. He was a good shot. He was one bastard of a shot. The first one had been within a meter, even as he moved. The second one had damned near taken his face off.

But there was something about the ego behind them that just begged for a retort. "Hell, Dagger, I'm not worried about the one with my name on it," he said, preparing to fire and move as soon as he said, "but all those ones you keep shooting addressed to 'occupant' or 'current resident' are really pissing me off."

That did it, Ferret realized as another bead ripped past. But he was committed, now. He had a slight depression for cover, only his face and arms were exposed, and any shot that hit him was going to kill him so fast he'd never know it.

His plan was to stay still, watch Dagger's movements and make his own shots as close to those of a sniper as he could manage. The sights on the punch gun weren't nearly those of a precision gauss rifle, but were plenty good enough for ranges less than a thousand meters, and the weapon was theoretically more accurate, being light speed and line of sight. It had more punch up close, hence its colloquial name, and any good shot would more than equalize things.

And that bead Dagger had just fired came from right there. Ferret zoomed in as best he could, saw a flicker that might be a camouflaged Dagger, and fired.

He missed, apparently, because another bead came in right afterwards. It tore at the grass and was so close he could feel the slap of the shockwave. From a projectile that tiny, that was impressive. He'd take one more shot and move, he decided, and shifted his weapon just slightly.

Dagger watched the shots come in. Ferret was right there, and if they kept swapping fire, he'd hit sooner or later. Of course, Ferret might, too. He was in the grass there, though he didn't show on infrared even in this late light. It might be wise to shift for cover.

But that insult had really stuck in his ass. Who the fuck was Ferret to criticize his shooting? Who the fuck was Tirdal? They'd been shooting as much as he had. Did they think they were special? Were they proud of the fact they couldn't do it?

No, Ferret was going to pay for that comment. And it was right then that Dagger saw it.

The grass shifted just slightly, and there was Ferret, hard to see but clearly outlined. He wasn't chameleoned. Either he'd had tech problems, or he'd just plain forgotten. And now was when it all paid off.

"Why, Ferret," he said, "you seem to have forgotten your chameleon." As he said the last word, he stroked the trigger.

For just a moment, the universe linked two minds.

It was that link between hunter and prey. The prey knew he had made a critical and final mistake, and looked up. The expression on Ferret's face wasn't of fear, though there was a hint of that beneath. There was also disgust at failure, after so tough a struggle. Mostly it was sadness and regret that the artifact was to leave the planet with one of the others.

The hunter knew he had the shot. Dagger smiled a cruel smile, an almost sexual thrill running through him. The tougher the target, the bigger the thrill, and Ferret had been a royal pain in the ass. He had all the time in the world, or less than a second. His finger brushed the trigger and the gauss rifle cracked its projectile.

At this range, flight time was negligible. Through the scope, a wake through the air was visible, ripples expanding from a shape that was a conical arc. What was that shape called? Dagger wondered idly. He'd have to look it up sometime.

Then the round ripped through Ferret's face, the husk peeling away to expose a few micrograms of antimatter. It had been a needless touch; any of the rounds would have killed. But Dagger was glad it would be excessive. There was a low, dull explosion that he wouldn't hear for a second or more, the reaction muffled for just a moment by flesh and bone that then expanded ahead of the shock wave, too fast for human eyes to see. Ferret just disappeared, everything above his abdomen vaporized by a combination of shock wave and steam explosion. His punch gun dropped, taking his disembodied hands with it, and his lower half gushed red, pink and gray innards into a fetid heap in front.

"Now that's sweet," Dagger said in a whisper, smile frozen on his face. One asshole down, one to go. "Hey, Tirdal," he transmitted, "Ferret's dead in front of me. You're next."

Tirdal replied of course. He always had a glib answer. "So I deduced. How unfortunate for Ferret. It does, however, simplify matters for me to have the weaker mind be the only pursuit. We shall see each other shortly, Dagger. Or at least one of us will see the other."

"Better hope it's you, Tirdal. Though you can't do

much except duck. You won't be within range of me with that shooter."

"'Hope' is not a Darhel concept," Tirdal replied. "We shall simply see. 'Good luck,' in human parlance."

"Yeah, screw you too, Darhel. It's six down and one to go," Dagger said.

Tirdal was just an annoyance, now. Dagger felt one hell of a lot better with a solid kill for his tally.

Still, it was getting dark in a hurry. Under his elation was a leaden wave of tiredness that kept dragging him down. It would be best to move a short distance away, and find a place to . . . hide . . . for the night. The word wasn't pleasant, but he would be hiding from Tirdal and local animals, not from the dark. He'd make it close by, so he could watch Tirdal's current location, and this chewed spot of the bluff, in case the Elf came up to look. Though he was betting Darhel boy was too timid and inexperienced for that.

In the meantime, food, water. His processor could produce lettuce-looking stuff that had a lot of moisture. That would have to suffice, he supposed. It would taste like grass, but it would keep him alive for now. And Tirdal wouldn't attack, because Tirdal couldn't be sure of getting within range without getting shot. The high ground was the best place, and Dagger had it.

Now, where to camp? He could roll against another crumbled dirt face and let it collapse across himself, his head and shoulders covered with the gear cover from his ruck propped up with rocks and sticks. Yes, that would work. It might even be cool, if he dialed the suit down. The dirt would absorb energy from him and radiate it away, and it would be dispersed enough not to be obvious.

First things first, though. He needed to swallow a nano for the ankle, stuff a lot of grass into the processor to get water from it, and clean the muzzle of his rifle.

He squirmed the rest of the way out of the scree, and gingerly took to a crawl. It would keep him low and protect both his screaming ankle and throbbing knee. Ripping whole fistfuls of grass, he stuffed them into the mouth of the processor until it was packed full. It worked more efficiently when lightly loaded, but this was an emergency. He opened the seal around his boot, hiked up the pant leg and pressed the nano carrier against his ankle. It seeped in, feeling cold, then the ankle began to itch, then go numb. Hopefully, it would be useable by dawn.

He had to settle for running a cleaning rod down the bore of the rifle, rather than a full stripping. He couldn't risk losing components. The charged brush seemed to clear everything, and he'd just have to assume the scope was still aligned and resight it if needed. It had been fine for Ferret, but that had been less than a thousand meters, and he didn't know how closely the round had hit his point of aim. A few microradians off was an angle of departure that would compound with distance. Also, it might have been loosened and any jarring could make shooting much less precise. For now, he couldn't change it.

It was near dark now, the light fading as fast as in Earth's tropics, even at this latitude. He checked the processor and was rewarded with the sight of crisp, wet rectangular sheets, reminiscent of lettuce leaves. He grabbed them as fast as they came out, stuffing them into his mouth and chewing. Yes, a half hour of this might get him another day's moisture. And he'd really need to take a dump when he awoke, he decided. Unbelievable that a stalk could take so long.

Much refreshed and healthier after eating, Dagger was at the same time exhausted beyond description. Pain tore at his leg still, along with the myriad aches and pains that were exacerbated between sleeps. He rolled back against the dirt face, pulled the cover over his head and shoulders, and kicked back with his good foot. A softly rumbling shower of dirt concealed all but his face, and with the chameleon circuits live he should be invisible.

And tomorrow, he thought, consciousness fading, he'd see about that damned Elf.

Tirdal decided he should rest a bit before continuing. With Dagger calm, he could do so, though there was no guarantee he'd have long. But that would wait until afterwards, if there was an afterwards. There were things to be done now, such as moving for solid defense against shots or predators. He wasn't sure of the difference in feel between Dagger asleep and Dagger in a shooting trance, so he intended to be cautious and maintain good cover. A Sense to the south didn't show any presence of Ferret, and there'd been a brief flash of fear when Dagger shot. Still, he called, "Ferret, are you there?" There was no reply. So assume Ferret was dead. That was unfortunate, really. The young human had definitely shown his mettle, stalking the two of them for days while crippled. He'd deserved better.

Tirdal had been getting rather disturbed by the flyers, but they were now circling off to the south in the failing daylight. It was likely the shot against Ferret had tossed enough vapor up that the smell of blood was clear. That would explain their interest. He didn't know if they were nocturnal, but losing their presence was a good thing.

Tirdal knew humans would feel unpleasant about the creatures eating one of their own. He wasn't bothered emotionally, and was glad of the distraction. Ferret had put on an impressive showing in this incident, and there would be much to consider and report. In the meantime, he was still of use to Tirdal, even if it was as bait. He wished he'd been able to examine that mind more. It had been frightened, hurt and overwhelmed, yet had stuck to a goal through all hindrance. Truly the mind of a warrior, as untrained and inexperienced as it had been.

But the universe wasn't fair, and dwelling on it wouldn't affect anything. Tirdal would meditate later and think of Ferret; for now, he had urgent needs in this world. He sank as low into the gully as he could, ensuring his head was below any line of sight.

First was the wound on his back. It was in a position where one would have a buddy treat it, but that was not an option. He opened his suit and peeled it down, avoiding inhaling the sweaty stink of himself. Two hundred and seventy Earth hours in the suit with no bathing. It was just one more of the glamorous aspects of military service.

Reaching back carefully, he was able to gingerly apply a nano-loaded bandage. It would heal in a couple of days, he decided, though it would leave a furrow that would have to be treated by professionals. In the meantime, he wouldn't be putting that box on his shoulder.

It would make sense to put it in his patrol pack,

distributing the load. If he snugged the hip belt and used the head band, too, he could distribute the mass well. However, he'd be less flexible thus constrained. Likely he'd just have to take the mass on his shoulders and deal with it.

To that end, he should remove excess mass. There were things in there he was not, frankly, going to need for this. He reached in and started sorting.

He was going to change suits, he decided. The damaged one could be left behind. He pondered for a moment, but yes, it could. Even if the chameleon circuits failed, he planned to be far enough away to dodge Dagger's fire, and the camouflage hadn't helped so far, so why keep a torn suit? He unzipped and shimmied between the two, shoulders stiff and keeping low. A considerable amount of sand came with him, but that was inevitable. Five kilos lighter, he considered what else could go.

Socks. He didn't really need socks, even though humans issued them, and he wouldn't be changing again soon. Keep one pair to swap off and dump the rest. He thought of using them for extra padding on the straps, but that was a field expedient and he'd be losing mass, so why bother?

Ammo. He had an energy pack in the punch gun that was good for eighty more full-power shots. That should be enough. He'd take one spare to be sure. That left four of them he could dump. He'd better keep his camera and recorder. It didn't mass much and contained information that was important.

That was about ten kilos removed. It would help considerably, and with the device strapped inside his pack it was far less bulky.

Why was he doing that, though? There was no question left in Tirdal's mind but that the sniper had a tracer somewhere, and the box was the logical place. He sat with it in his lap, turning the box over and over until he found it. It was an almost undetectable spot, which could have been a bit of dirt except that it didn't come off. And it wouldn't come off, either. The tracers required a special solvent to remove. He tried digging at it with his monomolecular blade but only just scratched the cover of the device.

So. He was being traced, not only tracked. Tracking he could have dealt with, eventually Dagger would come in close and he would have a reasonable chance. He should have pushed things at the camp, kept them almost in contact. But between the damage from the hornet round and the ultimate prohibition against killing a sentient he'd chosen the other path. He should have pushed the issue further when Ferret started shooting. He hadn't been able to see Dagger at that point, but a few cover shots wouldn't have hurt the situation. It would have been a morale issue at least, helping Ferret and disturbing Dagger. The truth was that his Darhel mind needed a very conscious decision to shoot and he hadn't made it. Now it was going to cost him.

He knew he was being traced. But did Dagger know that he knew? That was the question. Since the meadow the sniper had been less responsive, but Tirdal could feel his anger out there, somewhere. Not close, but definitely still on the track. If he didn't realize Tirdal had left the device somewhere . . . Yes, that was an idea.

Things were quiet now, too. Quiet to his Sense in this fading light. Had Dagger decided to rest? If so, Tirdal could approach and kill him.

The problem with that was that he'd have to not use his Sense to do so, lest the reaction from battle throw him over the edge into lintatai. And without using his Sense, he was vulnerable to a shot from Dagger.

No, Dagger had to get close enough to him, but not be allowed take a shot. A resting Dagger was a bad Dagger, in that regard. Tirdal needed him off balance. He could wake the man, but that would give away what he planned. Dagger would fatigue further, but he'd know Tirdal couldn't approach him. That was an advantage he needed to keep.

He thought about retreating to the south, back to the site of the murders. That's where the gear was. But there was nothing there he needed that justified the hike, and it would put Dagger between him and the second extraction point, thus reducing his options. It would be nice to have some of the gear, but it wasn't a fair tradeoff. Ferret's lifesigns tracker might be useful, and he likely had ammunition and water. But he wasn't skilled in the tracker's use, and he'd expose himself considerably trying to get it. Not worth it.

So, rest for now, move as soon as Dagger stirred. Tirdal stretched out his Sense for weather, animals, and one specific animal, then leaned back with his ruck as a chair back to rest. His overmind could relax and recover while his submind stayed alert. It wasn't as good as real sleep, but a solid meditation would help.

Chapter 17

DAGGER TWITCHED and said, "Unh?"

Coming awake, he realized he'd slept for some hours. It was dawn again, the sky above him just purple. He felt much better, too. Now to nail that damned Darhel.

He crawled cautiously out of his ersatz shelter, and opened his suit to drain and dump. He pinched out a turd that was hard and sore, because he was dehydrated, but it took pressure off. It was so hard he could feel his ass slam shut as it dropped, but he hurt a hell of a lot less afterwards. That accomplished and dust wiped off his hands and face, he chewed some more of the moist leaves. They helped a bit, but real food was called for. Well, that would just have to wait. He'd taken care of the rest.

"Good morning, Tirdal!" he greeted, trying to sound even more cheerful than he was. He donned gear and brought up the sensors.

"Good morning, Dagger. Did you enjoy sleeping in?" Dammit, the Elf still didn't sound distressed. What was he, a machine? No, not a machine. He was in about the same area, so he'd rested, too. Just an alien prick. Don't credit him with any more than that.

"Very much, Tirdal," he replied. It wouldn't do to act bothered. "I thought the extra time would let you consider your position. Alone. Down there. Burdened with the box and a short-range weapon. Running out of time. Might be a good idea to negotiate a surrender, hmm?"

"You make good points, Dagger," was the reply. "But I'm not sure we can trust each other at this juncture."

"Sure we can, Tirdal," he said. He'd thought this through. "You can tell when I've dropped my rifle . . . hell, I'll even throw it down. You drop the punch gun as I come in range and you can tell I'm not armed. Then we both unload our pistols and hold them up to prove it. Then we can talk about the box." While I stick a knife in your throat, asshole.

"That's a good idea, Dagger," Tirdal said, and Dagger smirked until he added, "but we should have done that three days ago. Your position has become clear and your 'soul' as you call it, is slimy and grotesque. Frankly, I'd rather attempt to negotiate with one of the predators. At least they are logical and have a defined goal I can understand."

Forcing calm upon himself, Dagger replied, "That is unfortunate, Tirdal. In that case, I'll have to kill you." And you're in a prime place for a shot.

"We knew that, Dagger, didn't we?" Tirdal replied. He was still calm, damn him! "And I just might kill you first."

The signal went dead.

All right, so he wanted to be that way. He was just about fifty meters north of where he'd been at dark yesterday. So, on a lower ledge, far enough back not to fall, settle in, set the rifle, and prepare to deliver God's Vengeance upon the Darhel.

Tirdal knew what was to happen. They both did. He'd move, Dagger would shoot. From there, Dagger assumed he'd be killed; he assumed he'd avoid taking fire. This stalemate, as it was called in chess, was tiresome and he was about to break it, but to do that he had to expose himself to the fire first. There was nothing doing but to get it over with.

He shrugged back into his ruck, feeling the soreness and tightness across his shoulders. That was made worse every time he moved his head with the added mass of helmet. It would do for now, and he counted himself lucky. A couple of centimeters deeper and the shot would have shattered both shoulders. Dagger really was that good. He'd have to force Dagger to take a shot, and be ready. He'd need tal in his system to boost his Sense. He reached inside himself and released a little.

That wasn't happening as quickly as he'd like. He

might be starting to suffer from fatigue himself, his submind less easy to control. So he recalled the feel of the kill, the taste of meat from yesterday. That did it. He could feel the energy flow, and then his Sense came on, detected the nearby herds, then Dagger, and the rate increased, pushing him toward . . .

A steady, controlled level of tal, regulated by Jem discipline. It was a bit easier to control today, though that might be due to the familiar conditions. How he'd handle a new set of factors he didn't know. But Dagger was there, so if he stepped out over here . . .

Dagger was drifting, drifting and was shooting now and Tirdal dropped forward and flat over a shelf of shale as the round cracked overhead and threw a mist of water up from the stream. Then he was up and moving and Dagger was there and angry and shooting now and Tirdal dropped sideways in case he'd anticipated the fall. He landed in a pile of sand as a rock erupted chips on the far bank. He stood and felt Dagger shoot at once and dug in his heels to change his momentum, then dropped as another crack presaged another cloud of mist.

That should do it, he thought. Dagger hated to miss more than just about anything else, would be easy to track with that storm of emotion roaring off him, and Tirdal could keep track as he decided how to execute his plan.

Then, only for a moment he could feel the human as if Dagger were he.

Dagger was pissed. Seriously pissed. He crushed another beetle on a rock before it could scuttle out of range and watched the rabbit-sized pseudoisopod writhe as he loped off. The damned Darhel had just dodged the bullets. Sure, it was vaguely possible, even with the high speeds of the "dumb" sniper rounds. But you had to know that a sniper had shot. That was the point of using a dumb round; it had no emissions to detect. You had to have an active system to detect it until it was too late.

But the goddamned sensat could feel him take the shot. The only way to stop that was to feel nothing when he killed the little shit. Which meant adopting a new shooting approach and, frankly, took all the fun out of it. What was the point if you couldn't get the rush from the kill?

So, to kill the Darhel he had to feel nothing. But the point of killing was to feel something, wasn't it? So what was the point of killing the Darhel? Oh, yeah. A billion credits.

So, this time, feel nothing. Not even excitement at getting a billion credits. Not until the box was in his hand. And the Darhel was dead. Feel nothing. That ought to be easy enough; it was his normal way of life.

The link severed as quickly as it had formed, tenuous threads of consciousness snapping away. That was Dagger's mind then. It was crass, paranoid, full of a fear of failure and incompetence, of showing fear or doubt. Any emotion, any humanity, was weakness to Dagger.

Tirdal sucked on the pulp from his processor while he sorted out the thoughts. He couldn't face killing something else in order to eat. His emotions were just too out of control and he was afraid he'd lose control the way he currently felt. Order was essential. Anarchy would lead to death, as it was leading to Dagger's.

Growing up, he never could understand the tal addicts, the Darhel who did things to push the edge of lintatai. Now he could. The tal was the most heady drug available to the Darhel and it was manufactured in their own bodies. After the pain, which was brief, came the rush of pleasure, then the long duration of nothingness, followed by a sated calm. It was too easy to lose oneself in it, accomplish nothing and feel little while doing so, and feel good about what little there was.

Tal addiction still killed thousands, millions every year; no Darhel would bother to care for one that had succumbed to lintatai. Those who failed the test would wither away, dying of dehydration usually. It was harsh, but necessary. It had taken hundreds of millennia to force their evolution back to this point, where tal could be used even if at great risk. It might take hundreds more before the Darhel became what they had once been, before the Aldenata interfered with their heritage and corrupted their destiny. The strong must continue, the weak must not, if they were to be a whole race again.

But he knew his own control and its limits. It had fluctuated throughout the pursuit, the game if you will, and now if it were pushed he wasn't sure he could hold back a full tal orgasm. Which would be death.

By the same token he was becoming more and more addicted to the tal himself. He had never experienced the range of emotions he was permitting himself. Even Dagger's discordant emotions were a pleasing sensation. They were spice, a delicacy, against the palate of known pleasures.

For that matter it seemed to be part of his enhanced

range. If he fully controlled the tal his ability to track the sniper decreased; it was only when he let some of the tal hormone trickle into his system that he could find his tracker.

He wasn't sure he could get the glinak back in the box. When he was done with this mission there would be plenty to meditate about. And much to discuss with his master. Perhaps even with the masters of the Art themselves.

He took a deep breath and considered his situation. The pod would move in another two or three days. If he headed directly for the next Extraction Point, Dagger would set up along the way, moving to intercept as necessary. If he headed up into the hills there would be even more areas for the sniper to ambush him, and he'd be approaching the fire. Not good.

It appeared it was time for a Darhel to enter once again upon the hunt. There was a thrill to that knowledge, with a foreboding cloud hanging over it. This was no game. The fates of three races and hundreds of planets, perhaps the galaxy, would balance on what Tirdal San Rintai did next, and how well his mind could fight genetic programming.

The question was what to do with the box. He pondered that for a few moments. He looked around on the plain. Then he smiled. It was a very predatory and devious smile.

The Elf had been moving steadily towards the Blob site but now he'd turned back to the west, crossing the stream to do so. There was lots of clear savanna in that direction, large enough that it was on the map. What Tirdal thought he was doing there Dagger couldn't decide. He moved north and west, down off the bluffs and the visual advantage they gave, aiming to cut the Darhel off. The Elf had headed across the stream and onto the savanna proper, all grass and shrubs, and probably intended to get well out of range and out of sight. But to get to the pickups he'd have to come back to the east and either north or south. Best to find a good spot on his probable route and wait for him. Dagger would lurk behind him until he turned, then take the hypotenuse to cut him off. If he started at an angle, Dagger would know which extraction point he intended to move toward, and could charge ahead, around the Elf, and be waiting for him. And if Tirdal took more than two more days, he'd have to head south anyway.

Perfect.

Dagger hunkered down in the grass to wait, nerves and sensors alert for any disturbance around him, and kept an eye on the box's movement.

This was a technique that Tirdal had rarely practiced. Alonial, the Indowy adept, was the master of projection, but Tirdal had never shown much ability at it. Still, he seemed to be managing adequately. He couldn't tell if the large browsers were seeing him as one of them, not at all, or simply as himself and were not afraid. Their primitive eyes didn't move to indicate the direction they were viewing, and the waving antennae were equally reticent. They weren't spooking, however, so something was right. It took only a trickle of tal to maintain the concentration for the illusion. Of course, that trickle was in addition to handling the stress on his twice-wounded body, and aiding his focus on Dagger, and . . .

The gargantuan insects were quiescent though, paying no attention to the strange biped in their midst. And everyone always said that thousand-klick-an-hour tape would stick to anything.

The "herd bull" was the size of a large bison or small elephant. To support that bulk with an exoskeleton required a material far stronger than chitin and the armored carapace of the bug was at least a hand span thick. It might be an impossible kill with a punch gun, depending on how the shell reacted to the blast. It would be difficult with the rounds Dagger carried. Not impossible perhaps. The antiarmor rounds might work. Antimatter would certainly work, though it might require blowing a deep crater with multiple rounds. But Tirdal wouldn't need to kill it and wasn't planning to.

He crouched for a moment then leapt up and over, free of the grass and with a clear, panoramic view. Even with his chameleon in effect, this was a dangerous time, and he'd have to work quickly lest Dagger see him and take a shot. That, and the insect might spook and toss him or dislodge him, possibly stampede or crush him.

He was atop it, sitting slightly astride as he swung his pack around and ripped open the top compartment flap. He heaved out the artifact, kept hold of the pack with one arm through it as it flopped down, and held the box still with his weight while he snagged the roll of tape with his left hand, reaching over his right and into the pack in a fashion that would impress an Earth acrobat.

It wasn't an easy task, with only one hand and his lips to get the tape going, but he succeeded. The first piece held the box just still enough for him to get a second piece on, then a third. He was stretching out a fourth piece when he suddenly found himself flying through the air from a truly elephantine buck. The giant pill bug had all the agility of a terrestrial beetle but, luckily, had the reaction speed of a slug. Perhaps it had slower neural paths, or was less sensitive on its back, or just stupid. But the herd bull now had the Aldenata artifact strapped to its magnificently striped and armored back, with the tape still hanging from the last strap he'd been fastening. And Tirdal was free to hunt. He grinned again and angled through the herd, crossing the paths of the large beasts just behind them.

Chapter 18

WHAT IN THE HELL did the Elf think he was doing? He'd moved along the east side of this savanna, which looked like it was probably a sinkhole lake that had emptied out, then moved rapidly west, then to the north. Now he was moving west again. Slowly. More meandering than moving. And all the while on the savanna. He had to have a better knowledge of tactics than that.

Dagger had found a lonely tree and climbed it for a good look. Generally he hated to shoot from trees. If you were detected it made you a perfect target and even without being detected it was a vulnerable

331

spot. Better to be hunkered down on the ground. But you did what you had to do and the savanna was a mixture of high pseudograss and bushes; there was no clear view from ground level. He referred to his tracker, then tried to spot the same general area on the savanna. It was several clicks away and the ground was rough but he couldn't spot anything that looked like the Darhel. There was a large herd of those damned beetle things that had gotten in his way before. The Darhel might be staying among them. That wasn't a bad tactic, actually. Dagger would have to get closer to take a shot, and there'd be a lot of interference.

Then he ratcheted up the magnification on his scope and swore. The box was attached to the broad gray back of one of the damned herbivores.

Without even thinking about it he was on his way to the ground. The Darhel would come looking for him now. He couldn't kill, though. There was one thing that all humans knew about Darhel; no matter how bad they were they couldn't kill.

So was the shoe on the other foot or not? Oh, this was just lovely.

Why couldn't the asshole have had the decency to die?

Tirdal paused and took a few breaths. This was really playing with the black side. The tal reacted to hatred, fear and aggression, all the demons that lurked in the Darhel soul. And it also accentuated them, causing a feedback loop. Now on the trail of his first kill, Tirdal constantly found himself forcing the glinak back in its cave. If it was this bad just trying to track in on the sniper, it would be nasty when it came time for the . . . the . . . kill.

That, and he'd have to dodge numerous shots. It was better than a draw that would leave him stranded, with Dagger in control of the pod's landing sites, or leave both of them stranded to die. Though that option was preferable, as a last resort, than to let Dagger have the artifact. If so, Tirdal was prepared to face that death. It would be an easy one. All he had to do was let tal push him into lintatai and he'd not care what happened next. Of course, the chewing of predators would drag him out of trance in order to die, but that could be avoided by hiding in a cave or depression.

Tal was still an enticing option, too. He needed it, and the dosage he required increased as he developed the taste and the accompanying Sense. Would it be possible to build immunity through exposure? Research said not, but Tirdal was certainly running at a level rarely encountered. If control was the reason, then it spoke well of him as an individual, but would not help the race. He let his thoughts continue as he rose and pushed off again, running in a low crouch to stay below the grass tops. He was uncomfortably aware of the trail he was leaving, smashed flat behind him. He could do nothing about that.

He summoned Jem and breathed deeply, regrouping his control. The breath caused an ache in his chestplate that was not gone yet. Had he been able to rest more, it would likely be healed by now. As it was, it had improved, but would need medical care afterwards, or the healed, misaligned crack would forever be a weak spot. The tight pain in his shoulders was still there, though discarding gear and the artifact had reduced it to a mere annoyance for now. Hunger gnawed at him, feeding the tal. Thirst hadn't hurt him yet; he'd been near water and able to resupply. But he was reaching a fatigue level that would begin to affect him, even with the brief nap he'd had. Tal seemed to increase strain on the metabolism, as well as causing him to use more energy.

Always the tal. Every problem in the Darhel psyche and physiology came back to tal. How had they accomplished so much with that stone tied to their feet, anchoring them? More questions to be asked afterwards. And more reasons to loathe the Aldenata.

But for now he must move, until Dagger reacted and he could Sense the activity and respond accordingly.

At a trot, he headed east, making no effort to mask his movement. His head stuck above the grass, making him feel exposed and naked as he bulled through it. Either Dagger would see him and start taking shots, or he'd get clear and be able to circle around, Dagger having no idea where he was. He couldn't get too far away, or Dagger would simply snag the artifact and go. That would leave him with no bait, and still risking stalemate and abandonment. But there could be no gain without risk.

He'd gone about three hundred meters when Dagger faded in his perception again. Likely a shot would follow. He gave no indication of his awareness, though part of him shouted to take cover. Instead, he breathed deeply, let his stride even out to a pace that didn't require thinking, and reached out with his Sense as tal rose, ready to respond.

Shot fired! his Sense shouted at him. He threw

himself sideways and low, rolled over the lump in his pack and stayed still as tufts and seeds drifted down, torn loose by the projectile's passage. The crack of tortured air rang his ears and echoed loudly from the hills. He breathed in the smell of the grass, and that of the earth just centimeters from his nose. His chin stung where the muzzle of the punch gun had smashed it as he landed. He took a breath to steady himself and held motionless. But staying still would simply let Dagger take a followup shot to end this, he realized at once. He scrambled forward and ran again, faster. He would keep this up until he had Dagger in a good frame of mind.

Shot fired! And again he dodged, this time dropping as soon as possible. A small eruption of dirt in front of him indicated Dagger was trying to catch his feet. That would be a difficult shot, but obviously Dagger thought he could make it. Not good. It might have been best not to provoke him in this terrain. Still, it was better than just running, hoping for a chance. He could also feel tal pushing at him.

Shot fired! Dagger was getting angry. Tirdal could feel it. This time he dove far forward, hoping Dagger wasn't leading him much, in response to his last two evasions. If he was right, he'd gain a few moments as Dagger repositioned for the next shot. If he was wrong, hopefully his armor would slow the round enough to reduce the injury. He arched in midair, landing flat on his abdomen and slapping the ground with his hands and toes to absorb the momentum. It was easier than he'd trained for, in this low gravity, although he got bashed in the head by his own gun again. At once he pushed up and went into a rapid crawl on toe and fingertips, scrabbling under the brush like a local scavenger. The tall grass and stalky growth reluctantly parted in front of him, bending but little from the narrow print of fingers and toes. The plant tops waved but little, leaving Dagger a broad potential target area to choose from. Dust and tiny insects blew past Tirdal's face.

He felt another shot and rolled to his right, where the shots were coming from, hoping a low round would pass over him. It did, the grass cushioning his mass for a moment before ripping away, leaving a flattened area. But Dagger now knew what he'd done there, and that round had already been close. It wouldn't take many more before this came to an end.

Another one came, this time a hornet round that cracked overhead as it targeted him. His suit snapped out a signal and the dead round banged into his hip, making him wince with pain but not causing major injury. That was good. It meant Dagger was getting frustrated, and doubted his own ability to make the shot. But he could shoot quite a few more rounds, and eventually one would hit Tirdal.

Then something happened.

The tenuous connection between them solidified again, and he could feel Dagger shooting. For just a moment, he could see what Dagger saw, a ghostly image over the reality in front of him. He closed his eyes for a moment to catch the scene, and moved. Dagger was aiming right at him and shooting now as Tirdal rolled away and rose to his feet, the shot chewing ground where he'd been, then another passing behind him. Dagger fired, leading him and he just stopped, standing precariously where he was for a moment, then moved at an angle then forward. Another hornet cracked, but he knew it was coming and dove forward. It missed him, barely.

Then the connection broke, feeling as if it were full of static. Dagger was furious, howling angry. He was panting and sweating and starting to shake. But he wasn't shooting.

And Tirdal knew where he was. He was on a low hummock of the rolling ground to north and east. Now he was heading for higher ground and trees to the north. Very well. Tirdal would meet him there. Should he follow behind Dagger, or circle around the east?

Follow. That would disturb Dagger even more. He grinned again, despite the sting in his hip now turning numb, the aches in his shoulders and chest, the itching from abraded skin irritated by sweat, the urgent, gnawing hunger and the cloying promise of tal.

It was time for Dagger to feel some of this.

He let tal build, slowly, until he was experiencing a dizzying, exhilarating rush. It was still controllable, though it took concentration, and he'd have to shut it down in a hurry before anything resembling a kill. He'd just have to hope nothing attacked him across this savanna. In the meantime, he could easily feel Dagger over there. That confirmed, he moved at a low crouch, helmet batting the grass aside as he strode. He reached out for other life, and found the herd, dumb and contented with its grass, and a buzz of lesser creatures underneath that, nonsentient and merely background. No predators reached him here, though there were some in the "distance," undefinable. They would not be close enough to worry about, so he drew his awareness in to focus on Dagger and anything in that range.

Dagger was moving for that small copse of trees, yes. Likely some trick of geology funneled water and nutrients to them, as they stood on solid ground, all alone. And Dagger intended, most likely, to climb one to use as a platform for a better shot. So while he moved that way, Tirdal could hurry closer.

Should he risk the kill? Should he risk trying to capture Dagger? Both had their dangers. He'd have to decide soon, but options were always desirable.

And there was Dagger, far ahead but visible. The range was about a kilometer, and Tirdal could see his head and rifle. The man was so enraged or so conceited he wasn't bothering with cover. Well, good. Some stray shots would serve to annoy him further . . . and just might hit him. Tirdal stopped, raised his punch gun and took careful aim.

The first shot caused an eruption of dirt ahead of the sniper, who sent out a mental shriek of fear but then dove for ground with trained reflexes. Tirdal fired again and again at the area, tossing stalks and dirt in cascades. Dagger's fear was palpable, edging up toward the level of his rage. And there . . . fatigue, despair. Emotions were piling on each other, wrestling to be the most important. Tirdal realized he could not ask Dagger to surrender. It would be perceived as weakness. He must push and keep pushing until something snapped. It was still possible, however unlikely, that Dagger might ask to surrender. That would be the best outcome. But it must be begged for, not offered.

Dagger was moving now, low and slow. Tirdal took

his best guess as to where and fired again. As long as a few of his shots were close, Dagger was too low to realize they were simply lucky, and would continue to panic. The occasional wisps of smoke from scorched grass couldn't hurt, either. It would be best to space the shots, so the seventy left would last a goodly number of minutes. Tirdal recalled a human joke about Murphy's Law of Thermodynamics: things get worse under pressure. So pressure there would be.

In fact, fire might not be a bad thing. Brush fires couldn't be too uncommon here, even though the oxygen level wasn't that high. It was a perfectly natural occurrence the Tslek shouldn't notice, and might serve to throw Dagger over the edge.

A tiny adjustment to the punch gun's controls, accomplished as two movements between the ongoing shots, and the beam would disperse just slightly more. However, that meant a lower-pressure plasma sheath around each bolt, which should encourage dry, stalky growth, covered in dust and flaky husks, to ignite.

It was a pity the weapon wouldn't fire faster. Still, four or five shots on the same area should do the trick, the subsequent beams providing more ignition sources and a slight wafting of air through the growth to fan the flames. Tirdal picked a spot he was sure was ahead of where Dagger was, drew it back to what seemed a good estimated distance, and started firing.

Dagger stopped prone and took a few breaths. He cringed as another scattering of dirt preceded the *poounk!* of the punch gun. The damned Darhel had figured out a way to track him. He thought at first that Tirdal had acquired some gear back at camp, and had finally figured out how to use it. His actions, however, indicated that he was only able to track sporadically, when Dagger was most frustrated. So it was his damned sensat crap. He seemed to notice when Dagger was going to take a shot, but only after the fact; he still could only sense emotions, not thoughts. So the thing to do would be to just . . . shut down. Get in that sort of meditation mode like when he was shooting. Just . . . become a rock, a blank spot . . . What was it that Darhel had said? "Think of a floating bubble . . ." He'd use that one, since he must. He shut out the earlier comparison to a pool and the surface. Had the slimy freak detected a residual thought of that time when he was eight, when the local bullies had held him under at the local swimming hole? Could it be coincidence, or was the Darhel trying to enrage him with bad memories? If so, it was working, and Dagger didn't believe in coincidence. So don't think about that. Think about that soap bubble bit. Ignore the implied insult about how simple and childish it was. There would be time to gloat after he took the shot.

Then he twitched again as another shot landed close enough for him to smell cooked lime from the ground. The Darhel bastard was learning quickly, and Dagger wondered if he'd managed to meet up or talk to Ferret. He was getting harder to kill, not easier.

How could something dodge so many rounds? He was sure a few of them had nicked, at least. Enough to slow the alien twerp down. Except they hadn't. Was his suit that good? If so, Dagger might be in deep shit. But that wasn't reasonable, or Tirdal wouldn't be running.

Except he wasn't running now. He was attacking. A sudden change in tactics indicated desperation. So

Tirdal was in bad shape. A faint grin crossed his face as he thought of that. The asshole was trying to keep him scared as he approached, but he still wasn't doing too well. His best attack so far had been to try to topple a bluff. No matter what happened, Tirdal still couldn't actually kill.

A familiar odor crept into his nostrils and brain. It was pleasant and relaxed him just slightly. That was nice. It wasn't something he'd smelled here, it was . . . grass smoke?

Then through the waving stems he saw an orange flicker that was also familiar. "You asshole!" he whispered hoarsely, and started to shimmy back in panic. A lucky beam must have caught something dry and flammable in this arid terrain.

Then Dagger realized there were more flames, making that crackling noise that meant they were spreading. Oily gray smoke hung low around him, and tickled his nose and stung his eyes. Shit. A whole area to his left was flaring up, between Tirdal and him.

Still, that meant he could use it as a screen, and he'd better damned well hurry, he realized, because that was the direction the prevailing winds were coming from. If that was a five kilometer breeze he felt, it was as fast as a brisk walk. He'd need to be faster than that.

Eyes wide again, feeling frustration, panic and fear fight with exhaustion and stress, Dagger rose to a crouch and sprinted the hell east and north. He'd had general plans to go that way anyway, but he hated, just hated, being forced into a course of action. But a grass fire was not something he could ignore, and it wouldn't react to his weapons.

He rode over his shivers and thought of how best to dispose of the rage and, and . . . fear . . . he was focusing and concentrating. How about as a mental attack for that sensat bastard? Throw some of this at him and see what happened?

Are you reading my mind, Tirdal the Darhel, cowardly little bastard? Read this, asshole.

Tirdal felt Dagger's mental outburst. Once again, he had a flashing connection to his enemy's brain, thoughts and feelings and sensory input cascading over him. Raw, seething hatred! Power and control. The strength of it caused his tal levels to rise, and he fought to lower them. That was the ongoing problem; maintaining the level high enough, without flying off that precipice.

But he had caught that brief glimpse of Dagger's surroundings. He was now farther to the northeast, almost to those trees at the edge of the prairie. The fire behind him and to Tirdal's right front was dying down to an angry black and red scar, the red fading to ashen gray as a pall of smoke rolled up and thinned, the upper edge flattening out in the stratified air.

Dagger's detectability was fading in and out as Tirdal fought the tal levels. Also, he seemed to be becoming "fainter." As if he was getting ready to take a shot. Or, more likely, trying to mask his emotions. There was a lot of rage there. Time to tweak it even further. Also time to stop shooting, so as not to provide a return target. He got low and began to belly crawl, arms stretched out ahead to minimize damage to the grass.

He called up Dagger and started playing mind

games again. "So, Dagger, how are you doing?" he asked as he slipped through the stalks, bending rather than breaking them again. "Of course, I don't really have to ask. I read your mind."

He paused at a thinning of the weeds, only to determine it was a path cleared by another herd of gargantuan insectoids. Good. He'd learned much in the last three days. This was something else for the Darhel to practice, on either cultivated "wild" areas or remote planets. The human monopoly on force became less of a potential threat as other tactical knowledge grew.

Dagger replied, a bit breathlessly but sounding surprisingly well controlled, "I take it you've never seen a real brush fire you little asshole? You do know they can go against prevailing winds, spread out in long lines, create firestorms that suck air in to feed them, and generally not do what you want them to do?"

Tirdal had known some of that. The rest sounded very reasonable and he realized he—they—had been lucky the grass was merely weather dry and not kindling dry from drought. That was not a mistake he should have let himself make from eagerness. On the other hand, risk was an essential part of war. He should push the man more, since he seemed worried.

"Dagger, a few degrees of flames and carbon monoxide with sulfur isn't bothersome to Darhel. I may decide to do that again. It's my turn to chase now."

"Oh, quit with the bullshit. I've seen Darhel burned in accidents. You're as easy to cook as we are. That was either an accident, or you're really clueless out here."

"If so, Dagger, it doesn't speak well for the humans I've been learning from," he said.

Dagger apparently decided to ignore that. He seemed to be getting smarter. Instead, he changed the subject. "That was rather clever, hiding the box on the bug. It would have been really clever to keep it low, where I couldn't see it sticking out like a saddle on a boar." There was a slight smugness pervading the control in his voice. And the control was obvious to Tirdal. Dagger was trying hard to suppress his emotions. Suppression, however, was not what he should do. They should flow, not be bottled up. And Dagger seemed to do exactly the opposite of what anyone wanted . . .

"I felt you needed the hint," he said to goad Dagger. "So far, you've shown little ability to outthink or out-track anything smaller and brighter than these bugs." The bugs were impressive, though, he thought as he skipped behind one and dropped back into the stalks. They were the size of Earth's extinct rhinoceri.

"I tracked Ferret, and he was supposed to be the vaunted master of it. You remember Ferret? I think he was wetting his pants when he realized I could see him. He was in good cover, too. Better than you've ever had. But the fickle finger of fate holds the trigger. And if you're so good I need a hint, why'd you drop the box and hide in the weeds?"

"Very simply, Dagger, I found your tracer some time back. It no longer serves my purposes to have you follow it. That was a ruse to keep you where Ferret could stalk you," he said. He also could use Ferret as a mythical ally. And as the man was now dead, Dagger couldn't cross check. "Now that Ferret is gone, I have no need to make things simple for you anymore. You'll have to do some real tracking. It's time for you to learn a few things."

With that, he rose back to a crawl, though this crawl was as fast as a good jog for a human, fingers and toes extended like a lizard's, but reaching far forward and behind to reduce the profile they cut in the grass.

"I'm going to kill you, you alien freak," Dagger said.

Tirdal spoke again to keep Dagger talking rather than shooting. "Really, Dagger, you should acquire calm, not just the outward symptoms. One should focus not upon the blankness within, but the blankness without, allowing it to draw the storm."

Dagger interrupted his spiel. "I've got a philosophical question for you, Tirdal."

"Yes, Dagger?"

"If a Darhel gets his head blown off in the middle of the forest, do the trees hear anything?"

"There, Dagger, you've made progress. You've acknowledged your anger. Now allow it to draw your fear of competence with it, and learn to feel. Only then will you be able to track a Darhel on flat ground without the tracer."

The crack of a projectile echoed across the savanna. One of the large herbivores twitched and staggered, trod in a circle as its sharp-edged feet threw clods of sod and grass. It was seeking its antagonist, and confused at not finding one. Moments later, it lined up on a nearby bull and charged. There was nothing wrong with its gait. The armor-piercing projectile had done no more than chip its carapace and annoy it. And that should be another lesson for Dagger, Tirdal thought. The beast's thoughts had spiked at the shot and were now subsiding back to normal. Dagger needed to do the same thing, and disappear behind the noise of the local life.

Dagger wasn't stupid. He knew the conversation had been designed to distract him. Anyway, a good sniper worked better in silence. To say nothing could be the scariest statement of all. And the damned Elf wasn't going to trick him into not using the tracking module. That whole jab had been an attempt to throw him off. It hinted of "fairness," and Dagger was not one for "fair" when "effective" was available. He'd use the tracker, the superior range of his weapon, his cunning and precision. And, he'd use his human ability to kill. To do otherwise would be silly. Let the Darhel mutter his philosophy. Dagger would shoot beads instead.

He took deep drafts of air, both to revitalize his flagging strength and to calm his nerves. Now he had to get into a state that Tirdal couldn't track. That would mean his tools would give him the advantage. His tools that didn't depend on emotion.

Tirdal really was desperate, he reminded himself. He was talking, running, hiding the box, setting fires. It was all very annoying, some of it was foolishly dangerous, and all of it meant he was out of practical ideas. This was a battle. A low-scale battle between only two combatants, but still a battle. Some damage was inevitable. Tirdal had trouble inflicting it directly—probably he couldn't kill and was hoping to push Dagger into getting injured, thus leaving him here in a cowardly fashion.

For a moment he remembered his own threat to Ferret, but that had been vengeful, not of necessity based on fear. Anyway, Ferret was dead, cleanly killed one-on-one.

Otherwise, Tirdal was just hoping for a lucky shot to catch Dagger, and all Dagger had to do was stand up to the fire, figuratively, and dish out what Tirdal couldn't take. He'd gone face-to-face with Ferret, this gutless troll should be easier. And that's what he was. Not an Elf, but a troll. A filthy little freak from a race of freaks who needed humans to fight for them. So here it came.

Dagger was going to head for those trees, get a good position, and at this range he could watch the Darhel's brains splatter as the round hit. That would be sweet.

Dammit! Calm! It's just an exercise. Locate the target, paint the target, shoot. Just like that bet with Thor. Just like the range. Afterwards was the time for a beer and a boast. And that artifact would be all the boasting he'd ever need. It would make him part of the war stories people passed around. Better yet, it would be one of the true ones.

He performed a maneuver that would have made his instructors proud. With an enemy at close range, he exfiltrated unseen and secured a new position. Chameleon at full power, because that was one of the things the Darhel couldn't track, and he really didn't care how much juice it ate up now, as he wouldn't need it after today, he squirmed snakelike, curving through the grass. Straight lines are a giveaway of intelligent activity, and a long, winding path would not only be harder to see, but if seen would be mistaken for an animal track. He did as little damage as possible. His rifle was slung over his shoulder, a loop of the sling held in his hand as a drag. Some of the beetle and flyer forms were disturbed at his passage, but nothing larger, and those only twitched because of the movement, not because they noticed this strange apparition.

Movement ahead made him stop short. He held utterly still, breath clenched, as he examined the shape. It was a small scavenger form, about a half meter long, and it trudged on past at an angle. Good. He resumed crawling, seeing the copse dark ahead. He'd pick one about three trees in, which would give him a clear enough field of fire, and provide both screen and some hard cover.

The grass thinned as he neared the outer reach of roots, and the ground rose slightly, too, built up from centuries of rot and decay. The tracking gear showed Tirdal to still be about fifteen hundred meters away, though the little asshole was moving at a hell of a clip. Well, that would make it easier. And with Tirdal heading straight at him, easier still. An upright, advancing target. The Darhel was a sucker if he thought that was a good tactic against a sniper. Still, Dagger would have to be quick across the exposed ground, as he couldn't spare the time to find the best approach or circle around behind. Then he'd have to be quick into position for a shot. He had perhaps two minutes.

Taking a breath for courage and for extra oxygen, he scurried like a lizard across open ground. His eyes were set on a tree ahead, and he made straight for it, then shifted sideways and dove around behind. No fire. Not detected by the Aggressor Team. Close eyes, avoid thinking, just breathe. We have a target, and that target is just a target. A pop-up, computerized dummy, just like a thousand others. It's a pass/fail shot. Show the general how good his troops are, then have a beer. Remember the old joke? One shot, one kill, drink coffee. A target was a target was a target.

In his best shooting trance, Dagger crawled low and quickly, seeking a good, climbable tree.

That one. Easy to climb, easy to evacuate, and it appeared to have a decent view from about five meters up. Perfect. And the target was now . . .

Less than seven hundred meters? How did the little bastard move that fast?

Dagger clambered quickly up the tree, trailing his sling. He found a solid limb about three meters above the ground, and paused to drag the rifle up. He made it up two more limbs, right to five meters or so, with a great view, even better than he expected. It was perfectly framed by the main trunks and limbs in front. He could lean over this angled limb while standing in that crotch, and would have cover from it. He linked all his sensors and his scope to make tracking fast, and gazed out quickly. He was going to pass this shot, so he'd have to take it fast.

The target was about there . . . and there was no movement there. There was only grass. He checked everything again. Right there . . . and nothing, not even the haze of a chameleon. There was an IR source, maybe, though the sunlight even filtered by haze made it only a ghost. . . .

The target was crawling, except it was the fastest damned crawl Dagger had ever seen. Holy shit, that was fast! And no clear target. Blue Team was being tricky. So for this exercise, switch between hornets and antiarmor, and fire as fast as possible. Outthink, outfight. Ready . . . and . . .

❖   ❖   ❖

Tirdal felt Dagger's presence. Dagger seemed to have learned, as his mind was reasonably calm and ordered. Ordinarily, that would have sufficed to mask him, but Tirdal was running tal to the very limits of his control. He had a Sense, a hunch of where Dagger was, and he was going to exploit that right now.

Dagger was still focusing on the fact that a Darhel would find it tough, if not impossible, to shoot a human. That thought stopped him from thinking about what else Tirdal could and might shoot at. Like that tree. That one right there.

Flashing a grin any human would recognize as triumphant, Tirdal eased his punch gun forward and fired.

A flash told him Dagger was firing, too, but there was nothing to do but follow through. His carefully aimed shot blew shreds of wet, fibrous wood out the back and into the tree behind it. Which was the tree Dagger was hiding in, if his estimation was right.

He tried to ignore the incoming fire as three hornet rounds cracked. The first blew dirt in his face. The second slammed into his boot and made his foot numb. The third he couldn't identify, except that it hadn't hit him. Then he was firing again, into the tree behind the first, shutting down his Sense in case he got lucky and hit Dagger. Twigs tumbled from the limb the shot had hit, and stray twigs blew out. They weren't much good as fragments, as they lacked mass. Still, they'd distract. In that time, he shifted his aim down near the base and started firing deliberately. Three shots took just over 1.5 seconds, and that particular tree had no base. The remains started to tumble sideways, its limbs whipping and crashing through the other trees. Then he turned his attention back to the one Dagger was hiding in. Another shot at a main limb blew chips in all directions. He'd not noticed Dagger's next shot, which had almost taken his hand off, but the next one cracked overhead, a clear miss because Dagger was too busy to think. That falling tree was crashing through the one he used as his platform.

Three more shots took out the base of Dagger's tree. That should have a positive effect. Tirdal grinned again and moved his aim to another.

Dagger was firing his third rapid hornet round at the warm spot in the grass when the tree in front of him exploded. Wet sap, splinters and chunks ripped past him and splashed over him. "Gah!" he yelled aloud, suddenly spooked. How the hell had the Darhel done that? And could he actually shoot to kill? The noise of the punch gun continued as Tirdal kept shooting.

There was nothing for it but to recover position and shoot again. This was where it ended. He shifted his grip, took a good stance and resumed firing, this time the dumb rounds. He'd march them along that line and hit something, he was sure.

Then the branch less than a meter above his head exploded. A chunk of it slammed into his helmet, dizzying him, and another jarred his rifle. Before he could recover, he was being whipped by tendrils and the tree was shaking as one off to his right fell across it. He shifted his balance, trying to recover position, as the tree shook convulsively. Then again. He figured out what was happening and quickly jumped out his escape route, wanting to be clear of the tree in a hurry.

His fall took him through the branches of the downed tree, and he scrambled through the obstacle, rifle held high to avoid tangling it. Branches caught at his feet and thighs as he fought to free himself. Already, he could hear his tree cracking angrily, and it just might fall backwards and crush him if he wasn't clear.

Off to his right, another tree was spewing splinters.

Dagger ran. He'd find cover some distance away and wait for Tirdal to follow. But this area was not safe. He tried to force his breathing back into control, but was scared. And admitting he was scared frightened him even more. He could hear trees crashing behind him, and wondered where the hell he could get a good shot and not be exposed? The farther away he was, the easier the Darhel could dodge his fire. Up close, he was in range of the punch gun, and it had been proven twice now that an inability to kill wasn't entirely a hindrance to the little turd. He needed to stalk better, wait for him to pick a route, then move to intercept. He batted at tendrils of stems, sacrificing stealth for speed.

Wasn't that little bastard ever going to sleep? That five-hour nap seemed a long time ago, and had barely taken the edge off his fatigue. But if the Darhel wouldn't rest, he couldn't. What would happen if it shot him while he slept? Or just buried him? Because Dagger knew he couldn't stay awake another three days until the pod left for its second point putting him between it and the Darhel.

Then he realized it was all moot. The Darhel was now tracking him. He'd have to move fast and switch roles again.

Ahead was clear grass and a slight rise. If he backed

up that hill, he could keep the copse in view and shoot the damned Darhel if he came through. Or, he'd be in a good position for a long shot, and there was nothing to collapse around him. Breath tearing at his parched throat as he tried to moderate it, he dropped to a sitting position and scrabbled backwards, rifle pointed out and ready to swing to any threat.

Tirdal wasn't about to follow Dagger into, through or around that copse. It was too likely he'd be targeted. The sniper was definitely still alive, though there was a hint of injury or pain in what Tirdal could Sense. All good, but not enough.

However, Tirdal was now confident he could ambush Dagger, on terrain of his choosing, pin him down and inflict injury by proxy or directly. Whether or not he could kill directly was another question, but a crippled Dagger put Tirdal in a much better bargaining position.

With Dagger confused, Tirdal beat a retreat for the stream, careless of the path he left. His plan was to reach a scrubby area he'd passed through not long before, all tangled and thick though not qualifying as "forest," merely brush. It was strewn with rocks and would provide several good places to dodge and shoot from. As Dagger's thoughts seemed to become coherent, again he began a series of zigzags to make himself somewhat less obvious.

He took long lopes down the slight slope to the stream's bluffs, then dropped over them. Dagger was alert now, and was starting to move. He was "far" and approaching "middle" in Tirdal's mind. Good. That gave Tirdal enough lead to get where he wanted to be.

He splashed across the stream, following a game trail southward that more or less paralleled the stream. He knew that he was leaving a trail but didn't know what to do about it. The terrain was karstic and there was a large chunk of limestone, a low bluff really, on this side. He looked at that, looked at the surrounding trees and his clear boot tracks in the mud and smiled.

Chapter 19

DAGGER HAD MOVED off to the east, trying to keep calm and think of nothing. But it was hard, very hard. The Darhel would be out there somewhere, and now the tracking was on the other foot; for the first time the Darhel was the hunter instead of the prey. Of course, that meant that he was closing. When Dagger saw him he would be too close to dodge a round. If Dagger saw him first.

That meant the hummocky terrain to the south. If he could bypass the Darhel, who was sure to be coming east, and get to the hills, especially to the southeast, he would have a good chance of getting the first shot in. If he moved by bounds, found an open area, set up, waited, then moved again, he had a good chance of getting the first shot in anyway. The Darhel didn't appear to be able to zero in on his position, just get a vague feel for his general locale. That would work. And keep calm.

Tirdal sensed the change in Dagger's demeanor. He was somewhere to the northeast, and even as a strong feeling of gloating came through the contact began to fade until it was almost impossible to discern. Apparently Dagger had taken his comments to heart about masking his feelings.

He let a little of his anger slip and felt the trickle of tal hormone fill his being with a feeling of lightness. But even with his enhancement he was back to "near/far" and the sniper was . . . somewhere in the middle.

Obviously Dagger was doing one of two things. Waiting, or swinging around to get on Tirdal's backtrail. Since the plan was to lead the sniper into another trap, it was important to make and then break contact. But with the feel of location fading it was going to be difficult. He or Dagger could walk right up to each other without even realizing it.

He marched into the scrub, and it was as bad as he'd hoped. Tendrils caught at his boots, coarse grass dragged at his suit, rocks of every size protruded into his path. Small flyers lofted past him, and once a boot-sized insect jumped from in front of him, digging frantically under the matted grass to find shelter. Then there were the choking vines, stiff plants and gnarled, low trees. It was sere and desolate and perfect.

Edging a little closer to the savanna, he headed due south, every sense alive for the slightest sign of Dagger.

Which was why he didn't notice the tiger beetles.

The creatures were not tigers, of course, and not beetles. But they were two meter long predators, albeit with short legs, and their mandibles were adapted to cut through the tough shells of the local herbivores like can openers; they were more than capable of taking apart a lone Darhel. Their evolution had taught them to be stealthy, lest the large prey crush them underfoot with their knife-edge hooves, or bite with their own jaws. Such a bite wasn't likely to be fatal at once, but would cripple the predator. That led to death from starvation, and improved the stealth and reactions of the surviving lines. The tiger beetles moved stealthily toward this strange little snack, darting and freezing.

Tirdal sensed the attack before the first rustle of underbrush and the things were on him. He dodged the first, but his Sense said "seven" and he knew he'd have to fire.

Dagger heard the hollow slap of the punch gun to the east and grinned. The Elf had run into something he couldn't run away from and it was going to cost him. The sniper cut immediately to the southeast where he knew the Darhel's trail would be. He listened to the shots, gauging direction and distance. He must be in that patch of crud across the stream. The Elf had been stupid not to press the attack when he could, and now Dagger would exploit it. At a run, weapon high, he bounded down the bluff, keeping ears open for the punch gun, eyes open for the Darhel and feet alert for tripping hazards.

It was a good kilometer, which was a long run on this terrain with this much crap. Add in lack of sleep and water, fatigue and a bad ankle plus a few new dings and Dagger was worn out and panting for breath by the time he neared the stream.

Tirdal wasn't sure how he had dodged the first rush but now it was a furball. Two of the predators were down, one of them twitching, one broken, but those were lucky shots. Two more had been hit but it wasn't stopping them; he had to hit a nerve center to kill the creatures. Neck or belly were the targets. Neck or belly, he reminded himself as he dodged another leap. They were pack hunters, and waited for cues from each other. They circled around at a run and dove in a tight sequence, one to distract, one from behind, the rest from the sides. He Sensed their leaps only instants before, but it had been enough so far. He knew their pattern, now, but could he maintain his luck and speed? His first evasion had sent pain shrieking through his lower chestplate. The second one had almost caused him unconsciousness. There was another danger; that of a reaction equivalent to human endorphin response. Part of his brain was Sensing his enemy, part clamping down tightly on agony, part controlling tal and preventing the cloying sweetness and urgency of lintatai, leaving badly eroded mental processes for wielding the punch gun, twisting through the blades of their jaws and staying mobile.

It took three quarters of a second for the punch gun to cycle and the pauses between shots were the most

incredibly long three-quarters of a second he could
imagine. He had accepted that he would have to fill each
of the beasts full of holes until he hit a nerve junction,
but the question was who would be dismembered first.
He ducked a leap, rolled to the left through thick weeds,
untangled from them and the matted grass beneath,
skipped back a step and fired. The gun went *poounk*,
his chosen target staggered, lintatai surged toward the
center of his brain and his training locked it back down.
The contortions and battle outside were a mere shadow
of the war within, of hormones versus self-control. It
was literally as hard as controlling an orgasm in progress,
that threatened to spill over at the slightest opening.
Except that this orgasm would kill him.

The insects scurried back into a circle around him.
He backed away through a gap, delaying the inevitable,
almost stumbling in the thick, close-spaced stalks, until
the punch gun recycled. He pointed and snap-shot just
as he'd been taught on the training range, pointing
for the head of the nearest beast, hoping for a stun,
blunt trauma or perhaps something better. The creature
was stretched out at the run, and the shot caught it
on the short but exposed neck. It wasn't dead-on, as
the head rolled between the forelegs but remained
attached by a sinewy string inside the articulated plates.
Still, the insect tumbled and began to twitch. It was
a kill. A surge of tal brought bright halos to everything in Tirdal's vision, and he took another breath,
laden with the coppery stench of blood, the earthy
smell of insect guts and the ozone tang of the shots.
He focused on the sensations, through them. See the
calmness of the lake. The currents run underneath.
Only the ripples wash the shore . . .

Pain lanced again, this time through his right thigh. His Sense had been distracted and missed this one. He drove the butt of the weapon down, tearing the mandibles free, fabric and flesh following them with an animated trail of blood droplets. The blow might have damaged the creature's jaw, as it seemed askew. A twist, point, shoot. Point-blank through the open mouth would also kill one, it seemed, and another surge swept through him. Forcing the searing pain in his chest and leg aside, he leapt over the horse-sized carcass, its legs thrumming the ground in death, and turned to face the remaining three as the tortured nerves in his shoulder, chestplate and thigh caused a cramp the entire length of his right side, from shoulder to ankle. The tiger beetles seemed to lack the rational sense to leave a losing battle. Or maybe they were starving. Or maybe Darhel smelled like chicken. They were going to leap now, and Tirdal dropped. It wasn't hard to let gravity do the work.

As they jumped, he fell behind the last corpse, its legs still twitching, brushing him in a macabre caress. But he was pointing straight up as they went overhead, and his shot caught one of them at the rear of the underside. That one split, its rear legs and joint tumbling free with a gout of entrails and yellow goo to land in a twitching heap. Tirdal dragged his feet painfully under himself in a squat, then shoved as hard as he could, rising up the curve of the carcass and over to the other side of the corpse, twisting as he went. The ankle on his already injured leg responded too slowly to the landing, and he felt it crunch, trauma inflaming the soft tissue into an instant sprain. He shot again and nothing happened. It had not been three-quarters of a second. The remaining pair spread wide, and he fired as the weapon recharged, getting one obliquely underneath as it left the ground. He dropped and rolled in close to the corpse behind him and waited for recharge and another attack.

The final tiger beetle continued its leap into a run and disappeared.

Tirdal did what any human martial artist would. He went into recovery breathing, slow and controlled, forcing his chestplate to obey. That alone reduced the pain somewhat, and he curled into a comfortable position. Sitting folded was preferred, but any position that helped an injury was the choice in the field. He grounded his thoughts and drifted for just a moment, pulling himself from the edge of unconsciousness. The cliff marks the edge. The edge can be walked. From the edge one can see into the distance. Behind is safety. Look not behind, but over the edge to the fear . . . He came back enough to feel the lintatai, and split his mind to deal with it. The wind stirs ripples through the leaves. The leaves sway the tree. The tree bends and flexes but does not yield. Supple is the tree. Supple is the mind. Emotions are but leaves in the wind of existence . . .

It took only a minute, but it was a minute well spent. Control returned, his mind aglow with the thudding of his heart and the warmth of emotion. All fell away into a cool, refreshed focus on a stalk in front of his eyes, its dun length covered in fuzzy white hairs.

That, and a gaping wound in his thigh and a sprained ankle. For the former, a self-healing bandage was called for. He cut away more of the damaged suit, keeping the hole as small as possible for protection. He eased the bandage inside, pressed it gently around the edges to seal it, then stroked its surface to activate it. It would disinfect the wound, staunch the bleeding, and drop nanites in to effect repair. It would be healed in a day, if he could only rest and eat. But of course, that was out of the question.

Rising painfully to his knees, then his feet, using his arms and the punch gun for support, he pressed a patch to his neck, letting a mild analgesic and more nanites into his bloodstream. What he needed was the Darhel equivalent of a narcotic and a muscle relaxer, but that, too, was out of the question.

The scrapes and minor tears he'd have to ignore. It was time to move. He lurched off deeper into the brush.

Dagger squatted low. The firing had stopped as he came down the hill. That could mean dead Elf, or crippled Elf, or that he'd won his engagement. It was time to be cautious again. That thick tangle of crud was definitely where he was, and there was nothing to do but ease in slowly, rifle raised at the ready and be prepared to shoot at any disturbance. This had to end soon, and there would be no better time. The Darhel had to be disoriented and possibly injured, too. Even likely injured. That had been a lot of shooting, indicating a predator.

So watch out for predators and wounded Darhel. Shoot both, ask questions later, he thought as he brushed fronds aside with the barrel of his rifle. The undergrowth was thick and matted, and he'd have to step carefully. What he needed was a hint as to where Tirdal's trail was. From there, he could stalk him down. And it would be damned near impossible for the little freak to dodge in this undergrowth.

Dagger was smiling faintly as he pushed forward. He raised branches carefully, stepping underneath and then lowering them to avoid swishes or snaps. Each step was thought through before the foot went down. He twisted as he walked, turning his torso to avoid growth where possible, so as to minimize his own trail. The sun was hot, flyers drifted up past him, disturbed by the movement, and pods and seeds clung to his skin and his gear. Rather than prickly like earth seeds, most here were gooey. That had to be because most life-forms had shells and not fur or feathers.

Then he came across a cracked stick. Near it was a flattened patch of grass. There, a turned log. This was trail, certainly. In a few moments, Dagger had it. A drop of violet blood glistened on a tall blade of grass.

He smiled; a drunk blind man could follow this trail. There were broken stalks from clumsy footsteps, bent and torn leaves from the passage of a body. Now to get in a good position to take the Darhel down. Though from the size of the blood trail the Darhel wasn't going to be much of a challenge anymore. More violet drops and faint greasy smears showed him to be injured.

Had Dagger seen the size of the area torn apart in the fight, resembling a tornado touchdown, and the corpses of six dead tiger beetles blown into pieces, he wouldn't have been so confident.

It was likely that Tirdal would seek shelter, some-where to patch himself up and rest. He might have major trauma from that fight. He might have a strain or other damage. A concussion, even, if Darhel were susceptible to them. Shock. All things that would slow him down. Dagger would exploit each one of those, find and nail him. He would be calm, methodical and professional, and afterwards he'd gloat.

The gloating would be very sweet. It had, after all, been a hell of a chase and a bastard of a fight. That made the coming victory that much more enjoyable.

Behind both combatants, the local scavengers had found the sign of the battle. Snuffling and twitching their antennae, those niche-fillers moved in to examine the area. There was protein in plenty here, with six large, well-fed predators dead, and their shells were already open. The meat would be efficiently disposed of in ever-smaller bites until the antlike legions scoured the skeletons clean. Then the insect borers would crumble those and the sun would break down the structure until it became merely crunchy soil underneath. But for now, best to feast quickly, lest some other predator dispute the rights. Most of them tore at the dead animals, but the area was crowded and blood had splashed widely. Some of that blood was interesting, different. What tasty flavor might such a wounded creature yield when dead?

A pack leader chittered, and brushed her antennae over her pack. At her lead, they trundled off through the scrub, following the scent of that strange blood. One stopped for a last bite of tiger beetle.

Tirdal could sense the sniper back on his trail; Dagger's control was slipping in the thrill of the hunt. Not that it mattered; there wasn't much he could do about it. Admittedly Dagger had been supposed to follow him but Tirdal wasn't supposed to have half his thigh bitten away at the time.

He splashed back across the shallow stream and up the other side, which was a dry rock shelf that might help hide his passage. He reached down to try to get his bandage into better position. He was dealing with a lot of problems at this point; multiple injuries, exhausting lack of sleep, the tal hormone which also responded to injury, general stress, and he hadn't eaten all day. But right now all he could do was hunker down and try to set his planned ambush.

Once across the water he headed along his backtrail for a distance, then swung back towards the stream. He could sense Dagger getting closer; the mental "scent" almost had horns attached to it. But he should have time to get into position. Whatever happened he should have the advantage at these ranges.

This would be a good spot, he decided. Solid rock would shield him from the gauss rifle. There wasn't much on the other side for Dagger to hide behind that a punch gun wouldn't blow gaping holes in, and if Dagger tried to cross the stream he'd be exposed. This was as good as it was going to get.

While Tirdal didn't have any dedicated tracking gear, there were motion sensors built into his suit. He slowly dialed up the sensitivity, so anything over twenty kilograms would register. That was overly sensitive, but he wasn't sure just how good Dagger was at sneaking. It might be that his audio or motion signature would be quite small. Twenty seemed a good number.

Then he sealed his suit. Gloves and boots hermetically joined to cuffs. A membrane dropped from his helmet and fastened to the neckline. The suit's fabric stiffened molecularly and became impermeable. Tirdal was now wearing an almost solid barrier that should keep any genetic or chemical scans from locating him. There was leakage through the hole on his thigh, but that could not be helped. He leaned back against the rock and brought the chameleon effect up slowly. At low level, it wasn't an easily detectable power source, would last several hours, and would make him as close as possible to invisible, provided he didn't move.

Of course, now he was in a pressure cooker. Air was thick and humid and would get worse, with only carbon dioxide escaping. Incoming radiation and heat, unradiated body heat, sweat and exhaled moisture would steam him. It was unpleasant already, in this environment hotter than the one he was used to, but he estimated he could survive an hour or so if he kept activity to a minimum. A bit of Jem meditation, without using tal, which was a change, reduced his awareness of the discomfort.

Slowly, he raised his awareness again. He'd have to be very sensitive until he had Dagger located, then withdraw his Sense and use his eyes and ears. If it came down to a direct shot, he'd have to lock everything down and hope for the best. He still wasn't sure he could kill, but a solid maiming would do as well, and even a moderate wound would keep Dagger and the artifact here, which was a less than optimum solution, but acceptable and preferred over the box leaving.

His awareness came up slowly, and there was Dagger, stalking him from "near." So he was likely just across the creek. Tirdal focused on that. He'd get an immediate warning of any predators, which would have to do, as he couldn't be distracted any further. Only Dagger should be in his Sense now. No distractions, nothing to require more tal. The trickle he was using was a dangerous level of itself, with all that had happened so far.

Now to wait.

The pack could tell that the prey had headed for the crossing and it knew a shortcut. It was aware that there were two smells ahead but it could expect to overtake at least one of them by the time they came to the stream. Then they would feed. They took their food where they could find it, and only from the weak. That was their role. The alpha female kept the others focused with chemical exudations. Wounded prey could be dangerous, and all might be needed to subdue it. It might even be that one or two of them would die. If so, they too would become food. There was little thought in the creatures, only hunger and focus.

Dagger consulted his HUD and frowned. The stream was ahead; the trail probably crossed it. He would need to be careful there; it was a good place for an ambush. He wasn't assuming Tirdal couldn't shoot him, no matter how strong the evidence so far was that he couldn't. There were no bluffs to fall on him, no trees to fall around him. Those memories momentarily shook his concentration, but he suppressed the anger. Calm. Stay calm. Locate target, shoot target, score points for the team on the exercise. Only an exercise, like so many others.

Yes, the trail led to the muddy banks of the stream. The target had jumped across there, not leaving footprints but leaving slickened grass and a silty eddy in the water. It couldn't have passed more than a few minutes before. Target was across there somewhere.

Dagger bristled alert, extending a human version of Tirdal's Sense. It was neither trained nor sophisticated, but anything out of place would send a warning to him. He moved to his knees in a slow sink, rather than a drop, taking more than a minute to do so. It was rough on his ankle and painful on abused and exhausted muscles, but it was a necessary step.

From his knees, he bent gradually to rest one hand on the ground. From there, it was simply a matter of patience. It was more than five minutes before he was settled. Another minute passed before the chameleoned muzzle of his rifle parted two stems of grass to overlook the stream.

Okay, Target. Where are you? I need those points for a win.

Tirdal settled on his rock with a quiet sigh. Nothing trying to eat him, no one trying to kill him for the moment. Just a big slab of limestone and dirt. And, shortly thereafter, a sniper, who would try to kill him. He breathed slowly, evenly, overmind controlling the pain and the rising core temperature, and alert for trouble with his normal senses. His submind kept alert with his Sense and worked on healing him. At this point, it might even be considered damage control. Medical care and recovery was certain to be involved.

Local small beetles and ant analogs crawled over his boots and suit. He was still enough to be part of the terrain to them. An odd, unseeable part to be sure, but not unusual enough to bother such sensitive but nonsentient creatures. There was nothing to do but wait until Dagger moved from "near" to "very near," unless an image came to him sooner.

Dagger was nearly close enough to see if Tirdal rose, but still obscured by brush. The punch gun would go through it but Tirdal wanted to make sure he got a good shot. So he calmed himself and waited for his nemesis to come fully into view, or expose himself by shooting.

Dagger had slipped into a perfect shooting trance. He wasn't even aware of it, of course. What he was aware of was that the Target was hiding over there, probably behind that rock. That would be the best place for hard cover. Should he toss a few hornet rounds and see what happened? But there might be additional cover he couldn't see. Hornets weren't magic. Frequently, they were only distractors. Too frequently, recently. For a moment, memories rippled his calm, but he recovered and was back in trance at once. Best to wait for a good, clean shot. He moved forward a few inches to get a better position with a wider field of view.

The pack could smell the prey ahead but they were wary. This was probably the "prey" that had killed the pack of tiger beetles. And the smells were wrong. But they were the smells of protein on the claw, the smells of meat. So it was worth the danger to try to take it down; meat was hard to find. Dangerous it might be, but hunger drove them. They too could be cautious slinks. The female retracted her legs in closely and cautiously probed ahead with her antennae. There was no movement, though wounded animals often didn't move much until attacked. There was something there, insubstantial as it was, but it was definitely an animal of some kind. She sprayed a hormone signal to the others, and squeezed between two more blades of grass.

The chemtracker function of the scope was off the scale. The Target had likely sealed up, but there would still be vapors in the air, especially after exhausting exercise. Sweat laced with ketones and pheromones dispersed slowly. So the Target was nearby, probably behind that rock on the right, waiting for Dagger to show himself or shoot. Where, exactly?

Dagger's helmet highlighted a small IR trace as a probable threat but he carefully stilled any rush of feeling. The Target was waiting for him to come fully into view before he took his shot. That would be his undoing. Dagger would shoot from right here. Then he would divert to the right and shoot again, and work his way around that cover. This was it. That protruding ripple might be a head or a hand, but an antimatter round would shatter it. He thumbed the selector, breathed, relaxed and squeeeezed.

Overhead, chunks of rock shattered, sharp pieces stinging through his suit though they did not penetrate. Tirdal cursed the Aldenata that had put him in this mess and flattened out on the rock, then hunched low. Dagger had him pinned down but the reverse was true as well. If he could get one shot he probably would be able to take the sniper. Unfortunately, if he tried to move he'd be a target. But . . . the punch gun could be set to repeat to the helmet systems. He toggled the punch gun's sight into his HUD and cleared the direct view. He could switch it back in a moment and he didn't need to see what was around him right now, but did need to see what the gun saw. Now, if he inched it around the rock . . .

Dagger triggered another round at the Darhel's position and grinned. Sure, if the Darhel got one good shot he was dead; there was no such thing as "cover" with a punch gun. But the Darhel's chosen spot had nowhere to crawl back from and he wasn't going anywhere so it came down to who could outwait who. And a sniper is the definition of patience. There was another faint disturbance, and he shot the edge of the rock. More chips flew.

He stilled his thrill as the heat sensor noted a movement to the side. He saw the edge of the Darhel's weapon come around the rock and took up slack on the firing button . . .

The pack paused at the crack of the shot and then the flurry that followed. However, again, the sounds were strange but meat was meat. They waved their antennae at the scents to the east. Close, very close that meat was. Tantalizing. And the insubstantial animal was barely moving.

Tirdal cursed his foolish eagerness as the weapon spun out of his hand, tumbling in two large pieces with innards hanging out. The weapon's casing was tough, but antimatter didn't care. He hunkered back down and carefully drew his rail pistol, it being mounted just above the wound on his thigh. One last chance. And it would really be bad to use it, because the EM field it emitted when fired was obvious to any sensor. It was all he had, though. Calm. He must remain calm. The ripples reflect the clearness of sky. The ripples are steady and even. The ripples wait for the shore, they do not rush to their fate.

The pack paused. They were scavengers, not predators. But this soft prey would be no threat. They waved their antennae in momentary indecision then leapt.

Dagger's first warning was the sound of scuttling behind him as the dog-sized pill bugs charged. Their mandibles were even more oversized than the predators, designed for rapidly ripping chunks of flesh from recent kills, and the first took his left leg and snipped the foot off at the ankle, right through the suit's tough fabric. Another ripped a hole in the thigh. Neither of those wounds registered at once; they were too quick and too clean for conscious thought to follow.

Then he was being chewed all over. Large bites, small bites, sawing and chewing through the fabric, his skin, muscle and grating on bone. He thrashed around in instinctive reaction, tried to swing his rifle around and realized there was no room. He reached for his pistol.

At the shriek, Tirdal froze. Then he peeked around the edge at a fusillade of pistol shots. He noted the scene and leaned back to wait. Dagger was occupied. It would be interesting to compare his abilities in this type of battle to Tirdal's. It would be best though, to wait for resolution before peeking again. Tirdal listened to the crunching of brush, the curses and screams and shots. Underneath, barely audible, were the chitters and the scrape of super chitin. Pistols, he recalled, were not likely to have any effect at all on these creatures, and it didn't sound as if Dagger were disposed to seek cover or evade. It was proof, after all the suspicions, that the man really was too cowardly to do the brave thing. His mental and physical courage was weighted by an emotional cowardice that was leading to this . . . In only a few seconds, the shots became scarcer, the screams softer. Shortly, they died down to rustling moans.

When Tirdal at last came out, the eerie quiet had returned to the woods. A glance suggested the pack and Dagger were about done with each other. Some had fled. The remaining creatures were each chewing on some severed part of Dagger.

Cautiously crossing and approaching from upstream, he located the shattered growth that pinpointed the battle. He crept in, wary of Dagger's thoughts, but found only the basic kernel of personality there. The man was badly injured. Still, he crawled into the area with only desiccated, crackly trees as cover. He kept his pistol low and ready in case of attack from either threat, or a new one entirely. His Sense was at minimum, tal tightly controlled to a trickle lest the feedback from a death throw him over the edge.

There was Dagger, and he was down and well bloodied. Some lobbed rocks and a couple of careful shots confused and drove off the scavengers, who chittered angrily but deferred to what seemed to them to be a superior predator. They knew their caste and moved off, dragging parts of Dagger with them, to seek other sustenance.

Tirdal pulled the gauss rifle away from Dagger's twitching form. The pistol was already well to the side, still clutched in the severed hand of the renegade.

Renegade, traitor, Quisling, sellout, turncoat. Humans had a rich array of words for this type of betrayal. They despised Darhel, who always abided by a contract for the sake of honor, yet saw nothing wrong with "screwing each other over" or "sticking it to them" or even "Jewing them down." That last one had taken some research, then a study of the concept of racism before Tirdal could define it. He still didn't understand it. That was something else that would require more meditation.

Back now to the business at hand. Tirdal stared for just a moment, then gave a very Darhel smile; all teeth. His ears flicked in appreciation of irony. Then he started applying tourniquets to the limp form before him. He was, after all, crosstrained as a medic.

Dagger muzzily regained consciousness. Pain throbbed through every fiber of his being. His skull pounded from both bruising and clashing hormones. There were stinks in the air, of blood and urine and scorched and putrefying flesh. He realized those were his. Reaching to shield his eyes with his right hand, he discovered anew that it was missing at the wrist. The stump bumped into his cheek, leaving a smear of jellied blood. It didn't hurt much; the tourniquet around it had killed the pain along with the flesh underneath it. Other sensations resolved as small insectoids underneath, stinging him with every tiny bite. His left leg was gone below the knee, he found when he tried to roll over. It too, had been tied off. Pain suffused his entire being, aches, sharp stabs and bites all fighting for attention. Chunks of flesh were missing all over his body, the gaping, ragged wounds covered with bandages but left not numbed. He rocked unsteadily over, iron control turning what would be shrieks into whimpers of agony. Every touch of the stiff weeds and spiky leaves around him hurt anew, and he looked through a red haze that might be the result of pain, or perhaps blood in his eyes.

There would be other animals, larger ones, coming soon, drawn to the strange but cloying scents of his meat. He'd need his rifle. Inside, never reaching his visage, a smile formed. The damned Elf hadn't been able to kill him. The smile inside became an insane smirk on the surface. He reached for the rifle. Even with just his left hand he could shoot.

It was gone. The depression in the growth and dug up dirt where it had plowed in were visible next to him. The rifle was not.

His pistol was there, still clutched in the shattered, glistening chunks of bone and shredded flesh that had been his right hand. It was holding down a note.

The note had been written in flawless block letters, as if by an engineer. Or someone who had learned English as a second language. It read: "I left you a bullet. Tirdal San Rintai."

From the bushes to the right, there came a rustling, followed by a chittering.

This time, Dagger's shrieks were unsuppressed.

Chapter 20

TIRDAL WAS NOW truly alone. He could rest and would, but first he must recover that box. Then, he must stay hidden while traveling. Certainly the Tslek base was a decoy, but if they'd detected any of this fight, they'd come to reconnoiter, and Tirdal could hardly hold off even a lone bot with just a pistol and Dagger's rifle. And it would be obvious from their presence that the team had discovered the Tslek ruse.

Once he had the box, he'd have to move fast, resting briefly. When he was at last aboard the pod he could relax. For now, the schedule remained to eat and move. At least he'd be able to reduce the pace and eat vegetable matter rather than meat. His overmind was calmed by that notion, his submind outraged. More meditation would be necessary to reconcile all the conflicts between thought and emotion.

For now, he had to recover the artifact. Dagger had had no idea of its real worth. It was worth far more than money. And it was worth more than life to Tirdal, who intended to recover it at once.

He still needed the damnable tal to operate! Injured, exhausted and hungry, it was all that could keep him functioning. He drew his awareness in to a bare few meters, alert only for predators. Should the Tslek show up, there was nothing he could do, so it was not something to be concerned about. With less noise intruding into his mind, meditation while hiking was a viable option. He ran simple exercises to calm his overmind. His submind would have to wait, a caged beast clawing at his consciousness.

He had the captain's tracer to find the box and the herd. The beasts had moved a good five kilometers, and it was getting dark again. That meant there were six days to reach the northern exfiltration point, and that was possible. Or might it be better to simply head south and use that day to gain distance?

The device was to his north. Additionally, he was running low on energy. A rough three- to four-day hike was better than a ten-day hike. If he failed in the first, he still had the option of the second. That decided him as much as the fatigue and even growing frustration did.

At a trot, his gait odd from accumulated wounds, Tirdal made his way to the north and west again, following the signal. Tangles gave way to low scrub to grass, and he swallowed water and food on the run, occasionally fortified with pain medication and nanites for healing. He could meditate the pain away, certainly, but his mind was busy enough as it was. He hoped his Masters wouldn't be too disappointed with that decision, under the circumstances.

It was an amusing thought. For the second time this day, his ears flicked.

He took a few bites from his processor and swallowed some water on the run. He still had a schedule to keep. The sun was oozing below the horizon, and the air was perfectly comfortable to him. Shortly, it would chill below even his tastes, and he'd simply adjust the suit accordingly. No longer did he need to cook or freeze, and the pleasant environment helped calm him, almost as much as the meditation and medication did.

It was full dark before he got near the herd, but if the tracer was correct, the animals ahead were his target. He approached slowly, alert for predators that might pursue them, or any kind of problem. Then he drew more tal (again!) and focused his thoughts for projection.

He wandered through the herd from the rear, still amazed that his projection was working, and he not seen. Or perhaps part of it was the chameleon. He'd elected to use it, since it wouldn't be needed for anything else. He would have appreciated the irony of Dagger having that same thought the day before, had he known.

The tracer simply told him that the box was ahead. There was a way to change the sensitivity and focus in closer, but it would take time for him to figure out how and there wasn't much point, as it had to be on one of these beasts.

There. That protrusion above the curving back of that one. It was visible by the starless shadow it left, and the visor showed it clearly in various frequencies. It was still securely taped.

Tirdal moved closer. The sounds of thick stalks being cropped echoed between the shells. Occasional rumbles of digestion or eruptions of gas provided cover for his footsteps. Whenever he'd seen this particular species, it had been eating. Did these creatures not sleep? Sleep only briefly? Sleep with part of the mind still alert? It was hard to tell, and not something he need concern himself with. What he needed to concern himself with was recovering that artifact. But they did seem to consume a prodigious amount of grass.

He was considering ways to climb or jump up and pull at the tape, the way he'd attached it, when it came to him that if he could cause one side to pull lose, the artifact's mass would cause it to drop off. That was easier than trying to jump in his present condition.

He lined up along one side, drew his pistol and sighted carefully. It was actually practical, given the animal's carapace, to simply shoot. The light load would cause no damage, indeed might not even be noticed. It would rip the tape, however. He thumbed the selector to automatic and fired. A ripping sound of projectiles tore through the night air.

He'd anticipated a reaction. The herd might scatter, spooked. They might charge each other or Tirdal or anything. They might rear and attack. He wasn't prepared for the reaction he got, however.

Nothing.

The tape had been sheared cleanly, and the artifact wobbled as the creature wandered forward. Tirdal followed, alert for trouble that never came, and within two hundred meters the box tumbled off one side, dangled from a strip of tape, then fell. He walked over, grabbed it by the handles and hefted it over his brutalized shoulders.

Step One accomplished.

He was quite loaded down with gear once again, but no one was pursuing so he could rest periodically and walk upright in the near silence. Those two simple things made it a much easier task. He decided to travel at night and rest days, as they had before. Daylight would make it easier to find a secure resting place, and the life here seemed in general to be diurnal, so predators would be stalking in the daytime and less likely to cross his path.

He turned again, back to the north and east. It would be his last direction change, he hoped.

The real advantage to the current state of affairs, Tirdal reflected, was that he could move as he should. The Tslek presence was far behind and no longer sensible. There were no humans to play down to, and he could trot at a good rate. He stopped twice a day for food and water and rest, slept once for five hours and was at the second extraction point in less than four local days. It was a moral victory only. Ferret had been wounded by the neural grenade and then shot. His own injured heel—from Dagger's shot—had gone numb and would need treatment. His injured shoulders—from Dagger's shot—were tight and painful, and might be becoming infected. The wound oozed and was starting to smell. His chest plate—from Dagger's shot—would need surgery to correct the way it was crookedly healing. The wound in his thigh from the beasts would need attention. His ankle was swollen and only medication and Jem discipline let him ignore it. In fact, he was only the winner by a lucky chance of the scavengers, but luck was an essential if unreliable part of warfare. The load he carried made it worse, but the artifact had to be recovered, and Dagger's rifle was the only weapon heavy enough for any real fighting at this point. He was reluctant to abandon its ten kilos, especially after a smaller predator form had tried to leap on him. There were other issues, too.

Converted leaves kept him fed sufficiently, though there was a demand for that taste of meat in his mind that would take much work to suppress. He would suffer the privations necessary to avoid meat, and further drowning in tal. His water was adequate; Darhel have very efficient "kidneys," and he didn't need that much to stay healthy if not comfortable.

He could see what was likely the shore ahead. He took a cautious look around, realized it was unnecessary, then decided to do so anyway. It would be a supreme irony to die so close to the end. He sent the signal, then repeated his surveillance.

Everything appearing clear, he crept forward over rolling hummocks of sand with tough grass clinging to them, dragging gear behind him, and slipped into the water among a patch of reeds. Shortly, he was submerged to his neck. Then he considered that there might be vicious aquatic predators, which might mean the shore was, in fact, safer. It was too late for indecision now, however. He'd remain here.

He was nervous for a while as the pod approached, slowly and deliberately, a rising dark dome like something from a human horror story . . . Cthulhu? But it came as ordered. Then there was another brutal swim. Swimming was not something Darhel did, because of their density, especially not when burdened with an Aldenata artifact. He'd abandoned everything else save one item in the grass behind, and left an enzymic package to hasten the destruction. Even on this duned shore, the plants should quickly grow over the nondegradable materials left, and it really wasn't a concern.

The gentle chop of the waves was enough to exhaust him. Still, swimming, while draining, was low impact, which relieved much of the pain in his heel. It hurt his ankle beyond what he could handle at the moment, so he reduced his stroke with that foot, letting himself bob in the water. He was gasping, pulse thudding, before he reached out a hand, grabbed an extruded stanchion, and swung himself up into the hatch. He took one last look around. Less than fifteen days he'd spent here, yet it would be part of him forever, with all that had happened. The team. The encounters with insects and flyers. The Tslek "base." The chase. Ferret, without question. Dagger most of all.

Part of the past. Now was time for the future.

Thrust tapered off as the ship injected into low orbit. Tirdal San Rintai looked at the hologram of the planet in the tank before him. An off-center quarter was visible from this angle, swelling toward him with the terminator a knife-edge across it. A pleasant enough place for humans, if they ever drove back the Tslek. With their enviable ability to kill, they could keep the predatory insectoids controlled. An interesting place for Darhel, but not a home, even if the climate was so enjoyable.

He touched the telltale from the garbage eject then and the Aldenata box began its slow tumble through space to annihilation. Attached to it was Dagger's rifle. He couldn't say why he'd done that, but it seemed appropriate. It was probably his imagination but he thought he could just see the box begin to burn up on reentry, an orange pinpoint in the hazy arc of atmosphere. It was a shame to destroy it after all this trouble, but it couldn't be allowed to fall into human hands. Or Tslek pseudopods. Atmospheric friction and impact would accomplish what heavy energy weapons would otherwise have been needed for.

He lay back in his contoured couch and pondered the humans' probable reactions.

Chapter 21

THE ROOM WOULD have been recognizable to a human martial artist. It had that spare look that avoided excess visual stimulation, while being elegant and attractive. Knifelike and spearlike weapons covered two of the walls in geometric precision that was inhuman but logical. A trained human fighter would have deduced the means of using most of them.

Tirdal sat, legs folded, near a small charcoal brazier above which was suspended the Darhel equivalent of a teapot. The steeping herbs within were fragrant and rich. All of this added to the environment, making it tastefully exotic to the untrained but familiar and conducive to proper mental energies in those who understood the Art. The mysticism surrounding any good martial art is not so much religion as mindset. One must feel the form. The clean, charred smell of the fire came to Tirdal, too. For a moment, the steeping beverage reminded him of Gorilla's tea. It had taken days to reach this level of calm, and he was almost back to normal, that "normal" having been imposed on his species by a race that dared to play deity. Then he reached the critical point and suddenly he was . . . there. In touch with himself mentally and physically, in touch with his Master, in touch with the universe. The pleading, demanding tendrils of tal, pulling at his mind and spirit, receded below the threshold to what was considered safe and untroublesome. Their retreat left only memories, which could be assimilated with his mastery of the Art into greater control for next time it became necessary to court lintatai for survival.

What to make of the ending? The "tiger beetle" attack was instructive in that he'd been able to kill, fortuitous in that Dagger had died as a result. Yet he had not been able to deliver that final death to the sentient, even though dealing death to the lesser forms was manageable. And Dagger had had the greater position until the very end, even exhausted, enraged and afraid. There was much to consider about humans, still. They were amazingly hard to kill, and could make very determined and deadly enemies. Generations long past had seen that. They had been correct in their assessment of the potential threat. A new study and evaluation would have to be made.

Which was not Tirdal's problem. Focus on Dagger,

his actions, thoughts and words. Remember all that took place, for the knowledge, evaluate it for its importance, for wisdom, and respect the strength of that mind, even in its sick and twisted state, for honor.

Focus on Ferret, who'd done what he must, not knowing why. He had been the only one whose motives were pure. Crippled, outclassed, seeing his own death, he'd fought anyway, stalking two physically superior enemies, knowing one outranged and outclassed him. He could have called an entire fleet using Gun Doll's gear, but had quietly and with dedication expended his life to maintain operational secrecy. No human would ever know of his valor. Only a very few Darhel. It was up to Tirdal to honor him.

Gluda San Rintalar entered from the panel behind Tirdal. He Sensed her presence before he heard her, and opened his eyes in deference as she padded around the hearth and sat across from him. She was a superior of his own line, and much respected.

Through the steam and hot gases of the brazier, her face rippled just slightly. That, too was part of the meditation. The Master had an etherealness when seen thusly, which reminded the Student that one's eyes were only one sense of many, and were not the Sense.

"I greet you, Rintai," she said.

"I thank you for the greeting, and return one, Rintalar."

"You are recovered?" she asked.

"I am untroubled. There are many memories to discuss," he said.

"We are most eager for your report. You were able to kill and eat animals, kill predators, even kill a sentient enemy, if indirectly. This is astounding news, and credits your training," she said. There was a trembling excitement to her body that not even her iron discipline could contain.

"If there is credit due, it is to you who trained me, Rintalar. I am but a Rintai," he said formally. Still, the compliment was real. He had impressed his instructors.

"Your humbleness is honest, Rintai, but incorrect. You have done what was thought still impossible. You will be noted."

"Then I thank you, Rintalar," Tirdal replied.

"There are, of course," she continued less formally, "still questions. Why, for example, did you dispose of the artifact? It would have been well to bring it. Especially since the humans are disturbed by the loss of a team without any hard evidence."

"Have they complained that much?" he asked.

"They have," she admitted. "They questioned whether Darhel could go insane. They have made inquiries as to you as the killer. Though their records of us in the subject of warfare and violence seem to make that a confusing and embarrassing question for them."

"I was the one to decide, having no superior to ask," Tirdal replied. "It seemed the most prudent course. They have the intelligence about the Tslek decoy, they have mapping data, drawn from my mind and from what memory remains of the cameras." His ears flicked at that statement. It had been hard to selectively erase scenes and make it appear a malfunction related to the "battle" they'd fought against Tslek bots. "As I understood, the humans were happy with the strategic result."

"Indeed they are, Tirdal San, and there is no mistrust of how you handled it. The caste is simply curious as to your motives."

"My motive was to find a way to get the artifact to our scientists, or have it destroyed. Beyond that, it was to stay alive to accomplish that task," he said.

"Yes, and it sounds as if that of itself was difficult."

"Very," he admitted. "Yet from it I learned the levels to which Jem can restrain tal and lintatai to turn them to use. Having survived and learned, I accept the event as positive. If I could have saved the artifact, I would have. But as the only survivor, I anticipated great inquiries as to the event, and decided it was safer destroyed.

"As to the other," he continued, "Earth seems to accept the story and has expressed great pleasure at learning of the Tslek trap. It also seems the cometary bases in that system were decoys. It is a shame that during the initial planetary engagement, the Tslek outer sentries killed the rest of the team. Nevertheless, they fought a valiant retreat to get the intelligence out. If not for my sensat skills and some luck, I also would have been killed. I was fortunate to have such competent professionals to learn from and who protected me. I only wish sensor data remained to show their true nature." Earflicks being insufficient, he grinned again.

"And of course," he said, "the humans have a fleet en route to clear the system and prosecute an offensive. It appears the fate of several worlds was affected by a lowly Darhel."

"So it does," Gluda agreed. "The fate of humanity

itself may have been affected." She shook her head and asked, "Was the artifact really a lindal?"

"Most certainly," Tirdal replied. "The markings were distinctive, even if the shape was odd. I speculate it was of the oldest type. There were images to confirm my analysis, but they suffered an accident." His ears flicked again.

"Yes, how unfortunate an accident," she replied, her own ears indicating wry amusement. It was unfortunate to both races for entirely different reasons. "It must have been an Aldenata research site from before they incorporated lintatai into our life coding. Perhaps even from before lindai was a Power they had."

"I concur," Tirdal said. "That was my thought upon seeing the device. It was a tense moment, but I was able to avoid indication of the depths of my interest."

"Yes," she agreed. "That has been noted. You did well there, too."

"I thank you," Tirdal replied and continued. "I also chose not to give humans the knowledge of the ability to artificially induce lintatai in Darhel."

"Yes, and we are grateful. It is a shame in many ways. The site would be a treasure trove for human and Darhel researchers. There are likely other devices in those mounds, and also elsewhere on the planet and in the system."

"It seems almost certain," Tirdal agreed. "But the system is currently in Tslek hands and would be just as useful to them. This must be avoided, I think. I know I personally prefer that neither gain access; some weapons are too evil to see the light of day."

"Indeed," was the reply. "And concurring, we are

working to that end. Favors are being called in from the O'Neal Bane Sidhe, plans made. If all goes well, we can avoid having that knowledge become available until after lintatai has been put in its proper perspective.

"You have done well, I say again, Tirdal San Rintai. Your performance was exemplary under conditions more extreme than anyone could have anticipated. Much new knowledge and data have you brought us to consider." She rose easily from her cross-legged position to stand. The meeting was over, and both had meditations and duties.

Tirdal did likewise. "I thank you, Rintalar. Please relay my thanks to those appropriate."

"I will, Tirdal. And you should begin preparations for the Rintanal examination."

A chance at advancement. It was not entirely unexpected, but appreciated nonetheless. And it showed respect for his abilities. "I am most honored, Rintalar. I shall endeavor to perform to that standard."

"You had best, Tirdal," she said with an earflick. "You will reflect on my training. And our Line will note how you do, youngling."

The destroyer flickered into existence barely a diameter from the planet. Such a jump had been risky, but it was not as dangerous as a long approach to such a target. For long milliseconds, nothing happened as factors and preset calculations were compared. Then a swarm of angry dots erupted forth, flying straight as the meteoroids they would imitate. The kinetic weapons entered the atmosphere in a reticulan spread as ground-based missiles and beams blazed to intercept.

Some were destroyed by counterfire. The lone Tslek desperately launched message drones, but the remaining weapons tracked in on the facility and adjusted their perfect courses into erratic terminal maneuvers. They hammered the ground, flashing into multikiloton incandescence and lifting the decoy base, now rubble, to the stratosphere and beyond. The bright spheres of the detonations subsided into mushroom clouds that would take days to dissipate, drifting around the globe in long, glowing streaks. Beams and more missiles fired space-to-space, destroying most of the few drones that had launched. The Tslek would find out what had happened sooner or later, but any delay was of tactical use.

Three of the planetary weapons, perhaps decoyed by the systems of the base, fell just to the south and west of the target area. The white flashes of the immolations were noted only by rough beasts.

✧ The End ✧

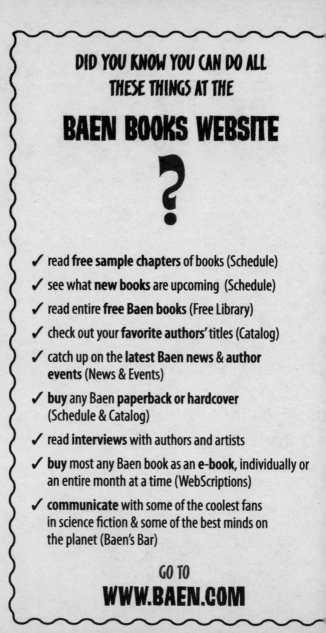